Steampunk London

Steampunk London

Neo-Victorian Urban Space and Popular Transmedia Memory

Helena Esser

BLOOMSBURY ACADEMIC
LONDON • NEW YORK • OXFORD • NEW DELHI • SYDNEY

BLOOMSBURY ACADEMIC
Bloomsbury Publishing Plc, 50 Bedford Square, London, WC1B 3DP, UK
Bloomsbury Publishing Inc, 1359 Broadway, New York, NY 10018, USA
Bloomsbury Publishing Ireland, 29 Earlsfort Terrace, Dublin 2, D02 AY28, Ireland

BLOOMSBURY, BLOOMSBURY ACADEMIC and the Diana logo are trademarks
of Bloomsbury Publishing Plc

First published in Great Britain 2024
Paperback edition published 2026

Copyright © Helena Esser, 2024

Helena Esser has asserted her right under the Copyright, Designs and Patents Act, 1988,
to be identified as Author of this work.

For legal purposes the Acknowledgements on p. vii constitute an
extension of this copyright page.

Cover design: Rebecca Heselton
Cover image: Dirigible balloon in the sky over a city © Rustic/ iStock

All rights reserved. No part of this publication may be: i) reproduced or transmitted in any form, electronic or mechanical, including photocopying, recording or by means of any information storage or retrieval system without prior permission in writing from the publishers; or ii) used or reproduced in any way for the training, development or operation of artificial intelligence (AI) technologies, including generative AI technologies. The rights holders expressly reserve this publication from the text and data mining exception as per Article 4(3) of the Digital Single Market Directive (EU) 2019/790.

Bloomsbury Publishing Plc does not have any control over, or responsibility for, any third-party websites referred to or in this book. All internet addresses given in this book were correct at the time of going to press. The author and publisher regret any inconvenience caused if addresses have changed or sites have ceased to exist, but can accept no responsibility for any such changes.

A catalogue record for this book is available from the British Library.

A catalog record for this book is available from the Library of Congress.

ISBN: HB: 978-1-3504-3390-8
PB: 978-1-3504-3394-6
ePDF: 978-1-3504-3391-5
eBook: 978-1-3504-3392-2

Typeset by RefineCatch Limited, Bungay, Suffolk

For product safety related questions contact productsafety@bloomsbury.com

To find out more about our authors and books visit www.bloomsbury.com
and sign up for our newsletters.

Contents

Acknowledgements   vii

Introduction: Punked Pasts and Cyborg Cities   1

1. Different Engines: Seminal Steampunk and the Foundations of Gonzo-Victorian London   15
   1.1 The California Trifecta: Time Travellers, Morlocks, and Mayhew's 'Shabby-Seedy' London   16
   1.2 Clackers, Computers, and Urban Revolution   28

2. East End Punk: Neo-Victorianism, Urban Gothic, and Collective Knowledge   51
   2.1 Devils, Detectives, and Deep Topographies   55
   2.2 Remixing Whitechapel: Marxist Body Horror in Second-Wave Steampunk   78

3. Hyper-City: Steampunk's Retro-Speculative Video Game Spaces   99
   3.1 Immersive Historical Play in *Assassin's Creed: Syndicate*   107
   3.2 Blade Running the Victorian City in *The Order 1886*   114

4. Re-claiming the Retrofuture: Feminism and Gender in Fin-de-Siècle and Steampunk London   141
   4.1 The New Woman as Modern Flâneuse   146
   4.2 In Hindsight: Fraught Feminisms, Action Girls, and the Steampunk Heroine   152
   4.3 Beyond the Binary: Anachronism as Queer Potential   176

Conclusion: An Exercise Bicycle for the Mind   199

Bibliography   205
Index   229

Acknowledgements

I would like to take this opportunity to thank my PhD supervisors at Birkbeck, David McAllister and Joe Brooker, for welcoming me and my project, and for providing support, enthusiasm, insightful questions, ambitious deadlines, and the freedom to pursue this milestone in my life with confidence and curiosity. I am also grateful for the generous engagement and invaluable advice of my viva examiners, Rachel Bowser and Scott McCracken. My thanks also to everyone at Birkbeck for their élan and encouragement, particularly Sue Wiseman and Ana Parejo Vadillo, to the Grace Morris studentship for the financial support, and to my PhD cohort for sharing and enlivening the otherwise so solitary PhD experience, whether in the historic Keynes Library, at cafés, or at conferences: Flore Janssen, Sasha Dovzhyk, Pauline Suwanban, Janette Leaf, Aren Roukema, Dickon Edwards, Katie Stone.

It was my privilege to live in the wonderful, both eternal and ever-changing metropolis I was writing about, to be flâneuse, explorer, scholar, and urban dweller in one, and I thank Christoph Heyl for supporting my first academic forays into steampunk, as well as for sharing enthusiasm, excursions, obscure anecdotes, and hidden treasures of and about London. Thanks to everyone at Duisburg-Essen who listened and encouraged me to keep going, especially Jens Gurr, Torsten and Stefanie Caeners, Lena Mattheis, and Claudia Drawe.

I am especially grateful to my parents, Andrea and Stefan Esser, for their unwavering continued support, and for moving me and all my books to, from, and across London. I would not have come this far without you. My special thanks also to my late grandmother Reni, who called me 'Frau Doktor' long before I merited the title, and all my friends and family who joined me in London, shared its wonders, and made my time there truly worthwhile.

Introduction: Punked Pasts and Cyborg Cities

Science fiction critic John Clute viscerally describes how William Gibson and Bruce Sterling's seminal steampunk novel *The Difference Engine* (1990) radically transforms the Victorian city of memory as follows:

> Very soon the face of London begins to convulse into a Freemason's wetdream of the City as a monologue of temples: parks and homes are demolished to make way for entrepreneurial edifices decorated with pharaonic runes and dedicated to Progress: new thoroughfares slice through the heart of town, steam gurneys choke the roadways and poison the air; and everywhere one can hear the *sound* of the new order being born.[1]

In so doing, he illustrates the central subject of this interdisciplinary study: By deconstructing and then re-mapping a vaguely familiar but commonly held urban imaginary, steampunk London emerges as a retro-speculative, alternative 'Victorian London' that both affirms and re-imagines its status as emblematic socio-economic nexus and collective symbol for the Victorian past.

This study explores why steampunk fiction, as a creative-critical, neo-Victorian, and popular memory practice, gravitates so often to Victorian London as its potent setting, and how its anachronistic impulses work both within and against a collective memory of the Victorian city. It contextualizes steampunk cities against Victorian cross-media strategies to represent the complexity, simultaneity, and social challenges of the modern metropolis, and so illustrates how and to what end steampunk creatively re-imagines London's urban environments across both spatial and temporal axes. In so doing, it illustrates how popular fiction at large, and neo-Victorianism in particular, invites participatory consumption and a playful, yet politically informed re-evaluation of the Victorian past's legacies, and considers its potential – and its failures – to interrogate and challenge our relationship with that Victorian past.

A Short History of Steampunk

Steampunk is notoriously difficult to define, although easily identifiable as retro-speculative, Victorian-looking universes populated by airships, automata, ray guns, or revenants: Steampunk, 'as a genre and a paradigm resists definition'.[2] It typically infuses neo-Victorian settings, be they fantastic secondary worlds or identifiably real-world Victorian past, with retrofuturism and technofantasy[3] as either aesthetic marker or temporal concept, and may incarnate across genres in literature, film, fashion, music, video games, or sculpture. Termed – although not invented[4] – by K.W. Jeter in 1987 for *Locus Magazine*,[5] steampunk initially synthesized 1980s anti-neo-liberal politics against the collapsing industrial paradigm and has re-emerged in the internet age as a cross-cultural, collaborative transmedia subculture that spans fiction, maker culture, music, art, and cosplay.

This maker culture most exemplifies steampunk's creative interrogation of our relationship with technology, and has most often garnered scholarship's attention.[6] It potently illustrates how steampunk synthesizes Victorian fictions, aesthetics, and materials – 'the dandified gear of aristocrats, peculiar brass gear, rather stilted personal relationships, and elaborate and slightly kinky underwear', as Sterling postulates – into a culturally charged visual shorthand,[7] and therefore merits a brief overview. Steampunk's quest to re-capture a knowability of the technology that saturates and defines our lives is illustrated by a much-quoted manifesto out of *SteamPunk Magazine* by the Catastrophone Orchestra:

> First and foremost, steampunk is a non-luddite critique of technology. [...] It revels in the concrete reality of technology instead of the over-analytical abstractness of cybernetics. [S]teampunk machines are real, breathing, coughing, struggling and rumbling parts of the world. They are not the airy intellectual fairies of algorithmic mathematics but the hulking manifestations of muscle and mind, the progeny of sweat, blood, tears and delusions. The technology of steampunk is natural; it moves, lives, ages and even dies.[8]

Attempting to 'rediscover the inherent dignity of created objects',[9] steampunk's online and collaborative maker culture seeks to re-humanize technology by externalizing its hidden functions in the Arts and Crafts spirit. Steampunk creations promise accessibility and offer a sensory experience: Their levers, gears, and boilers can be seen, heard, and touched, in opposition to the streamlined digital black boxes that refuse us users access or agency over their inner workings. The Victorian design aesthetic here signifies a complex network of meta-historical interrelations between production, workmanship, materiality, capitalism, and identity that are firmly identified with, and located in, the Victorian past. It so rethinks and re-applies Victorian critiques of industrial production and the mass market by Karl Marx, John Ruskin, or William Morris, and employs similar strategies of reclaiming agency and dignity through manufacture. However, the industrial design which Victorian critics rejected now becomes itself the object of reverence, because, now outdated, it is perceived as picturesque and intriguing. As a postmodern and post-industrial aesthetic, steampunk also illustrates our collective re-evaluation of a technological aesthetic once perceived as daunting and infernal as now quaint and clanky: 'Steampunk's key lessons are not about the past,' reflects Sterling in the *Steampunk Bible*:

> They are about the instability and obsolescence of our own times. A host of objects and services that we see each day all around us are not sustainable. [...] Once they're gone, they'll seem every bit as weird and archaic as top hats, crinolines, magic lanterns, clockwork automatons, absinthe, walking-sticks and paper-scrolled player pianos.[10]

As such, steampunk is intrinsically bound up with the neo-Victorian project of re-assessing the nineteenth century's legacies, here from a technological perspective. It condenses ideas about agency, artistry, and accessibility that defined object-user relationships amid the Industrial Revolution into a retro-speculative aesthetic shorthand[11] and adds irony and adventure. Its anachronistic, (re-)created objects become understandable, emotionally valuable, and full of (dangerous) possibility: 'Through the recovery of the everyday danger of interacting with volatile objects, steampunk practitioners desire to re-engage with the physical world, subverting the sterile and safe relationships they perceive to exist between people and objects in contemporary society'.[12]

Despite its semi-ironic reverence for Victorian materiality and aesthetic, steampunk remains conscious of the social and ecological cost of Victorian industrial production, and steampunks are called to 'punk responsibly' and remember that 'steampunking is a political act'.[13] Ultimately, steampunk is animated by a semi-nostalgic, semi-ironic celebration of a perceived sense of escalation and hubris associated with the Victorian age as a riotous, dirty, adventurous age of invention, romance, and exploration. As Diana Pho explains: 'Modern science fiction tells us: "Oh god, don't go build giant robots. They'll kill us all!" But Victorian science fiction says: "Yay! Let's go build giant robots! Oh shoot, they killed us"'.[14]

Steampunk is a self-aware, meta-historical, transmedia aesthetic that flaunts playful, retro-speculative anachronisms as its defining feature, and so collapses linear timelines into an imaginative and often semi-ironical triple exposure of past, present, and future. It usually includes techno-fantastical impulses and incorporates multiple, often paradoxical tensions. Marked by an inherent hybridity that blends genres and modes, such as the neo-Victorian with science fiction, it resists ontological coherence and unsettles dichotomies between fact and fiction, past and present, history and speculation, irony and nostalgia, the familiar and the strange. As such, it resembles Donna Haraway's cyborg in that it may 'contain contradictions that do not resolve into larger wholes', instead holding 'incompatible things together, because both or all are necessary and true'.[15]

It is the thesis of this study that, for steampunk fiction to function and deliver a satisfactory audience experience, it mobilizes a variety of popular cross-genre, transmedia tropes and mechanisms, with which its contemporary, transmedia-literate and globally connected audience of what one might call post-modern natives is intrinsically, if subconsciously, familiar. Through its anachronistic remix, steampunk creates ludic, irreverent relationships with space and time, here centred on and embodied through the Victorian metropolis, opening the past to interventions that play on the tensions and ironies of our hindsight position towards history. As such, it creates an active reader position and invites audiences to re-imagine their subject position in relation to material culture, here the shared memory of 'the Victorian', and urban space, and to evaluate competing collective narratives of the Victorian past. Steampunk so creates a unique interplay between (perceived) past and present, which in turn reflects back on our contemporary identity politics. Thus, depending on which historical meta-narratives are mobilized and how, steampunk holds the potential to shape its audiences as active political agents in pop culture discourse. Indeed, ongoing debates about the re-signification of post-colonial legacies and reparative re-shaping have been an integral part of the steampunk culture since its beginnings,[16] and so align it with the neo-Victorian project.

Neo-Victorianism and the Popular Imagination

As a meta-historical remix of popular memory, steampunk is always, if sometimes unconsciously so, engaged in what has been established as neo-Victorianism's core-principle, namely that it must 'in some respect be *self-consciously engaged with the act of (re)interpretation, (re)discovery and (re)vision concerning the Victorians.*'[17] It is also a decidedly popular incarnation of post-modern 'historiographic metafiction', 'those well-known and popular novels which are both intensely self-reflexive and yet paradoxically also lay claim to historical events and personages',[18] and, in its re-evaluation of the conditions, enduring traumas, and legacies of the nineteenth century in light of the present moment and its (usually) post-colonial and post-neo-liberal identity politics,[19] is likewise

> resurrecting the ghost(s) of the past, searching out its dark secrets and shameful mysteries, insisting obsessively on the lurid details of Victorian life, reliving the period's nightmares and traumas. At the same time, neo-Victorianism also tries to understand the nineteenth century as the contemporary self's uncanny *Doppelgänger*, exploring the uncertain limit between what is vanished (dead) and surviving (still living), celebrating the bygone even while lauding the demise of some of the period's most oppressive aspects, like institutionalised slavery and legally sanctioned sexism and racism.[20]

Steampunk, while its origins lie somewhat far afield of those of neo-Victorianism, is then nonetheless an essentially neo-Victorian mode, as it, too, constitutes an active site of interpretive struggle over the (re-)signification of cultural memory and, by extension, the collective identity of imagined communities,[21] only steampunk's neo-Victorian re-interpretation is infused with playful retro-speculation.

That the question of 'what it means to fashion the past for consumption in the present'[22] is as contested today as it was in the wake of neo-liberalism is painfully evident in Britain's Brexit era. Indeed, whereas the 'Victorian' marker, delineating Great Britain between 1837 and 1901, or what Eric Hobsbawm has termed the Long Nineteenth Century (1789–1914), is as potent as it is constricting and Anglo-centric, steampunk, like neo-Victorianism, is a global phenomenon with global potential.[23] What, then, comprises 'Victorian-ness' for international popular audiences? What is the symbolic significance of Victorian London especially as a potent essence of and emblem for that 'Victorian-ness' across national boundaries? How does steampunk London encapsulate, re-negotiate, or re-inscribe collective cultural memory which, as Jan Assmann suggests, is both externalized in symbolic spaces such as the urban sphere, and repeatedly communicated in and through everyday interaction?[24]

This study's aim is to pry apart and interrogate the multiple cultural mechanisms and meta-narratives about 'the Victorian' at play in the steampunk city in order to gain a deeper understanding of how a popular cultural memory of the Victorian past is shaped and transmitted. Steampunk emblematizes the production of communicative and cultural memory, not by relegated specialized authorities, but through the participatory space of popular culture, which Stuart Hall, after all, defines as a dynamic, ongoing process that both produces and reproduces a dominant cultural order: 'Popular culture is one of the sites where this struggle for and against a culture of the powerful is engaged: it is also the stake to be won or lost *in* that struggle. It is the arena of consent and resistance. It is partly where hegemony arises, and where it is secured.'[25] Notably, he also identifies popular culture as deeply rooted in nineteenth-century mass media, which is why a comparative approach to collectively constructed notions of Victorian London – both Victorian and neo-Victorian – will be especially productive: Considering that widely consumed media lastingly shape popular perception and illustrate 'what we want to imagine the period to have been like for diverse reasons, including affirmations of national identity, the struggle for symbolic restorative justice, and indulgence in escapist exoticism',[26] which persisting meta-narratives about the city reflect back our projected fantasies about the nineteenth-century? Which narratives are prioritized in an imagined teleological genealogy towards our present collective identity? Which stereotypes persist in the popular reception, potentially hampering a productive re-negotiation of the past? For example, given that, as Diana M. Pho argues, steampunk's ironically self-reflexive play dismantles homogeneous historical narratives, and rejects nostalgia in favour of transformative critique,[27] how does it reckon – or fail to reckon – with the nineteenth century's colonial legacies, especially regarding London as the Empire's capital?

Indeed, as Antonija Primorac notes, 'audiences' expectations are moulded less by a knowledge of the period based on the archival data (maps, blueprints, lithographs, paintings, photographs, life-writing, fictional and newspaper accounts), but more by the images generated by other, preceding, films and TV series set in the same period'.[28] 'In a sense', Kohlke and Gutleben diagnose, 'the neo-Victorian is by definition hyperreal, since it has no direct access to the Victorian real, instead relying entirely on Victorian texts and documents, that is, on signs of the past'.[29] Popular neo-Victoriana, sourcing from a pre-established collective idea of 'the Victorian', therefore often re-construct and perpetuate 'already accepted ideas about the Victorians for the sake of period authenticity. [...] [This means:] stereotypes about the Victorian past are (still) an important foundation on which popular adaptations rely'.[30] This may include persistent stereotypes about gender, or the almost reflexive, non-critical perpetuation of Gothic tropes, which are entangled in fraught Victorian ideas about race and Otherness. Popular neo-Victoriana and steampunk fiction may thus powerfully illustrate how our collective, politically conscious desire to reckon with the legacies of the Victorian past may be shaped by and entangled with shared fantasies and stereotypes about the period – and embodied, not least, through the 'Victorian' urban imaginary.

Cognitive Mapping and the Urban Imaginary

Collective memory is palimpsestically enshrined in the city. Its urban space is, as Henri Lefebvre conceptualizes, socially produced[31] and, whether in answering the logistic and economic demands of everyday life or encoding collective identity through *lieux de mémoire*,[32] continually accumulates layers of meaning. Perhaps no modern metropolis embodies this like London, where Roman ruins can be found near the brutalist sprawl of the Barbican performing arts centre, or where Leadenhall Market, a colourful Victorian arcade built on a market site dating from the fourteenth century, stands next to the 1980s' futuristic Lloyd's Building. Indeed, London has been the subject of literary production for centuries, and this study considers prominent approaches such as urban Gothic, flânerie, and psychogeography,[33] as well as literary urban studies.[34]

Here, mobilizing Roland Barthes' notion of the city as semiotic and symbolic,[35] the material city is conceived as a multilayered narrative, and the literary text may in turn become an urban model capturing or simulating the cityscape. Accordingly, my interest lies in how Victorian media (journalism, fiction, maps, paintings, and illustrations) aim to represent London's 'citiness'[36] – its socio-economic networks, palimpsestic infrastructures, simultaneous movements – and how their strategies lastingly shape the collectively imagined Victorian city against which steampunk London is juxtaposed. Literary cities, so Lieven Ameel states, can be considered 'realms of the imagination, constellations of tropes in an intertextual network'.[37] Consequently, collective memory of Victorian London emerges as a transmedia phenomenon in the vein of Henry Jenkins' notion of convergence culture, that is as a communally fostered imaginary constructed and consumed across multiple different media.[38] After all, neo-Victorian cities of memory are 'spaces in which memory is not just continually fostered, produced, and preserved, but also contested, deconstructed, and sometimes deliberately distorted or fabricated'.[39]

This study's main interests are in understanding how a shared urban imaginary is constructed, maintained, or re-framed across media and across time, and how that imaginary informs collective identity politics. Following Edward Said's concept of imagined geographies, it conceives of identity as spatial: Identity arises from how and where we locate, in our mental map of the world, the local and the strange, them and us, here and there, and is as such inherently political.[40] The city, too, functions as a microcosm of what Fredric Jameson terms cognitive mapping: Its paths and cornerstones externalize Lacanian notions of ideology as 'the representation of the subject's Imaginary relationship to his or her Real conditions of existence',[41] and so 'enable a situational representation on the part of the individual subject to that vaster and properly unrepresentable totality which is the ensemble of society's structures as a whole'.[42] The urban environment serves as an embodied, spatial analogy for how we situate ourselves in relation to larger social systems, and so serves as 'our mental and cognitive mapping of urban reality, and the interpretive grids through which we think about, experience, evaluate, and decide to act in these places, spaces, and communities in which we live'.[43] However, urban imaginaries, here of Victorian London, may function not only as mental maps of real spaces, but also as spatialized metaphors for our social and historical relationships.

This is why the steampunk city, albeit purely virtual because inherently fantastic and anachronistic, may illustrate how and to what end collective memory works in unique ways. As David Pike notes, 'a key element to the allure of Victorian London for steampunk is its limitless capacity to contain not only the world, as the imperial narrative would maintain, but also the multiverse—this world, all alternative worlds, and all the holes, fissures, and folds in between'[44] – all encoded in and through the city. Steampunk London acts as a projected theatre of 'Victorian-ness' that is open to participatory play. It re-calibrates our 'interpretive grids' and so acts a heterotopic counter-site to historical memory, 'a kind of effectively enacted utopia in which the real sites, all the other real sites that can be found within the culture, are simultaneously represented, contested, and inverted'.[45] Putting into play Kohlke and Gutleben's claim that, '[p]alimpsestically, we read the past city through the overlaid present, but conversely, we also read the present city backwards through the underlying and resurfacing past',[46] the steampunk city understands urban space as a cumulative texture, but also re-shuffles its palimpsestic layers. It draws attention to the process of memory-making and playfully invites audiences to re-think their subject position in relation to those processes and the identities they produce.

Book Overview

This book approaches the complex, multilayered nature of steampunk London from a variety of different angles and a multitude of texts. While the first two chapters focus on how steampunk comes into being through various cultural influences and collective memory-making, the latter two chapters ask why, that is for what purpose, and for whom, steampunk re-imagines the Victorian past. In all of them, Victorian London, whether imagined from a nineteenth-century perspective or through a steampunk lens, serves as a focalizing prism in which identity and memory are spatially encoded. While my focus lies largely on prose fiction, where steampunk Londons are typically most thoroughly imagined, I also discuss film, graphic novels, the visual arts, and video games at various points throughout, as my aim is to interrogate steampunk London as a transmedia phenomenon. As such, this study considers steampunk fiction from across the anglophone world, including the US, the UK, Canada, and New Zealand. The fact that writers and creators of steampunk Londons, just like their audiences, are at once globally scattered and connected through social media and a popular culture shared through the internet, demonstrates that steampunk imaginaries of Victorian London function as de-localized shared memory figures – illustrated by the international success of games like *Assassin's Creed*, or the globally sourced and read book reviews on sites such as Goodreads or YouTube, dedicated online forums, and blogs.

Chapter One examines the origins of seminal steampunk in 1980s California. I consider the impact of H. G. Wells' *The Time Machine* (1895) and Henry Mayhew's *London Labour and the London Poor* (1851) on the steampunk imaginary and argue that, while authors K. W. Jeter, James Blaylock, and Tim Powers semi-ironically coined the term steampunk in reference to cyberpunk, a coherent and recognizable steampunk aesthetic emerges later with William Gibson and Bruce Sterling's *The Difference Engine* (1990). My analysis situates early steampunk in the context of cyberpunk's counter-cultural agenda and the re-signification of the industrial paradigm at the dawn of the digital age. It examines how the novel utilizes the Victorian city in order to discuss the impact of cybertechnology and considers its re-use of urban space against the backdrop of Marxist urban theory, namely Henri Lefebvre's concept of the 'right to the city', and David Harvey's reading thereof.

Chapter Two is concerned with how steampunk functions in the context of collective memory, adaptation, and remix. I use London's East End as an example of how Victorian transmedia discourse constructed a palimpsestic urban mythology that encoded Victorian social anxieties through Gothic tropes. Focusing especially on Gustave Doré's illustrations, Arthur Morrison's *A Child of the Jago* (1896), and media generated around the Jack the Ripper murders (1888), I show how Gothic 'knowledge' is transmitted through popular culture. Against this backdrop, I examine how Kim Newman's *Anno Dracula* (1992) mines and remixes real and fictional events and people into a newly resonant, counter-fictional collage in order to satirize British 1980s neo-liberalism, positing that counter-fictionality is a staple of steampunk. I contrast Newman's popular fiction archive against the psychogeography of Peter Ackroyd and finally present George Mann's *The Affinity Bridge* (2008) and S. M. Peters' novel *Whitechapel Gods* (2008) as examples of how stereotypically or radically steampunk may re-purpose the legacy of East End mythologies in new ways going beyond the Gothic legacy.

Chapter Three considers how popular video games *Assassin's Creed: Syndicate* and *The Order 1886* (both 2015) actualize Victorian representations of London into a spatial simulation that aligns narrative progress with movement through space. Against the backdrop of Doreen Massey's theory of space as an active process of interlinking trajectories, I examine how Charles Dickens' London and the London of Sherlock Holmes have represented London's complexity through immersive and panoptic perspectives and analyse how game spaces synthesize the two. With brief recourse to the retro-speculative game spaces of *BioShock* (2007–2013) and *Dishonored* (2012), I show how game spaces become legible textures and storytelling devices in themselves. I argue that *Assassin's Creed* implements a fantasy of agency within urban spaces, whereas *The Order* uses cyberpunk impulses to build a dystopian hyper-city that undermines and challenges popular stereotypes about the Victorian era.

Chapter Four explores the ideological undercurrents informing steampunk imaginaries by discussing gender and feminist rebellion in *fin-de-siècle* London and steampunk fiction. I briefly consider the figure of the flâneur as a gendered phenomenon to offset how and why self-directed mobility in the modern metropolis was a central tenet of the New Woman's transgressive potential. However, I also consider how different or successive feminist agendas have shaped our perception of the nineteenth century, and how a monolithic feminist genealogy informs modern stereotypes about femininity and emancipation. Against this backdrop, I consider the progressive and paradoxically conservative agendas that inform how sexually liberated neo-Victorian and steampunk action heroines are configured and where their shortcomings lie by considering them within a framework of post-feminist and fourth-wave-feminist theory. I then provide a close reading of Gail Carriger's Parasolverse novels (2009 to present) as a positive example of how steampunk may imagine empowered and feminine heroines. By discussing how the same series reimagines LGBTQA+ characters through steampunk, I interrogate steampunk's potential to provide radical alternative histories.

Steampunk's retro-speculative play provides us with playfully anachronistic and unique meta-historical approaches towards a collectively remembered Victorian past. Here, we may highlight, redress, satirize, or re-experience its glories, quirks, and failures with utopian or dystopian impulses and nostalgic or radical outlooks. Free to re-imagine an era we understand as both socially, economically, and technologically formative, yet also fundamentally outdated and strange, steampunk's adventurous re-calibration of the nineteenth century bears a uniquely radical potential to address, even re-dress, the era's enduring traumas, such as its gender, class, and race hierarchies or colonial violence. However, as a popular phenomenon sourced from and aimed at a wide audience, steampunk's retro-speculative interventions also reflect back on us. They reveal what and how much we think we know about the Victorian past, which perceived historical failures we believe we can amend, and whether or not we have the imaginative tools to actually re-think them. Indeed, as this study will reveal, steampunk may (often unintentionally) re-iterate fraught assumptions about both past and present, and so expose our own blind spots. Fundamentally, however, steampunk playfully highlights and challenges our relationship with history and deepens our understanding of human agency in the outcome of historical processes, seeking to inspire us to approach the future with the same creativity. After all, as Sterling notes, 'the past is a kind of future that has already happened.'[47]

Notes

1. John Clute, 'Vive?', in *Look at the Evidence* (London: Gollancz, 1996 [1991]), p. 310.
2. Rachel A. Bowser and Brian Croxall, 'Introduction: Industrial Evolution', *Neo-Victorian Studies*, 3:1 (2010), 1–45, p. 29.
3. Mike Perschon, *Steampunk FAQ. All That's Left to Know About the World of Goggles, Airships, and Time Travel* (Milwaukee: Applause Theatre & Cinema Books, 2018), pp. 2–12.
4. For example: Disney's *20,000 Leagues Under the Sea* (1954), Karel Zeman's films (e.g. *The Fabulous World of Jules Verne*, 1958; *The Fabulous Baron Munchausen*, 1962), CBS's *The Wild Wild West* series (1965), the BBC's *Doctor Who* (1963 to present). For more, see John C. Tibbetts, '"Fulminations and Fulgurators": Jules Verne, Karel Zeman, and Steampunk Cinema', in *Steaming Into a Victorian Future*, ed. by Julie Anne Taddeo and Cynthia J. Miller (Lanham: Scarecrow Press, 2013.), pp. 125–144.
5. Cory Gross, 'A History of Misapplied Technology. The History and Development of the Steampunk Genre', *Steampunk Magazine*, 2 (2007), 54–61, p. 57.

6   Rebecca Onion, 'Reclaiming the Machine: An Introductory Look at Steampunk in Everyday Practise', *Neo-Victorian Studies*, 1.1 (2008), 138–163. Bowser & Croxall, 'Industrial Evolution', 2010. Stefania Forlini, 'Technology and Morality: The Stuff of Steampunk', *Neo-Victorian Studies*, 3.1 (2010), 72–98. Christine Ferguson, 'Surface Tensions: Steampunk, Subculture, and the Ideology of Style', *Neo-Victorian Studies*, 4:2 (2011), 66–90. Sally-Anne Huxtable, '"Love the Machine, Hate the Factory": Steampunk Design and the Vision of a Victorian Future', in *Steaming Into A Victorian Future*, ed. by Julie Anne Taddeo and Cynthia J. Miller (Lanham: Scarecrow Press, 2013), pp. 213–234. Suzanne Barber and Matt Hale, 'Enacting the Never-Was: Upcycling the Past, Present, and Future in Steampunk', in S*teaming Into a Victorian Future*, ed. by Julie Anne Taddeo and Cynthia J. Miller (Lanham: Scarecrow Press, 2013.), pp. 165–183. Martin Danahay, 'Steampunk as a Postindustrial Aesthetic: "All that is solid melts in air"', *Neo-Victorian Studies*, 8:2 (2016), 28–56.
7   Bruce Sterling, 'The User's Guide to Steampunk', in *The Steampunk Bible*, ed. by Jeff VanderMeer and S.J. Chambers (New York: Abrams Image, 2011), pp. 11–12, p. 12.
8   The Catastrophone Orchestra and Arts Collective, 'What then, is Steampunk? Colonizing the Past So We Can Dream The Future', *Steampunk Magazine*, 1 (2006), 4–5, p. 4.
9   Professor Calamity, 'My Machine, My Comrade', *Steampunk Magazine*, 3:1 (2007), 24–25, p. 25.
10 Sterling, 'User's Guide', p. 13.
11 See Huxtable, '"Love the Machine, Hate the Factory"', p. 214 and Ferguson, 'Surface Tensions', p. 67–69.
12 Onion, 'Reclaiming the Machine', p. 151.
13 James H. Carrott, 'Punking the Past: Politics of Possibility', *Steampunk Magazine*, 9 (2012), 70–71, p. 71.
14 James H. Carrott and Brian David Johnson, *Vintage Tomorrows* (Sebastopol: O'Reilly, 2013), p. 107.
15 Donna Haraway, 'A Cyborg Manifesto. Science, Technology and Socialist-feminism in the Late Twentieth Century', in *The Cybercultures Reader*, ed. by David Bell and Barbara M. Kennedy (London: Routledge, 2000) pp. 291–324, p. 291.
16 For example: Diana M. Pho, 'Objectified and Politicized: The Dynamics of Ideology and Consumerism in Steampunk Subculture', in Taddeo and Miller (2013): 185–212. Diana M. Pho, 'Punking the Other: On the Performance of Racial and National Identities in Steampunk', in *Like Clockwork. Steampunk Pasts, Presents & Futures*, ed. by Rachel A. Bowser and Brian Croxall (Minneapolis: Minnesota UP, 2016), pp. 127–152.
17 Ann Heilmann and Mark Llewellyn, *Neo-Victorianism: The Victorians in the Twenty-First Century, 1999–2009* (London: Palgrave Macmillan, 2010), p. 4, original emphasis.
18 Linda Hutcheon, *A Poetics of Postmodernism. History, Theory, Fiction* (Routledge: New York, 1988), p. 5.

19 Marie-Luise Kohlke, 'Introduction: Speculations in and on the Neo-Victorian Encounter', *Neo-Victorian Studies*. 1.1 (2008), 1–18 , pp. 3–4.
20 Marie-Luise Kohlke and Christian Gutleben, 'The (Mis)Shapes of Neo-Victorian Gothic: Continuations, Adaptations, Transformations', in *Neo-Victorian Gothic. Horror, Violence, and Degeneration in the Re-Imagined Nineteenth Century*, ed. by Marie-Luise Kohlke and Christian Gutleben (Leiden: Brill Rodopi, 2012), pp. 1–50, p. 4.
21 See Benedict Anderson, *Imagined Communities: Reflections on the Origin and Spread of Nationalism* (London: Verso, 1983).
22 Kate Mitchell, *History and Cultural Memory in Neo-Victorian Fiction. Victorian Afterimages* (London: Palgrave Macmillan, 2010), p. 3.
23 See Elizabeth Ho, *Neo-Victorianism and the Memory of Empire* (London: Bloomsbury, 2012). Antonija Primorac and Monika Pietrzak-Franger (eds.), Special Issue: Neo-Victorianism and Globalisation: Transnational Dissemination of Nineteenth-Century Cultural Texts, *Neo-Victorian Studies*, 8:1 (2015). Elizabeth Ho (ed.), Special Issue: Neo-Victorian Asia, *Neo-Victorian Studies*, 11:2 (2019).
24 Jan Assmann, 'Cultural Memory', in *Cultural Memory Studies. An International and Interdisciplinary Handbook*, eds. by Erll, Astrid and Ansgar Nünning (Berlin, New York 2008), pp. 109–118.
25 Stuart Hall, 'Notes on deconstructing "the popular"', [1981], republished in *Essential Essays, Volume* (Durham: Duke University Press, 2019), pp. 347–361.
26 Marie-Luise Kohlke, 'Mining the neo-Victorian Vein: Prospecting for Gold, Buried Treasure, and Uncertain Metal', in *Neo-Victorian Literature and Culture: Immersions and Revisitations*, ed. by Nadine Böhm-Schnitker and Susanne Gruss (London: Routledge, 2014), pp. 21–37, p. 21.
27 Pho, 'Punking the Other', pp. 128, 135.
28 Antonija Primorac, *Neo-Victorianism on Screen: Postfeminism and Contemporary Adaptations of Victorian Women* (London: Palgrave Macmillan, 2018), p. 12.
29 Marie-Luise Kohlke and Christian Gutleben, 'The (Mis)Shapes of Neo-Victorian Gothic: Continuations, Adaptations, Transformations', in *Neo-Victorian Gothic. Horror, Violence, and Degeneration in the Re-Imagined Nineteenth Century*, ed. by Marie-Luise Kohlke and Christian Gutleben (Leiden: Brill Rodopi, 2012), pp. 1–50, p. 41.
30 Primorac, *Neo-Victorianism on Screen*, p. 18.
31 Henri Lefebvre, *The Production of Space* (Oxford: Basil Blackwell, 1991), p. 26.
32 See Pierre Nora, *The realms of memory: Rethinking the French Past* (New York: Columbia University Press, 1999), p. 14.
33 See, for example: Julian Wolfreys, *Writing London: The Trace of the Urban Text from Blake to Dickens* (London: Palgrave Macmillan, 1998). Robert Mighall, *A Geography of Victorian Gothic Fiction. Mapping History's Nightmares* (Oxford: Oxford University Press, 1999). Julian Wolfreys, *Writing London. Materiality, Memory, Spectrality* (London: Palgrace Macmillan, 2002). Matthew Beaumont, *Nightwalking. A Nocturnal*

History of London (London: Verso, 2015). Estelle Murail and Sara Thornton (eds.), *Dickens and the Virtual City: Urban Perception and the Production of Social Space* (London: Palgrave Macmillan, 2017).

34 Notably: Jens Martin Gurr, *Charting Literary Urban Studies. Texts as Models of and for the City* (London: Palgrave Macmillan, 2021). Lieven Ameel (ed.), *The Routledge Companion to Literary Urban Studies* (London: Routledge, 2023).

35 Roland Barthes, 'Semiology and the Urban', in *The City and the Sign. An Introduction to Urban Semiotics*, ed. by M. Gottdiener and Alexandros Ph. Lagopoulos (New York: Columbia University Press, 1986), pp. 87–98.

36 See: Jason Finch, *Literary Urban Studies and How to Practice It* (London: Routledge, 2021). Lieven Ameel, et al. (eds.), *The Materiality of Literary Narratives in Urban History* (London: Routledge, 2019).

37 Lieven Ameel, 'Literary Urban Studies. An Introduction', in Lieven Ameel (ed.), *The Routledge Companion to Literary Urban Studies* (London: Routledge, 2023), pp. 1–10, p. 3.

38 Henry Jenkins, *Convergence Culture. Where Old and New Media Collide* (New York: New York University Press, 2008), p. 116. Jenkins' definition pertains to modern popular media franchises, but as recent studies exemplify, it is also easily applicable to a nineteenth-century context as well. See: Christina Meyer and Monika Pietrzak-Franger (eds.), *Transmedia Practices in the Long Nineteenth Century* (London: Routledge, 2022). Erica Haugtvedt, *Transfictional Character and Transmedia Storyworlds in the British Nineteenth Century* (London: Palgrave Macmillan, 2022).

39 Marie-Louise Kohlke and Christian Gutleben, 'Troping the Neo-Victorian City', in *Neo-Victorian Cities. Reassessing Urban Politics and Poetics*, ed. by Marie-Louise Kohlke and Christian Gutleben (Leiden: Brill Rodopi, 2015), pp. 1–42, p. 7.

40 See: Edward Said, *Orientalism* (London: Penguin Classics, 2003 [1978]).

41 Louis Althusser, quoted in: Fredric Jameson, *Postmodernism. Or, The Cultural Logic of Late Capitalism* (London: Verso, 1991), p. 51. Also: Kevin Lynch's *The Image of the City* (1960).

42 Jameson, *Postmodernism*, p. 51.

43 Edward Soja, *Postmetropolis: Critical Studies of Cities and Regions* (Oxford: Basil Blackwell, 2000), p. 324.

44 David Pike, 'Steampunk and the Victorian City', in *Like Clockwork. Steampunk Pasts, Presents & Futures,* ed. by Rachel A. Bowser and Brian Croxall (Minneapolis: Minnesota UP, 2016), pp. 3–31, p. 4.

45 Michel Foucault, 'Of Other Spaces', trans. by Jay Miskowiec, in *Architecture / Mouvement/ Continuité,* October 1984. pp. 1–9. Unpublished lecture, given 1967.

46 Kohlke and Gutleben, 'Troping the Neo-Victorian City', p. 6.

47 Sterling, 'The User's Guide', p. 12.

1

Different Engines: Seminal Steampunk and the Foundations of Gonzo-Victorian London

Introduction: Genealogies of Punk

This chapter explores the origins of steampunk, especially its synthesis of nineteenth-century urban ethnography and 1980s cyberpunk, and considers how first-wave fiction conceives of, and re-maps, social relationships with and within the Victorian metropolis. Indeed, as a term inadvertently and half-jokingly coined in 1987 by Californian science fiction writer K. W. Jeter in a letter to *Locus* magazine, trying to describe fiction recently written by him, Tim Powers, and James Blaylock in a 'gonzo-historical manner',[1] steampunk emerged without any agenda or clearly delineated aesthetic in mind. In fact, Jeter's suggestion was an ironic nod towards cyberpunk, which had emerged with Ridley Scott's *Blade Runner* (1982) and William Gibson's *Neuromancer* (1984). Thus, whereas the trio was perhaps inspired by 1950s and 1960s adaptations of Victorian literature,[2] early steampunk was as yet far removed from the neo-Victorian, which flourished later and predominantly in 1990s Britain.

Second-wave steampunk, emerging as a transmedia subculture rather than a niche subgenre of fiction and seeking to establish a canon, has repeatedly solidified the California trifecta's origin myth,[3] and invested in the serious and political implications of the '-punk' suffix: counter-culture, the deconstruction of historical meaning, dismantling of hegemonic structures.[4] However, as Perschon also notes, neither the trifecta's early novels nor second-wave popular fiction necessarily make overt political claims,[5] and as we will see, the trifecta's novels are hardly 'dark and subversive',[6] so this is certainly a misinterpretation. Nonetheless, as this chapter aims to show, even at its most whimsical and escapist, '[s]teampunk seems precisely to illustrate, and perhaps even perform, a kind of cultural memory work'[7] – even if unwittingly so. This is evident not least through the trifecta's gravitation towards the idea of Victorian London as their novels' epicentre, that is a setting that most enshrines both an imagined 'Victorian-ness' and of 'citiness' of that era. Why, then, is an urban setting so central to these authors' conception of 'the Victorian'? How do they conceptualize, interrogate, and re-purpose their retro-speculative gonzo-adventure stories through and within a Victorian aesthetic, and how does that illustrate steampunk's re-signification of our relationship with the past?

This chapter examines how Blaylock's, Jeter's, and Power's early steampunk novels re-adapt H. G. Wells' *The Time Machine* and Henry Mayhew's *London Labour and the London Poor* to re-focus their new urban imaginaries, here especially through the rationalizing narrative device of time travel. By considering William Gibson and Bruce Sterling's genre-defining 1990 novel *The Difference Engine* in the context of cyberpunk, I then examine how the novel synthesizes steampunk into a more coherent vision which lastingly shaped the movement. Central to my analysis, which is informed by the urban theories of Georg Simmel, Henri Lefebvre, and David Harvey, is the question of how early steampunk novels conceive of the Victorian city, both in conjunction and in contrast with the Victorian intertexts from which they source, and to what end they re-deploy a re-imagined Victorian urban setting.

1.1 The California Trifecta: Time Travellers, Morlocks, and Mayhew's 'Shabby-Seedy' London

Jeter's 1979 novel *Morlock Night*, firmly installed by steampunk discourse as 'the book that started it all',[8] is a fantasy-infused, escapist sequel to H. G. Wells' 1895 novella *The Time Machine*, 'in plot and action, not in politics or ideology'.[9] As an adventure odyssey through Victorian London in which a reincarnated King Arthur and Merlin search for Excalibur to defeat the Morlocks which have used the time machine to invade and colonize the alternative past, *Morlock Night* offers little in the way of subversive urban politics, or indeed Victorian aesthetics. Its most interesting feature is perhaps its usage of Wells' time machine for its premise, as now Well's speculative foray into the future is overlaid with the returned gaze from our hindsight perspective, establishing that playful double exposure of past and present so intrinsic to steampunk. I want therefore to briefly outline how speculation has informed speculative fiction and our relationship with temporal axes since Wells' classic text.

Indeed, projection and speculation as narrative models (here into the future), as David Wittenberg argues, are themselves rooted in a nineteenth-century, post-Darwinian shift 'toward specifically temporal models of sociopolitical extrapolation: plausible utopian futures must be directly "evolved" from actual present-day conditions.'[10] Utopian romances, as he terms them, develop into time travel fictions which 'link present and future realistically, and thereby [...] legitimize social prognostications'.[11] This is most clearly illustrated by Wells' account of future London in *The Time Machine* (1895). While the time traveller must constantly correct and re-adjust his anthropological deductions about the future he encounters, they are deeply rooted in an evolutionary logic he perceives as coherent, namely a logic of teleological progress and decline. In so doing, it mobilizes contemporary anxieties about degeneration. After all, 1895 saw the translation of Max Nordau's *Degeneration*, which made the term notorious as a defamation of *fin-de-siècle* culture through a logic of social Darwinism. Considering Nordau's spiteful attacks on the decadent movement, it is all the more ironic that the traveller's 'first evocation of London is a satirical biologizing of [...] 1890s Aestheticism (all those beautiful, dying, effeminate consumptives)'.[12] Indeed, the Eloi are insipid, child-like, post-bourgeois creatures, 'dwindling in size, strength, and intellect'.[13] Indolent and alienated from the decaying ruins of future London, they have lost any trace of urban sophistication alongside basic technologies such as fire-making and written language. They are continually preyed on by their antithesis, the 'ape-like', carnivorous, underground-dwelling Morlocks, characterized as primitive monsters, Lemurs, and 'human spiders'. (p. 45). The Morlocks are 'strongly associated [...] with the mythic landscape of the night and the underground', as well as the haunting echoes of technology.[14] The nameless traveller associates their subterranean dwellings with 'the Metropolitan Railway in London' (p. 47), where he hears 'the throb and hum of machinery' (p. 52). In fact, while the traveller may sympathize with the primitive Eloi, he shares with the abject Morlocks 'the same mechanical bent, the same longing for meat, the same disordered nights, the same bloodlust to kill'.[15] Wells' portrait of the future remains deliberately ambiguous about our alignment with these futuristic dwellers.

Naturally, Wells' pursuit of this Darwinist-Marxist imaginative trajectory along the lines of human evolution serves as socio-cultural critique of his late-Victorian present, hinging on the mediating, commenting presence of the time traveller who can only understand the future on the terms of his present. As such, he identifies the effeminate Eloi as the heirs of 'the Haves, pursuing pleasure and comfort and beauty', and the Morlocks 'below ground [as] the Have-nots, the Workers getting continually adapted to the conditions of their labour' (p. 48) who now in turn oppress their oppressors. Wells' imaginative playground is also viscerally realized in and through the urban landscape: 'Even now, does not an

East-End worker live in such artificial conditions as practically to be cut off from the natural surface of the earth?' (p. 48). In addition to such speculations about the Morlocks, the traveller configures the 'exquisite beauty of the buildings' to exemplify 'the last surgings of the now purposeless energy of mankind before it settled down into perfect harmony with the conditions under which it lived – the flourish of that triumph which began the last great peace' (p. 48). Such an assessment mirrors once again the self-perception of late-Victorian decadence, seemingly evolved to such heights of civilization that, as the traveller predicts, 'it takes to art and eroticism, and then come languor and decay' (p. 33).

Socially and physically, Victorian London is overlaid with its own future. Pinpointing geographical areas such as Wimbledon, Wandsworth, or Battersea, or examining future archaeologies in 'the ruins of some latter-day Kensington Museum', the traveller continues to see Victorian London underneath this future cityscape (p. 64). As Luckhurst remarks: 'The Traveller only sketches his moralistic degenerationalism onto the cosmos, making the end of the world a rather local, late Victorian affair.'[16] This in turn illustrates Louis Montrose's New Historicist claim about the 'historicity of texts', especially their rootedness in the socio-historical, political, and cultural contexts of their production.[17] It draws our attention to an important distinction: as Wells' traveller can only see and understand the future on Victorian terms, so steampunk can only re-imagine the past from a twentieth-century (later twenty-first) perspective, and although the imagined future and historical space with which both are concerned is, in a manner, 'Victorian', those ideas about what constitutes 'Victorian' must necessarily be at variance.

Speculative fiction, as Wittenberg outlines, undergoes paradigm shifts throughout the twentieth century, for example through Einstein's theory of relativity and Heisenberg's uncertainty principle, which make thinkable models of multiplication and recombination, or Freudian or Jungian psychoanalysis, which provides for 'temporal dilation or reversal, physical access to one's own past or future (or alternative presents), [...] "narcisstic" or "oedipal" meetings'.[18] Together with 1950s and 1960s developments in quantum mechanics, which popularize many-worlds and alternative, parallel universe tropes, time travel fiction increasingly plays with 'pivotal incidents' and divergent realities.[19] In short, speculative fiction, in the run up to the 1980s, increasingly de-centres the 'meaning of the individual historical event and its capacity to affect and define the broader historical record, as well as, alternatively, the capacity of the historical record to define and characterize the individual event'[20] and so puts into play Hayden White's notion of the fundamental ambiguity of the term 'history' in a way that differs significantly from Wells' approach.

After all, history, defined by White as 'a verbal structure in the form of a narrative prose discourse that purports to be a model, or icon, of past structures and processes in the interest of explaining what they were by representing them',[21] is itself narrative in nature. It is 'emplotted in some way'[22] – a term central to Paul Ricoeur's hermeneutic phenomenological philosophy as the organization of a series of events into a meaningful narrative.[23] In Ricoeur's work, emplotment is not only integral to historiography, but to his conception of identity itself, in which subjectivity emerges out of narrative: 'To answer the question "Who?" [...] is to tell the story of a life. [...] And the identity of this who therefore itself must be a narrative identity'.[24] Historiography and identity are then closely intertwined because both are founded on a hermeneutic process of sense-making, namely the synthesis of historical events into a 'plot': 'The plot, therefore, places us at the crossing point of temporality and narrativity'.[25] Steampunk, by using time travel conceits and retro-speculation, intervenes in and re-calibrates mutually constitutive notions of time, history, and identity, in new ways, namely by opening them up to experiment and adventurous play.

This becomes evident through Tim Powers' 1983 novel *The Anubis Gates*. Set in the pre-Victorian Regency era, the novel exemplifies the experimental spirit of early steampunk. Here, the academic and amateur biographer of the obscure Romantic poet William Ashbless, Brendan Doyle, is hired to accompany wealthy tourists through a hole in the time stream to visit a lecture by Samuel Taylor Coleridge in 1810. He becomes stranded there and, through a series of misadventures, comes to realize that he himself is, or will always have been, Ashbless. In constructing such a meta-literary, paradoxical, closed-loop time travel narrative, the novel so narcissistically interrogates the inevitability of history and enquires into 'the ontology of the event itself':[26]

> Is 'the historical event, in and of itself, a blankly preliminary cause, an overdetermined revisionist effect, or a mere component or signifier of some even larger story or signifier? Or, [...] is the inevitability of [(here: becoming Ashbless)] the result of the somehow unalterable pastness of that event, the result of the deliberate intervention of the time traveller from out of the present [(here: the biographer)], or the result of a powerful inertia or causelike weight of history itself?'[27]

After all, Doyle more or less seamlessly adapts into his new identity through the historical knowledge he assembled about himself in a now-distant future. Moreover, as he becomes quite literally his own subject, Doyle's journey stages, not as allegory but as part of the plot itself, what Lacan defined as the psychoanalytic session, the 'realization of the [subject's] history' in a present discourse, or even 'the restitution of the subject's wholeness ... in the guise of a restoration of the past'.[28] The novel establishes steampunk as a mode that destabilizes, subverts, and disassembles conservative notions of the past and our place in it.

In his 1992 novel *Lord Kelvin's Machine*, Blaylock's scientist hero Langdon St. Ives, in accordance with the Victorian inventor archetype, quite literally hijacks the past to experiment on it. In the attempt to undo his wife Alice's death at the hands of his arch-enemy Dr Ignacio Narbondo, St. Ives travels along complex non-linear trajectories, is transformed emotionally along the way, and in ultimately saving Alice, creates an alternative future which negates those parts of the 'present' which the reader has hitherto followed. It also relativizes his own identity, posing a dilemma about his own, multiple selves:

> He looked out into the street, where his past-time self lay invisible in the water and muck of the road. You fool, he said in his mind. I *earned* this, but I've got to give it to you, when all you would have done is botch it utterly. But even as he thought this, he knew the truth—that he wasn't the man now that he had been then. Alice didn't deserve the declined copy; what she wanted was the genuine article. And maybe he could become that article—but not by staying here. He had to go home again, to the future, in order to catch up with himself once more.[29]

The instability of the historical record is here built into the very fabric of Blaylock's steampunk universe. In this first phase of steampunk, revisiting the past is often a literal journey on the level of plot, that is, in Russian formalist terminology, narrative devices such as repetitions, flash forwards or backwards, or time lapse are staged not just in the *sjuzhet* (how the plot is mediated), but the *fabula* (the story that happens).[30] As such, time travel helps rationalize steampunk's experimental recourse to the Victorian past, as well as its intervention into and re-routing of a layered historiography. Mobilizing the post-Victorian relativity paradigm, early steampunk both destabilizes notions of history and identity, and plays out irreverent alternative outcomes in and through the Victorian era as one characterized by (imagined) philosophical coherence and stability. We must therefore investigate early steampunk's conception of what constitutes 'the Victorian' next.

The trifecta's early novels purposely draw from and re-work Henry Mayhew's journalistic account, *London Labour and the London Poor* (1851, reissued with additions in 1861, 1862, 1864 and 1865). They have termed it as 'the corner stone of Victorian London research work (at least when you need some seedy low-life colour)'.[31] It is interesting and important to note that, whereas Mayhew's near-Dickensian, sentimental, and picturesque descriptions of London's shabby-vivacious urban life are intrinsically informed by his (British Victorian) middle-class perspective and its prejudices, Jeter, Blaylock, and Powers, culturally and temporally distant, now ascribe to his work the authenticity of the journalist. To them, it becomes a 'source book' of, and key to, the gritty, hitherto undiscovered Victorian urban underbelly,[32] and inspires their fantastic re-workings. In *Morlock Night*, for example, we meet Rich Tom, a 'sewer-hunter', a group who according to Mayhew, find among the 'pieces of iron, nails, various scraps of metal [...] shillings, sixpences, half-crowns, and occasionally half-sovereigns and sovereigns', but are also 'improvident'. With 'but ordinary prudence', the shore-men might

> live well, have comfortable homes, and even be able to have sufficient to provide for themselves in their old age. Their practice, however, is directly the reverse. They no sooner make a 'haul', as they say, than they adjourn to some low public-house in the neighbourhood, and seldom leave till empty pockets and hungry stomachs drive them forth to procure the means for a fresh debauch.[33]

Yet Jeter's Rich Tom, having been converted by the journalist himself to middle-class virtues of prudence and foresight, has managed to amass a fortune.[34] There is, of course, a certain ironic humour at play here. Mayhew's portraits, driven both by his own bourgeois background and empathy, depict London street folk as nomadic, independent urban cultures who share codes of meanings and behaviour which are coherent in themselves and differ from those of the working or middle class.[35] Jeter picks up on this and adds his own, ironic twist, but Rich Tom's turn towards prudence indicates a degree of assimilation, not counter-culture.

In *The Anubis Gates*, a stranded, half-drowned Brendan Doyle is fished out of the Thames by costermongers. Mayhew outlines this community in painstaking detail over more than sixty pages, mapping out their trade routes, contrivances, their language, attitudes towards marriage, police, education, and religion, even their gambling habits, dress, and diet. In Powers' novel however, they merely convey Doyle to Billingsgate market and act as an omen that 'the advantage of all his twentieth-century knowledge' might not 'turn the scales in his favour'.[36] This encounter with the costermongers here functions as a gateway of Doyle's journey deeper into London's 'seedy' underworld, as it is at Billingsgate where he is introduced to the peculiar, even bizarre members of the beggars' guilds.

It is Blaylock's Langdon St. Ives series which makes most fruitful use of Mayhew's work. In *Homunculus*, we encounter Bill Kraken, a pea pod man holding 'an oval pot with a swing handle, the pot swaddled in a length of cloth' and 'a small closed basket' around his neck in which he carries 'salt, pepper, and vinegar'.[37] In this and many other descriptions, Blaylock closely echoes Mayhew's detailed, anthropological descriptions, but it is through Kraken, this versatile 'jack-of-all-Mayhew-trades'[38] who becomes a reliable part of St. Ives' crew of heroes and as such a main character, that most of Mayhew's characteristic tone of a somewhat romantic type of ethnography is re-presented.

All three novelists make conscious use of Mayhew as a source book to include characters and voices from the margins. Why this endeavour to portray an 'authentic' urban population in these adventurous Victorian fantasies? Costermongers, pea pod men and sewer-hunters appear in early steampunk rather to add that 'seedy low-life colour' rather than to deliver subversive social critique, and yet they are more than mere window dressing. They embody the 'citiness' of Victorian London, albeit an alternative and potentially subversive one. Their presence recalls Max Weber's urban theory of cities as originating in Medieval Europe as commercial centres in which guilds and free labour provided autonomy from feudalistic influences.[39] Trade and mobility are therefore quintessentially urban characteristics, and Mayhew' subjects embody both.

That they are relegated to the streets of London's East End illustrates how urban space is socially produced. As Henri Lefebvre's defines: '(Social) space is a (social) product. [...] [It] has taken on, [...] a sort of reality of its own [...]. [T]he space thus produced also serves as a tool of thought and of action; [...] in addition to being a means of production it is also a means of control, and hence of domination, of power.'[40] The physical city, according to David Harvey, eternally made and re-made, encodes our 'relationship to nature, lifestyles, technologies and aesthetic values.'[41] Mayhew's ethnographic work shows how the urban poor, barred from the central bastion of Victorian middle-class respectability, namely the domestic sphere, and with no access to the means of production, have developed their own urban habitus and ways of inhabiting that urban space which is open to them. Indeed, they embody what Walter Benjamin has observed about working-class communal life in twentieth-century Europe, namely that it crosses private-public boundaries: '[T]he house is far less the refuge into which people retreat than the inexhaustible reservoir from which they flood out. [...] Poverty has brought about a stretching of frontiers that mirrors the most radiant freedom of thought'.[42] Similarly, Benjamin's description of Moscow, where 'Shoe polish and writing materials, handkerchiefs, dolls' sleighs, swings for children, ladies' underwear, stuffed birds, clothes-hangers' are sprawled out in the street echoes the clutter of Mayhew's East End with its 'plaids, hats, dressing gowns, shirts [...][in] the dull brown-green of velveteen; the deep blue of a pilot jacket; the variegated figures of the shawl dressing-gown; the glossy black of the restored garments [...]'.[43] Even such cursory comparison implies an alternative, somewhat folkloric community in the city, a sort of inside-out lifestyle in defiance of a traditional middle-class 'Victorian-ness', centred around separated public and private spheres. Mayhew's urban tribes lead a life of invention and bravado which a writer in the 1980s, particularly one acquainted with the philosophy of 'punk', might have read as the subversive bricolage of styles and behaviours Dick Hebdige identified as integral to subculture.[44]

Indeed, early steampunk seems wholly uninterested in the domestic sphere of the respectable Victorian middle class: their heroes often gallivant around with gypsies, costermongers, shady coachmen, and beggars who all live and work in the open street, pursuing and being pursued by adventure in the ever-shifting cityscape. Here, what the trifecta identifies as Mayhew's shabby-vivacious subcultures proudly inhabit an urban space of precocity with wit, savvy, and defiance. Their social and economic vulnerability, nomadic living, and the whimsical exoticism of the Victorian city gives rise to opportunities for discovery and excitement among a hidden alternative urban world existing within and alongside the visible, tangible world of the Victorian middle and upper class. Jeter, Blaylock, and Powers re-prioritize previously obscured or at least to them unknown meta-narratives about what constitutes 'the Victorian' in favour of a new sense of adventure and whimsy.

'Gonzo Historical': The Urban Weird

Early steampunk's picturesque urban tribes infuse Victorian London with what Steffen Hantke calls an 'authorial whimsy in mixing history, fiction, and fantasy'.[45] Christine Ferguson refers to steampunk's 'whimsical' practices in her discussion of surface and style.[46] Perschon, too, describes Blaylock's steampunk as 'a fun place to play, a place where aliens arriving in London are met with the hope for a smoke, a chat, and a pint of bitter, rather than the London of today, where an alien might be met by the military. In short, Blaylock's steampunk is a world where whimsy rules'.[47] From early on, steampunk infuses the Victorian past with an 'interplay of the familiar and the alien, the sense of distortion, hyperbole, and defamiliarization' which oscillates between 'ironic and relativized absurdity'[48] and forms of escapism.[49] This can take on whimsical notes; a sort of irreverent but ultimately inconsequential quirkiness that, much like Sianne Ngai's concept of cuteness ('an aesthetic response to the diminutive, the weak, and the subordinate') renders the Victorian past safe and unthreatening, at least partly.[50] We are certainly drawn to the nineteenth century, as Kohlke and Gutleben note, for its 'its (would-be) *transcended otherness*, alternately gothically horrid and cheerfully quaint',[51] but it is precisely that tension between the two which in early steampunk finds expression through a 'post-nostalgic'[52] stance and elements of weird fiction.

In so doing, steampunk loops back to the late nineteenth and early twentieth century and to writers such as Arthur Machen, Ambrose Bierce, or H. P. Lovecraft.[53] The weird characteristically blends horror, fantasy, and science fiction into tales often saturated with a spiritual or cosmic dread and has famously been characterized by Lovecraft as follows:

> The true weird tale must have something more than secret murder, bloody bones, or a sheeted form clanking chains according to rule. A certain atmosphere of breathless and unexplainable dread of outer, unknown forces must be present; and there must be a hint, expressed with a seriousness and portentousness becoming its subject, of that most terrible conception of the human brain – a malign and particular suspension or defeat of those fixed laws of Nature which are our only safeguard against the assaults of chaos and the daemons of unplumbed space.[54]

To a certain degree, the weird relies on notions of the uncanny.[55] However, unlike in Gothic fiction (examined more closely in Chapter Two), where uncanniness arises out of repressed memories and fears and is therefore psychological and internal, weird fiction's terror is located without and saturated by a sense of foreboding (after all, the word 'weird' is derived from the Old-English concept 'wyrd', meaning fate or destiny). It explores the cosmic indifference of a universe continually widened and transformed by scientific discovery, and revels in undermining and dislodging the anthropocentric, late-Victorian perception, deploying transgressive or obscure content as what Luckhurst identifies as 'emblems of aesthetic resistance to the [middle-brow] market'.[56] Its boundaries remain deliberately slippery and 'wayward',[57] so that a certain influence on early steampunk, itself a hybrid mode, is discernible. Here, too, we find an audacious, inventive irreverence for the ontologies of the universe, an indifference for commercial good taste, and an exploration of a world constantly in flux. Perhaps this is why, in first-wave steampunk, we encounter a number of oddities, such as horror clowns and subterranean monsters in *The*

Anubis Gates, East End fish people in *Infernal Devices* (1987), or alien airships and homunculi in *Homunculus*. However, just as early steampunk's gaze is turned inward on the Victorian urban past, not to outward forces or the future, so do these oddities bear little resemblance with the tentacled weird monsters which Lovecraft's Cthulhu infamously embodies.[58] Whereas, as Mark Fisher notes, time travel in *The Anubis Gates* takes on elements of the weird,[59] it would be wrong to assume that these imaginative flourishes in early steampunk are concerned with an unfathomable cosmic indifference, a hostile urbanity, or dread and uncertainty in general.

On the contrary, imagined from the safe position of hindsight, they appear as part and parcel of the re-imagined urban environment itself. As Karl Bell posits: 'Beyond small, routine behaviours, the urban dweller lives in an environment in which s/he lacks personal influence, in circumstances defined by fragmented, impressionistic, and limited knowledge. Such an atmosphere is ripe for the intrusion of the urban weird'.[60] Early steampunk's homunculi, horror clowns, and fish people characterize a Victorian city that seems, in and of itself, a curiosity. Here, the unexpected, the outrageous, and the supernatural are perfectly at home.

The Regency London in which Brendan Doyle finds himself in *The Anubis Gates*, for example, is populated by gypsies, Egyptian sorcerers, Lord Byron homunculi, and body-switching werewolves. It is also warred over, unbeknown to most, by two rivalling beggar guilds: the Dolorous Brethren, led by the grotesque clown Horrabin, who disfigures his minions until they resemble a bizarre menagerie, and the Pye Street Beggars who elaborately perform archetypes such as the 'Decayed Gentlemen', the 'Shipwrecked Mariners' or the 'Distressed Hindoos' to a middle-class public, perhaps as ironic parodies of Mayhew's urban types.[61] Neither Dog-Face Joe, the body-switcher werewolf, nor Horrabin's Mistakes, those failed experiments with their 'roars and growls and wails, and the wet slitherings, and the rustling of heavy, scaled limbs being shifted and the rattle of claws' impact the adventure narrative through anything more than their grotesque outer characteristics (p. 436). As Bell argues, we have become familiar with the folkloric and mass cultural monsters such as werewolves and vampires through film and literature, and 'we have become comfortable thinking with and employing the mercurial, metaphorical value of such entities.'[62] Urban weird monsters, by contrast, tend to be less traditionally legible: 'The weird serves as a signal that our frameworks and our habituated ways of thinking have been rendered insufficient' (p. 9). Rather than challenge our fundamental assumptions about the universe, early steampunk's decoratively grotesque antagonists challenge our imaginary of the Victorian city. They may be absurd and whimsical, but their presence defamiliarizes and 'weirds' the urban space. What we encounter here cannot be categorized or rationalized through familiar pathways of memory, nor explained to satisfaction. 'The urban weird', notes Bell, 'reminds us that we are not masters of our cities', (p. 8) but at the same time, through destabilizing 'our former ways of seeing and knowing', it 'holds the potential for liberation from accepted norms' (p. 13). As such, the weird serves as ironic markers of the meta-historical steampunk fantasy which does not follow familiar conventions or offer knowable scenarios and, like the steampunk city itself, can only be explored gradually.

The whimsical and weird extend to the urban cityscape: Powers' London is overlaid at once by its own past and future. Holes in the time stream connect specific locales in and around the city, so that 1980s London is invisibly layered over 1810, which in turn reveals a passage to 1660 Southwark. Such palimpsestic moments are amplified by Doyle's own, anachronistic observations and actions, for example when he whistles the Beatles' song 'Yesterday' 'only a block, he realized, from Keats' birthplace',[63] or when he associates Horrabin's own whistles with 'the Nazi Gestapo sirens in old movies about World War Two' (p. 134). However, the palimpsestic city is also translated into a network of underground tunnels beneath St. Giles, an a-chronic underworld that houses the monstrous Mistakes as well as a 'subterranean river' complete with docks and boats (p. 187). From the outside, 'brick in every degree of size, shade, and age – and half-timbered, [...] linked to the dark bulk of other buildings at every level by flimsy bridges and ratlines, [...] pierced by windows in such an uneven pattern that they couldn't [...] reflect the arrangement of floors inside', Horrabin's 'Rat's Castle' 'had been constructed on the foundations and around the remains of a hospital built in the twelfth century' (p. 432). The whole structure suggests an eclectic, near-organic urban growth:

> [T]he hospital's bell-tower still survived, but over the centuries the various owners of the site had, largely for warehousing purposes, steadily added new floors and walls around it, until now its arched Norman windows looked, instead of out across the city, into narrow rooms fronted right up against them and moored to the ancient stone; the cap of the tower was the only bit of structure still exposed to the open air, and it would have been hard to find in the rooftop wilderness of chimney pots, airshafts and wildly uneven architecture.[64]

It is a haphazard conglomerate of styles and temporalities which is reflected above ground as well as below: '[A] subterranean grotto formed by the collapse

[...] of twelve levels of sewers, 'floored with stones laid by the Romans in the days when Londinium was a military out-post in a hostile Celtic wilderness'.[65] In this surreal, a-historic counter-space, it is no surprise that a displaced Samuel Taylor Coleridge suddenly finds himself several miles below ground in a 'dimly torchlit stairwell, whose architecture he recognized as debased provincial Roman', and, believing himself in a vivid opium dream, pens the beginning of 'Kubla Khan'.[66] Victorian London, in Powers' vision, is a labyrinth of waywardly accumulated times and spaces, many of which are hidden from view and can only be discovered by (involuntary) adventurers. Similarly, George, the protagonist of Jeter's *Infernal Devices*, discoverers a hidden population of fish people living in the East End, 'denizens of a London previously unknown'.[67] This 'Wetwick', a destination for slumming gentlemen with peculiar tastes,[68] is a secret accessible only for those who know its secret codes and habits: a mysterious coin of 'St. Monkfish' and a seedy-looking cab driver accompany George's foray into this alternative London.

Early steampunk novels formulate a vision of steampunk London as a city which retains an ontological peculiarity due to its unfathomable age, its physically and spatially palimpsestic character, and its vastness. It is a city grown, near organically, over centuries. Its physical structures have been modified, re-purposed, forgotten, and outlasted their inhabitants. Times and spaces co-exist simultaneously or layered over one another. With its secret or forgotten passageways and cellars, architectural features that have lost their use and meaning, and its changing populations, it is always in flux, shifting, adapting and being adapted – a space, in short, of tantalizing obscurity and infinite possibilities, open to the curious, the inventive, and the adventurous.

Such a vision of Victorian London as fundamentally weird and whimsical is inextricably tied to the reception of the 'Victorian' in all its sweeping generalization. The whimsy and weird function as symptoms which illustrate that steampunk takes the historical past as a retro-speculative playground in which 'to establish and then violate and modify a set of ontological ground rules' – among which we must count history, realism, or notions of 'the Victorian'.[69] From early on, 'the Victorian', an epoch that is 'fractured, multiple, and monstrous', intermingles freely with whimsy and weird elements in steampunk because to the 1980s writer of speculative fiction as well as to the millennial steampunk, 'the Victorian' itself is no less unfamiliar or otherworldly than the fantastical offspring of late-Victorian fiction by which it is inspired.[70] Indeed, when Bruce Sterling is called on to define steampunk, he foregrounds our contemporary re-signification of the industrial paradigm: 'The Industrial Revolution has grown old. So, machines that Romantics considered satanic now look romantic.'[71] What was once the height of technology is now 'crude, limited and clanky'[72] and relegated to the quaint, 'the queeny, chintzy, and merely ornamental flotsam of history'.[73] As such, however, it serves to Sterling as a comment on our present:

> Steampunk's key lessons are not about the past. They are about the instability and obsolescence of our own times. A host of objects and services that we see each day all around us are not sustainable. [...] Once they're gone, they'll seem every bit as weird and archaic as top hats, crinolines, magic lanterns, clockwork automatons, absinthe, walking-sticks and paper-scrolled player pianos.[74]

Whimsicality in steampunk does not mean thoughtlessly frivolous, absurd, or nostalgic. Instead, while it certainly perceives aspects of the Victorian past as abstruse or comical, when balanced with echoes of the weird, it also frames the Victorian past as potentially wayward, obscure, and resistant to both established taste and notions of historicity, inviting us to re-consider and re-approach the Victorian city as something we have not fully catalogued, mapped, and conquered – a space as yet open to play, exploration, and uncanny surprises.

In its re-imagining of the Victorian industrial paradigm, steampunk emerges at a formative historical moment. It is certainly no coincidence that its first iterations coincide with the decline of the American Rust Belt in the 1980s, or, as yet further afield, the violent deconstruction of Britain's mining industry.

1.2 Clackers, Computers, and Urban Revolution

Steampunk emerges in an era that, for both the US and the UK, is marked by neo-liberal politics under the respective leadership of Ronald Reagen and Margaret Thatcher. Both introduced an era of radical change characterized by economic liberalism and social conservatism which, through deregulation, privatization of public services, curtailing of worker's unions' rights, and discontinuing social welfare programmes gave rise to an unfettered capitalism with tangible social cost. Culturally, as Luckhurst observes, 'this transformation has been allied to the emergence of postmodernism',[75] of which Bruce Sterling and William Gibson's 1990 novel *The Difference Engine*, 'the closest text that steampunk has to a canonical novel'[76] is a potent example.

Fredric Jameson, who seminally defines postmodernism as a 'parody [...] without vocation' and 'the random cannibalization of all the styles of the past'[77] after all considers cyberpunk, Gibson's genre of choice, as the 'supreme *literary* expression if not of postmodernism, then of late capitalism itself'.[78] Gibson's 1984 novel *Neuromancer* is generally credited with launching the science fiction subgenre cyberpunk, preceded only by Ridley Scott's film *Blade Runner* (1982).[79] Cyberpunk contributes important contextual impulses to *The Difference Engine* which synthesizes steampunk into the more coherent, more radical counter-culturally potent vision which inspires the burgeoning subculture in the twenty-first century, and is therefore worth a closer consideration.[80]

Gibson's *Neuromancer* exhibits classical postmodern characteristics, such as the emphasis on style over content, the deconstruction of meaningful semiotic connections, or ironic performance instead of sincere expression. It is characterized by a dense linguistic style littered with neologisms, references to and pastiches of hard-boiled detective novels by the likes of Raymond Chandler and Dashiell Hammett, and a general atmosphere of cool defeatism so characteristic of the noir genre. Here, multi-national corporations murderously compete with one another in vast hyper-cities, Artificial Intelligences move about in the 'consensual hallucination' cyberspace, and cybertechnology saturates lives, bodies, and realities to such an extent that they can be hacked.[81] In accordance with Jameson's claim that the postmodern dissolves the boundaries between so-called high culture and pop culture, fascinated by the '"degraded" landscape of schlock and kitsch', *Neuromancer* glories in a sophisticated, rebellious pulp-ness, which has become a staple of the genre.[82] Gibson's speculative vision of the hyper-capitalist, info-technology-dominated future embodies a counter-cultural resistance to neo-liberal politics, which had appropriated science fiction boosterism: '[C]yberpunk was formulated in the way it was precisely because of the prominence of the SF megatext in the fantasy life of the American New Right'.[83] Instead, cyberpunk turned towards counter-culture and the underdog. In the preface of his *Mirrorshades* anthology (1986), Sterling outlines the movement as an 'unholy alliance of the technical world and the world of organized dissent – the underground world of pop culture, visionary fluidity, and street-level anarchy'.[84] Console-cowboy hackers like Gibson's Henry Case, then, are inspired by 'the technical revolution reshaping our society' and the thriving urban youth cultures of the 1970s and 1980s: rockers, punks, hip hop street dancers, graffiti artists, and skateboarders.[85] These are notably urban subcultures. Indeed, in cyberpunk, the mega-city embodies corporate domination and capitalist ideology, but urban space also breeds and accommodates dissenters, rebels, and subversive agents of change. Where the California trifecta gravitated towards an alternative, shabby-seedy Victorian London, Sterling and Gibson likewise draw from alternative urban lifestyles in *The Difference Engine* to craft a steampunk London full of 'violent, polluted, *laissez-faire* anarchy', that may serve 'as a precursor of the post-industrial near-future ecological wastelands of cyberpunk'.[86]

The novel certainly re-casts the Victorian past as an ancestor to the dawning computer age.[87] It imagines that Charles Babbage's Analytical Engine has been built, caused a revolution in the 1830s in which Luddites are defeated by the Radical Industrials, and thoroughly transformed the Victorian London of 1855. Mad scientists and gentleman inventors had appeared in Jeter's and Blaylock's work, imagined as a pre-corporate, individualist tinkerer – perhaps a romantically envisioned predecessor of the 1980s hacker – but it is *The Difference Engine* which fully re-purposes Herbert Sussman's claim that the Victorians were 'the first people to live in a culture dominated by technology',[88] and thus a formative precursor to the present not just socially or economically, but technologically.

To a world on the brink of transformation by computer technology, the nineteenth century now seemingly offered potent parallels as the first fully industrialized and global society affected by rapidly evolving technology such as the railway, the telegraph, mass media, electricity, or early automobiles. Now, the era which has long passed out of living memory and is separated from the 1980s by two world wars, modernism, the atom bomb, the Cold War, and American imperialism, and which Sterling imagines as embodied by 'the dandified gear of aristocrats, peculiar brass gadgets, rather stilted personal relationships and elaborate and slightly kinky underwear',[89] may seem newly attractive through both its strangeness and familiarity. As the industrial paradigm failed, Victorian Britain might have represented an era of perceived coherence, optimism in progress, and even hubris, a captivating paradoxical mixture of the seemingly historically inevitable, and the might-have-been. 'At its best', as Pike observes, 'steampunk simultaneously critiques ossified attitudes toward the past and pillages that same past for alternatives to a present-day status quo to which it is violently opposed'.[90] As such, the Victorian city becomes a powerful, unfamiliar and yet newly relevant nexus point in and through which to play out counter-cultural fantasies.

The Difference Engine

Charles Babbage's first Difference Engine never developed past a small model built in 1822 and had to be abandoned in 1842 when funding ceased. With Ada Lovelace, Lord Byron's only legitimate daughter and a mathematics prodigy, his new Analytical Engine evolved, through Lovelace's notes on Luigi Menabra's report on it, from a calculator into a proto-computer. Lovelace is nowadays regarded as the first programmer and her notes as the first algorithm. Nevertheless, conceived perhaps too early on and not yet as relevant as telegraphs, steam ships, or electricity,[91] the engine was never successfully built until 1991 by the London Science Museum and has been relegated to the fantastic imaginations of steampunk.[92] In *The Difference Engine*, it causes a radical paradigm shift and generates the novel's alternative history. Whereas it is the Analytical Engine that is considered to be the true precursor of modern computers, Gibson and Sterling here circle back to the Difference Engine, perhaps for its suggestive metaphorical power, since it produces a radically different timeline: the Marxist revolution is relocated to the United States, itself fragmented into British territories and small republics, and Japan aspires to be a 'Britain of Asia' a good twenty years early. The Duke of Wellington, misjudging the 'revolutionary tenor of the coming age of industry and science', becomes a casualty of the new age:

> And the England that Wellington had known and misruled, the England of Mallory's childhood, had slid through strikes, manifestos, and demonstrations, to riots, martial law, massacres, open class-warfare, and near-total anarchy. Only the Industrial Radical Party, with their boldly rational vision of a comprehensive new order, had saved England from the abyss.[93]

A surviving Lord Byron becomes the Industrial Radical Prime minister and society re-structures into a meritocracy, with the new Lords in Parliament being Lords Darwin, Huxley, Brunel, Galton, and Babbage. Their new-found power as 'savants' is emblematic of a complex and extensive socio-political development inducing and induced by a 'full-blown information order, complete with massive databases on citizens, surveillance apparatus, photo IDs, credit cards, rapid international data transmission via telegraph, and scientific societies that serve as unofficial intelligence arms of the military'.[94]

Gibson and Sterling's vision is a postmodern pastiche not only of history, but also literature. Through a characteristically dark-humoured re-writing of Benjamin Disraeli's condition-of-England novel *Sybil* (1845), they disassemble Disraeli's Young England conservative romantic ideology. *Sybil* critiques the idea of an oligarchy of the newly rich industrialists, hoping instead for a restoration of a noble aristocracy – yet Gibson and Sterling virtually dethrone the aristocracy in favour of a new, scientific elite.[95] The way in which *The Difference Engine* re-writes both history and literature has been examined by Herbert Sussman,[96] Jay Clayton and Patrick Jagoda, who trace the intricate interconnectedness of socio-historical and techno-political transformation which inform the novel's vision of a computer revolution played out a century and a half earlier. The novel's cross-textual synthesis establishes counterfiction, which I will examine in Chapter Two, as a staple of steampunk world-building. More pertinent here, however, is how this transformation is encoded through the city, a steampunk space which paradoxically, 'both *is* and *is not* a representation of nineteenth-century London'.[97]

Cityscape and alternative history are re-built in tandem. In playfully re-arranging the past, steampunk both calls up and deconstructs a shared knowledge about London's urban spaces: physical landmarks, topographies of meaning, architectural semiotics. In doing so, *The Difference Engine* engages what Istvan Csicsery-Ronay terms our '*science fictionality* as a way of thinking about the world', of 'entertaining incongruous experiences, in which judgement is suspended'.[98] Such an ability to comprehend the steampunk mode lets us navigate the alternative city and discern the implications of such a 'monologue of temples':

> Cromwell Road, Thurloe Place, Brompton Road—in their vast rebuilding schemes, the Government had reserved these sections of Kensington and Brompton to a vast concourse of Museums and Royal Society Palaces. One by one they passed his window in their sober majesty of cupolas and colonnades: Physics, Economics, Chemistry ... [...] Surely, in their aid to Science, the Palaces had repaid the lavish cost of their construction at least a dozen times.[99]

Here, the cityscape inscribes the new, rational world order. In Gibson and Sterling's universe, the Great Exhibition of 1851 seems not to have taken place and as consequences, Exhibition Road in South Kensington, with the Victoria and Albert Museum, the Science Museum, and the Natural History Museum with adjacent College, built between the 1850s and 1880s, never existed. Nevertheless, the same space remains firmly associated with a 'Victorian' spirit of scientific curiosity which here leads to an intensified version of history, in which each scientific discipline is physically enshrined in, and represented by, an expensively built Palace. The 'cupolas and colonnades' hint towards a neo-classical architecture, underscoring the scientific, rational spirit of this new age, but also implying a near-religious reverence. Clute's impression of a 'monologue of temples' hints at a similar reading. This 'hyper-Kensington' embodies the Industrial Radical ideology which re-builds London in its own image. Another manifestation of this is the erasure of the Duke of Wellington and with him the politics of the 'decadent Tory blue-bloods' who he championed from public space.[100] The absence of physical sites of remembrance, termed by Pierre Nora as *lieux de mémoire* in which cultural memory and urban space intersect, re-shapes the collective identity.[101] Control is exerted through a manipulation of the urban physical space as a social text.[102]

Indeed, the novel, as Patrick Jagoda argues, puts into motion Foucault's idea of biopolitics by playing out a transition to a disciplinary society in combination with Deleuze's notion of a control society.[103] Whereas the disciplinary society relies on centralized institutions of power managing the human collective through accumulated knowledge about it, the control society 'is characterized by the establishment of an individual identity that is marked through "signatures" and "numbers", exerting control through the regulation of "codes" and "passwords" that determine access to information'.[104] Nowhere is this more clearly embodied than in the Central Statistics Bureau, an institution whose domestic surveillance is made possible by innovations such as photo IDs, databases, or telegraph transactions.

> The Central Statistics Bureau, vaguely pyramidal in form and excessively Egyptianate in its ornamental detail, squatted solidly in the governmental heart of Westminster, its uppermost stories slanting to a limestone apex. For the sake of increased space, the building's lower section was swollen out-of-true, like some great stone turnip. Its walls, pierced by towering smokestacks, supported a scattered forest of spinning ventilators, their vanes annoyingly hawk-winged. The whole vast pile was riddled top to bottom with thick black telegraph-lines, as though individual streams of the Empire's information had bored through solid stone. A dense growth of wiring swooped down, from conduits and brackets to telegraph-poles crowed thick as the rigging in a busy harbor.[105]

Like the complex of Palaces in Kensington, a space associated with power, the Statistics Bureau is imposed into and over a space of socio-political resonance: Westminster, the seat of government. Its pseudo-Egyptian architecture, exemplified also in the 'fortress-doors, framed by lotus-topped columns and Briticized sphinxes, loom[ing] some twenty feet in height' (p. 145), hints at the godlike, central power of the pharaohs and ancient, universal, perhaps even a spiritual knowledge, kept hidden behind the intimidating gates of this 'fortress'. Here, in divisions named 'Quantitative Criminology', 'Deterrence Research' (p. 149), or 'Criminal Anthropometry' (p. 157) process and store record of every British citizen: 'Everyone who's ever applied for work, or paid taxes, or been arrested' (p. 160). Dr Edward Mallory, our focal character, observes 'men whose business it was to acquire and retail knowledge of the attitudes and influence of the public. Political men, in short, who dealt entirely in the intangible' (p. 147). If this reads like an Orwellian delusion, that is certainly the desired inference: 'We naturally keep a brotherly eye on the telegram-traffic, credit-records, and such' (p. 152) confides a head of division with a nod to *1984*'s all-seeing Big Brother.

The Statistics Bureau is a vast institution of domestic surveillance, monitoring citizens through every computer-technological innovation available, and embedded comfortably into a symbolic topography.

However, the Bureau's physical character also enacts its functional demands. On the outside, it is almost haphazardly marked by ventilators and telegraph lines. Inside, every space and every act are subservient to meticulous cleanliness, as a single crumb or speck of dust might contaminate the 'giant identical Engines, clock-like constructions of intricately interlocking brass, big as rail-cars set on end.' (p. 156). Everything inside this space, from the 'dry and static' (p. 147) atmosphere to the clerks on wheeled boots, shooting up and down the corridors delivering decks of punch cards like data in an information circuit, seems to be an extension of the engines at the building's core. As a windowless, dust-less, highly efficient structure in which humans are dwarfed and determined by machinery, the Bureau reads as a gigantic processor of human information, installed at the primal intersection of an urban infrastructure from which it collects its data. The city itself, by extension, is configured as one vast information-processing machine, in which human interactions, from telegrams and telegraphic communication to arrest or employment records, act as data.

This processor, however, proves not to be entirely stable. The eco-catastrophe of 1858, the Great Stink, in which the hot weather exacerbated the smell of human waste on the banks of the river Thames, as yet without Joseph Bazalgette's Embankment, here erupts somewhat earlier as a symptom of strain and overheating. The Bureau prompts in Mallory a vision of Darwin's earthworms, 'always invisibly busy underfoot, so that even great sarsen-stones slowly sank into the loam', 'churning in catastrophic frenzy, till the soil roiled and bubbled like a witches' brew' (p. 148). As a mechanistic organism traversing the soil as an allegory for the streams of data traversing the city, the earthworms' slow corrosion of the environment reads as foreboding. Their movements, unnaturally accelerated, produce a demonic energy that unsettle the soil, and soon, the Great Stink transforms the city into an apocalyptic vision:

> Outside the Palace, the London sky was a canopy of yellow haze. It hung above the city in gloomy grandeur, like some storm-fleshed jellied man-o-war. Its tentacles, the uprising filth of the city's smokestacks, twisted and fluted like candle-smoke in utter stillness, to splash against a lidded ceiling of glowering cloud. The invisible sun cast a drowned and watery light (p. 205).

Under this static, portentous sky, a result of accumulated ecologic irresponsibility and an omen of 'extinction' and 'chaos' (p. 271), the city ceases to function:

> The streets were such a crush as only London could produce. The omnibuses and cabriolets were all taken, every intersection jammed with rattle-traps and dogcarts, with cursing drivers and panting, black-nostrilled horses. Steam-gurneys chugged sluggishly by, many towing rubber-tired freight-cars loaded with provisions. It seemed the gentry's summer exodus from London was becoming a rout (p. 206).

London's networks are congested as those who can afford to leave. Others go on strike or begin to riot and loot. Increasingly, the city resembles a broken-down machine as ash rains from the sky and a grotesquely yellow fog obscures the cityscape. Mallory, usually navigating the city with ease, is stranded in Whitechapel and must find his way back to Kensington through '[s]even miles of roiling chaos' (p. 273). Though he masters the task and even journeys back to the East End to quell an uprising, the city begins to become overwhelming in its sheer, unfathomable vastness:

> It was a very weariness of London, of the city's sheer physicality, its nightmare endlessness, of streets, courts, crescents, terraces, and alleys, of fog-shrouded stone and soot-blackened brick. A nausea of awnings, a nastiness of casements, an ugliness of scaffoldings lashed together with rope; a horrible prevalence of iron street lamps and granite bollards, of pawn-shops, haberdashers, and tobacconists. The city seemed to stretch about them like some pitiless abyss of geologic time (p. 131).

Here is a vision of the city as an eternal, a-chronic physical structure, man-made and yet also independent from and eerily devoid of, humanity. Its material manifestations, from courts and crescents to shops, become grotesque and even weird when deserted, as urban space is disassociated from its purpose and meaning. The socially produced space disintegrates as the social networks that produced it collapse. As a labyrinth stretching endlessly through time and space, it is imbued with faint notions of sentiment; nauseating, nasty, uncanny. Mallory experiences a moment of cosmic dread, in which not the universe, but the city as an entity in itself, is indifferent to its inhabitants. Ironically, his vision is less a moment of delirious exhaustion, but more of total clarity in which he catches a glimpse of a larger truth hidden beyond the city and even the narrative itself before it begins to disintegrate as follows:

> Recede.
> Reiterate.
> Rise above these black patterns of wheel-tracks,
> These snow-swept streets,

> Into the great map of London,
> Forgetting (p. 450)

Here, the narrative voice simultaneously rises above and merges into the city, ceasing its account of events in a meta-narrative moment of self-awareness. The sudden dissolution of this mediative tether is performed through a movement away from the urban patterns of 'wheel-tracks' and 'streets' into the larger pattern of the abstract 'map' and can only be explained by a closer look at the ending of the novel, the last 'iteration', called 'Modus'.

Merely a post-modern assortment of letters, chronicle excerpts, and seemingly unconnected scenes, the final iteration serves as an eclectic collection of evidence about the alternative history, such as a diary entry by Lord Babbage or an account of the funeral of Prime Minister Lord Byron. In the last portion, Lady Ada Byron, the 'Queen of Engines', 'Enchantress of Numbers', delivers a lecture on the Modus Program, that mysterious set of punch cards which connects the narrative throughout. '[T]he execution of the so-called Modus Program', she claims, 'demonstrated that any formal system must be both *incomplete* and *unable to establish its own consistency.* [...] The Modus Program initiated a series of nested loops, which, though difficult to establish, were yet more difficult to extinguish' (p. 477, original emphasis). The speaker believes that '*self-referentiality* will someday form the bedrock of a genuinely transcendent meta-system of calculatory mathematics' in which 'such an Engine *lives,* and could indeed *prove* its own life' (pp. 277–278, original emphasis). Lady Byron's subject here is sentience. She envisions the possibility of an Artificial Intelligence gaining consciousness through a series of nested feedback loops. Whereas Sussman and Jagoda both discuss this speech and comment on the final scene, which I want to discuss next, they neglect to consider the implications of this final, but crucial moment, which Gibson characterized as follows in a 1991 interview:

> The story purports in the end to tell you that the narrative you have just read is not the narrative in the ordinary sense; rather it's a long self-iteration as this thing attempts to boot itself up, which it does in the final exclamation point. [...] But, yeah, the author of the book is the narratron; it's sitting there telling itself a novel as it studies its own origins.[106]

This certainly sheds new light on the narrative and its vision of London. The city, envisioned as an information-processing machine in which human activity is recorded as data, seems to have never 'really' existed outside the circuits of the entity re-constructing its own origin myth. The eclectic assortment of scenes and narrative strands emphasize, as Roger Whitson deduces, 'the non-human experience of complying and processing each of *The Difference Engine*'s historical events into signal. The signals processed by the Modus, in turn, comprize [instances] [...] of micro temporal history that it registers as it gains sentience.'[107] The city, then, is intrinsically intertwined with the now conscious 'narratron' and its notion of self-hood. The final scene, in which Ada Byron looks into a mirror and sees London in 1991, illustrates this:

> It is 1991. It is London. Ten thousand towers, the cyclonic hum of a trillion twisting gears, all air gone earthquake-dark in a mist of oil, in the fractioned heat of intermeshing wheels. Black seamless pavements, uncounted tributary rivulets for the frantic travels of the punched-out lace of data, the ghosts of history loosed in this hot shining necropolis. Paper-thin faces billow like sails, twisting, yawning, tumbling through the empty streets, human faces that are borrowed masks, and lenses for a peering Eye. And when a given face has served its purpose, it crumbles, frail as ash, bursting into a dry foam of data, its constituent bits and motes. But new fabrics of conjecture are knitted in the City's shining cores, swift tireless spindles flinging off invisible loops in their millions, while in the hot unhuman dark, data melts and mingles, churned by gear-work to a skeletal bubbling pumice, dipped in a dreaming wax that forms a simulated flesh, perfect as thought— (p. 485)

This, then, is a steampunk London envisioned through the prism of cyberpunk. Its towers evoke a modern skyline and the stacked columns of gears in an Analytical Engine alike, pavements become data circuits, and the flow of human movement morphs into de-humanized information through which the 'Eye' finally realizes what it sees is '*not* London—but mirrored plazas of sheerest crystal, the avenues atomic lighting, the sky a super cooled gas, as the Eye chases its own gaze through the labyrinth, leaping quantum gaps that are causation, contingency, chance' (p. 486). City and Engine become indistinguishable as the city dissolves into a vision of informational patterns and abstract movements.

The novel enacts Gibson's vision from *Neuromancer*, which coined the term cyberspace and configured it as a 'consensual hallucination [...] a graphic representation of data' that appears like '[l]ines of light ranged in the non-space of the mind, clusters and constellations of data [...] like city lights receding...'[108] This vision, as Edward Soja notes, configures cyberspace as 'intrinsically spatial in [its] rhetoric and referencing', as well as 'peculiarly urban'[109]: Steampunk London, itself ultimately virtual, here performs a process of self-recognition enacted through the metaphor of city, out of which the 'Eye' finally emerges sentient:

In this City's centre, a thing grows, an auto-catalytic tree, in almost-life, feeding
through the roots of thought [...] up, up, toward the hidden light of vision,
   Dying to be born.
[...] The Eye at last must see itself
   Myself...
   I see:
   I see,
   I see
   I
   !   (p. 486)

Right to the City? The Urban Habitus

In conjunction with configuring steampunk London as an information processor in which humanity loses significance and is present only as data, *The Difference Engine* also re-imagines a Victorian identity and an urban habitus constituted in and through the city through the prism of social upheaval during the Great Stink. Specifically, it takes the trifecta's vision of alternative urban communities, which also intrinsically inspire the cyberpunk vision, one step further to ask, what is the material city and who is it for?

These questions inform Henri Lefebvre's 1968 *The Right to the City*, characteristically published in a year in which international leftist counter-cultural movements realized the urban space as a terrain of protest. In it, he claims that '*the right to the city* is like a cry and a demand' to a 'transformed and renewed *right to urban life*',[110] and argues that urban dwellers, especially the working class which builds and sustains the city, have not merely a material right to what they produce, but also to more fundamentally anthropological social needs:

> [T]hey include the need for security and opening, the need for certainty and adventure, that of organization of work and of play, the needs for the predictable and the unpredictable, of similarity and difference, of isolation and encounter, exchange and investments, of independence (even solitude) and communication, of immediate and long-term prospects.[111]

As Harvey summarizes: '[W]hat kind of city we want cannot be divorced from the question of what kind of people we want to be'.[112] The right to the city is, then, a collective right to shape the process of urbanization and 'to rebuild and re-create the city as a socialist body politic in a completely different image—one that eradicates poverty and social inequality, and one that heals the wounds of disastrous environmental degradation'.[113] As such it is inextricably tied to a Marxist ideology opposing capitalist systems and the logic of commodification. In Harvey's thinking, the 1848 revolutions in Europe or the Paris Commune become examples of a dispossessed population reclaiming 'their' urban space. Considering that *The Difference Engine* features societal disintegration and a 'socialist' uprising, can the novel be productively read as putting the right to the city as a concept into motion? Is its concern the nature of, and the right to, urban life?

The novel's re-imagined ideology of ratio and scientific progress is inscribed firmly into its urban landscape and embodied by the Industrial Radical Party. Yet as the Great Stink erupts like a cataclysm through the city, this ideology, hard-won through revolution and reform, quite literally comes under attack. In Camera Square, Chelsea, Mallory finds himself in front of a shop selling an array of fantastic, steampunk 'fancy optical goods: talbotypes, magic-lanterns, phenakistoscopes, telescopes for the amateur star-gazer' to 'boy-savants' (p. 241), young scientists-to-be. The place epitomizes the prestige associated with a scientific career, and Mallory is lost in fond reminiscence when a 'London boy, thirteen or so' approaches on 'rubber-heeled boots', and with 'a yowling whoop', 'a pair of walking sticks doubled up under his arms.' He is followed by 'a pack of boys [...] leaping and yelping in devilish glee' (p. 242) and masked against the debris in the air, bringing with him an atmosphere of unbridled energy and youthful malice. Mallory's remark, 'Far too well-dressed to be street-arabs' (p. 243), hints at the notion that these boys are prospective middle-class customers of the optics seller, yet they too are caught up in their anarchic play. The gang leader, dubbed 'Panther Bill', skidding without restraint, crashes into the shop front, 'glass [...] toppling like guillotine blades', and is left unconscious or dead. Far from concerned or deterred, the others begin looting the shop 'with maddened shrieks' (p. 243). The characterization of these wild boys certainly plays with Victorian sociology which saw childhood as re-enacting the stages of teleological evolution, as the boys begin to 'revert' to a form of 'savage behaviour' in stark contrast with both their respectable clothing and their urban surroundings.

Such a reversion into mindless anarchy is not limited to children. In the East End, Mallory encounters not a neighbourhood but a post-apocalyptic wasteland:

> There was scarcely a window intact. Cobbles, grubbed up from side-streets, had been flung right and left like a shower of meteors. A seeming whirlwind had descended on a nearby grocery, leaving the street ankle-deep in dirty snow-

drifts of flour and sugar. Mallory picked his way through battered cabbages, squashed greengages, crushed jars of syrupped peaches, and the booted footballs of whole smoked hams. Scatterings of damp flour showed a stampede of men's brogues, the small bare feet of street-urchins, the dainty trace of women's shoes, and the sweep of their skirt-hems (pp. 271–272).

This is hardly the image of an urban population reclaiming urban space for more sustained or responsible ways of living. Instead, we find the traces of wanton vandalism that leaves valuable foods trampled underfoot, destroying only for the sake of destruction. The novel here cynically undermines and subverts notions of a progressive, enlightened Victorian urban habitus marked by respectability and ratio. Whether in Chelsea or Whitechapel, London has become 'a locus of anarchy' (p. 272) in which people are motivated by greed and pleasure alone:

> These Londoners were like gas, thought Mallory, like a cloud of minute atomies. The bonds of society broken, they had simply flown apart, like the perfectly elastic gassy spheres in Boyle's Law of Physics. Most of them looked respectable enough by their dress; they were merely reckless now, stripped by Chaos to a moral vacuity. [...] They had become puppets of base impulse. Like the Cheyenne tribesmen of Wyoming, dancing in the devil's grip of drink, the good men of civilized London had surrendered themselves to primitive madness. [...] It was exaltation to them, a wicked freedom more perfect and desirable than they had ever known (p. 277).

These 'Victorians' become wildlings in a cathartic frenzy of base instinct. Suddenly in stark contrast with their respectable dress and disconnected from the urban space built to encode an identity of sophistication, they appear so out of place to Mallory that he likens them to 'primitive tribesmen'; their carefully constructed, 'civilized', 'Victorian' identity undermined and deconstructed through this portrait of, not revolution, but a mad saturnalia.

One revolution, however, is supposedly underway in the East India docks, where a number of self-proclaimed socialists, led by a 'Captain Swing', have seized London's nexus of international trade. Swing's choice of name allies him with the (real world) Luddite riots of the 1830s and therefore suggests an anti-industrialist motivation. Rioters call one another 'comrade' and speak of the liberation of 'the common folk of London, the masses, the oppressed, the sweated labour, those who produce all the riches of this city' (p. 333). They propose to seize London from urban sites inhabited by the poor and vulnerable: 'We will fight them from the rooftops, from doorways, alleyways, sewers, and rookeries!' (p. 335). Apart from these hints at Marxist rhetoric, however, the revolution is more a darkly ironic comedy and an excuse for a machismo action show-down than a discussion of a more productive and enfranchized collective ownership of the cityscape. The rhetoric itself falls short in an alternative timeline in which the Marxist revolution is being displaced to the 'Manhattan Commune'. Mallory, having no concept of 'the oppressor-class' or 'the means of production', thinks himself in the presence of a lunatic. Indeed, he and his colleagues are guided through the docklands fortress by a man styling himself the 'Marquis of Hastings', the title a pre-Radical 'relic' (p. 329). This would-be aristocrat who seems, in addition, to own a black slave, is hardly an appropriate figurehead for the socialist reclamation of the city: '"What, my man Jupiter?" The Marquess blinked. "Jupiter belongs to all of us too, of course!"' (pp. 337–338).

It seems that the socialist uprising serves mainly as a reflection of the course of (alternative) history, for example through semi-ironic takes on Marxist determinist historiography such as this: '[I]t has come to me that some dire violence has been done to the true and natural course of historical development' (p. 343). This remark, by hinting self-reflexively at the narrative's character as alternative history, somewhat ironically calls into question whether such a 'natural course of history' exists at all. Perhaps this is why, ultimately, the conflict between Mallory and Swing turns to the Modus, the uprising is quenched in a bloody shoot-out and the dominant Industrial Radical order re-asserts their own right to the city. As Harvey states, the concept is, after all, an 'empty signifier full of immanent but not transcendent possibilities. This does not mean it is irrelevant or politically impotent; everything depends on who gets to fill the signifier with [...] meaning.'[114]

The Difference Engine, however, refuses to do just that. Its objective is not to examine the city as a nexus of capitalist relations in which the urban habitus is ultimately defined through commodification, labour, or surplus value. On the contrary, the novel imagines a scenario in which the Luddites are thoroughly defeated, economic power is synonymous with governmental power, and Karl Marx is exiled out of the realm of the British Empire. Instead, the novel delights in dethroning an imagined Victorian urban identity of superiority and respectability. Taking quite seriously Hayden White's notion of 'historical consciousness as a specifically Western prejudice by which the presumed superiority of modern, industrial society can be retroactively substantiated',[115] Gibson and Sterling's steampunk undermines such historiographies through a playfully postmodern mockery.

Conclusion: Three Steampunks walk into a bar . . .

According to the *Steampunk Bible*, steampunk begins in the early 1980s in 'a bar called O'Hara's in Orange, California'.[116] Whereas that is a neat origin myth, steampunk as a retro-speculative aesthetic itself constantly challenges, undermines, and re-writes historiographies in a playful and ironic manner, and its synthesis into a readable mode is suitably complex.

Jeter's, Blaylock's, and Power's 'Victorian fantasies', now canonized as early steampunk novels, did not necessarily share a coherent aesthetic or ideology about the genre they were inadvertently inventing. They do, however, instinctively conceive of history as represented through an emplotted narrative structure, and as such open to manipulation and play. Using time travel, a speculative fiction subgenre which similarly investigates the relationship between narrative identity and historiography, as a rationalizing trope, these early steampunk works journey into the Victorian past and infuse it with anachronisms. As such, they synthesize, as Istvan Csicsery-Ronay notes, 'every type of sf: time-travel tales, alternative histories, revolutionary and evolutionary future histories, and extraordinary voyages, all set in hypermodernized pasts',[117] and ponder the genre's origins with late-Victorian writers such as Wells. Nonetheless, even early steampunk is more than science fictional navel-gazing. In its gleefully anachronistic re-imagining of a more nostalgic memory of the Victorian era, embodied in and through the city, the trifecta's novels re-work Henry Mayhew's urban ethnography, perceived as an 'authentic' account of a less familiar, less respectable, and more shabby-seedy Victorian London in which urban communities carve out spaces and practises for themselves like the urban subcultures of the 1970s and 1980s. Inspired by Mayhew's vivid accounts, they fabricate a vision of Victorian London that is 'punk' not because it is openly political, but because it is intrinsically linked to the urban space in which alternative styles of living are performed and lived in defiance of respectable middle-class values. Uninterested in the private sphere of the home, the trifecta re-imagines their alternative cities as spaces of experiment and adventure.

Their steampunk Londons are populated by oddities such as fish people, beggar guilds, subterranean monsters, or horror clowns, which illustrates Hantke's claim that steampunk 'employs strategies borrowed from science fiction but modified in deliberate violation of their inherited uses' in order to distance itself from 'crucial postmodern tenets about historiographic metafiction', as it 'neither allegorizes Victorianism specifically, nor the process of historical periodization in general'.[118] Indeed, these elements preclude any simple reading of early steampunk as either neo-Victorian metafiction or retro-science fiction, as they re-purpose aspects of late-Victorian and early twentieth-century weird fiction, not to challenge anthropocentric identities through cosmic dread, but rather to distort and defamiliarize the Victorian past, foreclosing any sense of historical realism or familiar strategies of reading that past. As such, early steampunk deliberately forecloses the nostalgia of British heritage culture and takes a semi-ironic approach to Englishness: The Victorian itself is configured as weird, quaint, and whimsical, and neither sewer-hunters nor fish people seem entirely out of place amongst the clunky technology embedded in a genealogy of obsolescence. From its beginning, then, steampunk, holding incompatible things together, is both indebted to Victorian intertexts and not Victorian at all.

Whimsical play and alternative urbanities also inform Gibson and Sterling's collaborative novel, *The Difference Engine*. Their experience with the deliberately counter-cultural science fiction subgenre cyberpunk allows them to synthesize the trifecta's 'Victorian fantasies' with a speculative interrogation of information technology motivated by resistance against the New Right's neo-liberal politics and inspired by urban subcultures into a coherent aesthetic vision. As a radical alternative history, their steampunk re-projects the information revolution into a Victorian past that is at once familiar and fundamentally peculiar. The novel is a 'dialectical mesh of fantasies of the Victorians' social, political, and cultural institutions, as both the Victorians themselves and *fin de millennium* U.S. techno-bohemians might imagine them'.[119]

Here, the city itself enshrines alternative history and ideology, and budding information technology is immediately misused for domestic surveillance. The city itself becomes configured as a spatialized information gathering machine in which human movements become data, and in a final twist, the Difference Engine recognizes itself through the vision of the city and achieves sentience. At the same time, the novel stages an ironic subversion of a progressive, respectable Victorian (British) urban identity and complicates a Marxist-urbanist reading. As Londoners' civilized masks crumble into an anarchic saturnalia during the Great Stink, so are the socialist revolutionaries exposed to be thieves and charlatans, and as the social order breaks down, the material city itself, de-coupled from function and de-voided of meaning, becomes uncanny, grotesque, and even weird.

Gibson and Sterling's stance towards Lefebvre's concept of the 'right to the city' is certainly cynical. However, Harvey also interprets the concept as follows: 'To claim the right to the city in the sense I mean it here is to claim some kind of shaping power over the processes of urbanization, over the ways in which our cities are made and remade, and to do so in a fundamental and radical way'.[120] First-wave steampunk not only troubles and undermines received notions of history and memory as stable and determined through its play with time travel, but also virtually re-enacts the implications around the right to the city. Using Victorian London as an emblem of the proto-postmodern megalopolis and as a meta-historical nexus, they re-imagine Victorian London as a space full of whimsical possibilities and adventure in which marginalized communities can sustain inventive alternative lifestyles, or as a vast entity in itself that threatens to overwhelm and subsume its human citizens. It asks: In what way do we shape the city, and how far does the city determine us? In what kind of city do we want to live, and to what extent is that choice up to us? As such, it recognizes the urban environment as a shaping influence on collective identity, and a material manifestation of identity politics. Unlike in real cityscapes or even the historical city of memory, however, in steampunk London, nothing is set in stone, and everything is open to intervention.

Notes

1 Gross, 'A History of Misapplied Technology', p. 57.
2 For example, Disney's *20,000 Leagues under the Sea* (1954), the Vincent Price movies *Master of the World* (1961) and *City Under the Sea* (1965), as well as George Pa's movie versions of Wells' stories *War of the Worlds* (1953) and *The Time Machine* (1960). See: Mike Perschon, 'Seminal Steampunk: Proper and True', in *Like Clockwork. Steampunk Pasts, Presents, & Futures*, eds. by Rachel A. Bowser and Brian Croxall (Minneapolis: Minnesota UP, 2016) pp. 153–178, p. 156. See also Onion, 'Reclaiming the Machine', p. 140.
3 See, for example, Gross, 'A History of Misapplied Technology', or: Jeff VanderMeer and S.J. Chambers (eds.), *The Steampunk Bible* (New York: Abrams Image, 2011).
4 See: Jess Nevins, 'Introduction: the 19th-Century Roots of Steampunk', in *Steampunk*, ed. by Ann and Jeff VanderMeer (San Francisco: Tachyon, 2008), p. 10–11. Also: Perschon, 'Seminal Steampunk', p. 155–156.
5 Perschon, 'Seminal Steampunk', p. 174.
6 David. L. Pike, 'Afterimages of the Victorian City', *Journal of Victorian Culture*, 15:2 (2010), 254–267, p. 264.
7 Bowser and Croxall, 'Introduction', p. 10.
8 Tim Powers, 'Introduction', in *Morlock Night*, by K.W. Jeter (Oxford: Angry Robot, 2011 [1979]), p. 11.
9 Perschon, 'Seminal Steampunk', p. 161.

10 David Wittenberg, *Time Travel. The Popular Philosophy of Narrative* (New York: Fordham University Press, 2013), p. 30.
11 Wittenberg, *Time Travel,* p. 30.
12 Luckhurst, *Science Fiction* (Cambridge: Polity Press, 2005), p. 37.
13 H. G. Wells, 'The Time Machine', in *H.G. Wells. The Great Science Fiction* (London: Penguin Classics, 2016 [1895]), pp. 1–90, p. 49.
14 Pike, 'Afterimages of the Victorian City', p. 259.
15 Luckhurst, *Science Fiction*, p. 38.
16 Luckhurst, *Science Fiction*, p. 39.
17 Louis Montrose, 'Renaissance Literary Studies and the Subject of History', *Studies in Renaissance Historicism,* 16:1 (1986), 5–12, p. 8.
18 Wittenberg, p. 31.
19 Wittenberg p. 15.
20 Wittenberg, p. 11–12.
21 Hayden White, *Metahistory: The Historical Imagination in Nineteenth-Century Europe* (Baltimore: Johns Hopkins Univ. Press, 1973), p. 2.
22 White, p. 8.
23 '[W]e may say that [plot] draws a meaningful story from a diversity of events or incidents [...] or that it transforms the events or incidents into a story. The two reciprocal relations expressed by from and into characterize the plot as mediating between events and a narrated story. [...] A story, too, must be more than just an enumeration of events in serial order; it must organize them into an intelligible whole [...]. In short, emplotment is the operation that draws a configuration out of a simple succession'. Paul Ricoeur, *Time and Narrative,* Vol.1. (Chicago: Chicago UP, 1984), p. 65.
24 Paul Ricoeur, *Time and Narrative,* Vol. 3. (Chicago: Chicago UP, 1988), p. 246.
25 Ricoeur, 'Narrative Time', *Critical Inquiry.* 7:1 (1980), 169–190, p. 171.
26 Wittenberg, p. 64.
27 Wittenberg, p. 13, my comments.
28 Quoted in Wittenberg, p. 64. Lacan, *Seminar, Book I: Freud's Papers on Technique, 1953–1954* (New York: Norton, 1998), p. 14.
29 James P. Blaylock, *Lord Kelvin's Machine* (London: Titan Books, 2013 [1992]). p. 270.
30 '*Fabula* is the ostensible underlying sequence of story events in a narrative, *sjuzhet* its re-formation as a specific plot, the reconstructed montage of story elements arranged by an author within a given set of generic rules or protocols.' Wittenberg, p. 6, original emphasis.
31 VanderMeer and Chambers, *The Steampunk Bible*, p. 48.
32 For more on Mayhew, see: Ole Münch. 'Henry Mayhew and the Street Traders of Victorian London — A Cultural Exchange with Material Consequences', *The London Journal,* 43:1 (2018), 53–71. Sarah Roddy, Julie-Marie Strange and Bertrand Taithe,

'Henry Mayhew at 200 – the "Other" Victorian Bicentenary', *Journal of Victorian Culture*, 19:4 (2014), 481–496.

33 Henry Mayhew, *London Labour and the London Poor. Vol. II.* (London: Frank Cass and Company Limited, 1967 [1862]), p. 152.

34 'Mr. Mayhew, bless his memory, was the one who pointed out to me the folly of such rude practices, and how fast a little put by from one's findings would soon amount to a tidy sum.' K.W. Jeter, *Morlock Night* (Oxford: Angry Robot, 2011 [1979]), p. 133.

35 Eileen Yeo, 'Mayhew as a Social Investigator', in *The Unknown Mayhew. Selections from the Morning Chronicle 1849–50*, eds. by Eileen Yeo and E. P. Thompson (Harmondsworth: Penguin, 1973), pp. 56–109. There is also a more recent German study which discusses this at length, using Clifford Geertz' method of 'thick description' as basis: N. Bauer, et al., 'Vom Charakter der Details. Henry Mayhews Costermonger als Proto-Subkultur', in *Die Zivilisierung der urbanen Nomaden*, ed. by R. Lindner (Berlin: LIT, 2005), pp. 63–81.

36 Tim Powers, 'Introduction', p. 84.

37 James P. Blaylock, *Homunculus* (London: Titan Books, 2013 [1986]), p. 8.

38 Perschon, 'Seminal Steampunk', p. 166.

39 Max Weber, *The City* (Glencoe, IL: Free Press, 1958).

40 Henri Lefebvre, *The Production of Space* (Oxford: Basil Blackwell, 1991), p. 26.

41 David Harvey, 'The Right to the City', *New Left Review*, 53 (2008), 23–40, p. 23.

42 Walter Benjamin, *One-Way Street* (London: Verso, 1997), p. 174–175.

43 Benjamin, p. 180; Mayhew, p. 38.

44 Dick Hebdige, *Subculture. The Meaning of Style* (London: Routledge, 1979).

45 Steffen Hantke, 'Difference Engines and Other Infernal Devices: History According to Steampunk', *Extrapolation* 40:3 (1999), 244–254, p. 248.

46 Ferguson, 'Surface Tensions', p. 72, 76.

47 Perschon, 'Seminal Steampunk', p. 167.

48 Hantke, p. 248–249.

49 Ferguson, p. 72.

50 Sianne Ngai, *Our Aesthetic Categories. Zany, Cute, Interesting* (Cambridge: Harvard University Press, 2012), pp. 53, 59.

51 Marie-Louise Kohlke and Christian Gutleben, 'The (Mis)Shapes of Neo-Victorian Gothic: Continuations, Adaptations, Transformations', in Marie-Louise Kohlke and Christian Gutleben (eds), *Neo-Victorian Gothic. Horror, Violence, and Degeneration in the Re-Imagined Nineteenth Century* (Leiden: Brill Rodopi, 2012), pp. 1–50, p. 12. Original emphasis.

52 Hantke, p. 252.

53 Emily Alder, *Weird Fiction and Science at the Fin de Siècle* (London: Palgrave Macmillan, 2020).

54 H. P. Lovecraft, *Supernatural Horror in Literature* (New York: Dover, 1973), p. 15.

55 Defined by Sigmund Freud in his essay of the same name (1919), 'uncanny' denotes a sense of the uncomfortably strange, located at an ambivalent border of the familiar and the unknown which is constantly on the verge of collapse. The German 'unheimlich' literally translates to 'un-home-ly' and has a disquieting effect of destabilising identity. Sigmund Freud, 'The "Uncanny"', in *The Standard Edition of the Complete Psychological Works of Sigmund Freud, Volume XVII (1917–1919): An Infantile Neurosis and Other Works,* (London: Hogarth Press, 1955 [1919]), pp. 217–256.
56 Roger Luckhurst, 'The weird: a dis/orientation', *Textual Practice* 31:6 (2017), 1041–1061.
57 Luckhurst, 'The weird', p. 1049.
58 'Perhaps this is why the signature of weird fiction and horror film is not the vampire or the zombie, those minimal allegorical displacements of the human, but the tentacle, that limb-tongue suggestive of absolute alterity.' Luckhurst, 'The weird', p. 1054.
59 Mark Fisher, *The Weird and the Eerie* (London: Repeater Books, 2017), p. 40.
60 Karl Bell, 'Through Purged Eyes. Folk Horror and the Affective Landscape of the Urban Weird', in *The Urban Wyrd 2: Spirits of Place*, ed. by Andy Paciorek and others (Wyrd Harvest Press, 2019), p. 4.
61 Tim Powers, *The Anubis Gates* (London: Orion Books, 1983), p. 110.
62 Bell, p. 4.
63 Powers, *Anubis Gates*, p. 193.
64 Powers, p. 152.
65 Powers, p. 99.
66 Powers, p. 441.
67 K. W. Jeter, *Infernal Devices* (Nottingham: Angry Robot, 2011 [1987]), p. 96.
68 For more on the context and history of slumming, see: Seth Koven, *Slumming: Sexual and Social Politics in Victorian London* (Princeton: Princeton University Press, 2004).
69 Hantke, p. 248.
70 Hantke, p. 253.
71 Sterling, 'User's Guide', p. 12.
72 Ibid., p. 12.
73 Grace E. Lavery, *Quaint, Exquisite. Victorian Aesthetics and the Idea of Japan* (Princeton: Princeton University Press, 2019), p. xii.
74 Sterling, 'User's Guide', p. 13.
75 Luckhurst, *Science Fiction*, p. 196.
76 Patrick Jagoda, 'Clacking Control Societies: Steampunk, History, and the Difference Engine of Escape', *Neo-Victorian Studies* 3.1 (2010), 46–71, p. 47. John Clute, 'Vive?', in *Look at the Evidence* (London: Gollancz, 1996 [1991]), pp. 243–245, p. 310.

77 Fredric Jameson, *Postmodernism. Or, The Cultural Logic of Late Capitalism* (London: Verso, 1991), pp. 16–17.
78 Jameson, p. 419, original emphasis.
79 Gibson, who was in the process of writing *Neuromancer* left the cinema because he 'was afraid the movie would be better than what [he himself] had been able to imagine'. William Gibson, 'The Art of Fiction', *The Paris Review*, 2011. https://www.theparisreview.org/interviews/6089/william-gibson-the-art-of-fiction-no-211-william-gibson (accessed 10 March 2018).
80 Notably, steampunk exists both as a subculture, that is a community of like-minded people that engage in steampunk recreationally through costume, music, and style, and for whom steampunk is a hobby or self-expression, as well as takes on more counter-cultural potential for those who deploy it politically, i.e. its capacity for anarchic or anti-capitalist thought.
81 William Gibson, *Neuromancer* (London: Gollancz, 2016 [1984]), p. 59.
82 Jameson, p. 2.
83 Luckhurst, *Science Fiction*, p. 200.
84 Bruce Sterling, (ed.), *Mirrorshades. The Cyberpunk Anthology* (New York: Ace Books, 1986), p. xii.
85 Sterling, *Mirrorshades*, p. xii.
86 Luckhurst, *Science Fiction*, p. 213.
87 See: Istvan Csicsery-Ronay, *The Seven Beauties of Science Fiction* (Conneticut: Wesleyan University Press, 2011), p. 109.
88 Herbert Sussman, *Victorians and the Machine: The Literary Response to Technology* (Cambridge: Harvard UP, 1968), p. vii.
89 Sterling, 'User's Guide', p. 13.
90 Pike, 'Afterimages of the Victorian City', p. 265.
91 Brandy Schillace, *Clockwork Futures. The Science of Steampunk and the Reinvention of the Modern World* (New York: Pegasus Books, 2017), p. 130.
92 Sydney Padua, '2D Goggles, or The Thrilling Adventures of Lovelace and Babbage', http://sydneypadua.com/2dgoggles/ (accessed 12 March 2018).
93 William Gibson and Bruce Sterling, *The Difference Engine*. 2nd. Edition (New York: Random House, 2011 [1990]). p. 175.
94 Jay Clayton, *Charles Dickens in Cyberspace: The Afterlife of the Nineteenth Century in Postmodern Culture* (Oxford: Oxford University Press, 2003), p. 110.
95 Benjamin Disraeli, *Sybil; or, The Two Nations,* ed. by Thom Braun (London: Penguin, 1980 [1845]), p. 354.
96 Herbert Sussman, 'Cyberpunk Meets Charles Babbage: The Difference Engine as Alternative Victorian History', *Victorian Studies,* 38:1 (Autumn 1994), 1–23.
97 Jagoda, p. 61.
98 Csicsery-Ronay, p. ix, p. 3.
99 Gibson and Sterling, p. 173.

100 Gibson and Sterling, pp. 173–174.
101 Nora defines *lieux de mémoire* as socio-historical reference points at which collective memory is synthesized into a symbolic representation. They are cornerstones of collective identity formation: 'At once natural and artificial, simple and ambiguous, concrete and abstract, they are lieux—places, sites, causes—in three senses—material, symbolic and functional', Pierre Nora, *The realms of memory: Rethinking the French Past* (New York: Columbia University Press, 1999), p. 14; Jan Assmann's theory of cultural memory as a historical narrative of origin for a community. Jan Assmann, 'Cultural Memory', in *Cultural Memory Studies. An International and Interdisciplinary Handbook,* ed. by Astrid Erll and Ansgar Nünning (Berlin, New York, 2008), pp. 109–118.
102 Henri Lefebvre, 'The Right to the City', in *Writings on Cities*, ed. by Eleonore Kofman and Elizabeth Lebas (London: Blackwell, 1996), pp. 147–159, p. 148.
103 Jagoda, pp. 51–52; Michel Foucault, 'The Birth of Biopolitics', in *Ethics: Subjectivity and Truth,* ed. by Rabinow, Paul (New York: New Press, 1997), pp. 73–80. Gilles Deleuze, 'Postscript on Control Societies', in *Negotiations: 1972–1990* (New York: Columbia University Press, 1990), pp. 177–182.
104 Jagoda, p. 52.
105 Gibson and Sterling, pp. 144–145.
106 Daniel Fischlin, Veronica Hollinger, Andrew Taylor, William Gibson and Bruce Sterling, '"The Charisma Leak": A Conversation with William Gibson and Bruce Sterling', *Science Fiction Studies,* 19:1 (1992), 1–16, p. 10.
107 Roger Whitsun, *Steampunk and Nineteenth-Century Digital Humanities. Literary Retrofuturisms, Media Archaeologies, Alternate Histories* (London: Routledge, 2017), p. 41.
108 Gibson, *Neuromancer,* p. 59.
109 Edward Soja, *Postmetropolis. Critical Studies of Cities and Regions* (Oxford: Blackwell Publishers, 2000). p. 336.
110 Lefebvre, 'Right to the City', p. 158.
111 Lefebvre, p. 147.
112 David Harvey, *Rebel Cities. From the Right to the City to the Urban Revolution* (London: Verso, 2012), p. 4.
113 Harvey, *Rebel Cities*, p. 138.
114 Harvey, *Rebel Cities*, p. 136.
115 White, p. 2.
116 VanderMeer and Chambers, *Steampunk Bible*, p. 48.
117 Csicsery-Ronay, p. 108.
118 Hantke, p. 253.
119 Csicsery-Ronay, p. 109, original emphasis.
120 Harvey, *Rebel Cities*, p. 5.

2

East End Punk: Neo-Victorianism, Urban Gothic, and Collective Knowledge

Introduction: Gothic of the City

'If space embodies social relationships,' as Lefebvre asks, 'how and why does it do so? And what relationships are they?'[1] Having established how early steampunk comes into being, this chapter interrogates the shared popular memory against which steampunk's retro-speculation functions: How does its neo-Victorian remix work, and why? How does it play out in and through the city? How does the Victorian city stage and encode tropes and memory figures that endure in collective memory, and what happens to the neo-Victorian collage when these tropes are recombined and so re-contextualized? How may steampunk's fantastical anachronisms deploy historical textures to create new meanings – and where fail to do so?

Whereas early American steampunk responded to the declining industrial paradigm and neo-liberal politics with whimsical anarchy and cyberpunk-inspired counter-culture, the 1990s and early 2000s in Britain witnessed a boom in neo-Victorian fiction, prominent examples being A. S. Byatt's *Possession: A Romance* (1990), Sarah Waters' *Tipping the Velvet* (1998), *Affinity* (1999), and *Fingersmith* (2002), or Michael Faber's *Crimson Petal and the White* (2002). Neo-Victorian fiction of this era, as Louisa Hadley notes, must be 'understood within the context of Margaret Thatcher's political appropriation of the Victorians' and the slogan 'Victorian values'[2] as a 'talisman for lost stabilities'.[3] In the wake of Thatcher's nostalgic myth-making, which built up Victorian heritage as a quaint, economically stable, and hetero-normative counter-narrative to a 1980s present in which imperial hegemony and the nuclear family were seen to be threatened, neo-Victorianism became a battleground for identity politics and the meaning of Englishness. Neo-Victorian Gothic in particular, such as Alan Moore and Eddie Campbell's graphic novel *From Hell: A Melodrama in Sixteen Parts* (1988–98), Kim Newman's *Anno Dracula* (1992), or Peter Ackroyd's

Dan Leno and the Limehouse Golem (1994), set out to challenge and undermine Thatcher's highly selective, 'radical and reactionary, modernistic and atavistic'[4] rhetoric and politics, which after all dismantled institutions of the welfare state rooted in the nineteenth century. Resisting, as Elizabeth Ho diagnoses, such deliberate and falsely corrective misconstructions of collective memory, in which 'celebrations of the national past [...] gloss over the dark spots of the Whitechapel murders or Britain's imperial history',[5] these works, which Ho terms 'Ripperature', gravitate to London's East End to re-stage 'a catalog of hypocrisy, misogyny, violence, poverty, and prurience often excised from the national past'.[6]

For such an endeavour, there is no richer imaginative soil than Whitechapel and the East End, that symbolic epicentre of Victorian social anxieties and the now-classic staging ground for the urban Gothic mode. Across the nineteenth century, the classic, feudally Catholic Gothic of Ann Radcliffe and Horace Walpole, having 'bequeathed to the nineteenth century a whole new rhetorical idiom for writing about evil and violence, fear and madness, grief and death'[7], moved into the city, for example through Thomas de Quincey's *Confessions of an Opium-Eater* (1821) and G. W. M. Reynolds's serial *The Mysteries of London* (1844–48),[8] and by the late nineteenth century, London was increasingly imagined in Gothic[9] terms: In the obscuring foggy, gaslit shadows of the vast, progressive, enlightened, cosmopolitan metropolis lurk haunting spectres such as the social ills of disease, crime, and poverty, which are encoded in and experienced through a sensationalist language of affect. In accordance with popular post-Darwinian notions of races, cultures and societies as teleologically evolving, theories endorsed by personalities such as Herbert Spencer, Edward Tylor, or Francis Galton, the Gothic mode productively encoded contemporary anxieties about what Freud would later term the 'return of the repressed'.[10] Atavisms, regressions, and monstrosities, such as violence, alcoholism, crime, or prostitution continued to erupt in the modern city, which retained elements of obscurity supposedly at odds with its enlightened, transparent character. The Gothic rhetoric 'helped articulate how certain places made people feel, the supernatural providing a useful vocabulary for otherness, the unsettled, the unseen, and the unsolid', as Karl Bell posits. 'They were a means of expressing the subconscious awareness that cities were not just bricks and mortar but rich psychical landscapes'.[11] By the end of the century, the haunting presences from Robert Louis Stevenson's *The Strange Case of Dr Jekyll and Mr Hyde* (1886), Oscar Wilde's *The Picture of Dorian Gray* (1890), or Bram Stoker's *Dracula* (1896), aberrations mutated into monstrous degeneration, transform London into a labyrinthine, mysterious, and potentially dangerous nightmare cityscape.[12] The urban space itself remains seemingly fraught with anachronisms. Slums and 'rookeries were contextual anomalies, out of place in modern mercantile, industrial, and clock-time-regulated London'.[13] A multitude of feared regressions and deviations, then, lurk in the psychologically charged streets and alleyways of Victorian London, contributing to what Mighall has termed no longer a 'Gothic in the City' but a 'Gothic *of* the City': 'Its terrors derive from situations peculiar to, and firmly located within, the urban experience'.[14]

Whitechapel, especially at the time of the Whitechapel murders (1888), came to epitomize the repressed and atavistic misery, depravity, and violence that seemingly haunted the enlightened present, and against which the Victorian cosmopolitan identity was defined. Orientalist discourse had already posited the East End, from the docklands to Limehouse, Spitalfields, Shadwell, and Whitechapel, as, if not 'Darkest Africa', then 'Darkest London', an exotic, heterotopic other within, a *terra incognita* which slumming gentlemen might explore as Sir Richard Burton, David Livingstone, or Henry Morton Stanley had explored the African continent. London's most notorious urban monster, the serial killer known as Jack the Ripper, then seemingly affirmed all that was feared about the wilderness of East London; that it was dark, dismal, and dangerous, a space in which vice and violence collided. Ripper media has, since 1888, eulogized and continuously re-iterated and re-shaped an enduring Gothic East End mythology, which this chapter interrogates as a prominent example of popular memory shaped in and through the urban environment.

After all, as Kohlke and Gutleben posit: 'Palimpsestically, we read the past city through the overlaid present, but conversely, we also read the present city backwards through the underlying and resurfacing past'.[15] How do these layers interact within a collective urban imagination, and how does their meaning change when they are re-shuffled? In the following, I posit that late-Victorian urban Gothic, due to its continued re-adaptation across multiple texts and genres over time, has come to signify a dominant and particularly potent imaginary of 'the Victorian city', readily available to the collective memory, and as such, a rich imaginary which neo-Victorianism and with it, steampunk, can activate. Tracing the interwoven and intertextual media history through which that urban Gothic emerges therefore illuminates those shared memory processes on which neo-Victorianism relies, and which act as backdrop to steampunk's anachronistic play. Accordingly, I examine the emergence and codification of a register of urban Gothic tropes centralized in 1880s Whitechapel through two of its most influential chroniclers, Gustave Doré and Arthur Morrison, before considering how Ripper media newly synthesized and perpetuated that pre-established Gothic mythology. The Victorian East End and Jack the Ripper emerge as mutually constitutive symbols for Gothic urbanity, crafted into a distinct set of influential aesthetic tropes that lastingly shape neo-Victorian narratives, which either purposefully or unconsciously (by force of habit) reproduce a Gothic gaze. Indeed, neo-Victorianism 'must also be understood as a *purveyor*' and 'tak[ing] part in the constant reactivation of the Gothic', being '*by nature quintessentially Gothic*'[16] and continually

> resurrecting the ghost(s) of the past, searching out its dark secrets and shameful mysteries, insisting obsessively on the lurid details of Victorian life, reliving the period's nightmares and traumas. At the same time, neo-Victorianism also tries to understand the nineteenth century as the contemporary self's uncanny *Doppelgänger*, exploring the uncertain limit between what is vanished (dead) and surviving (still living) [...].[17]

Considering, then, that neo-Victorianism re-posits the Victorian past as new Gothic Other, I examine Kim Newman's *Anno Dracula* as an example of hyper-Gothic counterfiction and remix that provides an important connection between neo-Victorianism and steampunk.[18] As such, it forms part of a range of post-modern, farcical neo-Gothic remixes which Megen de Bruin-Molé identifies as 'deliberately inauthentic texts' that delight in 'fakery for the sake of spectacle and pleasure, and for the sheer enjoyment of the many modes of reflecting pastness', and that mobilize the 'popularity of its appropriated source texts, through which it is defined and assessed'.[19] Importantly, however, while neo-Victorianism, Gothic, and steampunk thus certainly share overlapping origins, modes, and aesthetics, they are not synonymous or interchangeable, or deploy neo-Victorian remix to the same ends, as this chapter seeks to demonstrate. For this purpose, I illustrate *Anno Dracula*'s creative leverage of popular memory through a brief juxtaposition with Peter Ackroyd's psychogeographical *Dan Leno and the Limehouse Golem*, a novel that interrogates urban memory in different ways. Both novels, I argue, demonstrate how neo-Victorian Londons may emerge from textual memory by way of the Gothic, but only *Anno Dracula*'s counterfictional remix rehearses both the mobilization of popular transmedia memory and the retro-speculative potential that lies at the heart of steampunk. This is illustrated by this chapter's final discussion of how second-wave steampunk may productively re-combine and re-purpose Victorian urban Gothic mythologies to re-organize meaning – or how it may fail to do so.

2.1 Devils, Detectives, and Deep Topographies

Darkest London: East End Mythologies

Considering that neo-Victorian Gothic texts such as *Anno Dracula* tap into a rich and palimpsestic urban mythology, as well as both activate and re-iterate a canon of narrative tropes, it pays to trace that tradition and contextualize the many cultural touchstones which Newman references and remixes as part of its steampunk collage. Indeed, neo-Victorianism, as Kohlke and Gutleben note, is '*by definition* hyperreal, since it has no direct access to the Victorian real, instead relying entirely on Victorian texts and documents, that is, on *signs* of the past'[20], but London itself has also long been chronicled as innately hyperreal,[21] ineffable, and labyrinthine, 'a sublime object,' as Luckhurst notes, 'that evokes awe and evades rational capture'.[22] Always already suffused and charged with imagination, the city becomes susceptible and 'more amenable to the disorderly mode of the Gothic'.[23] In other words, the sublimity of the modern metropolis which, if defined in Burkean terms as 'terror and awe', is not unlike the uncanny, can be potently expressed via the urban Gothic mode. Uncanny, or *unheimlich*, after all, literally translates to un-home-ly, and as such is intrinsically connected to identity and how we inhabit spaces.[24] By the mid- to late nineteenth century, an underlying Gothic rhetoric had been assimilated into the popular register with which urban London, and especially its social ills, were portrayed:

> For Dickens, as for nineteenth-century literary culture in general, it was this Gothic rhetoric which would come to dominate almost all depictions of human evil and misery, until by the time of *Bleak House* (1853) it no longer seemed strange to describe old men as vampires, detectives as ghosts, curtains as banshees, money-lenders as changelings, or court regalia as demons, even in a novel set in almost-contemporary London and notionally lacking any supernatural content.[25]

In addition, de Quincey had established the metaphor which encoded slums such as St Giles, Seven Dials, or Whitechapel as *terrae incognitae* – exotic, atemporal, and lawless spaces in which the civilizing effects of modernity were given no foothold, and which therefore remained significantly 'behind the times'.[26] It is then in discourse about the slum especially that Gothic imageries converge to identify it as what Mighall calls an 'anachronistic vestige of the "errors of our forefathers"', haunted by 'the vengeful spirit of pathology and plunder, the nemesis of neglect'.[27] As reformer William Booth's survey, *In Darkest*

England and the way Out (1890) shows by referencing Henry Morton Stanley's travelogue *In Darkest Africa* (1890),

> Social investigators, missionaries, and reformers often imagined the East End as an urban jungle filled with danger and sin and infested with 'savages' or 'beasts of prey in human shape'. The oxymoronic metaphor of the urban jungle enabled social investigators to fancy themselves as hardy adventurers entering what would today be called a 'combat zone', armed with nothing more than a map, a compass, and a Bible.[28]

Indeed, Booth's bestseller teems with analogies about savagery, sins, and disease.[29] Whereas Margaret Harkness' novel *Captain Lobe: A Story of the Salvation Army* (1889) eschewed strategies of Othering in favour of a more authentic portrayal designed to effect change,[30] her re-naming of the novel *In Darkest London* contributed to rather than undermined a popular reception of the East End as *terra incognita*, pandering to middle-class, Orientalist receptions of its inhabitants (Irish Catholics, sailors from China and India, and Ashkenazim Jews fleeing pogroms in Russia) as outlandish, foreign, and exotic.[31]

To what degree notions of the Gothic metropolis are intertwined with a reception of the physical urban landscape is illustrated in the work of the French artist and engraver Gustave Doré. His evocative illustrations for *London. A Pilgrimage* (1872), produced in collaboration with Blanchard Jerrold, have lastingly shaped imaginaries of Victorian London, but it is prudent to remember that, whereas Doré and Jerrold undertook field research through guided tours throughout London, many sketches were produced in retrospect from memory, not on location.[32] Doré, accused by some contemporaries of exaggerating in his depictions of misery, squalor, and deprivation, certainly envisions London as a mega-city of superlatives and extremes. Ludgate Hill, for example, proved a popular subject of 1880s urban artists, encapsulating with its multi-layered vista towards St Paul's cathedral, its traffic-crowded street, and urban railway bridge London's networked multiplicity, simultaneity, and tempo. Artists such as Wilhelm Trübner (*Ludgate Hill*, 1884), John Atkinson Grimshaw (*St Paul's from Ludgate Circus*, 1885), John O'Connor (*Ludgate, Evening*, 1887), William Logsdail (*St. Paul's and Ludgate Hill*, 1887), or Jacques-Emile Blanche (*Ludgate Circus: Entrée de la City* (Novembre, midi), 1910) were drawn to this vista of layered buildings. Doré, too, rendered this iconic vista as exemplifying the modern metropolis,[33] but in comparison also exaggerating its crowdedness for dramatic effect and casting the faceless multitudes and portentous sky through a tangibly Gothic vision. Other images, such as *Warehousing in the City*,[34] evoke endlessness through the absence of horizons, its warehouse fronts undefined by pavement or roof, stretching uncannily and endlessly into the shadows. In *Over London – By Rail*, a fish-eye perspective amplifies innumerable uniform brick houses stretching into the distance, forming a labyrinth of walls and chimneys in which dwarfed citizens are isolated and quite literally faceless.[35] Instead of a sky, high railway bridges stretch over the houses, invoking claustrophobia and gloom. Doré's London is a sublime megalopolis whose sheer physicality acquires Gothic qualities and which is nowhere so dreary and dark as in the slums, which Jerrold's descriptions complement through their vivid descriptions of the picturesque, yet bizarre:

> We plunge into a maze of courts and narrow streets of low houses—nearly all the doors of which are open, showing kitchen fires blazing far in the interior, and strange figures moving about. Whistles, shouts, oaths, growls, and the brazen laughter of tipsy women: sullen 'good nights' to the police escort; frequent recognition of notorious rogues by the superintendent and his men; black pools of water under our feet—only a riband of violet grey sky overhead![36]

In this passage alone, we find sensory staples of Gothic portrayals that later texts and films tend to take up: the juxtaposition of unusual light and dark, making strange the rowdy, promiscuous women and drunk men, the cacophonous soundscape, and the unfamiliar, oddly coloured sky all contribute to a vision of intriguing distortion and evocative shadows. In Doré's accompanying illustrations, urchins and street-dwellers in ill-fitting clothing crowd in melancholy shadows, highlighting sources of light only deepening the contrast.[37]

This is particularly evocative in the illustration of *Opium Smoking – The Lascar's Room in 'Edwin Drood'*,[38] where the solitary light source illuminates the Orientalized, alien face of the genderless Lascar woman: 'It was difficult to see any humanity in that face, as the enormous grey lips lapped about the rough wood pipe and drew in the poison.'[39] The scene relies on the notoriety of Dickens' intertext (1870) in which John Jasper finds himself in 'in the meanest and closest of small rooms', where '[t]hrough ragged window-curtain, the light of early day steals in from a miserable court'.[40] In this squalid and murky place in Shadwell, Jasper's visions of a romanticized, atemporal, and feudal Orient exemplifies the exotic mysticism with which middle-class Westerners imagined the East and, by proxy, the East End.[41] In later visions, opium smoking is associated with the London docks and Limehouse (settled by Chinese immigrants at the time), for example in Wilde's *The Picture of Dorian Gray*, or Doyle's Sherlock Holmes short story, *The Man with the Twisted Lip* (1891). Soon, Orientalist meta-narratives about the 'Yellow Peril', epitomized by Sax Rohmer's (Arthur Henry Ward) Fu Manchu (1913–1959), enshrined East London in the collective imagination as 'a place of exotic danger, where subterranean tunnels link gambling dens and brothels, and electric buttons hidden under the linoleum are used to communicate early warnings of police raids'.[42] Already, these texts, referencing each other rather than a lived local experience, accumulated a multi-textual register of (Gothic) East End tropes.

This is especially evident in Arthur Morrison's classic slum novel, *A Child of the Jago* (1896), a key intertext for Newman and later steampunk novels. The story of Dicky Perrot, a boy who, though clever and good-natured, is fated to a life of petty theft and poverty in London's worst slum, the Old Nichol (fictionalized as the Jago), impressed its readers with the brutality that characterized mob violence in Morrison's Jago, a space which policemen scarcely enter for fear of being attacked. Some reviewers noted the pathos with which Morrison outlined neglected, hungry children, others, like H. D. Traill, criticized the novel's 'extraordinary unreality' and called it a 'fairyland of horror': 'Mr Morrison has simply taken all the types of London misery, foulness and rascality, and "dumped them down" on the area aforesaid ... It is certainly not realism'.[43] Others again asserted they were acquainted with the very real types in the novel[44] – including Father Arthur Osborne Jay himself (who inspired the figure of Father Sturt). Jay, vicar of Holy Trinity in Shoreditch, had invited Morrison to explore his parish in 1895, which included the notorious Old Nichol,[45] which appeared on Charles Booth's *Poverty Map* (1889–90) in dark blue ('Very Poor, casual. Chronic want.') and black ('Lowest class. Vicious, semi-criminal').[46] The more than thirty streets and courts had housed 5,700 of the poorest Londoners, but by the time Morrison gathered his evidence, the slum had already been cleared by the London County Council for a rebuilding scheme.[47] Visions of the Jago then depended considerably on Father Jay's own, and often collected and re-mediated, narrative.[48] Morrison's portrait is therefore crucially built on narrative rather than authentic experience, which in no way hampered its lasting influence as the Old Nichol and the Jago became synonymous in the collective imagination.[49] Jack London's slum narrative *The People of the Abyss* (1903), for example, references to 'the municipal dwelling erected by the London County Council on the site of the slums where lived Arthur Morrison's "Child of the Jago",[50] exemplifying how his urban imaginary was shaped by fiction fused over already obscured facts.

Eulogized, then, as convoluted labyrinth of shabby streets and alleyways, in which people live in small rooms like vermin ('Here lies the Jago, a nest of rats, breeding, breeding, as only rats can; and we say it is well'[51]), the Nichol/Jago conjured up the slum's 'illegal sprouting of sheds, workshops and stables – slung up without parish surveyors' say-so in courts'[52] that constitute a parallel world which only residents may navigate. Dicky Perrot, corrupted by his surroundings despite his best intentions, navigates these urban spaces of vice and violence with ease and familiarity, but is also – literally and metaphorically– caught in its dismal maze: Sometimes evading pursuers after a theft through his knowledge of its intricate alleyways, sometimes exhausted by them, he is curtailed by an urban labyrinth which facilitates only corruption and forecloses escape. Morrison's vision exemplifies not only how Gothic tropes about destitution and atavism converged with a defiantly opaque cityscape, but also how narrative shapes the collective imagination of urban space.

Transmedia scholarship pioneered by Henry Jenkins discusses such convergence of media into what Pierre Lévy has termed 'collective intelligence' in the digital age, but we can also trace how Victorian discourse slowly accumulates an intertextual, palimpsestic mythology in the same, albeit analogue, manner.[53] Lévy defined collective intelligence as 'a form of universally distributed intelligence, constantly enhanced, coordinated, in real time, and resulting in the effective mobilization of skills. [...] No one knows everything, everyone knows something, all knowledge resides in humanity. There is no transcendent store of knowledge and knowledge is simply the sum of what we know.'[54] In Jenkins' work, collective intelligence interacts with the two concepts media convergence and participatory culture to create knowledge communities. 'Each of us constructs our own personal mythology from bits and fragments of information extracted from the media flow and transformed into resources through which we make sense of our everyday lives.'[55] In the same way, textual and visual representations of the Victorian East End contributed to a media flow which in turn created a collective knowledge shared by a predominantly middle-class demographic of Londoners. As recent research demonstrates, pre-digital transmedia practices and experiences thrived amid the nineteenth century's mass media landscape.[56] This is not least evident through the notorious Whitechapel murders, which newly activated and re-synthesized (Gothic) tropes migrating across multiple media.

Jack the Ripper's Shadow

No event seemed to epitomize contemporary anxieties around the East End as an a-chronic, lawless Other to a cosmopolitan Victorian identity as the Jack the Ripper murders of 1888,[57] and which also engendered a Gothic mythology that has dominated perceptions and depictions of the area ever since. The sexualized violence that informed the killings of destitute women in a locale already heavily charged with Gothic imagery shone an unwelcome light on persistent social shortcomings of the seemingly progressive late-Victorian metropolis. Reactions to and media coverage of the events represent dominant socio-cultural facets of the contemporary zeitgeist: the outrage at poverty and squalor and cries for reform, or the hysteric, xenophobic and often anti-Semitic treatment of 'usual suspects', contemporary attitudes towards criminality, criminology and the police, the ready use of sensationalist-Gothic rhetoric in the media and the co-influence of the murders on the success of the detective novel have all been chronicled and examined in scholarship.[58] In addition, Ripper stories have been told and re-told across various media since John Francis Brewer's *The Curse Upon Mitre Square* (1888), Frank Wedekind's drama *Die Büchse der Pandora* (1903) or Marie Belloc-Lowndes' novel *The Lodger* (1913) which imbued the killer with the famous iconography of top hat, Gladstone bag, and opera coat.[59]

Although scholarship has recently shone a necessary spotlight on their own stories,[60] the five canonical victims Mary Ann Nichols (31 August, Buck's Row), Annie Chapman (8 September, Hanbury Street), Elizabeth Stride (30 September, Dutfield's Yard), Catherine Eddowes (30 September, the so-called 'double-event', Mitre Square), and Mary Jane Kelly (9 November, Miller's Court) have long been assimilated into a geographically rooted catalogue of Ripper mythology as mere signifiers, commonly associated with the location of their murder and remembered largely through frequently reproduced renderings of their mutilated bodies in the *Illustrated Police News*. Indeed, influenced by W. T. Stead's New Journalism, a mixture of investigative and sensationalist reporting that focused on 'exposing' social ills and dangers,[61] the Whitechapel murders created the first serial-killer inspired media frenzy,[62] not least because their extreme violence defied usual strategies of (narrative) sense-making:

> These murders remained an impenetrable mystery and an unprecedented horror, with the killer seemingly capable of striking again at any time. Not only did this narrative have an ambiguous beginning [...], and an uncertain middle [...], it also lacked a clear ending [...]. Here was a series of shocking crimes without any closure.[63]

Without recourse to a criminological vocabulary regarding serial killers, journalists resorted to sensationalist tropes about urban monsters such as Spring-Heeled Jack or Sweeney Todd,[64] employing such terms as 'fiend', 'ghoul', 'beast', and a 'vampire' to describe what was imagined as a sort of *genius loci* embodying the East End's (perceived) depravity and violence. The *Star* outlined the crime in terms of Gothic fiction and the Gothic monster:

> Nothing so appalling, so devilish, so inhuman — or, rather non-human — as the three Whitechapel crimes has ever happened outside the pages of Poe or De Quincey. The unravelled mystery of 'The Whitechapel Murders' would make a page of detective romance as ghastly as 'The Murders in the Rue Morgue'. The hellish violence and malignity of the crime which we described yesterday resemble in almost every particular the two other deeds of darkness which preceded it. Rational motive there appears to be none. The murderer must be a Man Monster [...][65]

From the outset, elements of fictionality and the supernatural clung to this 'devilish', 'non-human' killer, who, as Alexandra Warwick cautions, 'has been a collective and collaborative invention since the moment of the murders taking place'.[66] From the beginning, 'Jack the Ripper' has been a collective symbol masking and absence, a black hole in the socio-historical fabric into which our communally created narratives may be projected. No wonder then, that the killer was often referred to as 'Mr. Hyde', especially considering that a stage adaptation of Stevenson's novella *The Strange Case of Dr. Jekyll and Mr. Hyde* (1886) had opened at the Lyceum shortly before Martha Tabram's murder (7 August 1888). The killer was all the more monstrous for his ambiguity and his anonymity, 'a dweller on the limits of society and yet fully integrated into it',[67] performing the assimilated urbanite and yet essentially split both in personality and morality – an imagery productively encoded in Jekyll's homicidal alter ego. Hyde, linking moral degeneration to physical regress and otherness in the 'ape-like', atavistic monster, seemed to inspire the Ripper to what the *Pall Mall Gazette* termed a 'tolerably realistic impersonification',[68] and drew comparisons to Sioux tribes, whereas the *Star* drew analogies to the 'Pawnee Indian'.[69] Such racist comparisons expose the Victorians' mental geography as intrinsically colonial, even – or perhaps, especially – when pertaining to London, the heart of Empire, imagined as a microcosm in which social Darwinist theories prevail.

How neatly the Ripper catalyzed threats to the British Victorian, and London identity is illustrated by the *Evening Standard*:

> The monstrous and wanton brutality by which they are distinguished is rather what we might expect from a race of savages than from even the most abandoned and most degraded classes in a civilised community. It is terrible to reflect that at the end of the nineteenth century, after all our efforts, religious, educational, and

philanthropic, such revolting and sickening barbarity should still be found in the heart of this great City, and be able to lurk undetected in close contact with all that is most refined, elegant, and cultivated in human society.[70]

From the outset, the Ripper was a phenomenon collectively constructed across multiple media, embodying collective anxieties about life in the city as an urban uncanny residing on the continually collapsing border between the familiar and the repressed, the ego and the id, progress and atavism, a duality also inherent in the Othering rhetoric about the East End.

However, newspapers and media not only shaped the Ripper myth through their rhetoric, but also by disseminating selected letters ascribed to the killer, most infamously the 'Dear Boss' letter in which the author self-identified as 'Jack the Ripper' for the first time, or the 'Saucy Jack postcard' signed with 'From Hell'. By disseminating the killer's – or, at least, the sender's – own myth-making, they enshrined that myth in the collective imagination, as Moore's graphic novel *From Hell* (1989) and its adaptation (1999) also illustrate. As Darren Oldridge concludes, 'the press launched the "Ripper industry"'[71] that ultimately fashioned the killer into an '*objet d'art*'.[72] Indeed, the Ripper's most enduring legacy lies in the realm of fiction.

The 1888 murders not least gave new, accelerating impulses to the developing genre of detective fiction, most notably through Sherlock Holmes, who penetrates the urban jungle with ordering logic and finds causality in contingency.[73] As a collective symbol for reason and order restored, the Holmesian detective usually navigates the city as an intricate labyrinth of traces with authority, negating the trauma of regressive violence with progressive deduction in opposition to the anarchic forces of crime. Jack the Ripper and Sherlock Holmes, then, are a match forged by destiny as the powerful early incarnation of that eternally popular and endlessly reproduced constellation of serial killer and urban detective. It is no wonder that subsequent Ripper fictions usually feature a detection plot or detective figure, especially considering that they represent the intersection at which 'real' and 'fictional' symbols converge: the heavily mythologized Ripper whose identity remains forever obscure, and the canonical detective who has become such an icon that people often think he really existed.

Indeed, every victim, suspect, locale, or investigator surrounding the events of 1888 has been assembled into an interconnected 'Ripper imaginary' that was continuously filtered through the collective imagination through cross-media representations and adaptations from the very beginning. They have become talismanic signifiers for 'Jack the Ripper' who himself acts as signifier for notions such as 'Victorian London' or 'the East End', which in turn signify crime, poverty, prostitution, exoticism, and so on. Through this medially constructed and interconnected web of signifiers, in which all signifiers associated with the Ripper are irretrievably bound up with one another, 'Jack the Ripper' and 'The East End' become mutually constitutive, and the actual, historical East End recedes from collective memory behind a communally constructed imaginary. As Clive Bloom notes, the Victorian East End has become a fantasy location delineated by an array of specific markers such as fog, brick walls, gaslight, and cobblestones, 'a ruined memory of a landscape now reduced to its significant effects, glimpses of a lost place that never quite existed'.[74] The East End imaginary emerges, as Bloom notes, as an 'East End of the mind', a trope-laden aesthetic fraught with insecurities: the obscuring fog or portentously dark shadows obscure pathways and hide predators and are only deepened by the sickly gaslight, the brick walls conjure up desolation, claustrophobia, and paranoia, and 'it is always 1888'.[75] Across time, its inhabitants remain the inevitable dubious drunkards, skulking sailors, lurking children, or shabby prostitutes, increasingly caricatured to create a 'hysterical, bigoted, and nasty' atmosphere.[76] We always recognize the Ripper from his top hat, opera cloak, and Gladstone bag, containing at least one surgical knife – aesthetic markers charged with the traces of historical meaning which accompanied their creation as an interlinked chain of signifiers. A multitude of discourses, anxieties, and images are so highly concentrated into symbols, none so iconic as 'Jack the Ripper', and they easily survive pop cultural modification or post-modern re-contextualization with the meaning attached to them still intact.

This becomes evident in Albert and Allen Hughes' film adaptation of Alan Moore and Edie Campbell's graphic novel *From Hell* (1989–1996/2001) which reflects an international popular reception, and which is based on Stephen Knight's 1976 Ripper theory *The Final Solution*.[77] The film exemplifies how neo-Victorian Gothic re-signifies the past through a communally legible Ripper iconography. It replicates the graphic novel's evocative compositions dominated by gloomy, uniform brick walls and shadowy doorways which echo Doré's endless cityscapes. So do the graphically eerie chiaroscuros that accompany the construction of Whitechapel as an indifferent maze full of shadows concealing malice and misery. Jack the Ripper, here the manic royal physician Sir William Gull, towers over his final victim as shadowy outline in top hat and opera coat, replicating at once the historical crime scene photographs and a fictional iconography rooted in Lowndes' *The Lodger*. As such, the film exemplifies Bloom's familiar 'Ripper aesthetic', but it also adds new, if equally Gothic imagery:

Masonic symbols and societies, portentously looming spires against an apocalyptic sky, Abberline's prophetic opium dreams, allusions to the Orientalist-imperialist, symbolized by Cleopatra's needle, accompanied by over-saturation, radically steep camera angles, and fragmentary distortion at once re-affirm Victorian London's and Gothic status, and re-calibrate it to re-position the Victorian past as Gothic Other.

Indeed, whereas Whitechapel remains the locus of Gothic Otherness, the whole city and all of society are portrayed as contaminated by Gothic corruption. *From Hell* deliberately implicates a complicit aristocracy as emblems of a corrupt authority in the form of Gull, who avenges the Duke of Clarence's slumming habits on the most destitute citizens, or through the shallow aristocrats who gawk at Joseph Merrick, the Elephant Man, under the guise of charity, or Abberline's bigoted superiors, conspiring in their Masonic secret societies. Corruption, like disease, deeply saturates this intrinsically uncanny Victorian London in which Whitechapel becomes but a symptom of an ever-present undercurrent of bigotry, decadence, and corruption. It is no longer the East End as an exceptional Other within that destabilizes a Victorian identity of teleological progress threatened by regressive 'savagery', but instead, Victorian society – and Victorian London – itself is encoded as a corrupt other. In accordance with Kohlke and Gutleben, the film, as neo-Victorian Gothic, 'participates in an implicit critique of the meta-narratives of civilization and progress, on which the Victorians prided themselves and for which they are still stereotypically celebrated today'.[78] It can do so productively in and through the Victorian metropolis because 'neo-Victorian crime and/or detective fictions, [are] quintessentially urban genres, in which cities simultaneously function as emblems of advanced civilization, culture, and progress and of atavistic corruption that threatens their undoing'.[79] Neo-Victorian Gothic so mines a shared imaginary of London Gothic to effect a critical re-evaluation of the past through the prism of today's identity politics.

Anno Dracula and its Counterfictional Story-World

Indeed, as Newman himself proclaims about *Anno Dracula*: 'I was trying, without being too solemn, to mix things I felt about the 1980s, when the British Government made "Victorian Values" a slogan, with the real and imagined 1880s, when blood was flowing in the fog and there was widespread social unrest'.[80] As such, the novel merits a close consideration not just for its Gothic resistance to neo-liberal meta-narratives about the Victorian past, but also as an example of creative counterfictional collage that re-assembles collectively shared visions off that past in a fundamentally steampunk way. Newman's novel, which is the first in a series of sequels and off-shoots, imagines itself as a sequel to a version of Stoker's *Dracula* in which the Count triumphs over the Harkers, Van Helsing, and their friends, and marries Queen Victoria to become the new Prince Consort, spreading vampirism throughout London and the Empire.[81] Inspired by Newman's affection for horror film and all sorts of vampire incarnations, the retelling is a vast, dense intertextual collage of historical, fictional, and pop cultural traces and characters, in which all intermingle freely: Oscar Wilde is seen at Florence Stoker's dinner parties, whereas Bram Stoker himself has mysteriously vanished, and Van Helsing has been executed for treason. Lord Alfred Tennyson remains poet laureate 'for dreary centuries', Polidori's Lord Ruthven has become Prime Minister, and in Whitechapel, where a rabid Jack Seward butchers vampire prostitutes, Inspector Abberline works with DI Lestrade, Dr Jekyll, and Dr Moreau. Mycroft Holmes, Sebastian Moran, and Professor Moriarty all move about in this novel's London, but Sherlock Holmes has been exiled to a work camp for political dissent – and, as Newman confesses, because 'the great detective would have identified, trapped, and convicted the murderer before tea-time'.[82] Naturally, at the heart of this intertextual reference work lies a quest to solve the Ripper murders, although the reader knows from the first chapter that, seeing that 'Stoker had obligingly called one of Van Helsing's disciples Jack, made him a doctor and indicated that his experiences in the novel were pretty much pushing him over the edge', the Ripper is none other than former psychiatrist Jack Seward.[83]

Other, smaller references point to the fiction of Alexandre Dumas *père*, Sheridan LeFanu, E. M. Forster, Count Stenbock, Frank Wedekind, or Anthony Hope, but also later intertexts such as Murnau's *Nosferatu* (1922), the films of George Romero, or the novels of Sax Rohmer or Anne Rice. These are intertwined with appearances of historical figures as diverse as Elizabeth Bathory, William Holman Hunt, Frank Harris, Arthur Morrison, Algernon Swinburne, or John Montague Druitt (a Ripper suspect), and Catherine Eddowes (the killer's fourth victim). This makes the novel, in Newman's words, 'as much a playground as a minefield' which goes 'beyond historical accuracy to evoke all those gaslit, fogbound London romances'.[84] Indeed, as a highly resonant collage of transmedia vampire fictions throughout the ages, Newman's story-verse is self-reflexively embedded in a canon of collective popular reception, recombining Count Dracula and Jack the Ripper as collective symbols for Victorian Gothic fact and fiction.[85]

This type of collage, 'beyond factual, counterfactual, and fictional', has been termed 'counterfictional' by Matt Hills to denote a story-world that 'not only needs to be distinguished from "factuality" but also from other preceding fictions'.[86] Counterfiction 'claims no fidelity to an originating fictional world. Instead, it deliberately sets out to re-construct, modify, and merge prior, existent fictional worlds'.[87] It relies on a reader's familiarity with the original text or an adaptation thereof to re-construct, subvert, or comment on said text or its context. A well-known example is Seth Graham-Smith's 2009 parody, *Pride and Prejudice and Zombies*, in which, as the title suggests, Austen's classic is re-combined with zombie-film genre tropes.

Counterfiction is also, I argue, a popular and indeed key steampunk strategy to craft retro-speculative universes that freely re-contextualize act and fiction into paradoxical parodies and pastiches which then act as meta-commentary, as exemplified by steampunk classics such as *The Difference Engine*, or Alan Moore's popular graphic novel *The League of Extraordinary Gentlemen* (2000). Importantly, because counterfiction involves 'texts self-consciously defining themselves in relation to their generic precursors',[88] it is directly affiliated with convergence and participatory culture as outlined in Jenkins' work on fan cultures,[89] in turn rooted in Michel de Certeau's notion of readers as textual poachers and 'travellers; [moving] across lands belonging to someone else, like nomads poaching their way across fields they did not write'.[90] Indebted also to Stuart Hall's encoding/decoding model of communication, Barthesian and Derridean post-structuralism, in which the meaning of a text is never fixed and authority over meaning does not reside with the author, and reader-reception theory, participatory culture emerges as 'that process of negotiating over the meaning of a text, and the terms of [fans'] relations with producers'.[91] In short, individual readings of popular or canonical texts may be subjective and varying, and although consensus arises through discourse which both constructs and sustains knowledge communities, the text remains open for negotiation. Both these seemingly contradictory impulses ensure that subsequent adaptations of the original texts reflect the consensus through identifiability and allow for alterations and re-interpretations.

Terry Pratchett, whose fantastical satires rely equally on the reader's pre-existing cultural knowledge, called this 'white knowledge' in reference to white noise in order to identify collective knowledge we merely absorb from our post-modern surroundings and can mobilize without recourse to an original text.[92] In reading *Anno Dracula*, for example, through 'white knowledge', we may deduce instantly that Seward is the Ripper from his allusion to 'Hanbury

Street – Chapman' (p. 15), or speculate on the fate of Catherine Eddowes or Mary Jane Kelly, even though the latter is seen through the prism of the memory of Lucy Westenra. By conflating the last Ripper victim with an eroticized vampiric woman, Kelly becomes the focus of Seward's obsessive grief and misogyny, which accounts for the barbaric violence inflicted on both the historical and the fictional body. However, as this overlay of the historical and fictional women also illustrates, the novel not only catalyzes a collectively shared 'white knowledge', but also capitalizes on the principles of participatory culture to engage in what Lawrence Lessing has termed 'remix culture'. The latter demands the active participation of knowledge communities by engaging readers as detectives,[93] providing clues that hint at an underlying network of shared knowledge and media literacy.[94] Newman effectively recombines the Ripper killings with Bram Stoker's *Dracula*, which indeed exerted some influence on the novel.[95] Both also reveal much about contemporary anxieties about sex, the first as the monstrous crusader, avenging vice,[96] the second through the charged imagery of the Count lapping young women's blood which has become a staple, if not a cliché, of subsequent vampire portrayals, for example in Hammer Horror films.[97] As such, they converge almost naturally: the unstable, lovelorn Doctor Seward who cannot overcome Lucy's death steps effortlessly into the footsteps of a nightly crusader, even more so if the women he kills recall to him that great loss. The prostitute and the vampire, with their connotations of sexual taboo, the night, bodily fluids, and female vulnerability converge equally easily. Similarly, Newman mobilizes a long tradition in post-Victorian pastiches and neo-Victorian thrillers in which Sherlock Holmes is sent out to catch Jack the Ripper, though of course he imports other Holmesian main characters and omits the Great Detective.[98] From here on, as the novel clearly demonstrates, it is only a small step towards importing every historical and fictional figure seemingly connected to the late-Victorian setting, its literature, or its afterlives, remixing them in clever ways. Like Lessing's example of image-sound remix, which articulates new meanings by trading collectively agreed-upon truths,[99] that is interpretations and meta-narratives, and showing rather than explaining them, counterfiction creates new meaning from juxtaposition and reference. It depends on a communally shared media literacy which identifies and actualizes the meaning with which pop cultural icons like Jack the Ripper or Sherlock Holmes are charged, to collage a depth and range of associated meaning which the text itself cannot hope to produce on its own, at least not without going to great lengths. Individual signifiers import associated meanings, as outlined above: Jack the Ripper signifies Whitechapel signifies gaslight and cobblestones signifies squalor and so on.

Steampunk, as seen in the last chapter, likewise 'succeeds by leveraging the meaning created by the reference to build something new',[100] especially by eliminating hierarchies between fact and fiction. In *Anno Dracula*, for example, the historical Goulston Street graffito, 'The Juwes are the men that will not be blamed for nothing', a testimony to anti-Semitic backlash in the wake of the Ripper murders,[101] here becomes: 'The vampyres are not the men that will be blamed for nothing' (205).[102] The re-contextualization, aside from serving as an inside joke, contributes to building the counterfictional world and also functions as a marker of general paranoia because it can import associations about xenophobia, anxiety, and aggressive tension which the original graffito encodes in its own context. Of course, there is also a certain ironic humour at play here, a strategy Christian Gutleben identifies as a metafictional distancing device which asserts an 'anti-nostalgic stance' within neo-Victorian Gothic through an ironic double discourse which both recreates and acknowledges the illusion of fiction.[103] Behind *Anno Dracula*'s disgruntled 'vampyres' lurk the real historical social frictions and anti-Semitism of a multi-cultural society strained by want and violence.

Indeed, the novel teems with (often sinister) irony, be it Jack 'the Ripper' Seward's daytime position as surgeon in the philanthropic institution Toynbee Hall, the fact that homosexuals implicated in the Cleveland Street Scandal (1889) are executed by being impaled on large wooden stakes, or the overall notion that a famously progressive and modern Victorian London slowly reverts to barbaric Medievalism. Such ironies are created through counterfictional juxtapositions of (fictional) appearance with the historical meaning which it can trade and activate.

In addition to conjuring up ironic resonances, counterfiction also assembles culturally charged markers in order to create a larger, underlying story-world. In Jenkins' concept of transmedia world-making, 'artists create compelling environments that cannot be fully explored or exhausted within a single work or a single medium. The world is bigger than the film, bigger than even the franchise – since fan speculations and elaborations also expand the world in a variety of directions'.[104] Whereas Jenkins' concept is geared towards popular franchises from *The Matrix*, *Star Wars*, or *Harry Potter* to the Marvel superhero films, Gothic East End mythologies and the Jack the Ripper aesthetic present, I suggest, a different incarnation of (cultural) transmediality. Gothic aesthetic conventions, such as the top hat, opera cape, and Gladstone bag combination, the fog and chiaroscuro, or gaslight and cobblestones serve as recurring motifs and aesthetic markers of the 'Ripper franchise', while also hinting at a larger story-world: Top hat and cape signifies Jack the Ripper signifies Victorian East End signifies drunkards and destitution signifies gaslight and fog, and so on. Moreover, the Ripper/East End story-world is continually adapted and expanded through films, novels, and comics, as well as questioned and re-imagined by its 'fans', the Ripperologists who share and debate theories within their own knowledge community. *Anno Dracula*, then, remixes such story-world markers from a large variety of interconnected Victorian and post-Victorian fictions, importing associated meanings alongside them into a new, counterfictional, and hyper-Gothic story-world designed both as homage to the genre and to satirize complacent and nostalgic fantasies about the Victorian past.

In so doing, the novel mobilizes, as Newman himself notes, Victorian and Edwardian invasion narratives,[105] as well as those underlying anxieties about reverse colonization which Stephen Arata has identified in *Dracula*.[106] Here, the Count, the foreign Other from the Eastern margins invades London, the heart of Empire, and 'British culture [not only] sees its own imperial practices mirrored back in monstrous forms',[107] but is overtaken and subsumed by it in the form of his vampirism. It is certainly no coincidence that London, the Empire's newly corrupted centre, likewise transforms into a distinctively Gothic cityscape dowsed in an ever-present fog. The 'London particular', so often a staple of the Ripper aesthetic, is tinged in sickly yellow, at times 'wispy, hanging like undersea fronds of yellow gauze'[108] (p. 86), others a thick, 'street-level sea of churning yellow that lapped at the buildings' (p. 375), or an obscuring 'sulphur-soup' (p. 364). In one particularly Gothic-surrealist visual image, the '[d]awn shot the fog full of blood' (p. 105). It obscures sight for human and vampire alike (p. 364), hinting at hidden predators (p. 109) and blending night and day, facilitating the Ripper's work (p. 174). As a visual metaphor, the persistent fog transforms London's cityscape into a maze characterized by precarity, uncertainty, and paranoia: the whole city becomes Bloom's 'East End of the mind'. That the fog is intrinsically connected to the Ripper, a symbol of such paranoia and precarity, becomes particularly evident when the fog begins to disperse as soon as Seward is discovered and killed (p. 393).

The novel similarly mobilizes the legacy of East End tropes when Charles Beauregard, agent of Mycroft Holmes' Diogenes Club and veteran of colonial spaces such as India, Shanghai, 'Afghanistan, Mexico, the Transvaal' (p. 51), is tasked with venturing into Whitechapel, which is likewise considered a *terra incognita* populated by regressive, lesser forms. The notion of Whitechapel as urban wilderness is enhanced by the presence of vampiric runts, mis-formed by Count Dracula's disseminated, diseased bloodline, which in turn externalizes

East Enders' disenfranchisement and Othering: Their lack of agency translates to their lack of control over their bodily shape, which, in conjunction with the 'beastly' imagery associated with the Count, often references reptiles and wolves. This calls up echoes of Morrison's (already fictionalized) Jago and its rat metaphors, and indeed a slum called the Old Jago here epitomizes the (imagined) East End:

> Red eyes glittered behind open windows. Rat-whiskered children sat on doorsteps, waiting to fight for the leavings of larger predators. [..] She was reminded of vultures. This was not England, this was a jungle. [...] Hunched, shambling creatures lurked in courtyards. Hate came off them in waves. The Jago was where the worst cases ended up, new-borns shape-shifted beyond any resemblance of humanity, criminals so vile other criminals would not tolerate their society. (pp. 281–282)

In Newman's hyper-Gothic East End, the Jago is continually evoked as a locus of Otherness, where violence, deprivation, and malice peak. The novel here literalizes Victorian rhetoric about atavism inherent in the East End imaginary, and creates a grotesque menagerie, a literal urban jungle populated in which (perceived) moral regressions like drunkenness or poverty translate into physical monstrosity. However, in presenting characters like the girl Lily, slowly poisoned and failing to shape-shift ('The animal she had tried to become was taking over, and that animal was dead' [p. 181]), the novel also evokes our sympathy and re-presents East Enders as victims of circumstance. Indeed, through the crusader figure John Jago, an anti-vampire Christian Crusader in full St George regalia (p. 254) no doubt modelled on Father Jay/ Father Sturt, who is secretly built up by the Diogenes Club as a rebel figure against the Count's regime, the novel also re-imagines the East End as a nexus of potential resistance.

At the same time, John Jago and his disciples, in their medieval crusader imagery, embody another trait vital to Newman's image of counterfictional London, namely that of a city gothically haunted by the crude and violent past which Vlad Tepes/the Count imports. Ironically, it is notably not the chivalrous, aesthetic Pre-Raphaelite or Revivalist Middle Ages of Alfred Tennyson and William Morris; in fact, Arthurian texts are deemed rebellious and banned as unrest stirs (p. 310). It is a classically Gothic Medievalism: Violent, ignorant, and feudal, jarringly out of place, recalling Radcliffe and Lewis – A Gothic of the Gothic, perhaps. Of course, in doing so, *Anno Dracula* takes up the resonances of xenophobia and Orientalism that characterize the Count as barbaric Eastern Other in classic Gothic fiction manner. The Count is, after all, also a Roman Catholic (p. 61): 'He missed the Renaissance, the Reformation, the Age of Enlightenment, the French Revolution, the rise of the Americas, the fall of the Ottoman' (p. 64).[109] Notions of the Oriental Other are complemented and somewhat alleviated by the vampire Geneviève Dieudonné's memories of the Hundred Years' War (p. 17, 193, 239, etc.), a European counterpart to the Transylvanian Count.

The latter's brand of Medievalism is represented by his Carpathian Guard, Kostaki, von Klatka, Cuda, General Iorga, who echo and satirize late-Victorian Ruritania stories like Anthony Hope's *The Prisoner of Zenda* (1894),[110] as well as the effeminate Count Vardalek, borrowed from Count Stenbock's 1884 story 'The Sad Story of a Vampire'. As the 'illegitimate children of Bismarck and Geronimo' they embody both a picturesque Ruritanian militarism and exoticized savagery conjured by the allusion to Native Americans:

> They [...] all wore highly polished boots and carried heavy swords, but their uniforms were augmented with oddments scavenged through the years. Von Klatka had around his neck a golden lanyard upon which were strung withered lumps of flesh [Geneviève] understood to be human ears. Cuda's helmet was adorned with a wolf's skin [...]. Vardalek was the most extraordinary figure, his jacket a puffy affair of pleats and flounces [...]. His face was powdered to conceal suppurating skin. Pantomime circles of rouge covered his cheeks [...]. His hair was stiff and golden, elaborately done up in bows and curls, twin braids dangling from the nape of his neck like rats' tails. (p. 80)

As an anachronistic assortment of 'barbaric' influences, they embody the Count's military vigour and his unenlightened cruelty. Roguish but crude, they are indeed later effectively joined and complemented by *Zenda*'s dashing and ruthless villain Rupert von Hentzau. Vardalek's somewhat inelegant rococo effeminacy meanwhile hints at his homosexuality, a trait that is dealt with in the episode about the Cleveland Street Scandal, in which every 'invert' and 'nancy-boy' (p. 127) is executed without trial and regardless of position by being publicly impaled in the 'well-lit, clean district': 'Cobblestones had been torn up and stake-holes were being rapidly dug' (p. 131). In addition to literally tearing into the Victorian city fabric, the gory episode demonstrates a callous homophobia (despite the ironic imagery), and a blind and presumably barbaric adherence to a backwards authority, exemplified by the fact that Vardalek is found among the patrons, and has to be executed among the others (p. 136). No doubt this part of the story sets out to undermine Thatcherite myth-making about quaintly heterosexual nuclear families, especially in an era of vocal LGBT activism and the AIDS crisis.

Altogether, London as city and mindscape is slowly poisoned by the corroding, diseased blood of the Gothic monster Dracula: 'The whole city seemed sick' (p. 110). 'Some quarters of the city have seen a resurgence of medieval diseases. It is as if the Prince Consort were a bubbling sink-hole, disgorging filth from where he sits, grinning his wolf's grin as sickness seeps through his realm' (p. 174). Dr Seward as Jack the Ripper, himself traumatized by the loss of his friends, the Count's invasion, and infected from Renfield's rabid bite, is then merely a symptom of the larger corruption as a catalyst for terror and moral panic. Yet the increasingly insane killer, fuelled by obsession and misogyny, also becomes a symbol of resistance, 'an outlaw hero, a Robin Hood of the gutters' (p. 160) who imagines himself a 'surgeon, cutting away diseased tissue' (p. 211). The fog accompanying the Ripper's reign seems analogous to a madness which clouds this city of the mind. As the government's authoritarian grip tightens, the city dissolves into a frenzied rebellion, tearing itself up in defiance: '[T]he remains of barricades still stood, and great stretches of St James Street had been torn up, cobbles converted into missiles' (pp. 397–398). The notion of the Ripper as a symptom of a city moving towards self-devouring insanity is strengthened by the fact that Geneviève and Charles Beauregard's discovery of the killer is not the final battle, nor was it the Diogenes Club's primary objective: The Ripper, somewhat paradoxically, has been appropriated as a symbol (encoding resistance and vengeance) to orchestrate the rebellion which lets Beauregard defeat the Count.[111] Similarly to his historical counterpart, the counterfictional Jack the Ripper serves as a catalyst for a complex network of societal debates, here amplified to volatility.

Anno Dracula's dense intertextuality demonstrates the potency of 'Victorian Vampires' as a transmedia story-world accumulated from two centuries of multi-layered adaptations that build on and reference one another, as well as how, within that story-world, Gothic encodes and transmits collective memory.

Dan Leno and the Limehouse Golem

Newman's neo-Victorian Gothic undermines heritage-driven fantasies of a stable Victorian past, as well as the politics which mobilized that fantasy, and so forms part of a larger trend of 'Ripperature'. Peter Ackroyd's *Dan Leno and the Limehouse Golem* (1994), a tale of serial murder and music halls in the Victorian East End, likewise forms part of that trend, but is informed by another counter-cultural movement: Psychogeography. Originating in 1950s Paris as a practice combining flânerie with eclectic spiritualism and historical discovery, psychogeography became an intellectual fashion in the 1990s, propagated by Iain Sinclair, Stewart Home, Will Self, and Ackroyd. I juxtapose the latter's 'Ripperature' novel[112] with *Anno Dracula* to throw into relief how steampunk's (often counterfictional) remix of a palimpsestic collective memory constructs steampunk London in relation to popular imaginaries. Accordingly, my attention lies not on how Ackroyd's London is configured as multi-temporal, a-chronic, and animated by innate *genius loci*, but on how his framing of the city as shaped by its Victorian past differs in crucial ways from Newman's – and as such, from steampunk's conception of the city.

The novel, set in 1880, is a post-modern array of textual fragments, such as transcripts of Elizabeth Cree's trial, the serial killer's (forged) diary, Cree's (unreliable) first person account of her past, or scenes told by a narrator positioned to comment from a post-Victorian perspective.[113] It is an array of familiar Ripper markers to tell a similar story about the uncanny city. Like the text itself, *The Limehouse Golem* imagines Victorian London as a dense web of interlinked traces which emerge and accumulate almost haphazardly, waiting for the psychogeographer to interpret their composite meaning. In this vein, we must eventually extrapolate that Elizabeth Cree is an unreliable narrator who has forged her husband's diary to implicate him and has been the serial killer, the golem, all along. Cree, too, finds inspiration in de Quincey's writing and religiously adheres to his essay 'On Murder Considered As one of the Fine Arts' (1827), in which he describes the Radcliffe Highway murders of 1812 with Gothic detail. Not only does Cree, failing to understand de Quincey's satirical stance, venture to re-create the violent murder of a family in the place which becomes to her 'as sacred to the memory as Tyborn or Golgotha' (p. 22), but George Gissing, moving through the novel as character, writes his own (fictional) journalistic evaluation of the work in a textual double echo.[114] Texts, in Ackroyd's novel, function as incarnated traces of a place's *genius loci*, articulating innate local spirits whose mysterious forces re-incarnate through being written about and amount to self-fulfilling prophecies in which space prescribes behaviour. In addition, as Chalupský notes: '[A]lthough Elizabeth willingly follows the vicious tradition of the area, her homicidal acts are still, according to Ackroyd, a result of the impact of the dark territorial forces which breed a monstrosity. She herself is aware of this power, noting that '"[i]nfinite London would always minister [to her] in [her] affliction"' (p. 182).[115] Next to Cree's re-staging of the multiple murder at Radcliffe Highway, Gissing is drawn into emotional turmoil and the East End through his unhappy marriage to an alcoholic prostitute, and the miserable day-to-day of the urban poor is elevated to Cockney humour on the music hall stage, where murder and violence become the subject of farcical comedy, casually re-inscribing crime as naturalized 'East End effect'.[116] As such, the events of the novel foreshadow the Ripper killings of 1888. Theatricality, spectacle, and performance play a dominant role in Ackroyd's vision and migrate from the music hall into the cityscape through Cree.

The simulated London of the stage 'seemed to Elizabeth the most wonderful sight in the world', and a street 'she had just walked' becomes 'much more glorious and iridescent': 'This was better than any memory' (pp. 15–16). To leave this space of illusion is 'like being expelled from some wonderful garden or palace, and now all I could see were the dirty bricks of the house fronts, the muck of the narrow street, and the shadows cast by the gas lamps in the Stand. [...] [E]verything was dark, and the sky and the rooftops merged together' (p. 48). Such inside/outside and performance/reality boundaries increasingly collapse when Cree, becoming a celebrated cross-dressing music hall performer, assumes a male disguise for exploring the city undisturbed (p. 145). Such performativity of gender enables her to live out her murderous alter ego, but Elizabeth herself becomes fictionalized in John Cree's unfinished play *Misery Junction* which configures her as innocent and virtuous heroine Catherine Dove, and which Elizabeth herself finishes and enacts on stage. Boundaries blur when Cree almost really strangles Leno on stage (p. 171), playing a 'mad butcher' (p. 170). In a final incarnation of this trope, her colleague and maid Aveline is actually hanged by accident in a re-enactment of Cree's execution on the music hall stage and her celebrity colleague dons her costume: 'Here was Elizabeth Cree in another guise, just as she had been before when she played the "Older Brother" or "Little Victor's Daughter", and it was a source of joy and exhilaration that the great Dan Leno should impersonate her' (p. 265). Naturally, Leno's catchphrase, 'Here we go again!' are the novel's and Elizabeth's final words, and they are words which emphasize recurrence and re-incarnation.

Theatricality also informs Cree's murderous activities which, in her diary, become a debut on a stage (p. 23) or 'a little piece' (p. 157) to be discussed alongside theatre plays. A register of performing, staging, and arranging saturates her self-presentation, and is one of many instances in the novel in which textuality recurs, is doubled or lastingly influences the movements or behaviours of characters until it is impossible to tell which determines which, and everything seems enactment and performance.[117] Consider this exchange between Dan Leno and Inspector Kildare:

> 'This murderer, this Limehouse Golem as they call him, seems to be acting as if he were in a blood tub off the Old Kent Road. Everything is very messy and very theatrical. It is a curious thing.'

Leno reflected for a few moments on this particular vision of the crimes. 'Much of it doesn't seem real at all. [...] [T]he atmosphere surrounding [the murders], the newspaper paragraphs, the crowds of spectators – it's like being in some kind of penny gaff or theatre of variety.' (p. 194)

As Wolfreys and Gibson note: 'Not merely the stage on which his narratives are enacted, the city of London is itself theatrical, a performative phenomenon more accurately described not as a place, but as that which takes place'.[118] City, performance, and texts are inevitably bound up with one another. Ironically, Cree once proclaims: 'I am not some mythological figure, as the newspaper reports continually suggest, or some exotic creature out of a Gothic novel; I am what I am, which is flesh and blood' (p. 151). The text here draws attention not only to the Victorian Gothic conventions surrounding urban serial killers such as Jack the Ripper, but also to its own fictionality. Doubly ironic is the fact that *The Limehouse Golem* does after all, re-present Cree as a Gothic monster rooted in the Victorian other which the novel both conjures up and examines critically, as well as the fact that, as 'Golem', the killer is absolutely embedded in a local mythology.[119] Patricia Pulham discusses these interrelations of the golem myth with the East End and its Jewish population, most notably the figure of David Rodinsky.[120] The scholar of the kabbalah vanished from his room above the synagogue in Princelet Street, Spitalfields in 1969. Rachel Lichtenstein, in her work on *Rodinsky's Room* (2000), describes finding 'hand-written notebooks revealing his knowledge of languages', 'hundreds of artefacts, thousands of scraps of small paper covered in coded messages', and 'hand-drawn maps, indications of journeys around London'.[121] The scholar, in his endeavour to unearth mystical ciphers in the Bible and his interest in exploring the city, becomes implicated in a psychogeographic reading of the cityscape, in which his presence also gives plausibility to the golem figure. Ackroyd's novel features Solomon Weil, the old scholar of Hasidic lore who not only possesses a collection of manuscripts identifying him as Rodinsky's *doppelgänger*, but also ventures daily to the Reading Room of the British Museum to sit beside Gissing, Karl Marx, and John Cree, his routes across the city a trace in the web that constitutes novel and city alike. As Wolfreys and Gibson conclude: '[T]he city, like the Golem, only comes into being through the multiplicity of enunciations and inscriptions, while never remaining the thing itself'.[122]

Weil's search for the hidden ciphers that determine the universe, here the city, is mirrored in Alice Stanton, the golem's third victim, who is found draped over 'the white pyramid outside the church of St. Anne, Limehouse' (p. 118). The pyramid evokes spiritualism and occultism, but Alice is connected to the hidden codes and patterns running through Ackroyd's London not least because 'she had been gazing at the workshop where the Analytical Engine waited to begin its life' (p. 118). We are introduced to Babbage's work through an article Gissing purports to write on it, understanding the Engine as a scientific tool in Benthamite social statistics, 'to calculate the greatest amount of need and misery in any given place, and then to predict its possible spread' (p. 107). Within the logic of the novel, it is imperative that a model of the Analytical Engine be hidden in a workshop in Commercial Street, in the heart of the East End where the collective 'need and misery' seem almost to have willed into existence this wondrous calculator, which 'gleamed like a hallucination' and 'was not in its proper time and, as yet, could have no real existence upon the earth' (p. 110). Whereas this model never actually existed, Gissing marvels at the 'giant form of rods and wheels and squared pieces of metal, so imposing and yet so alien an artifice that he was tempted to kneel down and worship it'.[123] At once anachronistic and woven tightly into the hidden patterns of Victorian London, the Analytical Engine becomes symbolic of underlying ciphers and currents which predict coming ages, for instance through H. G. Wells and Karl Marx, who take inspiration from Gissing's essay for their own forays into science fiction and communism, so the novel implies: 'The journey of a half starved novelist to Limehouse might in that sense be said to have affected the course of human history' (p. 117).

Ackroyd's London is a sublime, magical, supernaturalized entity pervaded, as Luckhurst notes, by 'the patterns of disappearance and return that crumple linear time into repeating cycles or unpredictable arabesques'.[124] The city is constantly 'taking place', weaving and being woven through chaotic, palimpsestic texts and the intersecting walking routes of the characters in it, who in turn are compelled by residual *genius loci*. For Luckhurst, *The Limehouse Golem* exemplifies a larger 1990s trend in which texts, not unlike in Ho's conception of Ripperature, enact a spectral modernity, that is, one intrinsically haunted by the resurfacing past. With recourse to Jean-François Lyotard, Bruno Latour, and Anthony Vidler, he outlines how '[a]ny proclamation of self-possessed modernity induces a haunting' and how '[t]he buried Gothic fragment thus operates as the emblem of resistance to the tyranny of planned space, but this resistance is necessarily occluded and interstitial, passed on only between initiates'.[125] 1990s Gothic, in which the genre's roots in the late-Victorian era become its *doppelgänger* other, so re-iterates Chris Baldick's observation that Gothic tales evoke 'a fear of historical reversion; that is, of the nagging possibility that the despotisms, buried by the modern age, may yet prove to be undead'.[126] At the same time, this recourse to the past which inevitably haunts the modern present can become a mode of aesthetic resistance against the commodified, neo-liberal city.[127]

This is where neo-Victorian Gothic intersects with psychogeography, which Iain Sinclair has characterized as 'the revenge of the disenfranchised'[128] and a 'necessary counter-conjuration, a protective hex against the advancing armies of orthodoxy'.[129] In psychogeography, also called 'deep topography', occult symbolism and archaeological knowledge serve as hidden codes that enable alternative re-mappings of the capitalist city, where, as Ho notes, 'glimpses of some originary trauma and suffering can still be felt'.[130] However, as Luckhurst notes, 'the discourse of spectralized modernity risks investing in the compulsive repetitions of a structure of melancholic entrapment'.[131] Psychogeography as part of the spectral turn may have its limits. It has become enough of a clichéd mode for Tom Gauld to effectively satirize it in a cartoon for the *Guardian* in 2017. Here, a pigeon describes psychogeography first as 'perambulating the liminal spaces of the submerged memory city', then, in simplified terms as 'mainly walking around, disapproving of gentrification'.[132]

Similarly, Coverley criticizes Ackroyd's vision: '[His] antiquarian sense of an endlessly recycled past negates any attempt by individuals to change the fundamental nature of their environment and renders them little more than passive observers in a city that is essentially self-regulating'.[133] We see this in *The Limehouse Golem*, where 'the old buried city extended as far as Limehouse with the Analytical Engine as its genius loci. [...] Perhaps Charles Babbage's creation was the true Limehouse Golem, draining away the life and spirit of those who approached it' (p. 138). In the novel's dense web of textual, spiritual, and geographical traces, individual agency seems superfluous: 'Ultimately, Ackroyd is expressing a form of behavioural determinism in which the city does not so much shape the lives of its inhabitants but dictates it'.[134]

Whereas both *Anno Dracula* and *The Limehouse Golem* mobilize neo-Victorian Gothic fiction, East End mythology, and the Ripper murders during the 1990s to resist neo-liberal myth-making, they differ fundamentally in their approach to textuality and history. Ackroyd conceives of London as sublime entity which stores historical traces as constantly re-incarnating energies and which inevitably always haunts itself. Newman's irreverent counterfiction, on the other hand, not only does not claim legitimacy as verisimilitude or memory – in true steampunk fashion, it flaunts its anachronistic play as feature, not bug – but it also draws attention to the role textuality plays in imbuing a space with the very mythology which Ackroyd presupposes to be ontological.

In *The Limehouse Golem*, the innate spirit of a locale is incarnated and reiterated through a multitude of texts and traces that intersect almost magically, subsuming figures like de Quincey, Gissing, or Cree as vessels. In contrast, *Anno Dracula* collages, retrospectively, the numerous figures and tropes through which we have collectively created an accumulated Gothic mythology in order to make sense of the East End, and the novel also leverages the (Orientalist, homophobic, or classist) anxieties and identity politics that have informed such constructions. It is a small, but crucial difference: in one version, Gothic disenfranchisement is the externalization of an eternal, a-chronic, and inescapable *genius loci*, in the other, Gothic interpretation is recognized as an ever-evolving sense-making strategy, resulting from, but not doomed to, that disenfranchisement. Ackroyd's Victorian London is a dense web of secret traces, the totality and reach of which however reveals itself only to the perceptive or knowledgeable reader able to follow and connect them. Neither Elizabeth Cree nor the omniscient narrator, though sensitive to it, is ever in a position to understand the full scope of the city's secret ciphers and irrational undercurrents. The text positions us readers as psychogeographers who gain a subjective, but partial insight into the mysterious, ineffable entity that is London through continuous excavation of hidden clues. *Anno Dracula*, on the other hand, maps the Victorian city through historical and fictional cultural icons, cataloguing the many versions and layers through which we have already collectively imagined the city. It remixes its own textual web from open-for-all sources which are part of a shared post-modern 'white knowledge', capitalizing on mythologies established in the collective imagination and readily mobilized to read the novel's counterfiction. *The Limehouse Golem*'s palimpsestic intertextuality imagines its collage to be both organic and ontological, and subjectively decipherable, but *Anno Dracula*'s remix is conscious, deliberate, and embedded in a collective reading of space. As such, it demonstrates how steampunk, too, relies on shared memory and popular transmedia story-worlds of 'Victorian London', activating the latter less as an innately mystical material place, but instead as a potent and endlessly mutable memory figure curated in real time through transmedia texts.

2.2 Remixing Whitechapel: Marxist Body Horror in Second-Wave Steampunk

Steampunk, then, likewise taps into a collectively shared knowledge of urban mythologies and mobilizes our resulting relationship with such urban spaces for its retro-speculative remix. For steampunk fiction of the second wave, that is after 2007, such mythologies are readily available through the internet. Here, steampunk makers and enthusiasts may build their own knowledge communities and so use convergence and remix culture to re-distribute individual agency across social and national borders.[135] As Jenkins notes: 'The biggest change [in consumption communities] may be the shift from individualized and personal media consumption toward consumption as a networked practice. [...] A man with one machine (a TV) is doomed to isolation, but a man with two machines (a TV and a computer) can belong to a community'.[136] This revolution in participation also gives license to a wider range of Ripper re-imaginations, for example through the steampunk band The Men That Will Not Be Blamed for Nothing, (named after a graffito found at the site of Catherine Eddowes' murder), but whether or not steampunk's semi-ironic remix contains the potential for new, radical relationships with the past crucially depends on how each steampunk text deploys the urban mythology it remixes.

This last section juxtaposes two second-wave steampunk novels to illustrate that steampunk's entanglement with the Gothic is sometimes for better, sometimes for worse.

George Mann's *The Affinity Bridge* (2009) features airship crashes, malfunctioning automata, and a mysterious zombie plague, and imagines Whitechapel as 'one of the seedier locales of the city, a refuge of beggars, criminals, and whores' (p. 32).[137] Readers find 'more factories, breaker's yards, and public houses' (p. 32), that it is a 'bleak morning' (p. 33), and that the corpse which our detectives, Sir Maurice Newbury and Veronica Hobbes, investigate, is found 'on the cobbles' and in 'surrounding fog' (p. 33). A mysterious series of stranglings is attributed to a 'phantom, a glowing policeman' (p. 36), and it is implied that the city-wide zombie plague manifests especially here: 'On the one hand, they're worried about the murderer; on the other, about the revenants that are walking the streets at night, hiding in the gutters like animals. Places like this, they ain't safe, ma'am. People keep themselves to themselves' (p. 36). This impression is strengthened by the constables' assertion that corpses found here are often either moved by their families or robbed and dumped in the river. All in all, the novel casts Whitechapel through social, rather than physical markers: The place is unfavourably – and stereotypically – defined by how people behave here. The presence of urban phantoms amplifies notions of Whitechapel as space of vice and misery in ways that are both fantastic and indebted to the Ripper mythology.

As such, it is no surprise that Newbury is attacked by zombies (supernatural, predatory relatives of the vampire) while examining another crime scene in the ever-present fog. Here, '[t]he confluence of three buildings and the cover of an arched alleyway had created a barrier of sorts against the thick smog. It still lay heavy in yellow wispy strands, but with the light of the three lanterns, [...] Newbury was able to ascertain the key elements of the scene' (pp. 194–195). Allusions to the 'blasted fog' and the lantern light are so liberally repeated throughout the scene that it creates a hyper-realistic, graphic chiaroscuro: in the 'thick and cloying', 'damp fog' and 'quiet darkness' (p. 198), the sight of revenants devouring two constables in a lonely alleyway becomes cinematic, even emblematic of a familiar Ripper iconography. The text re-enacts a popular Gothic mythology of the East End as a space of misery, murder, and fog, but does not consider or challenge the stereotypes it invokes. The abundance of fog is an aesthetic device, not symptomatic as in *Anno Dracula*.

Despite the descriptive shortcomings, the novel remains a favourite with readers. It has been reviewed as a 'genuinely *fun* book' and 'a light, highly enjoyable read'. The Book Smugglers' review states: 'Mr. Mann's turn of the century London feels pretty spot on', and SF Reviews attests: 'Mann has created a world rich in texture.'[138] Kirkus Reviews notes: 'Seething melodrama set against a vividly imagined backdrop', and Pop Matters agrees: 'The book is masterfully planned and is an interesting combination of sci-fi, detective fiction, and Victorian literature.'[139] Altogether, *The Affinity Bridge* seems to exemplify exactly what readers imagine they will find when new to steampunk and are generally satisfied and intrigued by the apparently typical steampunk setting. While of course the novel is the sum of its parts, my close reading of how Whitechapel is re-presented does not quite reveal this 'rich texture' and 'vividly imagined backdrop' – only a graphic evocation of well-known types through broad brushstrokes.

What this suggests is that Mann's vision succeeds in leveraging the meaning attached to a collectively shared 'white knowledge' about the East End with little effort. Despite the scant and graphic descriptive markers, the novel can depend on reader's collective knowledge and ready-made imaginary of the 'Victorian East End' to fill the gaps and perceive the area outlined only through a few bold strokes as a fully-fledged transmedia story-world, larger and deeper than the novel alone. *The Affinity Bridge* can create a 'richly textured' steampunk London simply by assembling markers embedded in a long tradition of East End mythology and thrive on leveraging the meaning already attached to them.

Whitechapel Gods

At the other end of steampunk's spectrum of re-imagining the Victorian East End lies S. M. Peters' novel *Whitechapel Gods* (2008).[140] By re-organizing the urban Victorian mythology in favour of body horror and pseudo-cyberpunk, the novel creates a unique steampunk vision of the East End.[141] Here, the eponymous district has been closed off from the rest of London through walls and become a world onto itself, dominated by the supernatural entities Father Clock and Mama Engine. Leading us into the text is a para-textual quotation from Arthur Morrison's 1889 essay on Whitechapel for *The Palace Journal*:

> A horrible black labyrinth, think many people, reeking from end to end with the vilest exhalations; its streets, mere kennels of horrent putrefaction; its every wall, its every object, slimy with the indigenous ooze of the place; swarming with human vermin, whose trade is robbery, and whose recreation is murder; the catacombs of London darker, more tortuous, and more dangerous than those of Rome, and supersaturated with foul life. (p. 5)[142]

This strikingly colourful description is, ironically, part of Morrison's re-iteration of stereotypes about Whitechapel which he then endeavours to dismantle, showing instead a 'commercial respectability'. *Whitechapel Gods*, however, chooses to root itself in this Gothic stereotype of a dark, exotic, and dangerous maze populated by atavisms and oozing malice – an image, as the date tells us, directly informed by the Ripper murders. Out of this imagery grows a hyper-Gothic nightmare city: 'Bailey stood a long minute with the door open, staring out. His gaze was dawn upwards, past the rotting rooftops of the neighbourhood [...]. He felt his jaw tighten as his eyes came to rest on the top of the looming iron mountain barely visible through the blackened air: the Stack, home to the gods' (pp. 10–11). This is a space of 'soot-stained streets and thick air' (p. 12), noisy factories, fizzling gaslights, and drab public houses, all of which are stacked, in an imaginative perversion of Doré's endless city, over one another in infinite levels: 'Oliver scanned the building lining the streets, apartments stretching the entire five storeys to the roof of the concourse. Some even went higher, tangling themselves in the braces of the next level' (p. 14). A familiar Victorian aesthetic with Dickensian echoes as the protagonist Oliver's name also implies, is twisted out of proportion until the uncanny city of the urban Gothic becomes a boundless, overwhelming monstrosity:

> Ahead, Stepneyside Tower slowly faded into life from within the clouds and the swirling ash. Its thick steel beams arched gracefully together, crossing and tangling, and at the top spilled back down in all directions, giving the tower the appearance of a huge black flower. The scattered lights of human habitation blinked between them like orphaned stars. [...] Oliver turned to look but saw only more grey sky, with the twisted shades of other towers lurking in that

direction. Somewhere beyond stood the impassable wall separating Whitechapel from the rest of London, topped with electric defences and guarded by untiring Boiler Men ...

Just beyond it, human soldiers of the British army stood ever ready [...]. (p. 35)

Whitechapel becomes a literal Other within, physically separated from the rest of London, its borders an impenetrable gateway into hostile territory, and not just *terra incognita*, but an actual foreign country: 'London wasn't his city. England wasn't his home. *Maybe it could be.*' (p. 158). This is, of course, a fantastical actualization of an urban Victorian metaphoric East End register. Below the endlessness of steely towers in a miasma of ash and smog, we find the Underbelly:

> The floor of the Underbelly was like a giant bowl of concrete, warped and misshapen to conform to the vagaries of the tower's steel supports. He traced the three strangers between two- and three-storey tenements, inexpertly constructed of whatever spare wood and plaster could be scrounged from the city above. The place had a ruined graveyard quality about it, enhanced by the few ghostly street lanterns that Missy had always detested. (p. 53)

This vertical geography literalizes social hierarchies into physical space, with the Underbelly as a dark slum supporting the towering structures above not only economically, but literally. This layering is also evidence of a literal palimpsest, considering that all this is built on Old Whitechapel, now an empty abyss under 'the maze of beams that held up the Shadwell Underbelly and went on to support the Concourse above' (p. 129). The old city 'had long since decayed into lumps of sodden debris' (p. 154), and we find here '[n]othing below but a mass of near-vertical pipes slick with condensation; nothing to the sides but silent ashfall', with an occasional 'angular assortment of pipes and wires that resembled a ladder as one may have looked in an opium dream' (p. 142). Nothing populates this abysmal counter-space but mechanical wild hounds preying on lost wanderers. This Whitechapel is a space of precarity, an endless cityscape that stretches into the horizontal, but more prominently into the vertical as a steampunk version of Doré's *Warehousing in the City*. Here, people are dwarfed and 'orphaned' among the concrete and lost in the noxious smoke. Navigation becomes an act of resistance, as exemplified by Oliver and his rebellious allies who traverse all layers of this endless cityscape in their quest to dismantle the tyranny of local gods.

Peters' Whitechapel is at once disturbingly inorganic in its vast materiality of steel, bricks, and concrete, but also seems somewhat organically grown. From the maze of beams that grow from the ground like a forest, to the makeshift wood and plaster constructions of the Underbelly and the gracefully tangling, flower-like steel beams of the towers, there is a paradoxical imagery at work here, but it ties in with the cyborgism and body horror which characterizes the novel at large. Father Clock, for example, is an entity with Orwellian powers of surveillance who represents a mechanized order whose paradigms are 'efficiency over emotion' and 'for all parts to work together according to a single Purpose' (p. 223). His minions, the cloaks, let themselves be crafted into cyborg automata with 'brass bones and copper nerves' (p. 233) or porcelain eyes (p. 33): 'Their mechanisms were their thirty pieces of silver, the price of their souls' (p. 34). In accordance with this imagery of computer automation, bodies and minds of dissenters are subsumed into the gigantic machinery of the Stack:

> He hung now in a chair, arms and legs supported by thin scraps of brass, six copper tines penetrating his neck. He spasmed randomly. He drooled. He bled dark oil from his eye and ears. To his left and right, above and below, thousands more trapped souls shuffled mindlessly, their bodies jerking in the indecipherable rhythm of the Great Machine. (pp. 49–50)

From here, the rebel Aaron's mind escapes into a virtual void, a sort of cyberspace: 'Aaron flaked apart and drifted away. What remained tightened securely, then began to spin at its designated frequency. It became part of a work greater than itself, part of an infallible string of physical logic inside the perfect machine' (p. 51).

Mama Engine, on the other hand, represents the volatile powers of energy. Her followers 'were rarely seen outside the Stack, preferring [...] to be near their goddess, working in her furnace deep inside that mountain of iron. The red glow of their own heart-furnaces leaked through burns and holes in their heavy clothes; some even had mechanical limbs, which held to no human shape' (p. 33). We find an example of this here: 'A black cloak scuttled by, moving on all fours like a spider, emitting an audible mechanical grinding as she moved' (p. 61). In portraying these different instances of humans transforming into machines, *Whitechapel Gods* imaginatively puts into play Karl Marx's critique of the capitalist factory:

> In handicrafts and manufacture, the workman makes use of a tool, in the factory, the machine makes use of him. There the movements of the instrument of labour proceed from him, here it is the movements of the machine that he must follow. In manufacture the workmen are parts of a living mechanism. In the factory we have a lifeless mechanism independent of the workman, who becomes its mere living appendage.[143]

In Marx's vision, a re-organization of human labour into a mechanized system means a reversal of power hierarchies and a shift from human dominance into servitude of the machine, equalling a loss of agency and dignity. The human worker is appropriated by the larger mechanism as interchangeable prosthesis, his ability and intellect drained away with his agency. This is actually the case in *Whitechapel Gods* where Marx's metaphorical concept is re-imagined in literal terms, and where a mysterious cancer, 'the clacks' disfigures ordinary, disenfranchised East End workers in one final iteration of the motif:

> The patient writhed and struggled in the bed, fighting a pain that distorted his features into something less than human. He was a comrade named Tor Kyrre, though Bailey could barely recognise him. Spikes of iron had sprouted from his bald pate and his bare chest was riddled with gears and bulbs of all types of metals, the tips of much larger growths festering beneath the skin. As the doctor made his second cut, lateral and shallow, across the base of the rib cage, black oil welled up, slipping down Tor's flanks and staining the sheets and blankets. (p. 7–8)

'Clacks' patients are literally consumed by the parasitic, semi-organic mechanic growths, such as brass bubbles, iron spikes, and gears beneath the skin. This corresponds to their social status in an oppressive industrial system dominated by the gods of industrial technology and efficiency, in which the 'clacks' become a symptom of these de-humanizing conditions:

> Below, dockworkers struggled to unload the goods descending by crane from two zeppelins tethered to the Aldgate spire. No single class seemed as afflicted with the mechanical growths as the dockworkers. They shambled around like parodies of men, covered in gleaming iron pustules, hobbling on malformed brass legs, and picking at ropes and crates with hooked hands and fingerless steel stubs. (p. 109)

The 'clacks', together with the other ways in which bodies are invaded, disfigured, dismembered, destroyed and deconstructed in this novel, become displaced external signifiers for the East Enders' lack of agency under an industrial tyranny productively encoded in a meta-Victorian aesthetic. This hyper-Victorian vision originates in the Ripper/East End mythology enshrined in collective memory, but *Whitechapel Gods* hardly re-iterates Gothic tropes about the eruption of atavism in the present, or psychological hauntings for the sake of repeating them. Instead, it adds other, non-Gothic Victorian impulses and techno-fantastical speculation and remixes them into a vision of the East End that is unfamiliar, yet can still be read through East End markers, such as industry, disenfranchisement, or factory work. The Gothic lingers not in roaming urban monsters, corrupting mania, or biological degeneration. Whitechapel citizens do not so much regress into ape-like Mr Hydes as evolve, more or less voluntarily, into un-human machine hybrids. Traces of the Gothic cityscape linger in the uncanny maze which, while not one of paranoia and isolation, is an overwhelming, labyrinthine, and grotesque wilderness of steel and concrete. Still, whereas the novel seems to externalize Gothic Victorian tropes into new, fantastical incarnations, it is the (anachronistic), industrialized future which haunts this East End, rather than the past. Through such a temporal reversal and overlay, *Whitechapel Gods* imagines the 'Victorian' past as an uncanny *doppelgänger* which is just as much – and very tangibly – haunted by us as we are by it.

Conclusion: 'She's alive!'

In their short video *Here Comes the Bride* (2014), the California-based performance art troupe The League of S.T.E.A.M re-imagines a steampunk version of *Frankenstein* – or rather, *Bride of Frankenstein*, the 1935 film.[144] The story, in which Coyote (Glenn Freund) and Baron von Fogel (Andrew Fogel) endeavour to build a female companion for their bookish friend Albert Able (Trip Hope), is not only clearly indebted to classic film interpretations of Shelley's original text, but also liberally peppered with allusions to other story universes, such as *Star Trek* or *Doctor Who*. Only eight minutes long, the short film manages to put humorous twists on a well-known story ('I can't believe I wasted my entire day getting dragged all over town, going to graveyards and stealing things . . .!', 0:05:00), by relying on their audience's media literacy and a prominent cultural 'white knowledge'. Even without knowledge of the classic texts, audiences intuitively identify Elsa Lanchester's iconic costume and hair-do, or deduce from a combination of bulky contraptions, thunderstorm and other 'mad scientist' iconography what is about to transpire because they can actualize and leverage a collective pop cultural knowledge.

Because of its easily identifiable aesthetic and tropes, and its prominence in popular media and memory, Gothic is particularly prone to neo-Victorian adaptation and remix, as Megen de Bruin-Molé's 2020 study, *Gothic Remixed*, interrogates at length. Accordingly, steampunk and Gothic are also inevitably affiliated, especially when it comes to Victorian London, where so many formative urban mythologies are rooted – as *Anno Dracula*, arguably a bit of both, also exemplifies. The Victorian East End increasingly encapsulated and epitomized contemporary social anxieties and was continually collectively constructed as a symbolic space through transmedia myth-making. Fiction and non-fiction converged to create a lasting catalogue of Gothic tropes, which were catalysed by, but not solely dependent on, the Ripper murders of 1888. This palimpsestic mythology has been mobilized across multiple adaptations and re-tellings, so that neo-Victorian Gothic and early steampunk, such as *Anno Dracula*, may creatively remix its aesthetic markers and fictional icons into a new, counterfictional collage to create new meanings. On the surface, both *Anno Dracula* and Ackroyd's *The Limehouse Golem* might be affiliated in their quest to unearth the Victorian past in order to craft darkly ironic counter-myths to the Thatcherite, neo-liberal meta-narrative. Both, after all, realize that 'the period's appeal lies in its (would-be) *transcendental otherness*, alternately gothically horrid and cheerfully quaint' and re-posit the nineteenth century as Gothic other.[145] However, where Ackroyd's psychogeography asks us to unearth hidden remnants of *genius loci* and find secret codes in the seemingly predefined 'deep topography', Newman's steampunk deliberately collapses history and fiction to highlight not just the textuality of history, but particularly the textuality of imagined space. Where classical Gothic as a mode is inherently invested in hauntings, echoes, repressions, and resurfacing trauma, which in neo-Victorian Gothic may serve to undermine nostalgic or overly conservative receptions of the past, steampunk's anachronistic play and alternative histories foreclose linear or reciprocal relationships between past and present in favour of a more volatile and multiple concept in which past and present continually invade, infuse, and shape one another. As Bowser and Croxall note: 'Through its own instability, enacted via nonlinear temporality and blended surfaces, steampunk reminds us of the instability and constructedness of our concepts of periodization and historical distance'.[146] In the counterfictional text, such 'blended surfaces' emerge as re-imagined characters, historical figures, and popular tropes. As Newman's Gothic satire of Thatcher's 'Victorian Values' illustrates, such re-organization of collectively transmitted signifiers may do ideological work.

However, whereas steampunk as a retro-speculative mode is intrinsically alert to how the present shapes past as much as vice versa through interlinked processes of memory and myth-making, whether or not that alertness translates into creative potential for such ideological work within the fictional text itself varies from iteration to iteration, according to their deployment of remix and the creator's intentions. Remix and participation are not just cornerstones of steampunk making,[147] but intrinsic factors of the steampunk collage itself. In first- and second-wave steampunk alike, both the historical past and the fictional canon become subject to remix and re-signification, relying on a collectively shared 'white knowledge' which readers actualize to decode the text and its underlying story-world. Indeed, steampunk's potential lies largely in its ability to activate a (Gothic-laden) memory, not to re-stage, but to re-shuffle the past.

The Affinity Bridge, by merely outlining the East End through stereotypical markers, can conjure up a classic Gothic setting outfitted with all that such a Gothic East End, always subconsciously catalyzed through an aesthetic Ripper register, entails. It demonstrates how deeply ingrained that aesthetic is in memory of Victorian city, but in its failure to interrogate the socio-cultural anxieties that inform such markers, also fails to say something new, and even risks perpetuating Victorian urban Gothic's classist or xenophobic aspects. *Whitechapel Gods*, on the other hand, radically remixes a labyrinthine, techno-fantastical Whitechapel to examine human-technology relationships, as well as agency and identity, within a (Victorian) industrial capitalism, and so creates a reciprocal dialogue between past and present: 'Indeed, steampunk looks to the present to illuminate the past, the past to illuminate the present, the future to illuminate the past, and the past to illuminate the future'.[148] Whereas our historical perspective inevitably colours our perception of the past, steampunk is free to let this mutual re-projection play out in new, creative, and externalized ways. Played out in historically charged urban settings such as London's East End, steampunk exemplifies how city spaces encode social relationships and become both the theatre and the battleground for collective re-signification of the historical past and its legacies in the present.

Notes

1 Lefebvre, *Production of Space*, p. 27.
2 Louisa Hadley, *Neo-Victorian Fiction and Historical Narrative. The Victorians and Us* (London: Palgrave Macmillan, 2010), p. 3.
3 Raphael Samuel, 'Mrs Thatcher's Return to Victorian Values', *Proceedings of the British Academy*, 78, 9–29, p. 9.
4 Samuel, p. 24.
5 Elizabeth Ho, *Neo-Victorianism and the Memory of Empire* (London: Bloomsbury, 2012), p. 28.
6 Ho, p. 29.
7 Joseph Crawford, *Gothic Fiction and the Invention of Terrorism. The Politics and Aesthetics of Fear in the Age of the Reign of Terror* (London: Bloomsbury, 2013), p. 154.
8 Mighall, *Geography of Victorian Gothic Fiction*, p. 28.

9 I have defined my understanding of the Gothic elsewhere as follows: 'In what follows, I understand what I will call the Gothic mode to be an array of aesthetic signifiers and narrative devices (such as fog, darkness, the grotesque, the uncanny, return of the repressed) which arouse dread, doubt, unease, or disgust in the viewer or reader, and which encode a person or space as monstrous, haunted, other, atavistic, or abject. Such signifiers are often aligned with the morbid and morose, or engage us by making use of our primordial fears and survival instincts. The Gothic mode helps to negotiate a wide variety of value systems and identities as it both destabilises and reaffirms what is seen as progressive, civilized, or enlightened, even if that progress is simultaneously called into question. [...] Gothic relies fundamentally on the effect of 'making strange' in order to open such spaces for re-negotiation: it destabilises identities and challenges our knowledge of the world by evoking the uncanny, the monstrous, and the other, for example through distortion or fragmentation. Considering that it also relies on inducing dread, doubt, and disgust, the Gothic mode evaluates, if not judges what it portrays to a certain extent.' Helena Esser, *'What Use Our Work: Crime and Justice in Ripper Street'*, Neo-Victorian Journal, 11:1 (2018), 141–173, pp. 145–146.

10 Spencer configured cultures as evolving hierarchies, Tylor applied evolution to colonial contexts, and Galton's eugenics were presented in a framework of Darwinist logic. Herbert Spencer, 'The Principles of Sociology', in *The Fin de Siècle. A Reader in Cultural History c.1880–1900*, ed. by Sally Ledger and Roger Luckhurst (Oxford: Oxford University Press, 2000 [1876]), pp. 321–326. Edward Tylor, 'Primitive Culture' in *The Fin de Siècle. A Reader in Cultural History c.1880–1900*, ed. by Sally Ledger and Roger Luckhurst (Oxford: Oxford University Press, 2000 [1871]), pp. 317–321. Francis Galton, 'Eugenics: Its Definition, Scope and Aims.' in *The Fin de Siècle. A Reader in Cultural History c.1880–1900*, ed. by Sally Ledger and Roger Luckhurst (Oxford: Oxford University Press, 2000 [1904]), pp. 329–333.

11 Karl Bell, 'Phantasmal Cities: The Construction and Function of Haunted Landscapes in Victorian English Cities', in *Haunted Landscapes. Super-Nature and the Environment*, ed. by Ruth Heholt and Niamh Downing (London: Rowman & Littlefield, 2016), pp. 95–110, p. 100.

12 These discourses are also linked to discussions of criminology, degeneration, and culture, most notoriously epitomized by the works of Cesare Lombroso and Max Nordau.

13 Mighall, p. 142.

14 Mighall, p. 30, original emphasis.

15 Kohlke and Gutleben, 'Troping the Neo-Victorian City', p. 11.

16 Kohlke and Gutleben, *Neo-Victorian Gothic*, p. 3–4, original emphasis.

17 Kohlke and Gutleben, *Neo-Victorian Gothic*, p. 4.

18 Whereas I consider the novel, with its irreverent remix, pseudo-scientifically encoded vampirism, and alternative history to be a steampunk text, those who prefer steampunk to include more obvious, openly techno-fantastical elements may not.

19 Megen de Bruin-Molé, *Gothic Remixed: Monster Mashups and Frankenfictions in 21st-Century Culture* (London: Bloomsbury, 2020), p. 11, 18.
20 Marie-Luise Kohlke and Christian Gutleben, 'The (Mis)Shapes of Neo-Victorian Gothic: Continuations, Adaptations, Transformations', in *Neo-Victorian Gothic. Horror, Violence, and Degeneration in the Re-Imagined Nineteenth Century*, ed. by Marie-Luise Kohlke and Christian Gutleben (Leiden: Brill Rodopi, 2012), pp. 1–50, p. 41.
21 Julian Wolfreys, *Writing London: The Trace of the Urban Text from Blake to Dickens* (London: Palgrave Macmillan, 1998), p. 8.
22 Roger Luckhurst, 'The contemporary London Gothic and the limits of the "spectral turn"', *Textual Practice* 16:3 (2002), 527–546, p. 531, Wolfreys, *Urban Text*, p. 8, 25.
23 Wolfreys, *Urban Text*, p. 21; Luckhurst, 'Spectral Turn', p. 531.
24 Martin Heidegger, *Being and Time*, trans. by Joan Stambaugh (New York: SUNY Press, 2010 [1927]).
25 Crawford, *Gothic Fiction*, p. 168–169.
26 Mighall, p. 35–36.
27 Mighall, p. 76–77. 'The Nemesis of Neglect' refers to a frequently reproduced Punch Cartoon from September 1888, in which the Phantom Jack the Ripper embodies social neglect and haunts darkened East End streets. John Tenniel, 'The Nemesis of Neglect', cartoon, in *Punch*, 29 Sept. 1888, https://commons.wikimedia.org/wiki/File:Jack-the-Ripper-The-Nemesis-of-Neglect-Punch-London-Charivari-cartoon-poem-1888-09-29.jpg (accessed 10 June 2018).
28 L. Perry Curtis Jr, *Jack the Ripper and the London Press* (New Haven: Yale University Press, 2001), p. 35.
29 'As there is a darkest Africa is there not also a darkest England? Civilisation, which can breed its own barbarians, does it not also breed its own pygmies? May we not find a parallel at our own doors, and discover within a stone's throw of our cathedrals and palaces similar horrors to those which Stanley has found existing in the great Equatorial forest? [. . .] [T]he stony streets of London, if they could but speak, would tell of tragedies as awful, of ruin as complete, of ravishments as horrible, as if we were in Central Africa; only the ghastly devastation is covered, corpselike, with the artificialities and hypocrisies of modern civilisation.' William Booth, *In Darkest England*, pp. 11–13, quoted in Curtis, *Jack the Ripper*, p. 36.
30 Flore Janssen, 'Margaret Harkness: "In Darkest London" – 1889', https://www.londonfictions.com/margaret-harkness-in-darkest-london.html# (accessed 10 June 2018).
31 John Marriot, 'The imaginative geography of the Whitechapel murders', in *Jack the Ripper and the East End*, ed. by Alex Werner (London: Chatto & Windus, 2008), pp. 31–63. Also Anne J. Kershen, 'The immigrant community of Whitechapel at the time of the Ripper murders', in *Jack the Ripper and the East End*, ed. by Alex Werner (London: Chatto & Windus, 2008), pp. 65–97.

32 David Kerr, 'Doré, (Louis Auguste) Gustave', Oxford Dictionary of National Biography, http://www.oxforddnb.com/view/10.1093/ref:odnb/9780198614128.001.0001/odnb-9780198614128-e-67162 (accessed 8 June 2018).
33 Gustave Doré and Blanchard Jerrold, *London. A Pilgrimage* (New York: Dover Publications, 1970 [1872]). Ludgate Hill – A Block in the Street, p. 119.
34 Doré, p. 115.
35 Doré, p. 121.
36 Doré, p. 145.
37 Wentworth Street, Whitechapel, Doré, p. 125, or Bull's-Eye, p. 145.
38 Doré, p. 147.
39 Doré, p. 148.
40 Charles Dickens, *The Mystery of Edwin Drood* (Cambridge: Penguin Classics, 2011 [1870]), p. 7; Mike Jay, *Emperors of Dreams: Drugs in the Nineteenth Century*, (Cambridgeshire: Dedalus, 2011).
41 Dickens, *Edwin Drood*, p. 6.
42 Matthew Sweet, *Inventing the Victorians* (London: Faber and Faber, 2001), p. 91.
43 H. D. Traill, 'The New Realism', *Fortnightly Review*, 67, 1897, pp. 63–73, reprinted in Arthur Morrison, *A Child of the Jago*, ed. by Peter Miles (Oxford: Oxford University Press, 2012), pp. 175–176.
44 Harold Boulton, 'A Novel of the Lowest Life', *British Review* (9 Jan. 1897), 349, reprinted in Arthur Morrison, *A Child of the Jago*, ed. by Peter Miles (Oxford: Oxford University Press, 2012), pp. 176–177. A. Osborne Jay, 'The New Realism: To the Editor of the Fortnightly Review', *Fortnightly Review,* 67, 1897, pp. 314, reprinted in Arthur Morrison, *A Child of the Jago*, ed. by Peter Miles (Oxford: Oxford University Press, 2012), pp. 178–179.
45 Arthur Morrison, 'What is a Realist?', *New Review*, 16/94 (Mar. 1894), 326–336, reprinted in Arthur Morrison, *A Child of the Jago*, ed. by Peter Miles (Oxford: Oxford University Press, 2012), pp. 179–181, p. 168.
46 Booth's evaluation exemplifies in which way poverty and criminality seemed confluent and inevitably linked in the Victorian imagination. Charles Booth, *Descriptive Map of London Poverty*, 1898; Laura Vaughan, 'Mapping the East End Labyrinth', in *Jack the Ripper and the East End*, ed. by Alex Werner (London: Chatto & Windus, 2008), pp. 219–237.
47 Sarah Wise, *The Blackest Streets. The Life and Death of a Victorian Slum* (London: Vintage Books, 2008). p. 8.
48 Sarah Wise, 'Arthur Morrison: "A Child of the Jago" – 1896', https://www.londonfictions.com/arthur-morrison-a-child-of-the-jago.html (accessed 15 June 2018). See also Wise, *Blackest Streets*, p. 231.
49 Wise, *Blackest Streets*, p. 226.
50 Jack London, *People of the Abyss* (London: [Penguin], 1977 [1903]), pp. 88–89.

51 Morrison, *Jago*, p. 133.
52 Wise, 'Child of the Jago'.
53 Pierre Lévy, *Collective Intelligence. Mankind's Emerging World in Cyberspace* (New York: Perseus Books, 1997).
54 Lévy, pp. 13–14.
55 Henry Jenkins, *Convergence Culture. Where Old and New Media Collide* (New York: New York University Press, 2008), p. 3, 23, 3–4.
56 See Christina Meyer and Monika Pietrzak-Franger (eds), *Transmedia Practices in the Long Nineteenth Century* (London: Routledge, 2022).
57 For a comprehensive overview, see: Paul Begg, *Jack the Ripper: The Definitive History* (London, Routledge, 2003).
58 *Jack the Ripper and the East End*, ed. by Alex Werner (London: Chatto & Windus, 2008). *Jack the Ripper. Media. Culture. History*, ed. by Alexandra Warwick and Martin Willis (Manchester: Manchester University Press, 2007). Curtis, *Ripper*. Drew Gary, *London's Shadows. The Dark Side of the Victorian City* (London: Bloomsbury, 2010). Mara Isabel Romero Ruiz, 'Detective Fiction and Neo-Victorian Sexploitation: Violence, Morality and Rescue Work in Lee Jackson's *The Last Pleasure Garden* (2007) and *Ripper Street*'s 'I Need Light' (2012–16)', *Neo-Victorian Journal*, 9:2 (2017), 41–69.
59 Clare Smith, *Jack the Ripper in Film and Culture. Top hat, Gladstone Bag, and Fog* (London: Palgrave Macmillan, 2016). Also: Clive Bloom, 'Jack the Ripper – a legacy in pictures', in *Jack the Ripper and the East End*, ed. by Alex Werner (London: Chatto & Windus, 2008), pp. 239–267.
60 Hallie Rubenhold, *The Five: The Untold Lives of the Women Killed by Jack the Ripper* (London: Transworld Publishers, 2019).
61 Curtis, *Ripper*, p. 79, Darren Oldridge, 'Casting the spell of terror: the press and the early Whitechapel murders', in *Jack the Ripper. Media. Culture. History.*, ed. by Alexandra Warwick and Martin Willis (Manchester: Manchester University Press, 2007), pp. 46–55, p. 47.
62 Oldridge, p. 46. Also: Sweet, Walkowitz, Judith R., *City of Dreadful Delight* (Chicago: University of Chicago Press, 1992).
63 Curtis, *Ripper*, p. 105.
64 Curtis, p. 113.
65 Alex Chisholm, 'The Star, 1st Sept 1888', http://www.casebook.org/press_reports/star/s880901.html (accessed 25 May 2018).
66 Alexandra Warwick, 'Blood and ink: narrating the Whitechapel murders', in *Jack the Ripper. Media. Culture. History.*, ed. by Alexandra Warwick and Martin Willis (Manchester: Manchester University Press, 2007), pp. 71–90, p. 71.
67 Clive Bloom, 'The Ripper writing: a cream of a nightmare dream', in *Jack the Ripper. Media. Culture. History*, ed. by Alexandra Warwick and Martin Willis (Manchester: Manchester University Press, 2007), pp. 91–109, p. 98.

68 Alex Chisholm, 'The Pall Mall Gazette, 8th Sept 1888', http://www.casebook.org/press_reports/pall_mall_gazette/18880908.html (accessed 25 May 2018).
69 Alex Chisholm, 'The Star, 8th Sept 1888', http://www.casebook.org/press_reports/star/s880908.html (accessed 25 May 2018). These racist comparisons to First Nation peoples also contextualizes Mallory's evocation of the 'Cherokee' in *The Difference Engine*.
70 Alex Chisholm, 'The Star, 1st Sept 1888'.
71 Oldridge, p. 54.
72 Gary Coville and Patrick Luciano, 'Order out of chaos', in *Jack the Ripper. Media. Culture. History.*, ed. by Alexandra Warwick and Martin Willis (Manchester: Manchester University Press, 2007), pp. 56–70, p. 56.
73 Martin Willis, 'Jack the Ripper, Sherlock Holmes and the narrative of detection', in *Jack the Ripper. Media. Culture. History.*, ed. by Alexandra Warwick and Martin Willis (Manchester: Manchester University Press, 2007), pp. 144–158. Romero Ruiz.
74 Bloom, 'Legacy in Pictures', p. 239, original emphasis.
75 Bloom, pp. 240–241.
76 Bloom, p. 249.
77 Max Duperray, '"Jack the Ripper" as Neo-Victorian Gothic Fiction: Twentieth-Century and Contemporary Sallies into a Late Victorian Case and Myth', in *Neo-Victorian Gothic. Horror, Violence, and Degeneration in the Re-Imagined Nineteenth Century*, ed. by Marie-Louise Kohlke and Christian Gutleben (Leiden: Brill Rodopi, 2012), pp. 167–196.
78 Kohlke and Gutleben, *Neo-Victorian Gothic*, p. 7.
79 Kohlke and Gutleben, *Neo-Victorian Cities*, p. 20.
80 Kim Newman, 'Afterword', in *Anno Dracula* (London: Titan Books, 2011 [1992]), pp. 449–456, p. 455.
81 *The Bloody Red Baron* (1995), *Dracula Cha Cha Cha* (1998), and *Johny Alucard* (2013), which continue with the same premise, but also stories set in the same universe or assembled in the same manner, namely *Angels of Music* (2016, Paris) and *One Thousand Monsters* (2017, Japan).
82 Kim Newman, 'Annotations', in *Anno Dracula* (London: Titan Books, 2011 [1992]), pp. 42–442, p. 429.
83 Kim Newman, 'Afterword', p. 454.
84 Newman, 'Afterword', p. 453.
85 This is rather interesting considering that both the epistolary cross-media Dracula and John Watson's frame-narrative in the Sherlock Holmes novels are themselves, self-aware fictions.
86 Matt Hills, 'Counterfictions in the Work of Kim Newman: Rewriting Gothic SF as "Alternate-Stories"', *Science Fiction Studies*, 30:3 (2003), 436–455, p. 439.
87 Hills, p. 440.

88 Hills, p. 452.
89 Henry Jenkins, *Textual Poachers: Television Fans and Participatory Culture* (London: Routledge, 2013 [1992]), pp. vii–li.
90 Michel De Certeau, *The Practice of Everyday Life*, trans. by Stephen F. Rendall (Berkeley: University of California Press, 1984), p. 174.
91 Henry Jenkins, '*Textual Poachers*, Twenty Years Later: A Conversation between Henry Jenkins and Suzanne Scott' in *Textual Poachers: Television Fans and Participatory Culture* (London: Routledge, 2013 [1992]), pp. vii–li., p. xxi.
92 'If I put a reference in a book I try to pick one that a generally well-read (well-viewed, well-listened) person has a sporting chance of picking up; I call this "white knowledge," the sort of stuff that fills up your brain without you really knowing where it came from. Enough people would've read [Fritz] Lieber, say, to pick up a generalized reference to Fafhrd, etc. and even more people would have some knowledge of Tolkien–but I wouldn't rely on people having read a specific story.' Terry Pratchett, quoted in 'White Knowledge and the Cauldron of Story: The Use of Allusion in Terry Pratchett's Discworld', by William T. Abbott, (unpublished Master thesis, East Tennessee State University, 2002).
93 Lawrence Lessing, *Remix. Making Art and Commerce Thrive in the Hybrid Economy* (London: Bloomsbury, 2008), p. 7.
94 Jenkins, *Convergence Culture*, pp. 175–177.
95 Nicholas Rance, '"Jonathan's great knife": *Dracula* meets Jack the Ripper', in *Jack the Ripper. Media. Culture. History.*, ed. by Alexandra Warwick and Martin Willis (Manchester: Manchester University Press, 2007), pp. 124–143.
96 Rance, Christopher Frayling, 'The house that Jack built', in *Jack the Ripper. Media. Culture. History.*, ed. by Alexandra Warwick and Martin Willis (Manchester: Manchester University Press, 2007), pp. 13–28., Robert F. Haggard, 'Jack the Ripper and the threat of outcast London', in *Jack the Ripper. Media. Culture. History.*, ed. by Alexandra Warwick and Martin Willis (Manchester: Manchester University Press, 2007), pp. 197–214. Walkowitz.
97 Denis Meikle, *A History of Horrors. The Rise and Fall of the House of Hammer* (Lanham: Scarecrow Press, 2009).
98 As early as 1907, a German publisher freely plagiarizing Holmes imagined a meeting of both in *Wie Jack, der Aufschlitzer, gefasst wurde*. Recent examples include Carole Nelson Douglas' *Chapel Noir* (2002), Lyndsay Faye's *Dust and Shadow* (2009) or Edward B. Hanna's *The Further Adventures of Sherlock Holmes: The Whitechapel Horror* (2010). There's also been film, TV, comic and video games adaptations such as *Sherlock Holmes Versus Jack the Ripper* (2009).
99 Lessing, p. 74.
100 Lessing, p. 76.
101 See Gray, Kershen, Begg.

102 Kim Newman, *Anno Dracula* (London: Titan Books, 2011 [1992]).
103 Christian Gutleben, '"Fear is Fun and Fun is Fear": A Reflexion on Humour in Neo-Victorian Gothic', in *Neo-Victorian Gothic. Horror, Violence, and Degeneration in the Re-Imagined Nineteenth Century*, ed. by Marie-Louise Kohlke and Christian Gutleben (Leiden: Brill Rodopi, 2012), pp. 301–326. p. 303, 310–311.
104 Jenkins, *Convergence Culture*, p. 116.
105 Newman, 'Afterword', p. 450.
106 Stephen D. Arata, 'The Occidental Tourist: "Dracula" and the Anxiety of Reverse Colonialization', *Victorian Studies* 33:4 (1990), 621–645, p. 623.
107 Arata, p. 623.
108 Newman, *Anno Dracula*. All subsequent quotations from the same edition unless indicated otherwise.
109 Andrew Smith, *Gothic Literature* (Edinburgh: Edinburgh University Press, 2007).
110 See, for example: Vera Goldsworthy. *Inventing Ruritania: The Imperialism of the Imagination* (New Haven: Yale University Press, 1998).
111 Amidst a grotesque setting of depravity and filth, Beauregard assists the Queen in committing suicide, thereby destroying the Count's claim to power in Britain.
112 Ackroyd's psychogeography and his novel have been the subject of extensive scholarly work. For example, on *Limehouse Golem* alone: Petr Chalupský, 'Crime Narratives in Peter Ackroyd's Historiographic Metafictions', *European Journal of English Studies*, 14:2 (2010), 121–131. Petr Chalupský, *A Horror and a Beauty: The World of Peter Ackroyd's London Novels* (Prague: Karolinum Press, 2017). Sidia Fiorato, 'Theatrical Role-Playing, Crime and Punishment in Peter Ackroyd's *Dan Leno and the Limehouse Golem*', *Pólemos: Journal of Law, Literature and Culture*, 6:1 (2012), 65–81. Duperray. Also: Jean-Michel Ganteau, 'Vulnerable Visibilities: Peter Ackroyd's Monstrous Victorian Metropolis', in *Neo-Victorian Cities. Reassessing Urban Politics and Poetics*, ed. by Marie-Louise Kohlke and Christian Gutleben (Leiden: Brill Rodopi, 2015), pp. 151–174. Barry Lewis, *My Words Echo Thus: Possessing the Past in Peter Ackroyd's Novels* (Columbia: University of South Carolina Press, 2007). Susana Onega, *Metafiction and Myth in the Novels of Peter Ackroyd* (Columbia: Camden House, 1999). Susana Onega, 'Family Traumas and Serial Killings in Peter Ackroyd's *Dan Leno and the Limehouse Golem*', in *Neo-Victorian Families. Gender, Sexual and Cultural Politics*, ed. by Marie-Louise Kohlke and Christian Gutleben (Leiden: Rodopi, 2011), pp. 267–296. Patricia Pulham, 'Mapping Histories: The Golem and the Serial Killer in *White Chappell: Scarlet Tracings*, and *Dan Leno and the Limehouse Golem*', in *Haunting and Spectrality in Neo-Victorian Fiction*, ed. by Rosario Aras and Patricia Pulham (London: Palgrave Macmillan, 2010), pp. 157–179. Aleksjs Taube, 'London's East End in Peter Ackroyd's *Dan Leno and the Limehouse Golem*', in *Literature and the Peripheral City*, ed. by Lieven Ameel, Jason Finch, and Markku Salmela (London: Palgrave

Macmillan, 2015), pp. 93–110. Julian Wolfreys and Jeremy Gibson, *Peter Ackroyd. The Ludic and Labyrinthine Text* (London: Palgrave Macmillan, 2000). Julian Wolfreys, *Writing London. Materiality, Memory, Spectrality* (London: Palgrave Macmillan, 2002).

113 Wolfreys and Gibson, p. 201.
114 Peter Ackroyd, *Dan Leno and the Limehouse Golem* (London: Vintage Books, 2017 [1994]).
115 Chalupský, *Beauty*, p. 84.
116 There is no historical evidence that Marianne Helen Harrison, known as Nell, was a prostitute. Ackroyd embellishes for dramatic effect here; pp. 104–105, in which his marriage is likened to a 'melodarama from the London stage', or something 'from the pages of Emile Zola.'
117 For example, when Eleanor Marx plays a role in Oscar Wilde's play, *Vera or. The Nihilists*, when Leno walks in the footsteps of his idol, Grimaldi, in a place described by Dickens in *The Pickwick Papers*, when Gissing reads Algernon Swinburne's essay on William Blake, when Cree picks up Gissing's novel *Workers of the Dawn* (1880), or when Gissing's essay on Babbage's engine lastingly influences H.G. Wells – who later discusses Marx's notes on the subject with Stalin.
118 Wolfreys and Gibson, p. 170.
119 Consider Cree's account of the *Pall Mall Gazette*, which 'depicted me with a top hat and cloak in general theatrical representation of a swell or masher' – in traditional Ripper iconography – but which 'smacked too much of the Gothic' as 'cheapest melodrama' (77).
120 In Jewish folklore, the golem is an animated, anthropomorphic creature usually formed from clay or mud. A versatile socio-religious metaphor, the golem, as affiliated to the homunculus, has also become a popular trope in fantasy writing. Pulham, 'Golem'.
121 Rachel Lichtenstein and Iain Sinclair, *Rodinsky's Room* (London: Granta Publications, 1999), p. 28.
122 Wolfreys and Gibson, p. 207.
123 Only a desk-sized demonstration-piece was built in 1832, and it did not feature a 'central engine rising some fifteen feet rising toward the roof' (111).
124 Luckhurst, 'Spectral Turn', p. 531.
125 Luckhurst, 'Spectral Turn', p. 532; Jean-François Lyotard, 'About the human', in *The Inhuman: Reflections on Time*, trans. by Geoffrey Bennington and Rachel Bowlby (Cambridge: Polity Press, 1991). Bruno Latour, *We Have Never Been Modern*, trans. by Catherine Porter (Hemel Hempstead: Harvester, 1993). Anthony Vidler, *The Architectural Uncanny* (Cambridge, MA: MIT Press, 1992).
126 Chris Baldick, 'Introduction', in *Oxford Book of Gothic Tales* (Oxford: Oxford University Press, 1992).

127 Luckhurst, 'Spectral Turn', p. 534.
128 Iain Sinclair, *Lights Out for the Territory: 9 Excursions in the Secret History of London* (London: Granta, 1997), p. 26.
129 Iain Sinclair, *Downriver (Or, The Vessels of Wrath): A Narrative in Twelve Tales* (London: Paladin, 1991), p. 265.
130 Ho, p. 45.
131 Luckhurst, 'Spectral Turn', p. 535.
132 Tom Gauld, *Tom Gauld on psychogeographers*, cartoon, *The Guardian*, 22 Sept. 2017, https://www.theguardian.com/books/picture/2017/sep/22/tom-gauld-on-psychogeographers-cartoon (zccessed 17 June 2018).
133 Merlin Coverley, *Psychogeography* (Harpenden: Pocket Essentials, 2006), p. 127.
134 Coverley, p. 127.
135 For more on connectivity, maker culture and steampunk as a subculture, see Carrott, Ferguson. Also: Suzanne Barber and Matt Hale, 'Enacting the Never-Was: Upcycling the Past, Present, and Future in Steampunk', in *Steaming Into a Victorian Future*, ed. by Julie Anne Taddeo and Cynthia J. Miller (Lanham: Scarecrow Press, 2013.), pp. 165–183.
136 Jenkins, *Convergence*, pp. 255–256, in reference to Marshal Sella, 'The Remote Controllers', https://www.nytimes.com/2002/10/20/magazine/the-remote-controllers.html (accessed 19 June 2018).
137 George Mann, *The Affinity Bridge*: A Newbury and Hobbes Investigation (New York: Tor Books, 2009).
138 Anon., 'Steampunk Week – Book Review: The Affinity Bridge by George Mann', https://www.thebooksmugglers.com/2010/04/steampunk-week-book-review-the-affinity-bridge-by-george-mann.html (accessed 19 June 2018); Thomas M. Wagner, 'The Affinity Bridge', http://www.sfreviews.net/mann_affinity_bridge.html (accessed 19 June 2018).
139 Anon., 'The Affinity Bridge', https://www.kirkusreviews.com/book-reviews/george-mann/the-affinity-bridge/ (accessed 19 June 2018); Catherine Ramsell, '"The Affinity Bridge" Is an Enormously Fun Steampunk Novel', https://www.popmatters.com/125702-the-affinity-bridge-by-george-mann-2496193023.html (accessed 19 June 2018).
140 S. M. Peters, *Whitechapel Gods* (New York: Roc Books, 2008).
141 For more on the interrelations between Gothic and body horror, see: Xavier Aldana Reyes, *Body Gothic. Corporeal in Contemporary Literature and Horror Film* (Cardiff: University of Wales Press, 2014).
142 Arthur Morrison, 'Whitechapel. From "The Palace Journal", April 24, 1889', https://www.casebook.org/victorian_london/whitechapel3.html?printer=true (accessed 19 June 2018).

143 Karl Marx, *Capital. A New Abridgement* (Oxford: Oxford World's Classics, 2008 [1867]), pp. 260–261.
144 The League of S.T.E.A.M., '"Here Comes the Bride" – Adventures of the League of STEAM', Video, YouTube, posted by The League of S.T.E.A.M., 24 November 2011, https://www.youtube.com/watch?v=CHY1U9wxv2o (accessed 20 June 2018).
145 Kohlke and Gutleben, *Neo-Victorian Gothic,* p. 12, original emphasis.
146 Bowser and Croxall, 'Introduction', p. 30.
147 For more, see: Forlini, 'Technology'.
148 Bowser and Croxall, p. 5.

3

Hyper-City: Steampunk's Retro-Speculative Video Game Spaces

Introduction: Of Other Spaces

Italo Calvino's much-referenced 1972 novel *Invisible Cities* lays out how urban spaces, charged with desires and fears, manifest social relationships, even if they are sometimes irrationally or palimpsestically coded:

> With cities, it is as with dreams: everything imaginable can be dreamed, but even the most unexpected dream is a rebus that conceals a desire or, its reverse, a fear. Cities, like dreams, are made of desires and fears, even if the thread of their discourse is secret, their rules are absurd, their perspectives deceitful, and everything conceals something else.[1]

As such, it not only calls up Lefebvre's notion of spaces as socially produced, but also illustrates steampunk cities' utopian potential as heterotopic counter-site in the Foucaultian sense, 'a kind of effectively enacted utopia in which the real sites, all the other real sites that can be found within the culture, are simultaneously represented, contested, and inverted'.[2] As retro-speculative heterotopias, steampunk cities re-present and reflect on 'real' space (in this case, our imaginaries of the Victorian city) and 'create a space of illusion that exposes every real space [...] as still more illusory'.[3] Cities of memory, like steampunk cities, are by necessity virtual, be they remembered or dreamed up, but both also illustrate that urban spaces are more than the sum of their physical parts. Edward Soja's concept of thirdspace, 'a purposefully tentative and flexible term', exemplifies this, as it 'attempts to capture what is actually a constantly shifting and changing milieu of ideas, events, appearances, and meanings'.[4]

Influenced by Lefebvre, Foucault, and Homi Bhabha among others, Soja defines thirdspace as 'a radically different way of looking at, interpreting and acting to change the embracing spatiality of human life'.[5] In his trialectics of space, firstspace is the concrete and material dimension of space, perceived, epistemological and empirically mappable.[6] Secondspace exemplifies how space is conceived, imagined, interpreted and represented, for example in art and fiction. This, then, is the aspect of spatiality which helps create a cumulative palimpsest of interpretations and imagery, and so informs cognitive mapping and the construction of urban imaginaries, especially of Victorian London. Thirdspace, finally, expresses the social dimension, encompassing both first- and secondspace and yet containing more than the sum of its parts. Radically open, thirdspace aims to express lived space in its simultaneities and complexities. '*Everything* comes together in Thirdspace: subjectivity and objectivity, the abstract and the concrete, the real and the imagined, the knowable and the unimaginable, the repetitive and the differential, structure and agency, mind and body, consciousness and the unconscious, the disciplined and the transdisciplinary, everyday life and unending history'.[7]

This chapter interrogates the role and function of space in the steampunk city: How does the experience of space shape our relationship with the city and the larger social order? What happens when that relationship is retro-speculatively re-routed? Or, in other words: How does steampunk's retro-speculative play intervene in and challenge the processes that contribute to the experience of thirdspace? In order to explore these questions, I examine how classic Victorian writers Charles Dickens and Sir Arthur Conan Doyle represent immersive secondspace imaginaries of London through the lens of Doreen Massey's notion of space as a process. I then turn to the popular video games *Assassin's Creed: Syndicate* and *The Order: 1886* (both 2015) as interactive simulations of Victorian London in which space assumes a central narrative function. Not only are video games the most popular, financially successful, and best-known iterations of steampunk cities, and as such both manifest and shape popular memory in important ways, they also provide unique opportunities to recombine historical, transmedia recordings of Victorian London – prose fiction, journalism, visual arts, maps – and realize steampunk London imaginaries as spatialized models.

Space in video games, according to Espen Aarseth, is their 'defining element', as they 'celebrate and explore spatial representation as a central motif and raison d'être'.[8] As three-dimensional visual constructs, they 'offload [the] cognitive overhead' of imagining space from text alone 'into the machine' so that 'gamers can focus on the flow of the game while learning the background mechanics through immersion and experimentation'.[9] Indeed, a defining feature of game spaces is that we may interact with them by proxy through a digital avatar. In addition, as neo-Victorian constructs sourced from collective memory, game spaces must be considered an example of hyper-reality in line with Baudrillard's simulacrum,[10] which Soja defines as 'a perfect copy of an original that may never have existed' and the 'cumulative replacement of the real with its simulated representations or images'.[11] Neo-Victorian and steampunk game spaces so tap into the collectively curated urban imaginary outlined in the last chapter: 'Today's video-gaming universe often draws on a Victorian novelistic *imaginaire* and the extrapolated cities which nineteenth-century print culture produced'.[12]

In *Assassin's Creed: Unity* (2014), for example, the virtual Notre Dame of revolutionary Paris was recreated with the help of 'more than 150 maps of the city', photographs, and historians' advice[13] and considered so accurate that, when the cathedral was damaged by fire in April 2019, Ubisoft both suggested its research be used in the reconstruction, and offered a free version of the game in which players could explore the building as they had hitherto 'known' it and might no longer be able to experience it. This illustrates how game spaces may provide unique relationships with both the real cityscape and our historical imaginaries of it, and although they are finitely coded and ultimately self-contained, they contain such aspects of thirdspace as subjectivity and objectivity, the abstract and the concrete, the real and the imagined, structure and agency, mind and body, everyday life and history. After all, Soja also links thirdspace to the Aleph as imagined by Jorge Luis Borges, 'the place "where all places are"'.[14] The Aleph, 'an allegory on the infinite complexities of space and time' and an 'all-inclusive simultaneity [that] opens up endless worlds to explore, and, at the same time, presents daunting challenges',[15] has been associated with virtual space. It is no wonder then, that William Gibson's cyberpunk *Sprawl* trilogy[16] originates the idea of cyberspace as the 'consensual hallucination [...] a graphic representation of data',[17] as the Aleph. Soja himself notes that *Neuromancer*'s conception of cyberspace as '[l]ines of light ranged in the non-space of the mind, clusters and constellations of data. Like city lights, receding...'[18] is 'intrinsically spatial in [its] rhetoric and referencing', as well as 'peculiarly urban'.[19] Urban and virtual space are, then, affiliated in interesting ways, as well as provide another instance in which steampunk may circle back to its cyberpunk roots in unexpected ways. This becomes not least evident in *The Order: 1886*'s leveraging of *Blade Runner*'s (1982) iconic hyper-city aesthetics, which re-configure Victorian London into an immersive steampunk city.

In this chapter, I interrogate urban space in Victorian literature and steampunk video games as a narrative strategy that encodes – and potentially re-calibrates – our mental and cognitive maps, that is, the 'interpretive grids'[20] through which we read and navigate our relationship with the larger social order.

Victorian London: Immersive and Panoptic Trajectories

Charles Dickens and Sir Arthur Conan Doyle both created widely formative imaginaries of Victorian London that successfully evoked its complex spatiality. A case in point is this passage from *Nicholas Nickleby*:

> They rattled on through the noisy, bustling, crowded streets of London, now displaying long double rows of brightly-burning lamps, dotted here and there with the chemists' glaring lights, and illuminated besides with the brilliant flood that streamed from the windows of the shops, where sparkling jewellery, silks and velvets of the richest colours, the most inviting delicacies, and most sumptuous articles of luxurious ornament, succeeded each other in rich and glittering profusion. Streams of people apparently without end poured on and on, jostling each other in the crowd and hurrying forward, scarcely seeming to notice the riches that surrounded them on every side; while vehicles of all shapes and makes, mingled up together in one moving mass, like running water, lent their ceaseless roar to swell the noise and tumult.[21]

London here is experienced in transit and produced through a succession of sensory impressions and indeed a network of interlinking movements. As such, it exemplifies Doreen Massey's concept of space as more than the sphere 'of a discrete multiplicity of inert things' and rather one that 'presents us with a heterogeneity of practices and processes': 'This is space as the sphere of dynamic simultaneity, constantly disconnected by new arrivals, constantly waiting to be determined (and therefore always undetermined) by the construction of new relations. It is always being made and always therefore, in a sense, unfinished (except that 'finishing' is not on the agenda)'.[22] Considering space a 'product of a multitude of histories whose resonances are still there', histories buried as well as still being made, she argues that to travel through space is to 'participate in its continuing production'.[23] This is evident in Dickens' evocation of ceaseless, crossing movements which, though transitory, create the experience of the metropolis as one of intersecting trajectories. Here, the temporal dimension converges with space as something more than the material surface: journeying through the city like Dickens' characters, or indeed the avatar in a video game, means to actively create space as one of a 'bundle of trajectories': 'Arriving at a new place means joining up with, somehow linking into, the collection of interwoven stories of which that place is made'.[24]

In this immersive passage, material space recedes behind the social and commercial relationships which constitute it and into which our focal characters now link and join up through their own journey. Massey illustrates this with recourse to a passage which she (mistakenly) attributes to Raymond Williams, in which the author, from the window of a moving train, catches a glimpse of

> a woman in her pinny bending over to clear the back drain with a stick. For the passenger on the train she will forever be doing this. She is held in that instant, almost immobilised [...], trapped in the timeless instant. Thinking space as the sphere of a multiplicity of trajectories, imagining a train journey (for example) as speeding across on-going stories, means bringing the woman in the pinny to life, acknowledging her as an ongoing life.[25]

Similarly, the characters' journey becomes one of countless intersecting trajectories which constitute the Victorian city of that moment: Linking into these threads of interwoven relationships, stories, and journeys here means 'weaving them into a more or less coherent feeling of being "here", "now"'.[26] While this passage illustrates how Dickens' immersive approach conjures up 'a city in production, rising and crumbling as it goes',[27] his work is also often attuned to the way in which his 'Dickensian London' was vanishing as he was writing it.[28] At the end of *The Old Curiosity Shop* (1840–41), we find the following passage:

> [Kit] sometimes took [his children] to the place where [Nell] had lived; but new improvements had altered it so much, it was not like the same. The old house had been long ago pulled down, and a fine broad road was in its place. At first he would draw with his stick a square upon the ground to show them where it used to stand. But soon he became uncertain of the spot, and could only say it was thereabouts, he thought, and that these alterations were confusing. Such are the changes which a few years bring about, and so do things pass away, like a tale that is told![29]

Here, Kit's mental map of the city becomes outdated in real time and his urban imaginary is troubled as the city changes. Indeed, his experience corresponds to the massive changes to London's cityscape during the Victorian era, as London transformed into the modern imperial capital whose structures have become essential cornerstones of a shared London imaginary; Among them Kew Gardens, Kensington Museum complex and colleges, Albert Memorial and Royal Albert Hall, Westminster Palace, Trafalgar Square's Nelson Monument, Liberty's department store, the British Museum, Victoria, Paddington, and Charing Cross railway stations, St Pancras Hotel, Tower Bridge, and Bazalgette's embankment and sewer system. Concurrently, railways, sewers, telegraphs, and the Underground, first built in 1863, also created connectivity and contributed to a large-scale modernization. As Lynda Nead notes however, London's modernity 'seemed to obey the spatial logic of the maze rather than that of the grid or *étoile*, and its characteristic experience was of disorientation, as opposed to purposeful movement'.[30] Unlike Haussmann's forcefully re-mapped Paris, London remained labyrinthine and multi-layered. Whereas city planners and chroniclers turned towards the panoptic view of the map, seeking a legible and comprehensive urban representation, no map could match the city's rapid development[31]: Maps, as Massey notes, misrepresent urban relationships by positioning the observer, 'themselves unobserved, outside and above the object of the gaze' and give the impression that space is 'a surface – that it is a sphere of completed horizontality'.[32] Hence, whereas Victorian London was routinely mapped through a panoptic view representing physical or social relationships such as the Ordnance Survey of 1851, John Snow's cholera map (1854) or Charles Booth's *Life and Labour of the People of London* (1889–1893), the 'logic of the cartographer', as Nead argues, 'cannot contain the city of memory and imagination'.[33]

In addition, London's sewers, underground railways, rail track overpasses, or telegraph lines expanded vertically into structures and levels not easily accommodated in the one-dimensional surface of the map. *Dombey and Son* (1848) captures a moment of upheaval and chaos during the city's transformation into a modern capital when describing the building of a railway:

> The first shock of a great earthquake had, just at that period, rent the whole neighbourhood to its centre. Traces of its course were visible on every side. Houses were knocked down; streets broken through and stopped; deep pits and trenches dug in the ground; enormous heaps of earth and clay thrown up; buildings that were undermined and shaking, propped by great beams of wood. Here, a chaos of carts, overthrown and jumbled together, lay topsy-turvy at the bottom of a steep unnatural hill; there, confused treasures of iron soaked and rusted in something that had accidentally become a pond. Everywhere were bridges that led nowhere; thoroughfares that were wholly impassable; Babel towers of chimneys, wanting half their height; temporary wooden houses and enclosures, in the most unlikely situations; carcases of ragged tenements, and fragments of unfinished walls and arches, and piles of scaffolding, and wildernesses of bricks, and giant forms of cranes, and tripods straddling above nothing. There were a hundred thousand shapes and substances of incompleteness, wildly mingled out of their places, upside down, burrowing in the earth, aspiring in the air, mouldering in the water, and unintelligible as any dream.[34]

Here is an overwhelming multiplicity of levels, layers, and open ends, of an intertwined and illegible cityscape always in flux, recalling Gustave Doré's

Piranesi-esque endlessness of London. Decoupled from purpose and flow, the cityscape becomes estranged as a 'wilderness of bricks' and 'ragged carcasses' and alive through active verbs such as 'mingle' or 'burrow', and so anticipates *The Difference Engine*'s 'nightmare endlessness of streets', its 'nausea of awnings' and 'ugliness of scaffoldings'.[35] While the panoptic view falsely conjures a complete and comprehensive cityscape, the actual, immersed experience is one of disorientation and confusion.

Yet, in 1887 there appears a character for whom London is a city of totality and certainty that can be read, understood, and securely navigated by the rational mind. Sherlock Holmes, the collective symbol of ordering logic presides in *fin de siècle* London, 'and it is with the London of those years that he has always been regarded as synonymous'.[36] This is not least because Holmes' knowledge of the late-Victorian city is unparalleled. When a mystery client has a cab transport Holmes, Watson, and Miss Morstan from the Lyceum theatre on the Strand to a secret location, Watson professes that 'soon, what with our pace, the fog, and my own limited knowledge of London, I lost my bearings and knew nothing save that we seemed to be going a very long way.' Holmes, however, 'was never at fault, however, and he muttered the names as the cab rattled through squares and in and out by tortuous bystreets'.[37] Holmes' knowledge of London is complete and unfailing. In *The Red-Headed League* (1891), he notes that 'It is a hobby of mine to have an exact knowledge of London'.[38] However, his own address at 221B in the real Baker Street is fictional: In Holmes' London, the real and imaginary converge into a mythic iconography of the modern metropolis. Doyle's use of street atlases and Post Office directories allowed him to map out trajectories across London which evoke the city's complexity through real pathways.[39] Indeed, we are never in doubt that London, 'that great cesspool into which all the loungers and idlers of the Empire are irresistibly drained', is *the* modern metropolis of the age, a capital of finance and trade, and a national and imperial nexus.[40]

David Cannadine notes that Holmes stories are 'often focused on the interlinked worlds of monarchy and government, aristocracy and plutocracy, financiers and rentiers, diplomats and military men, that were spreading across much of the city itself'.[41] The crimes which prompt the story are often domestic, conspiratorial, or professional, such as fraud, embezzlement, or forgery. Quite often, they are not legally crimes, but rather deceptions, scandals, oddities, and mysteries. Whereas this characterizes Holmes' London as one of the middle and upper classes, it also underlines that the detective is less concerned with mundane criminality, but rather, as he puts it, with 'those whimsical incidents which will happen when you have four million human beings jostling each other within the space of a few square miles. Amid the action and reaction of so dense a swarm of humanity, every possible combination of events may be expected to take place'.[42] Here, the modern metropolis is configured as a multiplicity of intersecting trajectories, physical journeys as much as narratives, which give rise to an incalculable variety of small eccentricities and puzzles. This is illustrated in 'The Blue Carbuncle' (1892), where a chance encounter between a commissionaire, a man with a Christmas goose, and a 'knot of roughs' on the corner of Tottenham Court Road and Goodge Street ends with the commissionaire in possession of a stolen gem hidden in the goose's crop.[43] Not only is this an example of three independent trajectories randomly intersecting in urban space, but Holmes' own, backwards tracking of the goose through a detailed knowledge of London's trade networks, leading him to Covent Garden, also exemplifies how his mastery of metropolis and modern life alike hinges on his understanding of networks, crosscurrents, and trajectories. The stories, and with them the London imaginary, arise less out of immersive observations (as in Dickens) but rather from the pathways traced by Holmes and Watson's journeys on foot, in a hansom cab, or via train, linking actively and purposefully into the network of stories and connections that constitute the city, and which remain centred on 221B Baker Street. At the beginning of 'The Resident Patient' (1894), Watson remarks: 'He loved to lie in the very centre of five million people, with his filaments stretching out and running through them, responsive to every little rumour or suspicion of unsolved crime.'[44] By using the image of the 'filament', which may be organic as well as electric, Doyle conjures up an idea of Holmes plugged into the city as hacker Henry Chase in *Neuromancer* plugs into cyberspace, which after all is intrinsically urban. In this image, Holmes, too, is linked into the very infrastructure of London.

This London with which Holmes is so synonymous in the collective imagination is firmly located in a Victorian context and cityscape. Even though Doyle wrote Holmesian adventures until the later 1920s, the stories are all set in and identified with the London of the 1880s and 1890s, as they eschew the new expansions and transformations London underwent during the Edwardian era[45]: Millbank, the Aldwych, Whitehall, or Regent Street were reconstructed in 'Edwardian Baroque', luxury hotels were built, and the cityscape altered significantly through electricity and motorcars. As Cannadine outlines, 'it has been suggestively argued that it would have been impossible for Holmes to have operated in such a different urban environment [...], which was why Conan Doyle retired his detective in 1903'.[46]

Where Dickens' London relies on an immersive perspective to create a memorable, complex and layered, if sometimes temporary and confusing urban texture, Conan Doyle's *fin de siècle* London is legible to Holmes through a combination of immersive and panoptic views, seeing that Holmes' journeys have actually been traced by the author with the help of a map. In addition, Holmes retains a comprehensive mental map of the modern metropolis that translates from its physical to is social relationships. His effortless mastery also creates a satisfying and reassuring urban habitus: Nonchalantly aloof and yet equipped with a detailed and useful knowledge of the city, Holmes exhibits many of the characteristics Georg Simmel's seminal 1903 essay, 'Die Großstädte und das Geistesleben', would identify as 'modern' and 'urban': Freed from social surveillance and anonymously free, the urban dweller fosters an indifferent attitude of cultivated privatism, and meets the incessant sensory over-stimulation of light and speed with a blasé mannerism which identifies them as thoroughly modern.[47] Holmes is so uniquely linked to and synonymous with a formative imaginary of Victorian London, whose mental map is defined by and created through a multitude of physical and social trajectories and journeys.

3.1 Immersive Historical Play in *Assassin's Creed: Syndicate*

Virtual game spaces may recreate Holmes' mental maps for modern audiences and invite players to forge a similar relationship with (an imagined) Victorian London. One of the most popular and widely-played blockbuster video games in the last decade, *Assassin's Creed: Syndicate* poses an opportunity to investigate how video games bring that London to life. It gravitates naturally to narratives of Dickens' and Doyle's city, presenting international audiences with a cityscape at once familiar through its landmarks, and excitingly strange through its temporal setting.[48] The ninth game in the *Assassin's Creed* franchise, *Syndicate* continues the frame narrative in which two rival orders, the Templars and the Assassins, wage a secret war for dominance throughout history by trying to gain control of magical artefacts. This provides a narrative and logical framework for the time travel and meta-stages of the game play which are less important for my purpose here. Far more compelling is the game's 1868 London.

Alternating between the twin avatars Jacob and Evie Frye, players attempt to dismantle the corrupting empire of the magnate Crawford Starrick, who controls London's networks of trade, transport, and production through his street gang, 'the Blighters' (easily recognizable through red jackets), and who so embodies Victorian evils such as colonialism and exploitative industrial capitalism. To go against Starrick, the game tells us, is to take on 'the city itself', if not the world at large: 'Whosoever controls London, controls the world.'[49] Not only does London here signify the larger, global nineteenth century, but it is also conjured and defined through its networks and externalized power structures, which the players dismantle and re-conquer. Taking on Starrick's city and, by implication, the 'Victorian' era itself, players assassinate his associates, free working children from dismal factories, regain city territory with their own, green-attired street gang, 'the Rogues', or solve puzzles and complete assignments set by a neo-Victorian collage of historical persons such as Alexander Graham Bell, Charles Dickens, Charles Darwin, Florence Nightingale, or Karl Marx, or hunt urban monsters Spring-Heeled Jack and Jack the Ripper. As such, players link into London as a nexus of power, production, and movement on both a narrative and spatial level, and the avatars' journeys participate in the (re-)construction of this hyper-real imaginary space, not least through the *Assassin's Creed* franchise's trademark extraordinary movements. In addition to sneaking across rooftops, into tunnels, and through secret laboratories and asylums, chasing thieving street urchins, sabotaging factories, zip-lining across Westminster Palace, or finding artefacts hidden on top of St Paul's Cathedral, the Tower of London, or inside Buckingham Palace, players may climb any structure and explore the virtual city at multiple angles and levels.

In positioning our avatars as heroic outlaws with the good intention to set right historical wrongs, the game offers a neo-Victorian narrative which broadly simplifies complex socio-economic and political realities of the real nineteenth century.[50] In line with the game's indulgence in 'genre conventions, such as the swashbuckling adventure,'[51] in which the complexities of the real world may momentarily cohere into clear choices, its neo-Victorian perspective pits players against a 'repressive patriarchal regime' which is 'convenient as it is morally and politically unambiguous'.[52] Relying on 'white knowledge' that its international audience may have picked up at school, through Dickens adaptations, or other (neo-)Victorian media, the game relies on a simple, stereotypical consensus about what characterizes Victorian London, who might move through it, and who its heroes and villains are. After all, *Syndicate*'s game space 'is always serving the primary purpose of gameplay' for a mainstream audience.[53] While as a simulacrum of a city of historical memory, it 'no longer needs to be rational, because it no longer measures itself against either an ideal or negative instance',[54] *Assassin's Creed* strives to synthesize a realist, believable representation with players' expectations and functional gameplay, and so relied on meticulous research and historical consultants, for example historian Judith Flanders.[55] It so brings a 'verisimilitudinous approach to the table, faithfully recreating cities and regions of the past' and a 'filmic reality effect'.[56] That effect in turn helps construct the virtual city and its meta-narratives as 'authentic'.

Not least, this reality effect is produced by the game's closely referencing Victorian visual art in creating the seven playable zones (Westminster, the Strand, City of London, Whitechapel, Southwark, Lambeth, and the Thames), which are extensively and intricately constructed game spaces with individual aesthetic identities that can be viewed at different times of the day and in different weather conditions. For example, John Crowther's *Panoramic View from the Top of the Monument* (c. 1890) is an example of how contemporary artists combined a panoptic gaze with 'the unfolding vista of the pedestrian at ground level'.[57] Other Victorian representations of London, such as the vistas from Ludgate Hill discussed in Chapter Two, John O'Connor's 1884 painting *From Pentonville Road Looking West: Evening*, or the paintings of John Atkinson Grimshaw which inspired the concept of *Syndicate* likewise create multi-layered vistas through a strategically placed vanishing point and urban layers which pale as they recede into the background.[58] O'Connor's painting captures the grandeur of the imperial city as 'the Gothic spires of St Pancras railway station rise above the humdrum banality of street life', but also accommodates ephemera of industry, transport, and business through the omnibuses, passers-by, and advertisements in the middle ground, and so uses the combined panoptic and immersive view to create 'opposing emotional registers'.[59] *Syndicate* recreates these influences in its concept art and gameplay through adept use of light, mood, and contrasting colours in building deep, evocative and layered vistas (over which, not seldom, St Paul's Cathedral presides) accompanied by audio cues and music which bring the three-dimensional paintings to life. Like Dickens' descriptions, it frequently foregrounds urban industrial textures such as bridges, underpasses, boat riggings, or lantern posts, chooses far away vanishing points to emphasize scale and dynamic, or foregrounds trains and railways, 'essential motifs of the modern city, indicating technological prowess, speed of communication and the fragmentary nature of society'.[60] In so doing, the game fuses scale and detail into a virtual model of London that can be experienced both on street level and from above, is indebted to secondspace Victoriana, and is fully mapped out, contains no blind spots and therefore seemingly portrays urban complexity as complete totality.

As Aarseth notes: 'As spatial practice, computer games are both representations of space (given their formal systems of relations) and representational spaces (given their symbolic imagery with a primarily aesthetic purpose)'.[61] Like previous games, *Syndicate*'s London offers meticulously and accurately recreated landmarks in their proper place and scale (such as Westminster Palace, Trafalgar Square, the Monument, or Buckingham Palace), but takes the liberty to rescale lesser known, surrounding architecture in order to accommodate the free-roaming movement required for the gameplay, so that the avatar may climb and zip-line across buildings or drive carriages through the streets.[62] 'The aim,' art director Mohamed Gambouz crucially notes, is 'to convey a believable setting, a believable city. And sometimes we even go for the perception people have, even if it's not 100 percent accurate.'[63] Ultimately, then, the game caters to shared urban imaginaries, and prioritizes them over historical data. This includes (game) spaces where the original nineteenth-century architecture is lost or has been substituted. Here, the game presents a sort of aesthetically distinct 'filler architecture' corresponding to the (imagined) visual identity of each borough: The Strand is palatial, colourful, and ornamented, whereas Whitechapel contains derelict half-timbered houses, and Southwark is the domain of industrial factories and smoking chimneys, and so on. *Syndicate*'s Victorian game world is a hyper-real simulacrum in which architecture and places act as cyphers for a collectively shared idea of 'Victorian-ness' and so shares qualities with steampunk at a fundamental mechanical level. Although its evocative hyper-real collage also utilizes an aesthetic shorthand to leverage aspects of the 'real' Victorian city and era, the simulation itself serves a primarily functional purpose: 'Computer games are allegories of space: they pretend to portray space in ever more realistic ways but rely on their deviation from reality in order to make the illusion playable.'[64]

Through the journey through such simulated, allegorical space, players interact with both gameplay and historical memory in tandem, as well as create narrative and spaces as they go: 'The moving perspective projection defines a film-like, interactive, space- and time-based narration, which enables the combination of commonly used reality-based design attributes and plot structures.'[65] In addition, as Mark J. P. Wolf suggests, game spaces invite 'audience participation in the form of speculation and fantasy' through 'conceptual immersion; the occupying of the audience's full attention and imagination, often with more detail than can be held in mind all at once.'[66] Accordingly in *Syndicate*, players must 'remember a wealth of details about the game's imaginary world in order to put together its backstory and solve puzzles,'[67] which are not only embedded in a larger narrative, but an interactive cityscape which extends beyond our immediate vision.

As we are tasked with locating stolen explosives hidden in St Pancras, for example, we must navigate the complex space, dodge, fight, and escape rival gang members, find an escape route, utilize tools, infrastructures, and people within the space, all the while being aware of how this operation pertains to the larger narrative and the city 'beyond'. As Wolf notes:

> Worlds offering a high degree of saturation are usually too big to be experienced completely in a single sitting or session. The amount of detail and information must be great enough to overwhelm the audience, imitating the vast amount of Primary World information which cannot be mastered or held in mind all at once. This overflow, beyond the point of saturation, is necessary if the world is to be kept alive in the imagination. If the world is too small, the audience may feel that they know all there is to know, and consider the world exhausted, feeling there is nothing more to be obtained from it. A world with an overflow beyond saturation, however, can never be held in the mind in its entirety; something will always be left out. What remains in the audience's mind then, is always changing, as lower levels of detail are forgotten and later re-experienced and re-imagined when they are encountered again.[68]

The city, then, is an environment pre-designed to simulate such a sensory overflow through its textures, vistas, possible pathways, its neo-Victorian collage, and technofantastical gadgets, to evoke the virtual city as a realistic simulation which requires and activates our transmedia competencies and cognitive mapping, compelling us to participate actively in navigating the simulated city and the narratives that play out in it.

History is Your Playground: The Assassin Fantasy

The *Assassin's Creed* franchise's success certainly lies in its providing a unique and adventurous approach to the past as a playground to be conquered: 'Video games are particularly successful when they combine a break with particular limitations of reality in some areas with a retention of reality in others, inviting both comparison with real life and with the spectacular.'[69] Evie and Jacob Frye, the twin avatars, offer the assassin as a fantasy of adventurous urban mastery by proxy: Throughout the game, we infiltrate factories, laboratories, asylums, prisons, haunted houses, and royal balls, pursue street urchins, hypnotists, and urban legends, engage in gang fights, steal carriages, trains, and Gatling guns, assassinate rival snipers from rooftops, and find hidden objects and passages before defeating Starrick in what is called a 'final boss battle' and receiving a knighthood from the Queen. Clearly, the game draws on the physical prowess and swashbuckling of the (characteristically Victorian) adventure genre in which disguises, deception, infiltration, investigation, chases, fights, and rescue missions evoke excitement and heroism in an exotic setting that provides hidden dangers and clues, as well as opportunities for exploration and intervention.[70] By adopting such a wide range of plots, objectives, and narrative conventions, *Syndicate* presents its Victorian London as a multiplicity of ongoing and intersecting narratives, in which, as in the London of Sherlock Holmes, all manners and combinations of events become possible. Like the great detective, we may link into these and so participate interactively in the construction of this hyper-real imaginary.

Moreover, like Holmes, the assassin is a figure set up to enact mastery of the city: where the detective's rational mind pervades the interlinked networks of urban life through extensive knowledge, the assassin masters the environment through physical prowess, secret knowledge, and access to forbidden routes. Moving outside the law and ethical demands that constrain others, the assassin is unencumbered by and independent from the social, economic and legal networks of urban space, and moves even outside the laws of physics, climbing facades, traversing rooftops, jumping on and off trains, carriages, and omnibuses, and being, even when immersed in a crowd, hidden and anonymous. In fact, the anonymity feature is a crucial element of the gameplay which, much like the X-ray-esque 'eagle vision' which highlights allies and foes in different colours and even through urban structures, enables us to navigate the city confidently and on multiple levels. Other features, such as the small hexagon which indicates the direction of and distance to our next objective, the small topographic schema which provides a map with which to observe our relation to objects and people, similarly use panoptic schematics to enhance and facilitate navigation through the city. Together with Evie and Jacob's skill set and weapons, these features enable us to, as the game itself puts it, 'conquer' the city through their movements and actions.

By re-creating Victorian London as a historical playground to be roamed, explored, and appropriated through our movements, the game assimilates the politics of parkour, created by Sebastian Foucan and David Belle in the 1980s Parisian suburbs. An 'extreme and subversive engagement' with the urban landscape and 'radical inhabitation' which 'makes use of the built environment in original and engaging ways that rely on a deeply reciprocal relationship with' it, seeking to challenge and redefine our 'experience of embodiment and presence',[71] parkour endeavours to re-imbue urban spaces with a sense of agency and purpose through a 'dialogical relationship between the built environment and [the traceur's] bodies and thus, challenge their subject positions'.[72] Traceurs (literally someone who draws a line or path) or free runners climb, jump or somersault over, across, and against urban structures, traversing urban space in ways not pre-designed architecturally or culturally. They effectively adapt Massey's notion of the trajectory as actively creating space into ways of forming a personal, embodied, and rebellious relationship with urban space, designed to generate 'the feeling of having a stake in a particular environment, even though one cannot claim legal ownership over it'.[73] Like our avatar in *Syndicate*, free runners re-claim urban space from its pre-designed functions and regulations through a 'socially symbolic act, a form of resistance to cityscapes that alienate, restrict and subjugate'[74] and to 'question the ideological parameters and disciplining structures of the socially produced, power-saturated and environmentally pathological city space'.[75] Through this, they 'create a parallel city'[76], 'of movement and free play within and against the city of obstacles and inhibitions'.[77] It is telling both that Ubisoft promoted the game through a real-life montage of traceurs in costume,[78] and that the behind-the-scenes video reveals the many locations and instances where London's physical and social regulations curtailed that endeavour.[79] In the game world at least, we may freely engage with a virtual Victorian London in ways not open to us in either the historical or the contemporary city, and feel a sense of resistance and ownership and of 'having a stake in a particular environment, even though one cannot claim legal ownership over it'.[80]

If not in the real world, in *Syndicate*, we may walk around and into Westminster Palace undetected and unimpeded by security protocols, or climb the building and discover its detailed, ornamental architecture up close and in spaces so high up they cannot be seen from below. Perching on its highest point, we may unlock access to the borough's embedded sequences and puzzles while gaining a comprehensive, panoptic overview over our surroundings and enacting a key feature of the *Assassin's Creed* franchise: the Leap of Faith. When the player reaches certain high points in the game space, the game slows and the 'camera' provides us with a 360° panoramic shot of the surroundings accompanied by a reverential, emotive musical score that suggests this is a near-spiritual experience in which a special relationship with the environment is formed. The player then launches Evie or Jacob off this point in a free fall, with outstretched arms conveying a feeling of dedication, power, and self-confidence.[81] The pose, according to Felix Marlo Flor of the Ubisoft creative team, enacts the credo that 'video games must feel for the player as if everything is under his control'[82]: It is the simulation and enactment of freedom, conquest, and agency over sumptuously imagined times and spaces that provides the *Assassin's Creed* franchise's key allure.

As such, *Syndicate* is a steampunk video game which re-presents Victorian London as a heterotopic space of play and exploration, in which 'history is your playground'. It re-scales and simplifies Victorian socio-economic and political networks as it does its city in order to offer a functional, playable experience, and invites players to form a unique relationship with a neo-Victorian London driven by their agency. Indeed, virtual game spaces 'can represent the past as it was, or as it never was, but they can also represent how players wish to remember it, revisiting or revising the past to make players yearn for it, and they can offer players the possibility of not only *being* there but of *doing* things there – of *playing the past*.'[83] This embodied experience may foster new relationships with that past as mediated through urban space because by placing the player in the midst of both space and narrative and configuring the latter as the direct outcome of a player's actions, 'games allow players to better understand the notion of agency in human history and to root out a deterministic image of the past.'[84] Through its spatializing of agency, power, and the alternative pathways of history into Victorian London, *Syndicate* puts the fundamentals of steampunk itself into play.

3.2 Blade Runnering the Victorian City in *The Order 1886*

Unlike *Syndicate* with its double frame narrative and loosely intersecting sequences of missions, *The Order 1886* (2015), a third-person action-adventure game developed by Ready at Dawn, is more stringently story-driven. It features one linear narrative and gameplay sequences which transition into cinematic or cut scenes. While its impressive production value and cinematic aesthetic have been lauded, players also criticized the lack of free roaming and exploration – which, however, may be the point. Nonetheless, I posit that the game, with its detailed cityscape, grounded period setting and style, steampunk impulses, and narrative twists, fully explores the possibilities of a heterotopic steampunk London that synthesizes urban memory with retro-speculative impulses, and that its re-calibrated urban environment is crucial in assessing and experiencing the potential of steampunk itself.

In the game's fantastical premise, King Arthur's Order of Knights has over centuries fought a genetically divergent 'half-breed' race of shapeshifters with the help of a life-prolonging elixir. As that Order's most appealing and adventure-prone time of existence, the game recognizes the industrialized nineteenth century, presenting a neo-Victorian London 'braced with the scaffolding of a coming modernity', in which mankind seems to have achieved dominance over the darker forces of nature (here, lycans and, later, vampires) through the mastery of emergent technologies: electricity, railways, airships, experimental new weapons, wireless communication.[85] As such, it seems to conceive emergent technological paradigms as effective antidote against Gothic monsters, but as in the previously discussed neo-Gothic narratives, social issues soon emerge as intrinsically entangled with, and within, the Victorian city[86]: A rebellious uprising originating in that epicentre of disenfranchisement, Whitechapel, is rising up against the United India Company, a fictionalized extension of the East India Company, and London becomes the battleground in which local and colonial power hegemonies are identified and contested.

As such, *The Order* synthesizes popular markers of the Victorian era such as Medievalism, Gothic monstrosity, social unrest, and colonialism and projects them into a steampunked London, perceived and mobilized as a socio-historical nexus and potent memory figure in which the real and the fictional intertwine and which can support and accommodate an unending variety of narratives.[87] Much like *Syndicate*, *The Order* recognizes Victorian London as 'truly the centre of the world in the late 1800s', but unlike the former, it realizes the city's potency as widely legible memory figure to construct an 'alternate history – a recognizable London, slightly ahead of its time'.[88] In the accompanying art book, *The Blackwater Archives* (2015), the game's developers articulate their commitment to investing this retro-speculative setting with 'authenticity' through atmosphere and textures, to 'heighten the game experience' and so facilitate immersion in an 'alternative yet still recognizable Victorian reality': 'This,' claims Kirk Ellis, 'is the kind of universe video games can manufacture better than any other medium, even cinema'[89]. Indeed, character designs, gadgetry, weapons, and clothing, or the urban environment itself become legible objects hinting at histories and cultural contexts. The game relies heavily on such potent visual storytelling, which is not supplemented by any frame narrative, and so offloads a significant portion of its narration into players' active interaction with, and constant re-interpretation of, the game space itself.

For example, players start the game in a flash forward, emerging into the perspective of a disoriented Grayson, or Sir Galahad, a Knight of the Order, who must escape from what turns out to be a dungeon under Westminster Palace. We gain understanding of gameplay and setting together, without additional schematics or X-ray modes to supplement or contextualize our initially blind cognitive map. Simulating total immersion at ground level, even if that is disorienting, the game prompts players to actively interpret setting and plot elements which are both familiar and steampunked, and so hermeneutically read the virtual space against shared memory. As such, it mobilizes reader-response theory in line with Hans-Georg Gadamer's hermeneutics (the cyclical and continuous re-interpretation of text based on new and cumulative understanding)[90] and Wolfgang Iser's phenomenological approach (the supplementation of the text's incomplete outline through the reader's own experience and imagination).[91]

The dynamics of reading a text in Iser's understanding – here, the virtual, steampunked city – involves a creative process of establishing connections, filling semantic gaps, and re-evaluating what one encounters against one's own preconceptions.[92] Indeed, as Gadamer posits, 'The anticipation of meaning that governs our understanding of a text is not an act of subjectivity, but proceeds from the commonality that binds us to the tradition', that is an evolving and culturally produced understanding of history.'[93] 'Hermeneutics must start from the position that a person seeking to understand something has a bond to the subject matter that comes into language through the traditionary text and has, or acquires, a connection with the tradition from which the text speaks'.[94] In other words, the hermeneutic act of interpreting and understanding a text, which Gadamer defines as ontologically circular and continually being (re-)formed,[95] takes place against a cultural tradition with which we expect it to cohere, and so mirrors our relationship to the historical tradition itself. In journeying through the steampunk city, readers likewise confront its urban signage with the aim to integrate what they encounter within a culturally determined and potentially evolving horizon of understanding, with the particular and distinguishing feature that readers must here also confront and seek to understand that which is counter-factual, anachronistic, and fantastical. Iser's argument that readers 'must reveal aspects of [themselves] in order to experience a reality which is different from [their] own'[96] therefore not only makes the reading process an imaginative, interactive, and inherently cultural activity, but is also especially, and exceptionally true for steampunk. Moreover, considering Gadamer's dictums that 'All self-knowledge arises from what is historically pregiven' and 'The horizon of the present cannot be formed without the past',[97] this continued re-engagement with the steampunk city during the players' immersed journey through it also holds the potential to impact their understanding of self, even if playfully: Players are invited to imagine alternative horizons of understanding, and as such, alternative parameters for their own cognitive mapping.

How the game puts into play this production of space through the literal journey, without extraneous clues or additional perspectives, becomes clear when avatar Galahad emerges onto a rooftop with a view of a steampunked

Mayfair and London cityscape, with a multitude of towering spires stretching into the distance, neo-Gothic skyscrapers rising up to and above the iconic dome of St Paul's Cathedral, and zeppelins floating in the sky.[98] This London is equally grounded in the creators' research, in which London's architectures, surfaces, and textures were systematically catalogued, and re-imagined through cyberpunk iconography as 'Victorian Blade Runner', creating interesting connections to its sister genre.[99] As it so imports new impulses and connotations through genre-specific signifiers, that iconography is worth a closer look.

Cyberpunk, 2019: Hyper-cities, Urban Futures

'My first city', says William Gibson, 'was Conan Doyle's London [...], a vast, cozy, populous mechanism, a comforting clockwork'.[100] To deem *fin de siècle* London 'cozy' and 'comforting' in its 'assumed orderliness and safety' is certainly the privilege of hindsight, but it is interesting that Gibson should locate his earliest understanding of cities as 'vast, multilayered engines' in the Victorian metropolis, considering that his work would launch the cyberpunk genre and lastingly influence our collective imaginary of urban futures and hyper-cities.[101] After all, whereas H. G. Wells's *When the Sleeper Wakes* (1898–1899) had once envisioned London as the mega-city of the future, after the First World War, this imaginary shifted towards 1920s New York City, then the world's most populous metropolitan area.[102] Conan Doyle himself had in 1914 remarked on the city's scale and 'big future', and in 1927, Fritz Lang's seminal film *Metropolis*, with its towering modernistic hyper-city seemingly anticipating the art deco skyscrapers of Manhattan (the Chrysler Building [1930], Empire State Building [1931], and Rockefeller Center [1939]), came to encapsulate and dominate both utopian and dystopian visions of the future megalopolis.[103] It is with the advent of cyberpunk, most notably through *Neuromancer* (1984) and Ridley Scott's classic film *Blade Runner* (1982), that this imaginary was lastingly transformed for the computer age, and to the point that Gibson, in a 2003 novel, simply used 'Blade Runnered' as a verb.[104] As Stephen Rowley notes:

> *Blade Runner* demands studying because it is has become so entrenched as the definitive screen depiction of the nightmare future city. Its imagery has become the standard visual iconography for the science fiction metropolis: super-tall buildings; poorly-lit streets and alleys; smog; rain; heavy industry belching fire into the sky; neon advertisements; overcrowding; ethnically diverse (that is, non-white) crowds; eclectic punk-inspired costumes and hairstyles; retrofitted buildings of varying architectural styles; scavenged props, and so on.[105]

Since its release, scholars such as Harvey, Jameson, Soja, or Massey have used the film as a reference point in their work on postmodern urbanisms,[106] and thereby enshrined *Blade Runner*'s 2019 Los Angeles as the defining urban imaginary of the future megalopolis. The film actualizes New York's modernist aesthetics in Los Angeles's urban sprawl, and, like cyberpunk at large, fuses markers of the noir genre with science fiction impulses and 1980s consumerism. Our first vision of future L.A. is a horizon-less vastness of light and belching chimneys, hinting at a limitless sprawl and immediately foreclosing the usually ordering perspective of the panoptic view. The camera pans across the pyramidic Tyrell Corporation and delves into a realm of bottomless verticality serving as canvas for huge, digital advertisements, the image of a geisha promoting Coca Cola conflating Orientalism and consumerism among this labyrinth of towering skyscrapers.[107] As Martin Dodge and Rob Kitchin describe:

> In the urban cores, space is at a premium, the cityscape is corporate, highly centralised and extremely dense both structurally and in terms of population. The value of space forces development both upwards and underground, to produce a vertical spectrum of stylised, mirrored, postmodern architecture – a riot of glass and steel.[108]

Below, what Dobraszczyk has described as 'containers of capitalist flow and elitism' characterized by 'hermetic isolation' and a 'visual dominance' that affects all citizens, is a densely populated underbelly defined by a heterogeneous amalgam of neon lights, traffic, street vendors, and small businesses, a retro-futuristic, cluttered, and anarchistic counterpoint to the sleekness above.[109] The city is stratified into extremes, a multi-layered matrix polarized between the rich and wealthy, located in the lofty, neo-modernist spires, and the anarchic sprawl at street level, where the disenfranchised must reclaim any space not yet appropriated and carve out alternative forms of urban life.[110] Far away from the monolithic, isolated towers whose sleek design bleeds into the smog-filled sky and where we may locate a pervasive sense of doom, we find the retrofitted, exposed underpinnings of the city (cables, ventilation units), 'the odd mechanical devices needed to keep human life palatable, counterpoints to a smoothly-operating exterior.'[111] No sleek modernism here, but, in set designer Syd Meade's own words, 'a curious accumulation of detail, a heuristic growth of odds and ends'[112] grounded in a materialistic aesthetic that functions as a heterotopic other to the city above: 'The postmodern aesthetic of *Blade Runner* is the result of recycling, fusion of levels, discontinuous signifiers, explosion of boundaries, and erosion.'[113] Through its visual density, *Blade Runner* finds an effective shorthand for an urban future characterized by a depletion of resources and living space, where overcrowding, social fragmentation, and environmental catastrophe converge into a largely dysfunctional city, constantly on the verge of collapse.[114] As such, it re-configures the vision of Lang's *Metropolis* for the neo-liberal 1980s.

Blade Runner's L.A. is illegible, oblique, and defies all agency. Its cityscape contextualizes characters' choices and movements among an alienating, almost delirious chaos where even flying police cars in their lofty isolation may not attain a panoptic view and remain immersed in a horizon-less mega-city.[115] In *Neuromancer*, in typical cyberpunk manner, global corporations like Tyrell Corp in *Blade Runner*, take the place of nations, their ruthless capitalism exiling the disenfranchised into a life of 'hustling' on the fringes of the city. Tokyo's Chiba City, where Case lives an outlaw life, is 'like a deranged experiment in social Darwinism' and configured through metaphors of material technology, clutter, and waste.[116] The infamous opening line conjures up a sense of synthetics: 'The sky above the port was the color of television, tuned to a dead channel.'[117] In both stories, we find postmodern heterogeneity and an uneasy composite of cultures and styles, extreme stratification into a dominating vertical and boundless horizontal axis, and a world in which incessant over-production and urbanization have overwhelmed and destroyed nature. Cyberpunk's overpowering cityscapes dictate flow and movement in disorienting, constricting, and dominating ways, and only the invisible flows of data in the 'bodiless exultation of cyberspace'[118] seem to provide a liberating experience of free roaming – not unlike game spaces today.

Blade Runner's L.A. is extrapolated from contemporary concerns about Asia's changing role on the global market, unchecked capitalism, pollution, cost of living, social fragmentation, and computer technology's impact on the social and economic fabric. It is also inspired by real urban metropoles: New York City's skyline, L.A.'s urban sprawl, the neon signage of Tokyo, and the density and texture of Hong Kong's Kowloon Walled City.[119] It remains a simulacrum, 'a hyperreal looking for an unattainable reality (a history)' which, beyond the real 2019, has yet to manifest in the West even though cities like Beijing or Shanghai have been likened to *Blade Runner*'s L.A.[120] As recent cyberpunk blockbusters show, the film's visual language is not only as potent as ever, but moving into mainstream culture, as what were once markers of a niche genre have become widely legible in the internet age.[121] *Blade Runner 2049*, the long-awaited sequel to the classic, *Ghost in the Shell*, a Hollywood adaptation of Mamoru Oshii's seminal anime (1995), and the Netflix series *Altered Carbon*, adapted from

Richard Morgan's novel (2002) all premiered in 2017, and are notably indebted to the imagery of the cyberpunk city.[122] *Ghost in the Shell*'s Japanese New Port City had, in the anime version, been modelled on Hong Kong and its counterpart was filmed there. It reads as an augmented, stylish hyper-city of towering skyscrapers and oversized advertisements, now hologram projections in neon colours, of inter-level highways, canals, and a bright, composite night life at street level. *Altered Carbon* re-presents San Francisco as Bay City, an urban jungle of towering spires connected by highways and bridges, petering out in the sky above until only the ultra-rich are left in lofty solitude quite literally above the clouds, while those on the margins live in graffiti-lined containers on the Golden Gate Bridge. These adaptations all reproduce a now-classic aesthetic of the cyberpunk city. *Blade Runner 2049*, directed by Denis Villeneuve and set thirty years later, is rooted in its predecessor's visual language, but also extrapolates from it and so is the only recent production to re-think and develop the cyberpunk aesthetic for the present. It imagines the cyberpunk city walled in against floods and complemented by radioactive deserts, horizon-less junkyards, drab protein farms, and empty wastelands: 'Mother Nature is dead, having lost the war against Capitalism'.[123] Here, the mega-city is characterized not just by clutter, density, and disorientation, but also by its colonizing and exploiting of spaces outside the city in service to it, and by prominent markers of climate catastrophe.

Crucially, cyberpunk hyper-cities extrapolate from and express real urban and social tensions through a dream-like, futuristic imagery. As Stephen Graham posits, 'they offer future allegories to act as a lens to look "back" at the contemporary, highlighting the political and ideological tensions within contemporary life'.[124] As such, they act as imagined heterotopias, counter-spaces to the present in which its concerns are translated into an allegorical shorthand of hyperbole and spatial exaggeration. Urban space itself becomes cyberpunk's primary vehicle of defamiliarization, reflection, and critique as the hyper-city becomes a distorted *doppelgänger* to the present.

Where *Assassin's Creed: Syndicate* offers up the modern Victorian metropolis for play and exploration, the cyberpunk city refuses to yield to the ordering logic of either the detective figure, like Sherlock Holmes, or the fantasy of the free runner or assassin. We may draw our own trajectories through this hyper-city, but we cannot gain a deeper understanding of it. We may, through our journeys, link into the complex matrix of ongoing networks of traffic, trade, or data flows, but the cyberpunk city remains a simulacrum without history and often forecloses meaningful understandings of what we are linking into. However, cyberpunk's visual language acts as a potent narrative environment legible to a wide audience and its mechanism may therefore be employed in constructing other speculative and retro-speculative scenarios, not least in video games.

Texture as Storytelling

Indeed, narrative environments in video games assume special importance in fantastic game spaces without real world, firstspace counterparts, and retro-speculation shapes virtual urban spaces into potent storytelling devices in and of themselves. As Henry Jenkins notes:

> [E]nvironmental storytelling creates the preconditions for an immersive narrative experience in up to four different ways: spatial stories can evoke preexisting narrative associations; they can provide a staging ground on which narrative events are enacted; they may embed narrative information within their mises-en-scène; or they provide resources for emergent narratives.[125]

Popular examples include Rapture, the underwater city of *BioShock* (2007) and *BioShock 2* (2010), the floating city of Columbia from *BioShock Infinite* (2013), and Dunwall from *Dishonored* (2012). Rapture, conceived as a 1940s, Ayn-Rand-ian alternative utopia out of the government's regulating reach, conjures the optimism and aesthetic of 1930s New York City through art deco skyscrapers, neon light, chrome, and glass, conveying its ideology through design. In approaching the game space, the player 'fills in the background narrative through exploration, through observation, and by listening to abandoned audio journals scattered throughout Rapture' – that is, by engaging with its environment.[126] That engagement slowly reveals the failure of Rapture's grandiose project, and markers of abandonment and decay signify a hidden dystopia calling up the 1920s and 1930s' social, political, and economic failures. In its film noir lighting, the game also leverages German Expressionist films such as Lang's *Metropolis* with its towering city and portrait of the 'impact of industrialized, urban modernity on the multitudes who are left behind in a competitive, capital-driven, and machine-driven environment',[127] as well as *Blade Runner*'s cyberpunk atmosphere, especially as a hyper-city collapsed under its own extreme social stratification. The game so references and remixes interconnected, legible aesthetic registers to convey important narrative cues: 'Rapture is therefore not just a world, it's an argument'.[128]

BioShock Infinite also uses its retro-futuristic game space as a narrative environment and extended argument. Its floating city in the sky, Columbia, is characterized by 'extreme architectural pastiche', accumulating a 'veritable cornucopia of late nineteenth-century buildings' to create a 'deliberately nostalgic feel'. With ornate airships floating around it, Columbia is a (deceptively utopian) steampunk vision of 'the memory of America that people think existed but never quite did', and as such another (fantastic) simulacrum of a city of memory.[129] The formation of an alternative society in the clouds also mirrors the cyberpunk trope in which an elite removes itself beyond the reach of the society below. Again, the urban texture, with its memorials, propagandist posters, and palatial architecture, is mobilized as a storytelling device which here conveys an ideological statement, and one which the player's exploration increasingly calls into question. Beneath Columbia's bucolic, utopian aesthetic, the player soon discovers a city saturated by xenophobic nationalism and white supremacy 'modelled on the segregationist past of the United States', and which is nonetheless dependent on the exploitation of a non-white labour force.[130] Here, too, the retro-speculative game space externalizes an interactive and immersive exploration of, and challenge to, (American) history and identity in its utopian visions their political biases.

Whereas the underwater and floating cities also allow the player to explore the city's verticality and layers in unusual ways, *Dishonored* creates its city of Dunwall as a claustrophobic, domineering, and plague-ridden space in which our avatar, royal bodyguard Corvo Attano, is framed for murder and becomes a vengeful assassin. The city is explicitly modelled on nineteenth-century London as a 'world city' with 'a historic past' familiar to European and American audiences, in which different eras can become aesthetically mixed, and inspired by Doré's illustrations, John Atkinson Grimshaw's paintings, and contemporary photographs of the 'London particular'.[131] Dunwall is then infused with aesthetics of Victorian London, such as obscuring fog, textures of brick and metal, or urban canyons, as well as present-day markers of control and regulation, such as barbed wire, gated control zones, guard cabins, spiked iron chains, bells, CCTV, door blockers, and hostile signage. Where *Syndicate* strives to create a cityscape in which the player may circumvent such mechanisms of regulation and curtailment, *Dishonored* incorporates them and finds itself 'clearly inspired by our urban experience in London': 'Everything looks under control'.[132] The effect is one of oppression and claustrophobia, and indeed, the stark perspectives, vertical re-scaling, expressionistic light, and a conceptual design that favours a murky blue night with isolated sources of light also mark Dunwall as a 'Blade Runnered' city, in which the assassin outsider (anti-)hero is not given the freedom to master the city, but must evade rabid plague victims, mechanistically enforced police, and a city-wide conspiracy.

These steampunk game spaces actively engage audiences' collective knowledge and narrative associations, that is their transmedia competencies and shared memory. They craft narrative environments that either enable or foreclose specific actions and movements and so shape the playing experience. Their urban textures, read hermeneutically against both popular memory and the evolving experience of the game space as it unfolds in real time, yield important clues about the game narrative and serve to either reinforce or subvert the ideology presented through urban designs. As such, they not only become vital storytelling devices, but also arguments in and of themselves.

Here Be Lycans

The Order's synthesis of the now imminently readable *Blade Runner* aesthetic likewise crafts an evocative narrative environment through its organization and texture of urban space. Its London is vertically expanded and populated by heavy Gothic-brutalist skyscrapers, mooring towers, lighthouses, and urban canyons, suffused in grey, blue, and black, punctuated by neon lights, purposefully importing *Blade Runner*'s height and scale, its 'dark tones, crowded streets, and oppressive atmosphere'.[133] By re-infusing the Victorian metropolis with the aesthetic markers of the universal nightmare city, the game both recognizes and re-imagines London as the original hyper-city. The aesthetic suggests, in a way that resonates powerfully with established Victorian Gothic and neo-Victorian imaginaries, that this is a city whose architectural stratification mirrors the gap between wealth and poverty, that below its confident grandeur hide not only the clumsy physical urban trappings such as wires, constructions sites, and elevated train tracks, or the barrels, papers, advertisements, and signage we encounter everywhere, but also a shabby underbelly – here, the East End. The cyberpunk visual language re-encodes and highlights what is already true or imagined about the Victorian city, while also hinting at an alternative history we may explore as players of the game. We do this, unlike in *Syndicate*'s episodic and contextualized gameplay, in a linear and immersed way in which city and narrative unfold in tandem.

In the wealthy and palatial Mayfair, avatar Galahad and his fellow knights track escaped 'Bedlamites' and lycans, not as outlaw assassins, but with the authority of the enforcing agent. However, they, too, may access hidden routes and unconventional pathways, showing that, like with Holmes, an extensive knowledge and mastery of the city is vital in supporting their authority. Regent Street, flanked by an elevated train track, and the rich texture of advertisements and signage, and railway bridges visible in the distance create a sense of the multi-layered, scaled-up metropolis of Dickens' imagination. After this episode, the knights return to Westminster Palace, whose medieval splendour houses the round table as well as hidden steampunk laboratories in which Nikola Tesla acts as a version of James Bond's 'Q'. The game so re-designs a well-known London imaginary to suit its steampunk narrative, collaging and re-imagining a variety of Victorian markers for its counterfictional set-up. For example, Charles Darwin's expeditions are funded by the United India Company and Arthur Conan Doyle is a police commissioner.

The Order debates whether to engage with the rebellions rising in the East End, but Galahad's mentor Mallory ultimately leads an expedition to Whitechapel. Like *Anno Dracula* or *Whitechapel Gods*, *The Order* configures the East End as its 'cauldron of resistance' where the margins of society are evocatively concentrated. This 'breeding ground for rebellion', gloomy, ramshackle and decrepit, is 'inspired by many celebrated authors of the time, most importantly Charles Dickens' and his 'almost palpable' descriptions.[134] As such, it mobilizes familiar Victorian and neo-Victorian Gothic stereotypes as a resonant backdrop for gameplay specific to the area. Shoddy, multilevel spaces and a Jago-esque labyrinth of alleyways, staircases, warehouses, and courtyards provide obstacles to evade or engage with during the fight sequences, and unlike in *Syndicate*, the absence of navigational interfaces and X-ray vision simulates an experience of urban guerrilla warfare at ground level. The London Hospital, a visual amalgam of historical and fictional influences assembled to maximum Gothic effect, must be searched, investigated, and interpreted, providing clues about a planned rebel attack on a United India Company airship.

In the next, quintessentially steampunk game sequence, the knights board a United India Company airship to prevent an assassination attempt on the Company's chairman, Lord Hastings, who is also an important politician. What begins with the adventure genre's typical, swashbuckling bravado, then turns to disaster when a bomb detonates and the airship crashes into and sets on fire the Crystal Palace in Hyde Park, killing Mallory. The tonal shift is effectively translated into the disorienting, burning airship wreck and ruined palace, re-shaping the cityscape and the narrative in tandem. Here, failure and catastrophe become part of the narrative itself, and that narrative, like the cityscape itself, becomes unexpectedly disorienting. During a heated debate in Westminster Palace, our avatar Galahad is called to fight a rebel ambush on Westminster Bridge, and the narrative escalates into a new direction: The bridge turns out to be a war zone riddled with multiple guard houses and fences, gates and sandbag stacks, suggesting shoot-outs and civil war in what the audience knows as a palatial London area, heavily regulated, and teeming with tourists, vendors, and traffic. Here, however, empty omnibuses and overturned carriages have turned into debris of past struggles, hinting at a steampunked alternative backstory in which audience expectations are defied, all the more because that backstory remains unexplored and embodied only through the cityscape. The latter's heavy fortifications so close to the heart of London's political power evoke a sense of dominance and anxiety, much as Dunwall's re-scaled environment. Indeed, Galahad interacts with a sentinel airship whose presence hints at domestic surveillance either prompted by the rebellion or as a feature of a police state. So Westminster Bridge not only illustrates how the game's narrative journey links into and is externalized by the steampunked urban texture, but also acts as a symbolic space of transience for Galahad, who chooses to disobey orders and pursue the rebels on a private vendetta to avenge Mallory's death.

Once more, Whitechapel is configured as a rebellious counter-space in keeping with neo-Victorian Ripperature tropes. Here, Galahad meets the rebel leader, Rani Lakshmibai of Jhansi, a key figure and subsequent symbol of resistance during the so-called Indian Mutiny in 1857, and who has stayed alive through the Order's elixir. As such, she has indeed travelled from the margins of Empire to challenge its centre, creating a post-colonial counterpoint to the United India Company. Speaking back to Galahad from a place marginalized through both race and gender, Lakshmibai suggests the Order has been manipulated by that corrupt Company, and takes Galahad to the Company's Blackwell Yards in the docklands through unfinished Underground tunnels. Destabilizing the narrative's seemingly clear boundaries, her words also configure the Company, with its private army of guards and secretive interests on India, as the steampunk version of the ruthless global corporations which operate in cyberpunk narratives. Now relegated from sanctioned agency to the secret byways of the outlaw, Galahad must navigate a different urban texture which, as in cyberpunk narratives, acts as counterpoint to the allegedly sleek and functional city.

The shipyards themselves, integrated evocatively amid a layered London background of cranes, smokestacks, and steam-powered ships, nonetheless call up larger trajectories of travel, trade, and colonial networks, and as such symbolize the British Empire's industrialized imperialism as effectively concentrated in its capital. The setting is both designed to offer new gameplay opportunities and 'impress the players with the influence and power wielded by the United India Company on both London and the rest of the world'.[135] In a warehouse large enough to also reflect on the Company's global reach, Galahad discovers several vampires sleeping in soil-filled crates (a nod towards Stoker's *Dracula*) and destined for 'the New Americas'. Lakshmibai is proven right: The Company exports such monstrous creatures into the colonies, so encoding its colonial affairs and economic interests metaphorically. As in *Anno Dracula*, the vampire may be read as a creature whose predation on others is physical as well as economic and political. Through Lakshmibai's conversion of Galahad to her cause, the game endeavours to critically interrogate the infrastructures and power networks supporting Empire as they are played out in and through the city from a post-colonial perspective.

Galahad, then also moves further from the centre of power when joining the rebels, and is now involved in a conspiracy narrative designed to challenge the dominant ideologies and status quo of the Victorian apparatus. The latter are highlighted, scaled up, and productively defamiliarized through the steampunk aesthetic. Galahad enlists the help of fellow knight Alastair to infiltrate the United India House, the Company's headquarters in Mayfair. Again, the game presents new gameplay opportunities such as sneaking around, climbing across rooftops, zip-lining into courtyards and navigating labyrinthine gardens, coming perhaps closest to what *Syndicate* offers as well. However, unlike *Syndicate*'s atmospheric aesthetic, *The Order* here deploys the *Blade Runner* aesthetic to characterize its setting: The palatial, neo-classical shrine to power identified with London's more prestigious social topography is seen on a hazy, blue-tinted night punctuated by isolated, yellow lights, and so becomes a treacherous, uncertain terrain. The rainy, noir-influenced atmosphere mirrors Galahad's newly ambivalent position and undermines our reading of the cityscape much in the same way as it does in *BioShock* or *Dishonored*. As with the dominant cultural narrative within the game about goodness and order against rebellion (supernatural, social, and post-colonial), the urban environment can no longer be read at face value but must be questioned and interrogated. Indeed, the Victorian *Blade Runner* city's dystopian impulses both complement and foreshadows the game's cynical plot twists.

Again, players interact with the game space to interpret clues, among them Tipu's Tiger, an eighteenth-century music box in the shape of a tiger devouring an East India Company soldier. The automaton, now on display at the Victoria and Albert Museum, symbolizes the complex and violent history of British colonialism in India and provides a connection to Lakshmibai's presence, but as a trophy now owned by the Company, it also turns its subversive potential into a harmless, exotic spectacle.[136] Other clues illustrate the Company's power networks across the Empire, but ultimately, the Company's predatory power is symbolically – and hyper-gothically – concentrated in its chairman, Lord Hastings. Capitalizing on the player's white knowledge of London Gothic, the game reveals he is not only a vampire himself, but the notorious Whitechapel killer Jack the Ripper[137] (who has appeared two years earlier than in real history). Again mobilizing Victorian stereotypes and popular conspiracy theories about slumming aristocrats, the game invokes the vampire's blood lust as a metaphor for social and economic exploitation, powerfully spatialized between a hypocritical and greedy aristocracy and the disenfranchised East End. In Lakshmibai's words, Whitechapel has, quite literally, 'become the country's feeding ground'.[138] The game here follows neo-Victorian 'Ripperature' like *From Hell* and *Anno Dracula* where the Ripper's violence becomes synonymous with colonial violence and a moral corruption which spreads from the centre to the margin, challenging heritage-based imaginaries of the Victorian era as cosy, quaint, or wholesome.[139] Hastings epitomizes a moral, social, and political corruption that seemingly saturates the Victorian world at its very centre and operates from a position of power. Through this (sensational) turn of events, *The Order*'s steampunk London, which initially seemed like an adventure playground, is re-posited as a corrupted Gothic other much as it is in those narratives.

It then only follows that Galahad is betrayed by Alastair, who turns out to be a lycan and frames him as rebel assassin, leading to Galahad's arrest, trial, and sentencing, and the incarceration under Westminster Palace from where our avatar finally escapes through the game's initial flash forward sequence. This time, the player understands that behind this steampunk London's palatial grandeur lurk the corruption and inequality which the neo-Gothic cyberpunk aesthetic has productively foreshadowed. In line with that tension, the game narrative has transitioned from an adventure plot with seemingly clear ideas of 'good' and 'bad', 'them' and 'us', 'heroes' and 'rebels' to cyberpunk's more ambiguous set-up of social underdogs confronting a ruthless company. Rescued by fellow rebel Tesla, Galahad undergoes a metaphorical rebirth as Grayson, no longer a knight.

Moving through the actual underground, that 'dark and invisible' heterotopic counter-space where 'revolutionary ideas' may 'ferment, undisturbed by above-world convention',[140] Grayson fights Alastair as the 'final boss' in the laboratory under the Palace, symbolic of how the Order's identity has been undermined and is threatened with collapse. Victory, when achieved by the player, is rendered profoundly ambivalent by Alastair's defensive claim that lycans, too, only fight for their right to live: 'My kind are no more evil than yours.' Speaking back as the

Othered monster as well as a decorated knight, he so troubles popular Gothic stereotypes. This is also evident in his final speech: 'I have lived too long not to know this day would come. [. . .] I have seen things I am condemned to remember. Civilisations born and destroyed by humanity's incessant greed. The pride of men slaughtering each other in the name of their so-called God . . .' Not least, his speech echoes Roy Batty's 'Tears in rain' monologue in *Blade Runner*, delivered as a death soliloquy: 'I've seen things you people wouldn't believe. Attack ships on fire off the shoulder of Orion. I watched C-beams glitter in the dark near the Tannhäuser Gate. All those moments will be lost in time, like tears in rain. Time to die.'[141]

Batty's status as replicant has, in the world of the film, denied him claims to humanity, yet his final act is saving the protagonist Deckard's life. By philosophizing on the scope and depth of his short existence, his capacity for memory and emotion, and his profoundly human awareness of his own transience, Batty is humanized, as is Alastair. As in cyberpunk's postmodern challenge to self-other or human-technology boundaries, those between human and 'half-breed', outlaw and traitor, here seem to blur, and that blurring likewise calls into question the Order's centuries-long feud, re-framed not as a noble defence of the realm, but instead a genocide perpetrated to shore up power. Alastair so literalizes the metaphoric qualities of the monster as discursive Other in opposition of the status quo because it reveals the monster to be merely another group disenfranchised and persecuted by the dominant order – a meta-narrative that echoes the unequal power dynamic both within the city (Westminster vs East End) and the world at large (London vs British Empire). In essential noir tradition, Grayson's discovery of the truth does not translate into victory: To quite literally keep (the) Order, he is sacrificed to the integrity of the organization and excised in disgrace, keeping his potentially incendiary knowledge secret and outlawed. In the game's final sequence, Grayson looks over the city once more, this time across the river over to Westminster, poised like a classic lone vigilante, while Tesla, over the communicator, tells us martial law has been declared. This time, London is transformed into an apocalyptic, starkly lit nightmare city. As the only times Grayson and with him, the player, attain a panoramic, semi-panoptic view of London, these parallel motifs gain potency as inversions of one another: Confidence and agency have become resistance and uncertainty. As such, the game mobilizes the genre markers and aesthetic tension between the neo-Victorian city and the cyberpunk register to re-investigate a received Victorian identity from a post-colonial perspective. Its narrative and physical journey through London enact a cynical contestation of the story-world's status quo as hypocritical and exploitative, prompting players to consider: Whom does it protect?

Where in *Syndicate*, the player takes over London piece by piece, and moves from margin to centre in a clandestine but triumphal conquest of a monolithic, corrupt enemy, *The Order* enacts a movement in the opposite direction. Players here ally with marginalized rebel identities in a conspiracy plot set amidst a civil war, and without navigational clues or panoptic context. Indeed, the game's ground-level immersion demands a continuous hermeneutic re-evaluation of the clues and cityscapes it presents, mobilizing the steampunk city as an intrinsic storytelling device. Through its heterotopic counter-space, steampunk London, it invites players to explore and re-examine not only the status quo presented in the game, but their own shared memories and assumptions about the Victorian imaginary, especially regarding its networks of power across London and the Empire. Using popular, simple, and often stereotypic, but also widely accessible genre markers and neo-Victorian ideas, the game literalizes steampunk's thought experiment of playfully re-evaluating the Victorian past into an immersive and interactive spatial simulation and so endeavours to enact steampunk itself as a meta-historical hermeneutic circle, constantly made and re-made in dialogue with the present like urban space itself.

Conclusion: The Hermeneutics of Steampunk

Marco Polo, in Calvino's *Invisible Cities*, describes Zaira, the city of memory so evocatively that the passage is worth quoting at length:

> In vain, great-hearted Kublai, shall I attempt to describe Zaira, city of high bastions. I could tell you how many steps make up the streets rising like stairways, and the degree of the arcades' curves, and what kind of zinc scales cover the roofs; but I already know this would be the same as telling you nothing. The city does not consist of this, but of relationships between the measurements of its space and the events of its past: the height of a lamppost and the distance from the ground of a hanged usurper's swaying feet; the line strung from the lamppost to the railing opposite and the festoons that decorate the course of the queen's nuptial procession; the height of that railing and the leap of the adulterer who climbed over it at dawn; the tilt of a guttering and a cat's progress along it as he slips into the same window; the firing range of a gunboat which has suddenly appeared beyond the cape and the bomb that destroys the guttering; the rips in the fish net and the three old men seated on the dock mending nets and telling

each other for the hundredth time the Story of the gun-boat of the usurper, who some say was the queen's illegitimate son, abandoned in his swaddling clothes there on the dock. As this wave from memories flows in, the city soaks it up like a sponge and expands.

A description of Zaira as it is today should contain all Zaira's past. The city, however, does not tell its past, but contains it like the lines of a hand, written in the corners of the streets, the gratings of the windows, the banisters of the steps, the antennae of the lightning rods, the poles of the Bags, every segment marked in turn with scratches, indentations, scrolls.[142]

Much of Polo's argument reflects this chapter's central concerns, namely that meticulous mapping cannot capture what a city truly is, especially Victorian London as a global metropolis which underwent significant changes throughout the nineteenth century. More than that, as Dickens attests through his alertness to the limits of mapping and his immersive portrayals of the multi-layered metropolis, the city arises out of a combination of urban space or firstspace ('the measurements of its space') and the ongoing, accumulating, and interlinking narratives which play out in it ('the events of its past'): 'the height of that railing and the leap of the adulterer who climbed over it at dawn'. Both Calvino and Dickens enact Massey's theory of space as 'dynamic simultaneity' and the product of a multitude of lingering histories, and so illustrate how Soja's concepts of firstspace and secondspace converge into a thirdspace that contains both but also much more. Conan Doyle's immortal detective Sherlock Holmes realizes Massey's notion of intersecting trajectories and ongoing narratives through his connectedness to the multitude of intersecting processes across London. His complete knowledge of social, economic, and political networks and the geography of London enable him to penetrate the chaos of the metropolis with ordering logic even if, and especially when, any and all possible combinations of events occur. Holmes has become emblematic of the Victorian city he so thoroughly understands, but he is also constituted by it and the way London's own history is 'written in the corners of the streets' during that age.

Video games such as *Assassin's Creed: Syndicate* mobilize and actualize this complex conjunction of the measurements of space and the history written into it by translating transmitted Victorian imaginaries into a virtual simulacrum. *Syndicate* provides a simulation of a collectively imagined but also re-configured memory city with which we, as players, may engage through participation. It re-imagines Victorian London as a historical playground in which we roam freely as assassin-outlaws and underdog heroes, setting right the wrongs of the past as exemplified in the evil industrial magnate Starrick. This gameplay depends on a simplified and even patronizing approach to the socio-economic complexities of that past in favour of an alternative, empowering urban experience in which clear choices can be made and lead to triumph. As Eckart Voigts outlines:

> It is convenient that the stereotyped Victorian characters are locked away safely in the past. The advantage of a historical hermeneutics of cultures are clear: it is less painful to attack, and easier to understand, the patriarchal orthodoxies of the Victorians than it is to achieve understanding for or to pass judgement on existing contemporary moral fundamentalisms. In reverse, supporting the plight of Victorian subcultures pitted against the repressive patriarchal regime of Victorianism is convenient as it is morally and politically unambiguous. The distant Victorian mainstream becomes a hetero-stereotype—the moral target of pre-liberation Western culture—and Victorian subcultures may reinforce the auto-stereotype—what it must have been like for us (i.e., sexually liberated, open-minded Westerners) to live furtively under the regime of Victorian repression.[143]

Whereas Voigts is here considering the portrayal of homosexuality in neo-Victorian novels, his argument also applies to the neo-Victorian tendency to re-position the nineteenth century as a Gothic or even a 'neo-Oriental other',[144] and so also to *Syndicate*'s simplistic conceptualization of its antagonists. Nonetheless, it is telling that this mainstream blockbuster games' alluring adventurous gameplay of 'playing the past' is also synonymous with the promise of exerting agency and righting wrongs, enacting liberation from repressive patriarchal and industrial orthodoxies. This narrative is effectively enhanced by and translated into our mastery of the cityscape by proxy, an experience we cannot attain outside the virtual space because both the Victorian past and the present-day city are equally inaccessible to us in such a way.

As such, the Victorian city is re-positioned as a space where the complexities of the present are suspended and, within a game space teeming with real, identifiable dangers, we may, quite literally, leap into action. Mobilizing the adventure genre's catalogue of gallantry and derring-do in exotic or romantic locales, here, the Victorian age itself becomes an exciting, exotic, and romantic past whose perceived failures may be easily identified, critiqued, and even remedied in a morally and politically unambiguous way. To this end, *Syndicate* may fruitfully mobilize a widely shared Victorian imaginary and set it up as a historical playground to be conquered.

The Order 1886, while following the same neo-Victorian formula of re-positing the Victorian status quo as a corrupt antagonist, renders such a triumph over the traumas of the past more difficult, not least because Grayson, for all his adventures in a visually interesting urban setting, fails to achieve larger systemic changes and ends up as an outlaw with insight, but little agency. Wrongs of the past, here identified as capitalist exploitation of a working class that is actually fed on by the elite, and colonialist greed, are intertwined and, although embodied by the United India Company, also saturate and corrupt government and the Order itself, making all power structures complicit. The game seeks to enact a more complex understanding that these wrongs, which still have tangible repercussions in the present, cannot easily be recognized, defeated, or set right, and so performs the widely shared steampunk credo that 'history has sharp edges': 'The fact is that steampunk's romance with the past can be dangerous. It's altogether too easy to become an unwitting accomplice in the crimes of the past.'[145] For our proxy Grayson (formerly Galahad), this is indeed the case, and ultimately his and our only agency lies in choosing to ally ourselves with those outlawed, marginalized, and rebellious. Where *Syndicate* offers us the outlaw assassin as a fantasy of freedom and mastery, here it eventually exiles Grayson from a city set up to disintegrate under martial law. Gothic monsters, while initially Othered, are humanized and our assumptions called into question. This is not a neo-Victorian past that we may master, but instead one whose dominant narratives must be interrogated, challenged, and sometimes even subverted. The game thereby enacts what James Carrot here flippantly outlines in his appeal to *Steampunk Magazine* readers to 'punk responsibly':

> You just can't dig into the nineteenth century without butting up against empire in one form or another. Imperialism is some seriously dangerous shit. Not just 'back then' but right the hell now. Handle with care. It ain't enough to say 'we want to keep the good and toss the bad'. History doesn't work that way. You can't strain the East India Company out of your cup of tea.[146]

Unlike in *Syndicate*, where we often remain separate from and above city and past alike, surgically removing whoever stands in the way of the larger meta-narrative we aim to construct, in *The Order* we remain immersed at ground level, and the disorientation of that perspective also enacts how difficult it is to attain a full understanding for or to judge the complexities of the Victorian past, even if the United India Company's corrupting influence is evident and tangible in narrative and cityscape alike. Its social failures are effectively encoded in and foreshadowed through, cyberpunk's aesthetic register, in which steep urban canyons, vanishing horizons, and brutalist neo-Gothic skyscrapers leverage a sense of social stratification, stark capitalism, and defeatism to create a labyrinthine hyper-city that defies mastery, both physically and historically. Like

Rapture or Columbia in *BioShock* and Dunwall in *Dishonored*, the retro-speculative aesthetic configures an urban narrative environment that is both legible because it imports genre markers, and unfamiliar because it adds its own retro-speculative twists. In these fantastical heterotopias, history, cityscape, technology, and society may be 'punked' and so re-evaluated through our interaction with and interrogation of the virtual game space.

In the same vein, *The Order*'s London literalizes steampunk's dialogue with the past into a cityscape in which the legacies of the past are remixed with speculations about the future. Our engagement with the narrative environment undermines and exposes the ideologies presented through its urban textures, which demand to be re-evaluated hermeneutically as both narrative and physical journey progress. Game spaces literalize the steampunk aesthetic and the narratives imagined within it into a virtual simulation in which meta-narratives, hermeneutic understanding, and the nature of steampunk itself are produced and enacted together through movement in space. They provide a heterotopic lens through which to form new and exciting relationships with urban space and in so doing playfully re-evaluate our relationships with real space and real history. Like steampunk itself, video games may, as Konrad Wojnowski notes, 'allow players to better understand the notion of agency in human history and to root out a deterministic image of the past'[147]: Both invite a playful re-experience of the past that ultimately invites us to imagine the same agency in our present and future.

Notes

1. Italo Calvino, *Invisible Cities*, translated by William Weaver (London: Harcourt Brace & Company, 1972), p. 44.
2. Michel Foucault, 'Of Other Spaces', p. 3.
3. Foucault, p. 8.
4. Edward Soja, *Thirdspace: Journeys to Los Angeles and Other Real-And-Imagined Places* (Oxford: Blackwell Publishing, 1996), p. 2.
5. Soja, *Thirdspace*, p. 29.
6. Soja, *Thirdspace*, p. 10.
7. Soja, *Thirdspace*, p. 56–57, original emphasis.
8. Espen Aarseth, 'Allegories of Space. The Question of Spatiality in Computer Games', in *Space Time Play. Computer Games, Architecture, and Urbanism: the Next Level*, ed. by Friedrich von Borries, Steffen P. Walz, and Matthias Böttger (Berlin: Birkhäuser Verlag, 2007), pp. 44–47, p. 44.

9   George Carstocea, 'Uchronias, Alternate Histories, and Counterfactuals', in *The Routledge Companion to Imaginary Worlds,* ed. by Mark J. P. Wolf (New York: Routledge, 2017), pp. 184–191, p. 189.
10 Jean Baudrillard, *Simulations,* trans. by Paul Foss, Paul Batton and Philip Beitchman (Los Angeles: Semiotext(e), 1983).
11 Edward Soja, *Postmetropolis. Critical Studies of Cities and Regions* (Oxford: Blackwell Publishers, 2000).
12 Estelle Murail and Sara Thornton, 'Dickensian Counter-Mapping, Overlaying, and Troping: Producing the Virtual City', in *Dickens and the Virtual City: Urban Perception and the Production of Social Space,* ed. by Estelle Murail and Sara Thornton (London: Palgrave Macmillan, 2017), pp. 3–34, p. 5.
13 Andrew Webster, 'Building a better Paris in Assassin's Creed Unity. Historical accuracy meets game design', *The Verge,* 17 April 2019, originally published 31 October 2014, https://www.theverge.com/2014/10/31/7132587/assassins-creed-unity-paris (accessed 15 February 2020).
14 Soja, *Thirdspace,* p. 54.
15 Soja, *Thirdspace,* p. 56–57.
16 *Neuromancer* (1982), *Mona Lisa Overdrive* (1986), *Count Zero* (1988).
17 Gibson, *Neuromancer,* p. 59
18 Gibson, *Neuromancer,* p. 59.
19 Soja, *Postmetroplis,* p. 336.
20 Soja, *Postmetroplis,* p. 324
21 Charles Dickens, *Nicholas Nickleby* ed. by Michael Slater (London: Penguin, 1986 [1838–39]), p. 488–489.
22 Doreen Massey, *For Space* (London: SAGE Publications, 2005), p. 107, original emphasis.
23 Massey, p. 118.
24 Massey, p. 119.
25 Ibid., p. 119. The original passage can be found in George Orwell's *The Road to Wigan Pier* (1937), Penguin edition from 1989, p. 15.
26 Massey, p. 119.
27 Murail and Thornton, 'Counter-Mapping', p. 5.
28 The idea of the 'Dickensian' is a vision of London tinted with the quaint and shabby, the eccentric and even grotesque, the sentimental and the dismal, a vision of crooked angles and clutter. In his writing, places are often imbued with a certain personality: Houses stare, windows frown, and doorways leer, and the 'meagre' or 'doleful' houses seem almost like living, somewhat strange creatures. This Dickensian mode harmonizes well with Mayhew's urban ethnography which I have discussed in Chapter One, especially his cataloguing of the shabby and genteel.
29 Dickens, Charles, *The Old Curiosity Shop* (Ware: Wordsworth Editions Limited, 2001 [1840]), p. 544.

30 Lynda Nead, *Victorian Babylon. People, Streets and Images in Nineteenth-Century London* (New Haven & London: Yale University Press, 2000), p. 4, original emphasis.
31 Nead, p. 13.
32 Massey, p. 107.
33 Nead, p. 26.
34 Charles Dickens, *Dombey and Son* (London: Penguin, 1970 [1848]), pp. 120–121.
35 Gibson and Sterling, p. 131.
36 David Cannadine, 'A case of [Mistaken?] Identity', in *Sherlock Holmes: The Man Who Never Lived and Will Never Die*, ed. by Alex Werner (London: Penguin Random House, 2014), pp. 13–55, p. 16.
37 Sir Arthur Conan Doyle, 'The Sign of Four', in *The Penguin Complete Sherlock Holmes* (London: Penguin, 2009 [1887]), pp. 15–87, p. 99.
38 Sir Arthur Conan Doyle, 'The Red-Headed League', in *The Penguin Complete Sherlock Holmes* (London: Penguin, 2009 [1892]), pp. 176–189, p. 185.
39 Cannadine, pp. 17–18.
40 Sir Arthur Conan Doyle, 'A Study in Scarlet', in *The Penguin Complete Sherlock Holmes* (London: Penguin, 2009 [1887]), pp. 15–87, p. 15.
41 Cannadine, p. 37.
42 Sir Arthur Conan Doyle, 'The Adventure of the Blue Carbuncle', in *The Penguin Complete Sherlock Holmes* (London: Penguin, 2009 [1892]), pp. 224–256, p. 245.
43 Doyle, 'The Blue Carbuncle', p. 245.
44 Sir Arthur Conan Doyle, 'The Resident Patient', in *The Penguin Complete Sherlock Holmes* (London: Penguin, 2009 [1894]), pp. 422–434, p. 423.
45 Cannadine, p. 46.
46 Cannadine, pp. 47–48.
47 Georg Simmel, 'The Metropolis and Mental Life', in *The Sociology of Georg Simmel*, ed. by K.H. Wolff (Glencoe, IL: Free Press, 1950 [1903]), pp. 409–426.
48 Indeed, games in the *Assassin's Creed* series have taken place in increasingly modern settings, such as the crusades, Renaissance Italy, or the French Revolution. After *Syndicate*, the game's chosen eras returned to ancient Egypt, Greece, and the Vikings era, suggesting that the nineteenth century is the last era that can be productively imagined as playfully adventurous or exciting to explore.
49 Ubisoft, *Assassin's Creed: Syndicate* (2015), dir. by Marc-Alexis Côté, Scott Phillips, and Wesley Pincombe, PlayStation 4, Ubisoft.
50 Holly Nielsen, 'Reductive, superficial, beautiful – a historian's view of Assassin's Creed: Syndicate', *The Guardian*, 9 December 2015, https://www.theguardian.com/technology/2015/dec/09/assassins-creed-syndicate-historian-ubisoft (accessed 15 February 2020).
51 Péter Kristóf Makai, 'Video Games as Objects and Vehicles of Nostalgia' *Humanities*, 7, 123 (2018), 1–14, p. 3.

52 Eckart Voigts-Virchow, 'In-yer-Victorian-face: A Subcultural Hermeneutics of Neo-Victorianism', *Lit: Literature Interpretation Theory*, 20 (2009), 108–125, p. 122.
53 Aarseth, p. 47.
54 Baudrillard, p. 7.
55 Webster, n.p.; Flanders has written *The Victorian House* (2003) and *The Victorian City* (2012,), among others.
56 Makai, p. 3, p. 11.
57 Pat Hardy, 'The Art of Sherlock Holmes', in *Sherlock Holmes: The Man Who Never Lived and Will Never Die*, ed. by Alex Werner (London: Penguin Random House, 2014), pp. 135–157, p. 135.
58 Paul Davies, *The Art of Assassin's Creed: Syndicate.* (London: Titan Books, 2015), p. 92.
59 Hardy, p. 156.
60 Hardy, p. 155.
61 Aarseth, p. 44.
62 Webster, n.p.
63 Webster, n.p.
64 Aarseth, p. 47.
65 Ulrich Götz, 'Load and Support. Architectural Realism in Video Games', in *Space Time Play. Computer Games, Architecture, and Urbanism: the Next Level*, ed. by Friedrich von Borries, Steffen P. Walz, and Matthias Böttger (Berlin: Birkhäuser Verlag, 2007), pp. 134–137, p. 135.
66 Mark J.P. Wolf, *Building Imaginary Worlds: The Theory and History of Subcreation* (London: Routledge, 2014), p. 29.
67 Wolf, p. 69.
68 Wolf, p. 70.
69 Götz, p. 135.
70 Makai, p. 11. Consider *The Three Musketeers* (1844), R.L. Stevenson's *Treasure Island* (1882), Anthony Hope's *The Prisoner of Zenda* (1894) and Emma Orczy's *The Scarlet Pimpernel* (1905), as well as the fiction of Rider Haggard and G.A. Henty.
71 Maria Daskalaki, Alexandra Starab and Miguel Imasa, 'The "Parkour Organisation": inhabitation of corporate spaces', *Culture and Organization*, 14:1 (2008), 49–64, p. 51.
72 Lieven Ameel and Sirpa Tani, 'Parkour: creating loose spaces? *Geografiska Annaler: Series B, Human Geography* 94 :1 (2012) 17–30, p. 18.
73 Ameel and Tani, p.18.
74 Daskalaki et al, p. 57.
75 Michael Atkinson, 'Parkour, anarcho-environmentalism, and poiesis', *Journal of Sport and Social Issues* 33: 2 (2009), 169–194, p. 175.
76 Ameel and Tani, p. 18.

77 Paula Geyh, 'Urban free flow: a poetics of parkour', *M/C Journal. A Journal of Media and Culture* 9: 3 (2006), n.p.
78 devinsupertramp, *Assassin's Creed Syndicate Meets Parkour in Real Life!* Video, YouTube, posted by Devin Graham, 7 July 2015, https://www.youtube.com/watch?v=HFRscoOkkb8 (accessed 15 February 2020).
79 TEAMSUPERTRAMP, *Behind The Scenes – Assassin's Creed Syndicate Meets Parkour in Real Life*, Video, YouTube, posted by Devin Graham, 6 July 2015, https://www.youtube.com/watch?v=c2dlOR4CdR4 (accessed 15 February 2020).
80 Ameel and Tani, p. 18.
81 Davies, p. 183.
82 Davies, p. 183.
83 Zach Whalen and Laurie N. Taylor, *Playing the Past: History and Nostalgia in Video Games* (Nashville: Vanderbilt University Press, 2008), p. 27.
84 Konrad Wojnowksi, 'Simulational Realism – Playing as Trying to Remember', *Art History & Criticism*, 14: 1 (2018), 86–98, p. 95.
85 Kirk Ellis and Ru Weerasuriya, *The Blackwater Archives. The Art of The Order: 1886* (San Francisco: Bluecanvas, Inc. 2015), p. 6.
86 For a concurrent reading of the game's Gothic city, see: Michael Fuchs, '"Things Are Not as They Seem": Colonialism, Capitalism and Neo-Victorian London in The Order: 1886', in *The New Urban Gothic. Global Gothic in the Age of the Anthropocene*, ed. by Holly-Gale Millette and Ruth Heholt (London: Palgrave Macmillan, 2020), pp. 41–56.
87 *Blackwater Archives*, p. 133.
88 *Blackwater Archives*, p. 133.
89 *Blackwater Archives*, p. 8.
90 Hans-Georg Gadamer, *Truth and Method* (Wahrheit und Methode), (New York: Continuum, 1989 [1960]).
91 Iser, Wolfgang, *The Implied Reader: Patterns of Communication in Prose Fiction from Bunyan to Beckett* (Baltimore: Johns Hopkins University Press, 1972). Wolfgang Iser, 'The Rudiments of a Theory of Aesthetic Response', in *The Act of Reading: A Theory of Aesthetic Response* (Baltimore: Johns Hopkins University Press, 1978).
92 Iser, *The Implied Reader*, pp. 192–193.
93 Gadamer, *Truth and Method*, pp. 292–293.
94 Gadamer, *Truth and Method*, p. 295.
95 Gadamer, *Truth and Method*, pp. 294, 301, 305.
96 Iser, *The Implied Reader*: 194.
97 Gadamer, *Truth and Method*, pp. 301, 305.
98 Ready At Dawn, *The Order 1886* (2015), developed by Ru Weerasuriya, PlayStation 4, Sony Computer Entertainment.
99 *Blackwater Archives*, p. 133, 139.

100 William Gibson, 'Life in the Meta City', *Scientific American*, posted September 2011, https://www.scientificamerican.com/article/life-in-a-meta-city/?redirect=1 (accessed 7 March 2020).
101 *Scientific American*, n. p.
102 Paul Dobraszczyk, *Future Cities: Architecture and the Imagination* (London: Reaktion Books, 2019), p. 106.
103 Cannadine, p. 51.
104 William Gibson, *Pattern Recognition* (London: Penguin Random House, 2003), p. 146; Will Brooker, 'Introduction: 2019 Vision', in *The Blade Runner Experience. The Legacy of a Science Fiction Classic*, ed. by Will Brooker (London & New York: Wallflower Press, 2005), pp. 13–24, p. 13.
105 Stephen Rowley, 'False LA: Blade Runner and the Nightmare City' in *The Blade Runner Experience. The Legacy of a Science Fiction Classic*, ed. by Will Brooker (London & New York: Wallflower Press, 2005), pp. 203–212, p. 250.
106 Brooker, p. 160.
107 Dobraszczyk notes how, when skyscrapers were first introduced, they were likened in the public imagination to the buildings of ancient civilizations, for example Egypt, Mesopotamia; p. 110. Notably, Tyrell Corp is a pyramid, and *The Difference Engine* also configures the Statistics Bureau as one.; Timothy Yu, 'Oriental Cities, Postmodern Futures: "Naked Lunch, Blade Runner", and "Neuromancer"', MELUS, 33:4 (2008), 45–71.
108 Martin Dodge and Rob Kitchin, *Mapping Cyberspace* (London: Routledge, 2017), p. 195.
109 Dobraszczyk, pp. 106–107.
110 Paul M. Sammon, *Future Noir: The Making of Blade Runner* (New York: HarperCollins, 2017 [1996]).
111 Aaron Barlow, 'Reel Toads and Imaginary Cities: Philip K. Dick, *Blade Runner*, and the Contemporary Science Fiction Movie', in *The Blade Runner Experience. The Legacy of a Science Fiction Classic*, ed. by Will Brooker (London & New York: Wallflower Press, 2005), pp. 63–82, p. 68.
112 Sammon, p. 89.
113 Giuliana Bruno, 'Ramble City: Postmodernism and "Blade Runner"', *October*, 41 (1987) pp. 61–74, p. 6.
114 Rowley, p. 252.
115 Barlow, p. 67.
116 Gibson, *Neuromancer*, p. 8.
117 Gibson, *Neuromancer*, p. 3.
118 Gibson, *Neuromancer*, p. 6.
119 Kowloon Walled City (1956–1993) was a notoriously densely populated and largely self-governed settlement in Hong Kong, housing between 35,000 and 50,000 people

on a 6.4 acre site; Dobraszczyk, p. 175.; Ian Lambot, 'Self-Build and Change: Kowloon Walled City, Hong Kong', *Architectural Design*, 87:5 (2017), 122–129. Ian Lambot and Greg Girard, *City of Darkness: Life in Kowloon Walled City* (Pewsey: Watermark Publications, 1993); Takayuki Tatsumi, 'Transpacific Cyberpunk: Transgeneric Interactions between Prose, Cinema, and Manga', *Arts*, 7:9 (2018), n.p.

120 Barlow, p. 68; Dobraszczyk reflects on how, in 2013, an image of an advertisement projected onto the smog-shrouded facade of a skyscraper in Beijing prompted international readings and marketing of the city as real life Blade Runner; Dobraszczyk, p. 7, Barlow, p. 68, Stephen Graham, 'Vertical Noir' *City*, 20:3 (2016), 389–406, p. 395.

121 *Blade Runner* failed at the box office, but a later Director's Cut version gathered a fan following.

122 Notably the 2020 video game and franchise, *Cyberpunk 2077* functions as an immersive collage of popularized cyberpunk tropes and styles, and its success testifies to the genre's wide reach and readability.

123 Tanya Lapointe and Denis Villeneuve, *The Art and Soul of Blade Runner 2049* (London: Titan Books, 2017), p. 45.

124 Graham, 'Vertical Noir', p. 395.

125 Henry Jenkins, 'Narrative Spaces', in *Space Time Play. Computer Games, Architecture, and Urbanism: the Next Level,* ed. by Friedrich von Borries, Steffen P. Walz, and Matthias Böttger (Berlin: Birkhäuser Verlag, 2007) pp. 56–60, p. 57.

126 Carstocea, p. 190.

127 Carstocea, p. 190.

128 Carstocea, p. 190.

129 Dobraszczyk, p. 83.

130 Rick Elmore, '"The bindings are there as a safeguard": Sovereignty and Political Decisions in *BioShock Infinite*', in *BioShock and Philosophy: Irrational Game, Rational Book*, ed. by Luke Cuddy (Oxford: Wiley Blackwell, 2015) pp. 97–105, pp. 100–101.

131 GDC, *World of Dishonoured: Raising Dunwall*, Video, YouTube, posted 22 February 2016, https://www.youtube.com/watch?v=LOQDbSvpFtY (accessed 15 February 2020).

132 GDC, 00:14:19.

133 *Blackwater Archives,* p. 139.

134 *Blackwater Archives*, p. 191, 192.

135 *Blackwater Archives*, p. 231, 244.

136 See Marie-Luise Kohlke 'Tipoo's Tiger on the Loose: Neo-Victorian Witness-Bearing and the Trauma of the Indian Mutiny', in *Neo-Victorian Tropes of Trauma: The Politics of Bearing After-Witness to Nineteenth-Century Suffering*, ed. by Marie-Luise Kohlke and Christian Gutleben (Amsterdam: Brill Rodopi 2010) pp. 367–398.

137 Longplay, 4:22:40.
138 Longplay, 3:33:06.
139 For more on neo-Victorian Gothic and the Ripper, see Ho, Mitchell, Flint, Kohlke.
140 Dobraszczyk, p. 141, 159.
141 *Blade Runner*, Final Cut, dir. by Ridley Scott, DVD (Los Angeles: Warner Brothers Entertainments, 2007 [1984]), 1:42:17–1:43:10.
142 Calvino, p. 10–11.
143 Eckart Voigts-Virchow, 'Hermeneutics', p. 113.
144 Marie-Luise Kohlke, 'Sexsation and the Neo-Victorian Novel: Orientalising the Nineteenth Century in Contemporary Fiction', in *Negotiating Sexual Idioms: Image, Text, Performance*, ed. by Marie-Luise Kohlke and Luisa Orza (Amsterdam: Brill Rodopi, 2008), pp. 53–79.
145 Carrott and Johnson, *Vintage Tomorrows*, p. 189.
146 Carrott, 'Punking the Past', p. 71.
147 Konrad Wojnowksi, 'Simulational Realism', p. 95.

4

Re-claiming the Retrofuture: Feminism and Gender in Fin de Siècle and Steampunk London

Introduction: The Woman in the Crowd

Steampunk spaces provide a theatre in and through which our collective memory of the Victorian age may be playfully re-evaluated in either comfortably stereotypical, or innovatively new ways. By re-routing present-day topics and concerns not just through a perceived Victorian past but also a retro-speculative lens, steampunk may make visible the ideological, social, and cultural undercurrents that continue to inform our present in new ways and contribute to ongoing debates. This last – and longest – chapter seeks to gain a deeper understanding of how these identity politics play out in steampunk, and why their radical potential sometimes falls flat. Steampunk, as previous chapters have shown, often identifies social failures such as economic disenfranchisement, environmental catastrophe, racism, and colonialism in the Victorian era and city with varying degrees of insight, but can it offer alternatives? This I interrogate through the lens of gender, particularly notions of feminism, femininity, and queerness.

In his examination of steampunk's 'Useful Troublemakers', Mike Perschon concludes that the female protagonists of Cherie Priest's and Gail Carriger's novels are 'amplified expressions of subtler ideas' about the Victorian New Woman: 'The steampunk New Woman, however, is not the New Woman as she was imagined in the nineteenth century, or even re-imagined by neo-Victorian writers in the twentieth and twenty-first centuries: she has far more agency than those women and is given the option to have her proverbial cake and eat it too'.[1] Claire Nally, however, claims that Carriger's heroine merely enacts a post-feminism 'which seeks to articulate choice and lifestyle as part of an emancipating agenda, whilst at the same time paradoxically presenting some very conservative visions of what it is to be a woman', and does 'very little to challenge the status quo'.² Already, scholarly assessments of the same texts reveal a complex and evolving understanding of gender and femininity. What is at stake in the perceived 'success' of feminist liberation? How might the New Woman or post-feminist theory figure in steampunk's ability to articulate gender in progressive, meaningful, and challenging ways? What does the way in which we re-imagine Victorian gender say about the ideological undercurrents that underlie this endeavour in the present? And, of course: What role does London play, both as a real setting and an urban imaginary, in such articulations and interrogations of gender?

In the nineteenth-century city, the modern urban experience was epitomized by Baudelaire's flâneur. Whereas Edgar Allen Poe's *Man in the Crowd* (1840) had already lost himself as idling observer in the bustle of London, it is usually with Baudelaire's *Painter of Modern Life* (1863) that both the seminal idea of 'modernity' and the flâneur are identified:

> The crowd is his element, as the air is that of birds and water of fishes. His passion and his profession are to become one flesh with the crowd. For the perfect flâneur, for the passionate spectator, it is an immense joy to set up house in the heart of the multitude, amid the ebb and flow of movement, in the midst of the fugitive and the infinite. To be away from home and yet to feel oneself everywhere at home; to see the world, to be at the centre of the world, and yet to remain hidden from the world—impartial natures which the tongue can but clumsily define. The spectator is a prince who everywhere rejoices in his incognito. The lover of life makes the whole world his family, just like the lover of the fair sex who builds up his family from all the beautiful women that he has ever found, or that are or are not—to be found; or the lover of pictures who lives in a magical society of dreams painted on canvas. Thus the lover of universal life enters into the crowd as though it were an immense reservoir of electrical energy. Or we might liken him to a mirror as vast as the crowd itself; or to a kaleidoscope gifted with consciousness, responding to each one of its movements and reproducing the multiplicity of life and the flickering grace of all the elements of life.³

Modernity, a concept with whose coinage Baudelaire is credited, is born in Haussmann's Paris with its boulevards, electric lights, and department stores. It is the exhilarating experience of the fleetingness, the anonymity, and the increasing pace of the metropolis. A phenomenon closely tied to the urban experience of large cities, modernity is most prominently connected to nineteenth-century Paris, London, and Berlin, inspiring new explorations of artistic expression. The flâneur figure, however, was crystallized into a literary concept by Walter Benjamin much later in 1930s Berlin and Paris, when the new century demanded its own re-conceptualization of modernity as modernism. Against the background of Simmel's 1903 conceptualization of the urban habitus, the flâneur became 'the individual sovereign of the order of things who, as the poet or as the artist, is able to transform faces and things so that for him they have only that meaning which he attributes to them. He therefore treats the objects of the city with a somewhat detached attitude.'[4] For him, 'metropolitan spaces are the landscape of art and existence [...] driven out of the private and into the public by his own search for meaning',[5] observing the transitoriness of modern life as connoisseur and detached consumer of spectacle. Part voyeur, part detective, he is concerned with traces in the urban crowd, his '[c]riminological sagacity coupled with the pleasant nonchalance'.[6]

As a leisurely observer and artistic consciousness blending seamlessly into the crowd, fantasizing idly or passionately about amorous encounters with strangers like Baudelaire's speaker in 'A une Passante', the flâneur is a gendered figure. Baudelaire's poem portrays modernity as a chance encounter with an unknown woman in the anonymous crowd and therefore locates it firmly in an urban setting. Though they exchange no more than a brief look, the speaker has a short but intense experience of love, perhaps infatuation, before she is swept away by the currents of the city. The poem is most often read as encapsulating, not just the experience of modernity as one of fleetingness, acceleration, and simultaneity, but also that of the flâneur as a man of the crowd who observes, experiences, and participates in this new urban, and therefore modern life. However, the poem also reveals the gender-related biases that have informed the construction of the flâneur figure, considering that the woman is also in, and presumably of, the crowd: If what the speaker describes is true, is she not meeting him on equal terms? Is she not also moving through the urban sphere, and, as the 'glance' through which the speaker 'was suddenly reborn' indicates, actively perceiving her environment? She might have been a flâneuse, but she is also visibly consumed through a male gaze.[7] The woman is outlined in flashes of physical, sensual attributes such as the glittering hand, the flouncing skirt, the graceful leg, and the eyes from which he drinks (thereby metaphorically consuming her), and yet we must assume that he fantasizes about a sexual encounter because 'the pleasure that kills' alludes to the 'petit mort', even though her being in mourning casts doubt on whether the same thing is on her mind. The urban experience of modernity, as outlined by Baudelaire in 1860s Paris, is inevitably gendered.

The question of whether a flâneuse, a female flâneur, exists, is a question intrinsically connected to receptions of Victorian gendered space, in which public/private is equated with male/female. Scholars' initial claims that flânerie was impossible for women have been increasingly challenged or re-thought. Janet Wolff seminally highlights conjunctions between the gendered constructions of space and dominant definitions of modernity, and posits that anonymity, freedom, and the fleeting impersonal encounters that fascinated Baudelaire were out of bounds for women: 'She could not adopt the non-existent role of a flâneuse. Women could not stroll alone in the city.'[8] Curiously, she draws this conclusion from a passage in which George Sand recounts her venture into the crowd in cross-dressed disguise. While Sand cannot reconcile a performance of femininity with flânerie, in this successful venture she both is and is not a woman of the crowd, and so certainly ambiguous. Nonetheless, Wolff concludes: 'There is no question of inventing the *flâneuse*: the essential point is that such a character was rendered impossible by the gendered divisions of the nineteenth century.'[9] Griselda Pollock notes that respectable women had no access to the public, gendered spaces which inspired impressionist artists and decadent poets, namely the street, the bar, the café, or the cabaret: 'There is no female equivalent to the quintessentially masculine figure, the *flâneur*: there is not and could not be a female *flâneuse*.'[10] As Teresa Gómez Reus and Aránzazu Usandizaga note, 'spatial confinement is one of the more obvious ways in which the life and destiny of women have been circumscribed: the socially imposed role in the private as opposed to the public sphere, in the home rather than in the street, inside rather than in the world outside.'[11] Deborah Epstein Nord outlines how the female urban rambler was associated with the figure of the Fallen Woman in Victorian culture: 'Just as there was no wholly adequate social or economic structure for the independent existence of the genteel single woman, so there was no wholly respectable context for her appearance in the city landscape.'[12] Deborah Parsons acknowledges that the 'opportunities and activities of flânerie were predominantly the privileges of the man of means, and it was hence implicit that the "artist of modern life" was necessarily the bourgeois male.'[13] However, she also aims to 'undercut the myth that the urban artist-observer is necessarily male and that the woman in the city is a labelled object of his gaze'[14] by considering alternative ways to experience the city and form an artistic or sensory relationship with it. Indeed, to seek the flâneuse solely on the terms of Baudelaire's flâneur reveals a monolithic understanding of urban space: Lynda Nead suggests that a more sophisticated approach should begin 'with a formulation of a more complex understanding of the public sphere than has been evident in previous studies of the metropolis. Rather than seeing public life as a monolithic entity, it is possible to conceive a variety of ways of accessing the public world and a number of different public arenas in which women could be involved.'[15]

The flâneur as quintessential urban figure throws into relief debates about gender and public space because the genealogy of women's emancipation is premised on their increasing participation in public, and therefore urban, and modern life. As Wendy Parkins suggests: 'Like modernity, mobility – with its connotations of escape, liberation, and adventure – has also been gendered masculine, not least through its differentiation from the home environment. It is perhaps surprising, then, that romanticizing mobility has been such a temptation for feminists in late modernity as for Baudelairian *flâneurs*.'[16] However, a flâneur figure evaluated solely on the terms of Baudelaire's male-defined experience may hardly reflect women's relationship with the metropolis in accurate or interesting ways. Instead, we must measure with different parameters: 'To suggest that there couldn't be a female *flâneur* is to limit the ways in which women have interacted with the city to the way *men* have interacted with the city. We can talk about social mores and restrictions, but we cannot rule out the fact that women were there: we must try to understand what walking the city meant to them. Perhaps the answer is not to attempt to make a woman fit a male concept, but to redefine the concept itself.'[17] Indeed, Wolff later acknowledges the potential inherent in refocusing on the 'blurring of boundaries, the negotiation of spaces and the contradictory and open-ended nature of urban social practices', of exploring 'the liminal space, the ambiguous situation, the unexpected moments of access [...], porosity, plasticity, thresholds, permeability, fluidity'.[18] Following this re-positioning, women's relationships with urban space have been productively re-examined, for example by positing philanthropy as female urban mobility, the drawing room as a female public forum, the female body as public space, or *fin-de-siècle* urban literature as precursors of Mrs Dalloway, the modernist flâneuse. Indeed, how Victorian women navigated and made use of public/private boundaries provides important insights into matters of gender and agency, as is not least illustrated by the New Woman.

Arising out of late-Victorian public discourse, the New Woman provides an alternative to the restrictive idea of the flâneuse, not least because she availed herself of modern technologies, such as the bicycle or the omnibus to chart a self-determined course through the metropolis, which makes her a valuable and productive alternative to the flâneur and companion figure to the steampunk heroine. The allegedly progressive and independent steampunk heroine, I argue, may be productively measured against the Victorian New Woman, as this reveals how steampunk feeds into the continuing history of feminism and its evolution.

Considering the different aims and agendas of the four phases, or waves of feminism (1880s–1920s, 1960s–1980s, 1990s–2000s, 2010s to present), this chapter considers George Mann's 'Newbury and Hobbes' series (2008 to present), Tee Morris and Pip Ballantine's 'Ministry of Peculiar Occurences' series (2011–2017), and Gail Carriger's 'Parasolverse' series (2009–2019)[19] and their successes and failures in (re-)imagining Victorian femininity. Lastly, Carriger's steampunk universe illustrates how steampunk may craft alternative queer genealogies through its social retrofuturism.

4.1 The New Woman as Modern Flâneuse

The New Woman figure has been continuously present in Victorian studies since the 1980s canon revision and, configured through a distinct iconography, has survived into a collectively shared cultural memory and so found her way into neo-Victorian media. However, it is crucial to first consider what she signified in her own age. Whereas in the popular imagination (both then and now), the New Woman may be identified by clear signifiers such as the bicycle, a bicycling outfit, or Girton Girl markers, she is of course a composite, complex ideal distilled from a multitude of media and debates, from earnest argument and satiric mockery, from novels and images. In this she shares qualities with the flâneur.

Like feminism throughout the twentieth and twenty-first century, *fin-de-siècle* feminism was far from a monolithic, absolute movement in pursuit of a clearly mapped-out, teleological 'progress'. Still, the 1890s New Woman came to epitomize Victorian feminism as a collective symbol for women seeking autonomy in a male-dominated society, mainly through problematizing marriage as an institution of violence and oppression and by demanding education, careers, sexual freedom, dress reforms, and the right to vote. While the term itself was coined by Ouida (the pseudonym of writer Marie Louise de la Ramée), ironically in a polemic response to an article on 'New Aspects of the Woman Question' by Sarah Grand in 1894, and subsequently became a constant presence in literature and public debate, the epithet merely gave shape to ongoing debates about 'the Woman Question', which had been discussed in the writing of, for example, Henry James, Thomas Hardy, Henrik Ibsen, Mona Caird, or Olive Schreiner since the 1880s.[20] Embedded in a longer history of women challenging 'their subordinate social and political position,'[21] as well as other movements, from socialism, the peace movement, or animal rights to aestheticism and decadence, the New Woman of the *fin de siècle* was widely perceived as radical and transgressive: 'They walked without chaperones, carried their own latchkeys, bicycled, and the more daring ones smoked cigarettes, cut their hair, or wore divided skirts and plain costume in accordance with the principles of rational dress'.[22] Talia Schaffer here demonstrates that the New Woman was to a large extent an imaginative nexus of behaviours and debates, a collective symbol mutable to 'whatever goal the writer has channeled it towards,' while inspired by and distilled from a wide variety of real working women, novelists, campaigners, and bicyclists into an ideal figure.[23] Albeit, as Sally Ledger puts it, 'semi-fictional', the New Woman as 'discursive phenomenon' is also 'just as "real" and historically significant as what she *actually* was.'[24] This is particularly true with regard to reception and widely shared Victorian imaginaries; much like the Gothic tropes in Chapter Two, the New Woman may be read as an array of signifiers, in which 'certain technologies come to work as "freedom machines", as visual emblems connected to the New Woman and signifying female emancipation.'[25]

This emancipation is to a large extent enacted in and expressed through space, and symbolized through the most prominent of New Women attributes, the bicycle. As Sarah Wintle summarizes, 'in different ways the freedom, physical independence and sense of personal control offered literally and symbolically by [the bicycle] was, when seized by women, a kind of trespass on traditionally masculine territory, as, among other things, the obvious anxiety about female dress [...] bears witness.'[26] This is not least evident from the New Woman's status as a popular subject of caricatures from the anti-feminist camp, depictions which ridicule her ambitions and question her femininity as an 'unsexed, terrifying, violent Amazon'.[27] Such cartoons, often published in *Punch* magazine, seemed imaginative and outrageous to their audience but in retrospect, they can seem almost steampunk-ish: speculative, yet not wholly implausible. 'Sartorial oddities', note Richardson and Willis, 'were a celebrated target for cartoonists: the eccentrically dressed minority were used to (mis)represent and undermine the various demands of *fin-de-siècle* feminisms.'[28] This pertains to bicycles in particular. Initially seen as a strange contraption that prompted women to adopt outlandish and unfeminine dress, the bicycle developed into an icon of athletic womanhood and feminism, not least because the bicyclist, newly mobile and autonomous, destabilized Victorian perceptions of gendered spheres. 'By 1897', concludes Lena Wånggren, 'women's rights and the bicycle were firmly bound together in the popular imagination.'[29]

Whereas *Punch*'s cartoon lampooned the New Woman and her pantaloons as fundamentally ridiculous, New Woman heroines such as H. G. Wells' Jessie in *The Wheels of Chance* (1896) or Grant Allen's Lois Cayley were presented as attractive, courageous, and formidable. Here, the spirited, proactive New Woman bicyclist was celebrated and marketed through fiction as an exciting ideal of optimistic progress and adventure. Alongside the bicycle, infrastructures such as the railway, the omnibus, and the Underground offered women the opportunity to participate in 'the wide, freely visitable world a world that normally men were entitled to and which was often identified with the fluidity and flux of the modern pace of living'.[30] By accessing public transport, women participated in modernity as well as exercising agency in choosing their destinations. Travelling alone across the metropolis, they created their own urban space through their individual trajectories which linked into larger transport networks and allowed them to witness the transient urban life. As a consequence, 'omnibuses and underground trains were tools not only to discuss modernity, but also to destabilize gender in the metropolis.'[31] Moreover, these modes of transportations could become a way for women to lose themselves in the crowd of passengers, and to become observers: 'The passenger is a nomad in the modern metropolis, and in her journeys she records life as it passes by'[32]. In her study of women writers of the *fin de siècle* and urban aestheticism, Ana Parejo Vadillo illustrates how writers Amy Levy, Alice Meynell, Graham R. Tomson (Rosamund Marriott Watson), or Michael Field (Katharine Bradley and Edith Cooper) derived subjective enjoyment from the cityscape as artist-poets, like Levy recording the busy ebb and flow of London with '*jouissance* and satisfaction': 'Amy Levy's aesthetic of the omnibus was both an instrument of modernity with which to rethink the position of the *fin-de-siècle* woman poet in an urban milieu, and a tool with which to create a new aesthetic theory based upon the cinematic character of urban transport.'[33] Meynell meanwhile, in her 1897 articles for the *Pall Mall Gazette*, observed the urban sphere from a position of 'intellectual and aesthetic detachment', her writing a 'reverie', and the 'representation of her panoramic impressions of the city'.[34] In this way, the city became a powerful conduit for women's changing sense of self. As Lisa Hager posits, 'women writers understood urban space in terms of women's mobility within that space both above and underground. These writers understood mobility, in turn, not only in terms of physical freedom, but also as a way to understand themselves, reconceiving their subjectivity'.[35]

Women moved across the city spaces for much of the late nineteenth century; promenading on Hyde Park's Rotten Row, populating the theatres, and restaurants of the West End, visiting art galleries and gardens, and exploring the newly created department stores such as Liberty's and John Lewis.[36] They enjoyed the freedom of open space amid anonymity and life and sought artistic inspiration for their writing in the crowded urban sphere, as illustrated in Ella Hepworth Dixon's 1894 novel *The Story of a Modern Woman*:

> Sunshine brightened the huge gilt letters over the newspaper offices; the crowded, brightly coloured omnibuses, the hansoms laden with portmanteaux on their way to Waterloo Station, the flaxen hair and beflowered hats of the little actresses hurrying along to rehearsal. An ever-moving procession of people poured like a torrent up and down the street; journalists, country folk, office boys, actors, betting men, loafers – all the curious shifting world of the Strand was jogging elbows on the pavement.[37]

In the protagonist's perception, the city appears as a tableau of spectacle, simultaneity, and intersecting networks of travel and commerce. We see here the multitude of ongoing trajectories that we have encountered with Dickens and Doyle in the last chapter, so that Hepworth Dixon's portrait of the city aligns her with prominent writers of Victorian London and, through emphasis on colour and sensory impressions, creates a flâneur-esque impression that anticipates later female city writers such as Virginia Woolf.

Dixon also draws attention to the role fashion might play in facilitating the passenger's progress: 'I told Worth when I was in Paris that I always went on the tops of omnibuses, and he designed me this little frock on purpose.'[38] With her fashionable 'little frock' designed by a famous Parisian couturier explicitly for urban travel, Dixon's protagonist fashions herself into a modern urban flâneuse. In an era where women's dresses were integral not merely to their communication of social status, but their purpose of activity (walking dress, visiting dress, evening dress) and range of movement (riding dress, bicycling costume, athletic wear), self-fashioning becomes an important factor in tailoring one's urban identity and exerting agency over the self, both for the Victorian New Woman and the steampunk heroines we will encounter later.

George Paston (Emily Morse Symonds)'s 1898 novel *A Writer of Books* can also be seen as anticipating Woolf's urban reflections, as its protagonist displays 'enjoyment of the freedom of the city and partakes of its various pleasures, even more intrepid than Elizabeth Dalloway twenty-five years later.'[39] This is evident form the following passage:

> Often, as she passed through the crowded streets, she felt tempted to slip between two lovers and listen to their whispered words, to follow the tired looking shop girls and chattering factory hands as they hurried home from their work, to eavesdrop at the doors of sinister-looking houses in narrow back streets, or to strike up an acquaintance with the sandwich-men and flowers-sellers who lined the Strand.[40]

Here, women become observers and chroniclers of distinctly urban phenomena, exploring the vast city and its hidden goings-on from out of the anonymous crowd. Modern London becomes the potent setting for aesthetic contemplation and self-discovery. In a similar vein, suffragists stepped into open public spaces and suited it to their purpose of campaigning. Certainly, their marches, rallies, and exhibitions have become firmly associated with urban spaces such as Hyde Park, where they gathered, or Oxford Street, where they protested. An icon of feminist activism, the suffragist is also characterized by her choice of dress, skillfully employed to project her values of sensibility and purity, femininity, and modernity across public space.[41] Suffragists employed their visibility as women in the city to support their demand for a voice in politics, as well as utilizing public space in order to visualize their demands in a tangible manner through sashes, flags, and banners in their signature colours. Lynne Walker outlines how suffragists also employed architecture to project their values and blurred private/public boundaries by using their private homes for meetings, and furthered their cause through effective neighbourly networking:

> Living and working in central London was a one of the strategies of suffrage politics. The apparatus of white middle-class British women – the well-ordered home; the 'good' address at the heart of London and of empire; the round of formal introductions, social calls, and duties; as well as a sense of neighborly connection for those who lived nearby – supplied a private, social matrix for public, political action.[42]

The New Woman was, among other things, an urban traveller. She availed herself of the technologies of the day and suited them to her purpose so much so that the bicycle has become a signifier intrinsically linked with her as a symbol of independence and mobility. Through her appropriation of urban space by traversing it without chaperones and at her own speed, by using its infrastructures and public spaces for her personal pleasure and political agendas, the New Woman created a female alternative geography of interlinking trajectories across the city, which included not just private drawing rooms, but parks, streets, department stores, and omnibuses. In so doing she did not just participate in the urban modernity outlined by Baudelaire, but actively shaped it.

At the same time, it pays to consider that the New Woman has become the defining cypher of feminist progress at the *fin de siècle* just as much through her canonization by 1980s, canon-revisionist feminist scholarship, which foregrounded resistance against systemic oppression of women in patriarchal Western society and history,[43] and actively sought to identify the New Woman as feminist foremother whose aims paralleled its own: The challenge of marriage as a patriarchal institution, and the participation in public life through political rights and access to the work place. This framework lastingly shaped which writers were and were not recuperated as worthwhile foremothers. Ouida, for example, although she coined the term and was deeply invested in concerns that influenced and aligned with the Woman Question, has (until recently) long been neglected because she was considered 'anti-feminist'.[44]

Post-Feminism, Steampunk Heroines, and the Action Girl

Third wave feminism (1990s to early 2000s) developed feminist ideas through post-colonial and queer theory, notably through the work of Gayatri Spivak and Chandra Mohanty, Judith Butler's work on gender performativity, or Donna Haraway's cyborg manifesto. However, it is also an era in which feminist ideals were appropriated by a neo-liberal media and global market and marketed back to the young women who could take feminist achievements of the previous wave for granted. Characterized by a backlash against the perceived brash manliness of the 1980s superwoman and a rebellious as well as commercialized re-claiming of traditional femininity through Girl Power, a movement which redefined women's rights and equality 'in terms of a liberal individualist politics that centers around lifestyle choices and personal consumer pleasures',[45] this complicated 'double entanglement' of anti-feminist and feminist ideas[46] is often theorized as 'post-feminism'.[47] This term may in turn denote a 'free market feminism' which sells an illusion of feminist progress via fashion and cosmetics,[48] a 'sense of intellectual fatigue and exhaustion as we seem to have run out of steam', the idea that 'suggests that the project of feminism has ended, either because it has been completed or because it has failed and is no longer valid',[49] or a treacherous 'kind of substitute for feminism'.[50] As Antonija Primorac notes, 'empowerment and choice have been appropriated by the neo-liberal media that seeks to inspire women (especially young women) to perceive their agency as that of active, self-monitoring, heterosexually desiring consumers who are now encouraged to choose traditional gender roles'.[51]

These complexities in the feminist project also affect neo-Victorian media and second-wave steampunk. Here, authors seek to re-articulate received notions about the Victorian woman as a symbol of femininity under patriarchal control through post-feminist strategies and create steampunk role models of empowerment that both highlight and overcome the limitations placed on their historical ancestors. In neo-Victorian post-feminism, a nostalgia for femininity and clear gender roles converges in complex ways with the desire to construct a teleological genealogy of steady female liberation and empowerment, giving rise to paradoxical relationships with femininity itself.[52] As Genz notes: 'Femininity in particular has been hampered by negative associations of female oppression and inferiority that stubbornly cling to its descriptions and expressions.'[53] Under the post-feminist lens, expressions of female agency and empowerment have become pluralistic and contradictory because they are entangled with the idea of lifestyle choices, and this ideology is in conflict with second-wave ideals which reject the 'traditional'. Femininity often becomes a casualty of this rejection and on the surface level, frills, flounces, or full skirts remain stereotyped markers of docile subservience, naivety, innocence, or bubbly superficiality. However, femininity also provides creative and flexible ways to re-fashion female identities and re-appropriate 'traditional' expressions of gender into a feminist discourse.[54] A post-millennial femininity allows for 'multiple layers of signification and female identification that go beyond the dualities of subject and object, perpetrator and victim, power and powerlessness' and is therefore worth investigating.[55]

In steampunk, the complex desires to portray empowered women while also enjoying a Victorian aesthetic received as elaborate, beautiful, whimsical, or romantic, may be solved by the fact that steampunk is able to craft anachronistic, independent heroines in the never-was space of the steampunk city. Here, the retrofuturistic element allows for counter-factual, anachronistic heroines who combine the best of past and present – for example through the figure of the New Woman.[56] However, steampunk's endeavours to do so are equally entangled in post-feminist ideas, conflicting notions of femininity, or the sexist tropes of mainstream culture, and therefore often fail to enact narratives of real empowerment. Moreover, they reveal our present's own agenda in approaching and re-imagining the Victorian age and, against the backdrop of 'real' history, reveal the blind spots of our collective memory. That the failure or success of articulating feminist ideals in a steampunk space also hinges on our sometimes-conflicting understandings of feminism and femininity is potently illustrated by neo-Victorian portrayals of, for example, Irene Adler and Mina Harker, as well as their scholarly reception.

4.2 In Hindsight: Fraught Feminisms, Action Girls, and the Steampunk Heroine

Popular films and TV series are perhaps the most widely consumed form of neo-Victorianism and may illustrate both how mainstream media conflates post-feminist ideas with a latent sexism, and how we collectively imagine Victorian femininity. Primorac's astute reading of Irene Adler's representations considers the *Sherlock Holmes* films directed by Guy Ritchie (2009 and 2011) and BBC's *Sherlock,* notably the episode *A Scandal in Belgravia* (2012). Her analysis

> demonstrates how Irene Adler's on-screen afterlives reflect the contemporary postfeminist media's use of the naked, sexualised, female body as the source of women's power and agency. [...] The spectacle of the naked or overtly sexualised body, coded as a liberation of the repressed Victorian heroine, is identified as a distraction from a significant diminishment of Adler's agency.[57]

After all, Doyle's Adler is an independent and cosmopolitan woman (an opera singer), who not only outsmarts the Greatest Detective, but eludes him and lives her life happily and undetermined by him or anyone else. In recent and popular re-tellings, however, 'the elision of female agency takes place through a paradoxical representation of Adler as supposedly strong and in control because of her overt sexuality and reliance on using her body as a weapon. Such use of a woman's body and sexuality – as a means of "empowerment" – belongs squarely to the postfeminist discourse present in popular culture and media, especially since the 1990s'.[58] While in theory, the reclamation of women's bodies under postfeminist sex positivity may seem empowering, it cannot be such if the narrative simultaneously curtails her movements and agency, scrutinizes her through a male gaze, or punishes her for her alleged transgression of boundaries. In both Ritchie's *Sherlock Holmes* and BBC's *Sherlock,* Adler uses her body and sexuality to manipulate the titular hero as part of a criminal and romantic cat-and-mouse game, but Ritchie's narrative lets Holmes arrest Adler at the end of the first film and kills her in the second: Employed here by Professor Moriarty, she is disposed of for falling in love with Holmes. As Primorac concludes, 'Adler in Ritchie's films fails to be more than a saucy, sexy criminal. Her agency, heavily reliant on her use of sexuality and her own body, is, in the end, safely neutralized by the coldblooded criminal mastermind Moriarty who turns out to be her employer'.[59] In the BBC version, the bisexual dominatrix is ultimately 'reduced to a crouching damsel in distress, miraculously saved from death by Holmes himself'.[60]

Adler is at once 'empowered' in a way that services the male gaze and marketed as a post-feminist ideal of choice, and at the same time robbed of the freedom and power she possessed in the original text. This process of 'updating' Victorian texts [...] through the – now almost routine – 'sexing up' of the proverbially prudish Victorians' highlights how present-day conceptions of 'feminism', especially as consumerist choice, can become entangled with our perception of the Victorian age in paradoxical ways.[61] The persistent and erroneous stereotype of the inherently prudish and sexually repressed Victorians seems to afford us, who like to imagine ourselves as sexually emancipated people and empowered women, the opportunity to liberate and rescue them in our retrospective imaginary. But really, 'the "updating" of Adler as a dominatrix and a sexual woman gives her only the temporary power of the female body as fetish and a very "Victorian" narrative destiny. As soon as she "over-reaches" her limits of agency as a sexualized body, Adler promptly falls/fails, is humiliated and punished.'[62] It is this trope of punishing the transgressive or Fallen Woman which constitutes an especially persistent echo of Victorian conventions, and one that neo-Victorian and steampunk narratives, as well as popular culture at large, often reproduce.

Claire Nally posits Mina Harker from Alan Moore's and Kevin O'Neill's graphic novel series *The League of Extraordinary Gentlemen* (1999 to present) as an empowered female character. She cites Harker's leadership, education, and independence as markers of the New Woman, as well as the fact that she smokes and is called 'a smelly little lesbian' by Moriarty, because she troubles and threatens conventional gender relations.[63] These markers seem indeed designed to characterize Harker as transgressive, but already she is defined by a man's (rather ugly) utterances which also re-iterate the more misogynistic stereotypes which were levelled at the New Woman in her own time. Nally also points to Harker's aggressive seduction of an elderly, seemingly emasculated version of Rider Haggard's imperial masculinist hero, Allan Quatermain, as evidence for her re-negotiation of gender relations: 'She then proceeds to undress in front of the bewildered older man [...] whilst he feebly protests [...] and in a graphic representation of their sexual encounter, Mina climbs on top of the aged Quatermain [...]'.[64] However, this episode reads as hardly more than a crude reversal of gendered power relations, and its implication that getting consent is beneath whoever is the empowered party is highly problematic. Harker's 'empowerment' is derived purely from the appropriation of male-coded behaviours of dominance – if not 'toxic masculinity' – and thereby only plays into stereotypes of the New Woman as a perversion.

While I agree with Nally that Harker's struggles with patriarchal structures, especially in trying to lead the team of heroes, 'represent the ways in which women are silenced or otherwise devalued',[65] I consider what she diagnoses as the graphic novel's attempt to 'address the toxic masculinity which we might more obviously associate with twenty-first century discourses around rape culture'[66] as highly ambivalent and potentially flawed. As Nally convincingly shows, Harker, whose assertiveness and independence threaten masculine identities, is continually under threat from such toxic masculinity, but the detailed, graphic, and 'highly sexualized' depiction of a patriarchal revenge fantasy in the form of a psychological rape by the Invisible Man also re-iterate and perpetuate a voyeuristic male gaze that makes the reader complicit and uses trauma to undermine Harker's perceived defiance of patriarchy.[67] In fact, she is introduced to the narrative in a situation where she is threatened with rape and saved by Quatermain, so her alleged empowerment as a New Woman is very much in question throughout the narrative.

The fact that Nally considers Harker to demonstrate that the 'value of steampunk narrative [...] is that women's agency is written back into the history, albeit fantastically and retrospectively',[68] while I find her a troubling example of how such attempts are nonetheless often thwarted by a pervasive sexism, illustrates how different conceptions of 'feminism' may come into conflict with one another. Nally's post-feminist lens approves of how Harker draws attention to the ways in which women, especially progressive ones, are under threat by toxic masculinity and rape culture, while my fourth-wave feminist lens foregrounds how that endeavour is compromised by the graphic novel's perpetuation of sexist tropes and its casual attitude towards sexual violence. Moreover, Harker's alleged empowerment is just as much centred around her sexuality, curtailed by the male gaze, and under threat from the patriarchy, as that of neo-Victorian Irene Adler.

Reclaiming the Retrofuture: Alexia Tarabotti

Gail Carriger's supernatural romance, the Parasol Protectorate series was initially derided for not being 'steampunk enough' because it prioritized social comedy over technological speculation.[69] As we see with Claire Nally's reading of the series as running 'counter to more radical literature within the subculture', Carriger's frivolous and whimsy fiction can still be misunderstood as reinforcing 'conservative' romance tropes such as 'heteronormativity' or as misusing the 'wealth of post-feminist choice [...] to make some very conventional decisions'.[70] Nally's disapproval of Alexia Tarabotti, Carriger's heroine's 'so-called choices'[71] is evident from her quoting Rosalind Gill on post-feminist romance:

> What is interesting, however, is the way in which they seem compelled to use their empowered postfeminist position to make choices that would be regarded

by many feminists as problematic, located as they are in the normative notions of femininity. They choose, for example, white weddings, downsizing, giving up work or taking their husband's name on marriage'.[72]

Again the ideals of second-wave feminism come into conflict with 'notions of femininity', as well as hierarchies of genres. I have already argued that the parameters of post-feminist criticism, which here deride pluralistic lifestyle choices for which previous generations have fought as somehow 'wrong' and 'not feminist enough', can overlook problematic sexist tropes such as the Faux Action Girl, and while Nally's diagnosis of conservatism may hold true for several steampunk romances, I posit that Carriger's fiction enacts a positive and inclusive steampunk vision in accordance with the ideals of fourth-wave feminism.[73]

Fourth-wave feminism (2008 to present) is informed by a politics of intersectionality and inclusion across race and class boundaries: It is 'transaffirmative and intersectional, attentive to how classism, racism, ableism, geographical location, and other forms of discrimination and privilege differentially shape women's lives'.[74] It also relies on the high speed connectivity of social media to initiate a grassroots activism: 'The internet has created a culture in which sexism or misogyny can be "called out" and challenged', diagnosed Elasaid Munro in 2013, when the term and movement gathered new momentum.[75] Social media 'facilitated the creation of a global community' of (largely millennial, digital native) feminists who engage in discussion and activism in these non-academic spaces.[76] Accordingly, fourth-wave feminism is embedded into the workings of convergence culture, 'the flow of content across multiple media platforms, the cooperation between multiple media industries, and the migratory behavior of media audiences'.[77] This both accounts for its plurality in the wake of post-feminism's complex legacies and indicates how fourth-wave feminism may interact with pop culture and fan criticism. Indeed, it has been endorsed by public figures and celebrities who recognize that championing social justice has become socially desirable.

The fourth wave, while continuing third-wave projects about intersectionality with civil rights and queer activism, also challenges conservative and white-centric feminisms, and has added its own foci in response to emerging and vocal right-wing populism, threats to women's reproductive rights, enduring pay gaps, and endemic sexual harassment. 'It is sobering,' so Jennifer Cooke, 'to recognise that women's hard-won legal rights and positions in society are more fragile than we might have supposed'.[78] Supplementing is critical vocabulary with queer registers and terms such as toxic masculinity, body shaming, and rape culture,[79] this wave has resulted in hashtag campaigns such as #YesAllWomen (2014) or #MeToo (2017) and intersecting with such movements as Black Lives Matter.[80] In fact, fourth-wave feminism has widely become known as the 'MeToo era', discussing how patriarchal power structures still influence and threaten women in the very spaces that previous feminist waves have fought to access. The movement has brought to light how these power structures have secretly re-captured the sexualized agency of female workers and appropriated it into systems of gate-keeping and exploitation. The fact that MeToo was catalyzed and made visible through and within the entertainment industry also highlights how mass media and popular culture are entangled in the dissemination of male-dominated cultural narratives, both behind the scenes and within the narratives themselves. Indeed, the way in which the fourth wave turns its 'attention to both media portrayals of women, and the impact of popular culture on women's lives'[81] is not least illustrated by the complex entanglements, desires, and failures of neo-Victorian heroines such as Irene Adler, Mina Harker, and Veronica Hobbes. Carriger's Alexia Tarabotti, I argue, poses an alternative.

On one hand, neo-Victorian media compulsively seeks to 'sex up' and 'liberate' Victorian women, stereotypically imagined as 'repressed both in terms of gender and sexuality',[82] on the other, it re-inscribes persistent narrative tropes that monitor those same women through a male gaze, curtail their agency or punish their transgression of gender boundaries. It seems that the Victorian woman, imagined in retrospect, provides a potent symbol onto which present-day desires and fears around femininity and gender are projected and becomes the Other against which contemporary feminism and post-feminism may define themselves. '[R]ebellious women', notes Eckart Voigts, 'repressed in their political as well as in their sexual expression, seem to be locked in a perennial battle with the Victorian patriarchy'.[83] Indeed, 'Victorian subcultures are rewarding because they are clearly defined by normative discourses and lend contrastive poignancy to portrayals of transgression.'[84] As such, both neo-Victorianism and steampunk tend to contrast their liberated and rebellious heroine, with which the post-feminist reader is invited to identify, against a backdrop of almost comically exaggerated stereotypes, such as the secret society in *Phoenix Rising*. Once again literalizing a popular trope, this society plots to build an automated robot workforce secretly sourced with organic material from working-class victims—yet another way that East End dwellers are literally consumed by capitalism. Almost as a matter of course, the members' upper-class wives are portrayed in turn as traumatised abuse victims and an 'erotic display' for the male gaze as well as a sort of harem (277). The repressed Victorian woman becomes a near-fetishistic object of Gothic fascination. 'We extract politically incorrect pleasure from what now appears comic, perverse, or ethically unimaginable as a focus of desire', diagnoses Kohlke. 'We enjoy neo-Victorian fiction in part to feel debased or outraged, to revel in degradation, reading for defilement. By projecting illicit and unmentionable desires onto the past, we conveniently reassert our own supposedly enlightened stance towards sexuality and social progress.'[85] As much as Victorian Gothic has become neo-Victorianism's new Other, Victorian gender becomes, as Kohlke astutely observes, 'the new Orientalism, a significant mode of imagining sexuality in our hedonistic, consumerist, sex-surfeited age.'[86]

These stereotypes thus shored up through endless repetition throughout popular culture become entangled with and obscure the gender politics at work in our present:

> Rather than exhibiting an unequivocally liberating potential, these neo-Victorian exposés of Victorian sexual hypocrisy and gendered oppression lose their impact in the sheer repetition of these tropes. When looked at cumulatively, this 'sexsation' turns into a dominant, prescriptive narrative that clouds the ideologically suspect undercurrents at work.[87]

In theory, Steampunk, as retro-speculative mode, is free to realise the transformative potential inherent in historical currents and events through play, distortion, and anachronism. However, despite its radical potential, it too often only reveals the limits of our imagination when it relapses into sexist tropes, even if unintentionally. *The Janus Affair*'s portrait of the suffragist movement, for example, uses action and adventure tropes in ways that accidentally undermine the New Woman's revolutionary potential.

Here, New Zealand's suffragist leader (and involuntary cyborg) Kate Sheppard, a personal friend to Eliza, has come to London with her delegation to support the suffragists, having won women the vote at home.[88] The novel takes up women's mobility when we encounter Lena, a suffragist on her way back from Edinburgh, on the hypersteam-train (a steampunk amplification). Notably, the chapter is titled as 'Wherein the Perils of Train Travel Are Made Plain' (1). Lena is followed by an unspecified evil and even seeks to evade it by hiding on the roof of the carriage (3-5) — a stunt we associate with action movies rather than a Victorian setting. The young woman cannot escape her predicament and, upon locating Eliza in another compartment, vanishes in a mysterious electric ball of light.

In London, we witness several suffragists take up the public space of Hyde Park's Speaker's Corner, visible and active, yet unable to fully evade a few opinionated 'cads' (22) whose presence is meant to illustrate (patriarchal) opposition. They soon retaliate, not with their morally superior arguments or resilience, but with a 'monstrosity of a rifle': 'The air around the rifle's barrel-bell distorted and wavered until brilliant pearlescent rings of heat and power burst from it' (25). By cooking a goose with this steampunk device, the suffragists apparently announce their strength and resolution, but it remains an ambivalent gesture of male-coded violence — perhaps a nod towards the later militant activism of the more radical Women's Social and Political Union, or simply an attempt to amplify the 'coolness factor' that often governs steampunk logic.[89] In a similar vein, the novel also equips the suffragists with an all-female group of bodyguards versed in the art of bartitsu, using steampunk retro-speculation and counter-fact to amplify and highlight how the suffragist movement, at least in Britain, was caught up in a spiral of escalating and often gendered violence against the activists and in general on both sides.[90] These are good examples of steampunk's meta-Victorian shorthand. However, it is the fact that suffragists like Lena become the victims of the mysterious electric beam kidnapping device and are targeted in specifically public places, which risks re-affirming the idea that public places are precarious for women and those who transgress are likely to be victimised. The kidnappers turn out to be women themselves: a pair of Indian twins posing as suffragists are revealed to be fundamentalist radicals who project their colonial psychosis of displacement onto the rising menace of the women's movement: '"My country does not believe in this movement, and yet this cheek—this effrontery— is tolerated! [...] You see how the sickness has spread, even in my own home country where women begin to gather. They watch. They plan. And they will rise. One day, they all will'" (371). Through her reactionary diatribe, the antagonist draws attention to feminist networks across the Empire. Her assertion that one day, 'they will all rise up' locates the beginning of a global, teleological meta-narrative of feminist activism and liberation in the late Victorian age — and specifically, in London. The public sphere of urban London becomes the stage on which first-wave feminism, and with it the foundation to later feminisms, is enacted, and which therefore becomes her target. Urban networks are here shown to play a significant role in steampunk's imaginary of feminist genealogies, and while their rebelliousness places the suffragists in danger especially in the public spaces in which that rebellion is enacted, it also becomes the conduit for it.

Steampunk heroines, while often presented as go-getting, feminist reader stand-ins, equally often only enact a flawed post-feminism. Miss Veronica Hobbes, assistant and partner-in-crime to Sir Maurice Newbury, the gentleman detective in Mann's Newbury & Hobbes series, is introduced as 'pretty: brunette, in her early twenties, with a dainty but full figure, and dressed in a white blouse, grey jacket, and matching skirt.'[91] Whereas the sensible blouse and skirt combination is meant to indicate a capable and forthright New Woman type, this first impression fails to communicate any characteristics not related to her (sexualised) body: she is seen through a male gaze.

We are repeatedly assured that Miss Hobbes 'can look after herself' (33), has a sharp mind, makes astute observations, and is generally practical. Newbury is regularly 'impressed', however, which indirectly suggests that he supposes other Victorian women to be frivolous, feminine, and largely useless. In line with Mann's reliance on superficial but familiar tropes, Veronica is never characterised in more depth. We infer from her manner of speech that she is a rational person intrigued by mystery, making her an appropriate sounding board for the detective hero, but she is supposedly a secret agent in her own right. In the second novel, *The Osiris Ritual* (2009), Veronica investigates a series of disappearances of women from a theatre in Soho, alone and 'expressly against the wishes of Sir Maurice' (164). We are assured that 'she was also an agent of Her Majesty Queen Victoria, and that she was quite capable of managing a case of her own. She was fully aware of the risks and saw nothing unduly dangerous about her choosing to tackle Alfonso on her own. If he proved difficult, she had the wherewithal to incapacitate him and call for the police' (164-165). This remains pure theory: although she does indeed demonstrate her skill in a sword duel with the suspect, Veronica is nonetheless outwitted by a trapdoor, ironically following the other kidnap victims in Alfonso's disappearing act. Captured by a mad scientist archetype, the woman 'who can take care of herself' must now be rescued by Newbury.

This episode both suggests that the city remains a space of danger for 'New Women'— even steampunk ones — and undermines Veronica's claims to capability and autonomy by repositioning her as an ingénue reduced to a Damsel in Distress. This clichéd staple of Western popular storytelling has been classified as a trope in itself, called 'Distress Ball', by the online wiki TvTropes, a repository of fan criticism:[92] 'If any female character, in a burst of anger or enthusiasm, decides to go off and accomplish something on her own without the hero, she will fail miserably and again have to be rescued.'[93] Popular fan criticism, fuelled by social media, routinely interrogates performances of gender and its place in popular narratives, and considering how deeply embedded steampunk is in the knowledge communities that pop culture creates (see Chapter Two), we must take into account how 'white knowledge' about narrative tropes must inevitably inform the steampunk heroine. This is evident not least in the action-adventure heroine, the default in many steampunk fictions: 'The action heroine's conflicting identifications involve a continuous play between passivity and activity, vulnerability and strength, feminism and femininity, individualism and communality', writes Genz: '[She] is either portrayed as a semi-tough pretender to male power who is ultimately too feminine to be as effectual as her male counterpart; or depicted as a de-feminized male impersonator, reinforcing the link between masculinity and toughness.'[94] In many ways, the action heroine 'epitomizes the multiple subject and agency positions that become available to women in a twenty-first-century context' as a character who is supposedly an empowered woman, confidently exerting agency by participating in action-oriented plots (p. 153). She 'adopts a number of characteristics and attitudes that have been deemed masculine or male and she challenges the essentialist dichotomy that denies women recourse to action and strength as means to empowerment' (p. 152). As such, however, she also runs the risk of becoming a token character in what is usually still a male-dominated narrative. Tokenism constitutes an 'alluring fantasy of transcendence and power' while it simultaneously 'works to secure the status quo as it glorifies the exception' (p. 152). In fan criticism, this type is known as the 'Strong Female Character'. Sophia McDougall's column echoes Genz when she explains:

> Part of the patronising promise of the Strong Female Character is that she's anomalous. 'Don't worry!' that puff piece or interview is saying when it boasts the hero's love interest is an SFC. 'Of course, normal women are weak and boring and can't do anything worthwhile. But this one is different. She is strong! See, she roundhouses people in the face.'[95]

Like Mina Harker above, the Strong Female Character is 'empowered' mainly through her imitation of male-coded behaviour, and often shown as being at variance with traditionally feminine characters or behaviours. Customarily, the action heroine is presented as remedial evidence of women's emancipation, designed as post-feminist proof that feminist goals have been achieved and feminism is obsolete. As Genz posits, she is an 'intrinsically ambiguous persona who walks a tightrope to achieve an almost impossible balance' (p. 152). Thus, the success of an action heroine's 'empowerment' hinges not on her physical strength or her ability to keep up with male characters, but rather on whether or not she may exert agency within the plot, and whether or not she is defined by a male gaze. Veronica Hobbes, on the terms of TvTropes, is only a 'Faux Action

Girl', who is 'supposed to be The Hero (or, one of the heroes), but never gets to actually do anything heroic. She has a well-grounded reputation as a strong fighter in her field, but always fails miserably in the line of battle'.[96] We will see why this matters through a closer look at Tee Morris and Pip Ballantine's popular series of novels, *The Ministry of Peculiar Occurrences* (2011-2017), which succeeds in presenting us with a variety of female characters, thereby foregoing tokenism, but which still becomes tangled up in contradictory representations which undermine its project of empowerment.

We are introduced to agent Eliza Braun, one half of the protagonist duo Books and Braun, through a cinematic trope:

> A lady emerged from the smoke and debris—though her improper fashions indicated that she was unworthy of the title. She was wearing pinstripe breeches tucked neatly into boots that stopped just above the knee. More disturbing than the fact that this 'lady' was wearing trousers were the sticks of dynamite strapped around her thighs. The boots also had several sheaths for knives. The bodice she was wearing was a black leather device, which not only served to lift the petite woman's bosom up but also provided a secure surface for the baldric she wore across it. All this was accented with an impressive, fur coat that flowed around her like a cape.[97]

Her visually coded emergence from the clearing smoke immediately identifies Eliza with popular action narratives in film and TV, which is strengthened by her male-coded attire. Identified from the first moment as an Action Girl, a 'female badass',[98] Eliza is vulnerable to the conflicting stereotypical descriptions that characterise the type. A vision of literally weaponised sexuality, she simultaneously manages to scandalise and titillate the supposedly modest, gentlemanly focal character, Agent Books. The latter, in keeping with steampunk's ironic fascination with 'Victorian' social conventions, is suitably shaken by Eliza not performing traditional femininity, even while she is saving his life. Through setting itself up with a gendered reversal of the Damsel in Distress trope, the novel promises an 'unconventional', that is an independent, daring, and forthright heroine who is at odds with everything we (and Books) have been made to expect from a Victorian woman. The *Ministry of Peculiar Occurrences* series here styles itself as a steampunk adventure in the vein of the 1960s television series *The Avengers*, and by inserting an action-spy heroine into a Victorian setting, purports to play with our expectations through subversion, humour, and irony.

This largely succeeds. Eliza is vocal, impulsive, stubborn, and fierce whereas Books is temperate, timid, and practical. Both are characterised through attributes usually associated with the opposite gender, especially in a Victorian context. In an added post-colonial dimension, many of Eliza's transgressive behaviours which continue to unsettle Books in humorous ways are ascribed to the fact that she is from New Zealand. Eliza, with her penchant for eclectic crossdressing in trousers, belts, and other masculine items, embodies the steampunk subculture's approach to style. Her initial ensemble of pinstripe breeches, bodice, and knee-high boots is certainly more at home at a steampunk convention or photo shoot than in any Victorian or neo-Victorian context. However, Eliza also dresses in traditionally feminine gowns for social occasions. This implies she evaluates clothing based on practicality and purpose and freely tailors her gender performance through fashion to the urban spaces through which she travels: in the realm of performing gender and femininity through fashion, Eliza certainly exerts agency. She does this also by securely and freely navigating the East End docklands, where the Ministry is located. She enjoys 'legwork' in Whitechapel, as it

> was very familiar. She and Harry had spent a great deal of time down here as many Peculiar Occurrences happened in the cramped houses and narrow alleyways in this part of London. This was the corner of the City, forgotten and ignored by the upper classes, full of rabble-rousers, Fabians, cut-throats, and Dollymops. It was dirty, dangerous, and dank.' (151)

Whereas the passage portrays some familiar stereotypes about Whitechapel, it also attests to Eliza a sort of alternative urban knowledge. Like Sherlock Holmes, she is familiar with its networks and idiosyncrasies, especially those shabby-genteel urban tribes which characterised the London of steampunk's first wave. As a detective walking a beat and listening in to conversations in the pub, she displays a combination of idleness, observation, and purpose reminiscent of the flâneur. Eliza also engages with her 'targets' in disguise or adopts specific feminine roles to gather her information, and self-fashions according to her purpose. In addition to her wandering on foot, Eliza also (literally) harnesses urban infrastructures, for example in a chase scene around Charing Cross. In accordance with her fiery temperament, she borrows a cab to pursue a suspect, becoming considerably more than an observant passenger (124–130). She similarly transgresses into masculine territory in the second novel, when we see her riding a 'lococycle' (stolen from another female character, a seductive villainess), which we can infer from its 'two wheels [...] like a bicycle', its 'valves, pistons and flyways', and the 'narrow tray [...] that flickered with blue flame', 'something the devil himself might have invented' (195) looks like a modern motorcycle.⁹⁹ As an upgraded, energetic and volatile bicycle, certainly not intended for 'genteel pursuits', the device becomes a sexually charged symbol of unstoppable mobility, especially when ridden astride by a woman in trousers. A male focal character perceives the villainess Sophia del Morte (who owned the lococycle before Eliza) as follows: 'She looked terrifying and arousing, clad in men's attire, atop a hissing, chugging machine' (196).

It is certainly telling that this sexualised machine is given first to the enticing assassin with a penchant for luxuries, both feminine and transgressive, and cast in the role of the alluring *femme fatale*. It is equally telling that Eliza later uses it for high-speed pursuits and launching herself at an airship. Both Eliza and Sophia, who by no small coincidence resemble one another in appearance, are presented as Action Girls. Sophia scales the Natural History Museum to steal a valuable artefact, demonstrating her mobility across vertical as well as horizontal axes and enacting a fantasy of freedom and agency much like the player in *Assassin's Creed* (see Chapter Three). As a criminal, she transgresses boundaries at every turn, but both she and Eliza freely traverse the city in ways only a steampunk heroine might. It is certainly no coincidence either that both Sophia and Eliza are outlined as sexual and sexually empowered women, one the sultry, cosmopolitan *femme fatale* with multiple lovers, the other an outgoing, flirtatious 'Colonial Pepperpot' with a predictable romantic weakness for the male hero.¹⁰⁰

It is here that Eliza's (self-)stylisation as an empowered Action Girl becomes complicated because the novel dismantles her performance. Contrary to her sexy persona, Eliza's real love life is revealed to be traditional, romantic, and much less intimidating for Books. Her sexual independence is toned down so that she may be romantically available for the hero. Such a desire to make independent or transgressive women more vulnerable and therefore palatable for male consumption is present in our wider popular culture, as Irene Adler's neo-Victorian afterlives show. Moreover, this desire to rein in the Fallen Woman, which in Victorian literature mostly means a tragic death, is here enacted through victimisation, violation, or humiliation, usually in gendered ways: Adler crouches before male aggressors, Harker is threatened with rape, Hobbes becomes a Damsel in Distress. In keeping with this unfortunate trope, Eliza is subjected to explicit and gendered abuse in *Phoenix Rising*, while the male hero is given a leisurely tour of the mad scientist's underground lair. The fact that this is not her first time in a dungeon, as she had 'spent some nightmarish weeks in the Kaiser's cells' (348) or that she banters, provokes, and insults her assailant does not negate this. The following passages show this:

> Using the short chain between the cuffs as a makeshift leash he tugged her over to the wall to take advantage of a 'convenient' hook overhead. When he hoisted her by the cuffs with his free arm onto the hook, she felt her arms and sides stretch. Eliza would be forced to stand on tiptoes to take the tension off her shoulders. [...]
>
> His tongue was lapping up the blood and on reaching the small wound he sucked slightly. With him so close to her, Eliza could feel his erection pressing against her. With a delighted gasp, he pulled away from her arm, grabbed Eliza's hair, and tugged hard. Her surprised wince was enough for Devane to shove his tongue into her mouth. [...] His moans were sickening, even more sickening than the feel of his hand cupping her breast through the muslin of her undergarments, his forefinger and thumb teasing her nipple. That was the mistake she was hoping for.' (350–352)

While Eliza soon overpowers her assailant without outside help, we must ask ourselves why we made voyeuristically complicit through such explicit descriptions before she does. Like Mina Harker's symbolic rape, this seems too much like a punishment for her transgressive sexuality, as it explicitly targets her sexually. And while she frees herself from this gendered victimisation, it is not long before Books must rescue her after all when the trigger-happy heroine is knocked out and it falls to the Archivist, who we suddenly find out is a secret master marksman, to carry her to safety (363–370). While Eliza is certainly empowered in some areas, she also frequently lapses back into Faux Action Girl territory. She is re-imagined 'as feisty, sexually and physically active, a heroine with her own agenda, reluctant to be tied down by the rules of propriety – yet, ultimately, a heroine whose agency is re-inscribed within a patriarchal system of power-play.'[101] It is then not surprising that the assassin Sophia del Morte, like Adler in Ritchie's film, also turns out to be working for a more powerful, male criminal mastermind. Fan criticism is also aware of this last-minute cop-out in popular media:

> Nowadays the princesses all know kung fu, and yet they're still the same princesses. They're still love interests, still the one girl in a team of five boys, and they're all kind of the same. They march on screen, punch someone to show how they don't take no shit, throw around a couple of one-liners or forcibly kiss someone because getting consent is for wimps, and then with ladylike discretion they back out of the narrative's way.[102]

In the Library, with the Hair Pin

We first meet Alexia, a spinster, having strayed into the library at a society ball in search for refreshments, 'only to happen on an unexpected vampire'.[103] What might have been a clichéd Gothic scene between a 'darkly shimmering' vampire and a lady in a 'low necked ball gown' (p. 1) is immediately recast in a Wodehousian tone. Alexia is a preternatural, which means her touch can negate supernatural abilities and she is more concerned with the vampire's bad manners than the threat to her life: 'I say!' said Alexia to the vampire. 'We have not even been introduced!' (p. 1). The damsel-and-vampire cliché is further subverted when Alexia 'issued the vampire a very dour look' and shoves him into a tray of treacle tart ('Miss Tarabotti was most distressed by this. She was particularly fond of treacle tart').

It is important to note that, unlike Veronica or Eliza, Alexia is not introduced through the male gaze of another focal character, but as an autonomous woman who not merely appears, but acts and reacts. In accordance with the chapter title, 'In Which Parasols Prove Useful' she wields her accessory, which was 'terribly tasteless for her to be carrying at an evening ball' and 'whacked the vampire right on top of the head': '"Manners!" instructed Miss Tarabotti' (p. 3). Undaunted and pragmatic, Alexia displays an unexpected set of personal priorities (for example, manners over physical safety) and re-purposes a traditionally feminine, 'frilly' (p. 3) accessory which we might assume to be quite useless into a useful weapon. Later in the novel, Alexia's friend Ivy will claim that she has 'parasoled' a man (p. 42), thereby, as Amy Montz notes, 'turning this seemingly useful feminine article into an active verb, and a violent one at that.'[104] Similarly, Alexia re-purposes a wooden hairpin into a 'hair *stake*' (p. 4, original emphasis), and kills the vampire with the wooden tip of her parasol. The scene subverts the familiar constellation of male Victorian vampire and young woman into one where the latter retains power and agency, not despite her femininity but because of it.

Moreover, Alexia ingenuously uses gendered behaviours to her advantage, even particularly feminine stereotypes about female delicacy, for example to evade the awkwardness of being questioned: 'With a resigned shrug, she screamed and collapsed into a faint. She stayed resolutely fainted, despite the liberal application of smelling salts, which made her eyes water most tremendously, a cramp in the back of one knee, and the fact that her new ball gown was getting most awfully wrinkled' (pp. 6–7). Given this ironic play with gender conventions and the connotations of Victorian femininity, it is unsurprising that the parasol becomes an icon for Alexia and the series at large. In the second novel, she is gifted one that is quite literally weaponized, as it is outfitted with hidden compartments, poisonous darts, and silver and wooden tips to ward off supernatural attacks. This characterizes Alexia, as Montz concludes, as a 'damsel, saving *herself* from distress.'[105]

Alexia is set up as active, decisive, and self-reliant, both defying 'normative notions of femininity' and re-purposing feminine behaviours and accoutrements in her own interest. Carriger's series simultaneously celebrates the Victorian aesthetic in a semi-nostalgic way and semi-ironically pokes fun at it through a light and witty narrative tone that channels Jane Austen's social comedy, Oscar Wilde's absurd paradoxes, P. G. Wodehouse's satire, and screwball comedy into a re-calibrated neo-Victorian collage. This becomes evident when she kills the vampire in self-defence: 'Alexia's books called this end of the vampire life cycle *dissanimation*. Alexia, who thought the action astoundingly similar to a soufflé going flat, decided to call it the Grand Collapse' (p. 6). The irony and parody always inherent in the steampunk mode is here foregrounded into a whimsical, but witty comedic style which at first seems to be at odds with the radical potential of steampunk, but which has caused Carriger's work to become 'easily one of the (if not the) most successful steampunk series ever published.'[106] Furthermore, this mode is designed to interrogate and re-present Victorian imaginaries in clever ways, because it thrives on the humour, irony, and parody that operate in steampunk at a fundamental level.

Poking Fun with Parasols

'Neo-Victorianism', as Kohlke and Gutleben note, 'relies in fairly equal measure on a vacillating sense of homage and irreverence, praise and condemnation, fascination and disgust', and catalyzes how '[p]ostmodernity's love-hate relationship with the nineteenth century throws up both comic convergences and incongruities between "then" and "now", "Them", and "Us".'[107] Indeed, ironic humour functions as a metafictional distancing device, and as something that is 'doubly double: both temporally and ideologically', neo-Victorian humour and steampunk especially play with our expectations, here regarding conventions of gender and genre.[108] In doing so, however, steampunk both re-activates and perpetuates persistent stereotypes about 'the Victorians' and then subverts, destabilizes, or undermines them.[109] The audience 'must subscribe to and be aware of the ironizing gestures'[110] at work for it to function, and hindsight can create a (false) sense of superiority, enacting 'a refusal to be gulled by appearances, reputation, propaganda, and spectacle. The extradiegetic audience participates in this superiority through its preparedness to be amused.'[111] This is especially important with regard to Victorian gender, already positioned as Other to our supposedly enlightened moment.

Nally's study provides an astute analysis of how steampunk artists Doctor Geof and Nick Simpson parody and lampoon the masculine ideals of late-nineteenth-century new imperialism through 'bathos, incongruous humour, carnivalesque excess and irony', and the same forces are certainly at work in Carriger's fiction.[112] These steampunk masculinities, expertly parodied through absurd conflations with the trivial (in form of a Tea Referendum or a rocking horse, for example) as they are, seem however content with identifying markers of toxic (Victorian) masculinity with a jovial self-irony that indirectly proclaims, 'Look how far we have come!' While they may reflect 'on ways in which our contemporary moment can rethink these stereotypes',[113] they also seem to lack the vocabulary to really formulate viable alternative masculinities.

Meanwhile, Carriger's 'Parasolverse's' steampunk comedy lovingly, but certainly also ironically, exaggerates Victorian fashions and manners, which, as part of Sterling's 'weird and archaic', seem fascinating and absurd in themselves, and by conflating genre tropes (especially urban fantasy) with the Victorian aesthetic. In this steampunk world, werewolves, vampires, and ghosts have been assimilated into British society, and so high necklines are made fashionable by vampires wanting to hide neck bites, and werewolf soldiers explain Britain's colonial power. The series avoids setting up a monolithic 'Victorian femininity', against which only the heroine stands out, by presenting us with a variety of different female characters. Alexia, pragmatic and intelligent because 'preternatural' and therefore 'soulless', has a 'bluestocking' curiosity and is unconventional in that she is buxom and half Italian, which is widely assumed to be an unfashionable disadvantage.[114] Alexia's aberrations are framed within the Victorian aesthetic – she does not depend on 'liberating' anachronisms in order to be a modern heroine, but can be so within the logic of the hyper-Victorian intertextual collage. In keeping with this, many of her personal freedoms and eccentricities are justified by her being either a spinster or, later on, an eccentric aristocrat. Alexia has been put 'on the shelf at fifteen' (p. 32), but does not mind this: 'Not that she had never actually coveted the burden of a husband, but it would have been nice to know she could get one if she ever changed her mind' (p. 32). As a spinster, she also enjoys her 'ever-increasing degree of freedom' (p. 30). Her mother in fact thinks of her as 'revoltingly independent' (p. 31). Such independence is also expressed in her mobility as it enables her to walk freely and unaccompanied through the genteel, but public urban space of Hyde Park, years before the advent of the bicycle: 'Under ordinary circumstances, walks in Hyde Park were the kind of thing a young lady of good breeding was not supposed to do without her mama and possibly an elderly female relation or two in attendance. Miss Tarabotti felt such rules did not entirely apply to her, as she was a spinster' (pp. 31–32). Alexia's independence as spinster, wife, outcast, or mother, is always expressed through her ability to travel on foot, via carriage, train, or dirigible.

On her walks in Hyde Park, Alexia is accompanied by her best friend Ivy Hisselpenny, who unfortunately is 'only-just-pretty, only-just-wealthy, and possessed of a terrible propensity for wearing extremely silly hats' (p. 33). Ivy, with her tendency towards a more frivolous (if not embarrassingly outrageous) femininity, throws into relief Alexia's eccentricities as a foil. Delivering feminine responses deemed appropriate such as 'It is simply not the done thing' (p. 36), and 'It's simply too outrageous' (p. 37), or simply 'blushing furiously' (p. 174), she both acts as a yardstick of conventional Victorian femininity and a caricature thereof – as indicated by her bad taste in garish hats, which is a running gag throughout the series. Ivy also acts as a guide for performing femininity to Alexia, who on multiple counts asks herself '*What would Ivy say?*' (p. 66, original emphasis) when wishing to do something considered particularly feminine such as flirting with a man. This again draws our attention to gender performance as a set of coded behaviours which, to some degree, are open for play, manipulation, and subversion.

Other female characters in the series include Evelyn and Felicity, Alexia's self-absorbed step-sisters who 'specialize [...] in being both inconvenient and asinine' (p. 24) and as 'pale insipid blondes with wide blue eyes and small rosebud mouths' (p. 27) represent a fashionable ideal of femininity, but Felicity also becomes a spy for Countess Nadasdy, a cunning vampire queen looking like a baroque shepherdess. There is also Sidheag Maccon, a sullen Scotswoman and first female leader of a werewolf clan. In the adjacent Young Adult series about a 'Finishing' School that trains socialites to become assassins, set a generation earlier, the girls' characters range from clever, cunning, or vain to timid, to upbeat or grouchy. In the 'Custard Protocol' series focused on Alexia's daughter Prudence, we find the titular character a wild, enthusiastic tomboy complemented by a soft, but pragmatic best friend (Ivy's daughter Primrose), a sultry and courageous shape-shifter, a morose mechanic, a soft-spoken trans-woman, and a smart and caring female doctor. Female characters in this series often play with archetypes and clichés but are also employed to explore femininity and femaleness as a multifaceted spectrum.

Fashion vs the Steampunk Heroine

In a steampunk universe so engaged with femininity and performance, self-fashioning symbolizes the heroine's exerting of agency over herself and her environment. Alexia implicitly understands that fashion is a legible system identifying her within a social context as a respectable woman of wealth and taste, which grants her powers and liberties:[115]

> She sat awaiting [the gentleman's] arrival calmly in the front parlour, wearing a forest green carriage dress with gold filigree buttons down the front, an elegant new broad-brimmed straw hat, and a cagey expression. The family surmised her imminent departure from the hat and gloves, but they had no idea who might be calling to take her out. Aside from Ivy Hisselpenny, Alexia did not entertain callers often, and everyone knew the Hisselpennys only owned one carriage, and it was not of sufficient quality to merit gold filigree buttons. The Loontwills were left to assume that Alexia was awaiting a *man*. (p. 135, original emphasis)

Here, Alexia's choice of dress is not only tailored towards her purpose of a carriage-ride, but also the company and her intentions towards him. It is therefore embedded in concerns of mobility within both a social and an urban sphere.

When Alexia's detecting uncovers a secret society of scientists performing illegal experiments on supernaturals, her attire becomes useful when she breaks a mirror and 'wrapped a sharp shard of glass carefully in a handkerchief and tucked it down the front of her bodice, between dress and corset, for safekeeping' (p. 264). Her garments here help her protect herself. It is certainly interesting that the corset should be instrumental in this venture, considering that, in neo-Victorian media and the popular imagination, the corset has 'become the accepted visual shorthand for the notion of the literally and metaphorically repressed Victorian woman' and thus created 'unquestioned visual stereotypes and assumptions that reinforce rather than question or dispel the received notions about the period.'[116] While some cite it as evidence that steampunk enacts a 'false feminism' or is in essence anti-feminist and 'retrosexual' instead of an accessory in steampunk self-fashioning, I agree with Julie Anne Taddeo's claim that the corset lets women 'safely and triumphantly play with and transgress boundaries', and indeed provides opportunities to reclaim femininity on their own terms.[117] Symbolic readings from a present-day perspective run the risk of obscuring corsets' primary function as an undergarment – forerunner to those still worn by women every day. As Montz argues, Victorian women '*existed* within a fashion system; that is, they lived within it, functioning and fashioning their lives while, through, and in spite of wearing corsets, gloves, crinolines, and veils.'[118] Carriger's text is alert to this.

The Parasolverse also explores 'the way fashions must change to accommodate new technologies of travel, particularly the dirigible', here the 'very real practicality of wearing Victorian dress in the air.'[119] In the second novel, *Changeless*, Alexia's status as Lady Maccon means her attire merits description in the society papers:

> Lady Maccon boarded the Giffard Long-Distance Airship, Standard Passenger Class Transport Mode, accompanied by an unusually large entourage. [...] The party was outfitted with the latest in air-travel goggles, earmuffs, and several other fashionable mechanical accessories designed to facilitate the most pleasant of dirigible experiences. [...] The lady herself wore a floating dress of the latest design, with tape-down skirt straps, weighted hem, a bustle of alternating ruffles of teal and black designed to flutter becomingly in the aether breezes, and a tightly fitted bodice. There were teal-velvet-trimmed goggles about her neck and a matching top hat with an appropriately modest veil and drop-down teal velvet earmuffs tied securely to her head. More than a few ladies walking through Hyde Park that afternoon stopped to wonder as to the maker of her dress [...] [120]

The retro-speculative impulses of Carriger's Parasolverse are re-integrated into a hyper-Victorian aesthetic that, although whimsical, privileges a logic of feminine performance. Instead of resorting to masculine trousers or a forerunner to the New Woman's bicycling outfit, her steampunk setting merely adapts the existent repertoire: skirt hems are weighted to preserve modesty, bustles designed to accentuate the feminine form, and goggles trimmed with velvet. Like the railway, the airship represents the cosmopolitanism and speed of modernity and to adapt women's fashion accordingly is to facilitate their participation in that modernity on their own terms. Alexia is even saved from falling to her death when her reinforced metal hem is caught in the docking mechanism of the airship (p. 173).

Carriger acknowledges fashion as an integral factor in performing femininity and functioning in society, undermining persistent stereotypes of Victorian fashions as instruments of restriction or repression. As Montz reminds us: 'Monumental events in women's history such as the Married Women's Property Act (1882), the repeal of the Contagious Diseases Acts (1886) and most especially the universal vote for women in England (1928), were fought for by women who wore – quite fashionably, in fact – the very trappings so shunned by contemporary Steampunk writers.'[121] The Parasolverse pays homage to this feminist genealogy by portraying Alexia as a woman who repeatedly saves herself from distress sometimes despite and sometimes because of her corset and bustle.

Taking Advantage

Alexia is portrayed as a woman of fortitude and pragmatism, an Action Girl who does not compromise her femininity to achieve agency or independence. Given that, in post-feminist neo-Victorian and steampunk depictions, sexuality can constitute both the means by which the contemporary heroine might assert her perceived liberations and the factor which entraps her in narratives of patriarchal power play, it is especially interesting to consider Alexia as a Romance heroine.

Alexia's relationship with Lord Connall Maccon, Earl of Woolsey, head of the Bureau of Unnatural Registry, Alpha werewolf, Scottish, scruffy, large, and loud, is governed by typical romance tropes around an attractive, rude, Byronic hero. Connall's masculinity is encoded in wildness and violence because he is a werewolf, and thus quite literally a beast for Alexia to tame with her preternatural touch. Whereas on the surface, he may so perpetuate common, rightfully problematic tropes that invoke dominance and allusions of rape, Carriger here, too, plays with the trope.[122] For one, Connall's untamed beastliness is played for laughs because his dishevelled appearance is at variance with the expected behaviour of a gentleman. He is physically attracted to Alexia, but also recognizes that she has 'got a jot more backbone than most females this century' (pp. 22–23) and, acknowledging her intelligence and competence, 'refused to be suckered into becoming sympathetic' (16). By not patronizing Alexia merely because she is female, he shows respect, but this may be conveniently misunderstood within Victorian etiquette so that Alexia and Lord Maccon spend the better part of the novel deliberately at odds. However, both parties see eye to eye, sometimes almost literally, even when at variance: 'Lord Maccon stood, slightly panicked, and said exactly the wrong thing. "I forbid you to go!" [...] Miss Tarabotti stood as well, instantaneously angry, her chest heaving in agitation. "You have no right!"' (p. 67) Alexia is never intimidated, and Connall specifically admires and courts her as an 'Alpha Female': 'He has been perceiving you as he would an Alpha female werewolf.' (p. 177).

Thus, while Connall initiates the romance by kissing her – 'in the middle of a public street' (p. 112), a gendered urban space – Alexia's exploration of her own sexuality is in the narrative's focus. She often takes charge, is in fact invited to 'stake a claim, indicate pursuit, or assert possession. Preferably all three' (p. 117). This she does when proclaiming 'I am going to take advantage of you' (p. 164) and later even suggesting Lord Maccon become her 'Mistress' (p. 206) in a comic subversion of the usual, gendered roles. These she also defies by not equating sex with love, and not relying on Connall marrying her in affecting or restoring her status and self-worth: '[I]f you are not interested in me as anything more than a [...] momentary plaything, you might at least have told me outright afterward. [....] I deserve *some* respect' (p. 155, original emphasis). Alexia's mother, however, is scandalized and attempts to pressure her into marrying Lord Maccon, and ironically it is Alexia who tries to 'do the honourable thing' by releasing him while he genuinely appreciates her as a potential partner on equal terms and pictures 'waking up next to her, seeing her across the dining table, discussing science and politics, having her advice on points of pack controversy and BUR difficulties' (p. 213). The idealistic, fantasy-fulfilling romance genre is here deployed with the premise that what women desire is a partner who desires them, but also respects their space and their agency.

Alexia evidently defies an image of Victorian women as passive and chaste, but her female sexuality does not compromise her as a steampunk heroine or implicate her in a contradictory display of false empowerment. She does not use it to project her alleged liberation, yet in refusing to accept that her honour needs restoring or to marry without love, while simultaneously exploring her sensuality, she is actually liberated. This contrast to Eliza Braun or Veronica Hobbs becomes most prominently during the novel's (somewhat literally) climactic showdown. During full moon, Alexia finds herself in a cell with the transformed Alpha and must now maintain physical contact with Conall at all times to keep him human with her preternatural touch. Such intimate contact with the naked man is a reversal of the male gaze which emphasizes female nudity and dependence, and in contrast to the events of *The Janus Affair*, where Eliza Braun is at the mercy of a male captor. Instead, Alexia and Connall join forces to solve the novel's mystery, and she retains agency, or example by 'deciding' that 'there was something excruciatingly erotic about being fully dressed with a large naked man pressed against her from head to foot' (p. 288) and then 'seiz[ing] the moment' (p. 288). It is here that the two resolve their tensions and profess their love before teaming up to overpower the mad scientists. Instead of being separated and treated in problematically gendered ways like in *The Janus Affair*, the male and female hero are brought closer together and operate on consent and consensus. Alexia is never victimized in gendered ways or punished for her sexual appetite or agency – on the contrary, she is rewarded with a marriage to a man who genuinely appreciates her and a position as an agent of the Crown, recruited by Queen Victoria herself (pp. 335–340).

Throughout the series, sexuality, like femininity, is treated as something that women may explore and enjoy on their own terms, a process which becomes part of a coming of age. It is not solely the domain of the unconventionally forward and assertive heroine: 'Miss Hisselpenny found most of the [erotic] books in Alexia's father's library shameful to read. She covered her ears and hummed whenever Miss Tarabotti even mentioned her papa, but she never hummed so loudly she could not hear what was said. But now that her friend possessed firsthand experience, she was simply too curious to be embarrassed'

(p. 121). Ivy's curiosity is portrayed as different, but no less valid than Alexia's, and in the 'Custard Protocol' series, we witness both Prudence and Primrose (as well as Primrose's twin brother Percy) go through a similar but individually attuned process in which their own agency and comfort is foregrounded. In line with the trappings of the popular romance genre, Carriger delivers female-centric fantasies that avoid the problematic entanglements of other portrayals, such as those discussed previously.

Dirigibles and Octopi

Alexia's independence is often externalized through her independent travel across London or Europe at large, which in the 1860s in which the series is set, constitutes her as a precursor of the New Woman. Her access to urban spheres is, however, linked to her status as spinster, wife, mother, or – briefly – Fallen Woman. During the third novel, *Blameless,* Connall falsely accuses Alexia of unfaithfulness, and she is disgraced, but hardly seems to mind. The paradoxical punishment which befalls her post-feminist colleagues fails to manifest. Having just escaped an assassination attempt via mechanical ladybugs, she hides out in a public tea shop on Cavendish Square in Marylebone, 'a popular watering hole among ladies of quality'[123] (p. 41) and causes a stir: 'One or two matrons, accompanied by impressionable young daughters, stood and left in a rustle of offended dignity' (p. 42). With her status altered from peeress to disgraced woman, Alexia is out of place in this semi-public urban space which serves as a stage for feminine respectability, yet she refuses to conform to expectations. When Lady Blingchester purports to shame her, suggesting she 'might have done [her family] a favour by casting yourself into the Thames' – a stereotypical destiny for the Fallen Woman – Alexia merely replies: 'I can swim, Lady Blingchester, Rather well, actually' (p. 57). Again, Alexia's sense of self is independent from social conventions, and she continues to move about the city as she pleases and in fact uses social conventions to obscure her more political goals in comedic ways: 'It went against her nature to be seen fleeing London because she was thought adulterous, but it was better than having the real reason known to the general public. Just imagine what the gossipmongers would say if they knew vampires were intent on assassinating her—so embarrassing' (pp. 76–77).

Throughout the series, Alexia remains firmly in control of where she goes and why, detained neither by public opinion nor her advancing pregnancy in the fourth novel *Heartless*, which sees her track a suspect to a warehouse in an unfashionable neighbourhood (p. 264), set fire to it (p. 271), then traverse the city in a small dirigible (p. 275), disrupt an evening ball in Mayfair to which she is unwelcome although she has been invited (p. 285), and pursue a gigantic mechanical octopus across London (p. 304).[124] Even when she goes into labour inside the octopus, Alexia refuses to be defined by her gendered body: 'Oh, that's not important. That can wait' (p. 350).

During the series, Alexia goes through several 'stages' of (Victorian) womanhood – spinster, wife, Fallen Woman, expecting mother, mother – without being wholly defined by any of them. Nally's accusation that Alexia uses her 'so-called choices' to opt for 'some very conservative visions of what it means to be a woman' seems curious considering that none of these choices actually change what Alexia does or where she goes.[125] While she navigates surely through and within a Victorian social system like any historical woman would have, she also readily bends or breaks the rules where they impede her, and is in fact at no point curtailed in her agency, re-presented through a male gaze, or punished for her sexuality. Neither does the narrative devalue these roles in favour of masculine entrepreneurship, pursuit of power, or deployment of violence: Alexia does not need trousers, explosives, or to dominate others in order to secure or express her own agency. Out of this chapter's neo-Victorian and steampunk heroines, Alexia alone is imagined and realized fully on her own terms, not re-appropriated into a patriarchal narrative logic.

Alexia certainly anticipates the New Women in some ways, and creates her own, individual vision of female empowerment in others. She does not travel by bicycle or omnibus, reject marriage, or campaign for suffrage, but she utilizes carriages, mechanical octopi, and dirigibles to go where she wants to, demands equality in her marriage as an Alpha Female, investigates supernatural cases as an agent of the Crown, and exerts agency over her journey and her sexuality with success. Her daughter Prudence, who later becomes the captain of her own airship, self-evidently considers 'herself a New Woman, [and] thus she did not think it odd to travel alone in public hire'.[126] No doubt she is modelling herself on her mother. Interestingly, Perschon considers Alexia an 'amped-up New Woman' as a steampunk incarnation of agency and feminist optimism within a Victorian aesthetic, while at the same time, Nally's post-feminist lens struggles to accommodate Alexia's actions within the catalogue of feminist achievements that has been constructed between the New Woman as collective symbol and second-wave feminism. However, I argue that Alexia puts into play the ideals of fourth-wave feminism and the popular fan criticism with which it cross-pollinates. She embodies Sophia McDougall's call for more nuanced female characters: 'I want her to be free to express herself/ I want her to have meaningful, emotional relationships with other women/ I want her to be weak sometimes/ I want her to be strong in a way that isn't about physical dominance or power/ I want her to cry if she feels like crying/ I want her to ask for help/ I want her to be who she is.'[127]

Fan criticism of the fourth wave focuses less on the validity of lifestyle choices, but demands that women be written three-dimensionally, represent female experience as a full spectrum, and be allowed to be feminine and strong at the same time. This criticism, interlinking with fourth-wave discussions about body shaming, sex positivity, rape culture, and other prominent concerns of the MeToo era, foregrounds representation and agency within the narrative frame, and independence from patriarchal narrative logic in the form of re-assimilating a 'Fallen Woman' character through punishment or a male gaze. Alexia Tarabotti, while inhabiting a genre often considered frivolous, un-serious, un-critical, and conservative (not least because it caters to women's romantic fantasies), emerges somewhat ironically as an example of how fourth-wave feminist ideas may be realized within a steampunk setting, and that such ideas can build on and supplement the parameters set up by previous feminist genealogies in creative ways.

4.3 Beyond the Binary: Anachronism as Queer Potential

Discussions about steampunk and gender often centre around feminist concerns, but the aesthetic presents unique opportunities to interrogate gender and sexuality as a full spectrum, even though it is sometimes read as a mode which re-inscribes 'traditional' gender binaries through what appears like a gendered fashion aesthetic. To read today's steampunk as 'retro-sexist', however, risks re-inscribing these heteronormative gender binaries which the aesthetic's creative play is geared towards challenging. After all, steampunk cosplay de-centres and re-assembles meaning through remix and juxtaposition, as Molly Westerman argues: '[M]any people use steampunk to play with those categories. In many steampunk texts, objects, and garments, masculinity and femininity are more like design elements than like absolutes of nature—which makes gender more fluid and far less moralizing than the nostalgic style might initially suggest.'[128] Here, men may don corsets and women may choose not to, as Lisa Hager notes: '[M]any steampunk women have a longstanding love affair with corsets, but, equally important here are the women who crossplay masculine personae, like myself, and the many men who have similar fondnesses for corsets and wear them exquisitely well.'[129] Moreover, through its play with gender binaries, steampunk may accommodate a full spectrum that includes LGBTQA+ identities, as Carriger's Parasolverse also exemplifies.

Alexia, Lord Akeldama, and Madame Lefoux

Alexia's marriage to Connall has been read as a 'recourse to a traditional narrative of heterosexual marriage', and the portrayal of homosexual characters Lord Akeldama and Madame Lefoux as ultimately governed by 'the pressures of heteronormativity'.[130] Considering that Carriger's universe is one of few steampunk works of fiction to actually feature queer characters, such claims merit investigation.

To begin with, Alexia's marriage to Lord Maccon may give the impression of heterosexuality, especially in the first novel, but as soon as Alexia meets Genevieve Lefoux the cross-dressing inventor, in *Changeless*, readers discover that she is actually coded as bisexual (and thus her marriage is not, in fact, heteronormative): 'Alexia thought, without envy, that this was quite probably the most beautiful female she had ever seen.' (p. 79). When Madame Lefoux 'reached up and stroked the back of her hand down the side of Alexia's face [...] it made her face feel hot even in the cold aether wind' (pp. 153–154). Alexia frequently reacts to Genevieve's flirtations as she reacts to Connall's, and Carriger has confirmed that in her Parasolverse, 'preternaturals are all pan, or at least bisexual', even though 'in Victorian times with her upbringing she doesn't have the language or understanding'.[131] About Alexia's bisexuality, Carriger notes: 'I think that there is always a small part of her half in love with Madame Lefoux but she could never understand that's what it was, so she never acknowledges it.'[132]

It is this lack of vocabulary about non-normative sexualities that makes steampunk's tension with the Victorian era from which it synthesizes itself so productive. Discourses around male homosexuality in the late-Victorian age were largely centred on 'sodomy' as a criminal offence formally encoded through the 1885 Labouchère Amendment and famously catalyzed through the Wilde trials in 1895. It is not surprising, then, that Lord Akeldama, a rogue vampire, is an amped-up emblem of the dandy-aesthete, himself a composite figure that synthesized Victorian debates around aestheticism, artisanship, gender, and 'degeneration', and who encapsulates many of steampunk's inherent ideals.[133] Akeldama is an ageless, flamboyant vampire who 'might look and act like a supercilious buffoon of the highest order, but he had one of the sharpest minds in the whole of London.' (*Soulless,* p. 47). With his long blond hair, 'queued back in a manner stylish hundreds of years ago' (p. 51), 'ethereal face' and his proclivity to 'speak predominantly in italics' (p. 46) particularly where the words 'darling' or 'daffodil' are concerned, he performs effeminacy and revels in the outrageous. His attire is eccentric: 'His coat was of exquisite plum-coloured velvet paired with a satin waistcoat of sea-foam green and mauve plaid. His britches were of a perfectly coordinated lavender [...]' (*Soulless*, p. 220). His cartoon-ish and somewhat anachronistic style always hints at the late Baroque: 'I am afraid I never quite left that particular era. It was *such* a glorious time to be alive, when men finally and *truly* got to wear sparkly things, and there was lace and velvet everywhere.' (*Soulless*, p. 225, original emphasis). However, there are also echoes of Oscar Wilde's aesthetic style, for example in the well-known series of photographs by Napoleon Sarony.[134] Indeed, Nally notes that Lord Akeldama's proclivity for 'yellow, orange, gold, pink, and lemon' echoes Wilde's ideals of 'joyous colour' for the Dress Reform movement.[135]

Matt Cook outlines how sexologists such as Krafft-Ebing attested homosexuals' vanity and a liking for fine fashions and luxury, 'characteristics [...] closely associated with the sophistry and luxury of a particular fashionable urban set, and more specifically to prevailing stereotypes of the decadent or dandy'.[136] Lord Akeldama certainly embodies these stereotypes, but not without irony.[137] By reminding us that laces and velvets were once integral to performing masculinity in previous centuries, he undermines purely binary ideas of gender, and his interior decorations hint at how thoroughly he enjoys his decadent tastes: 'The carpets were [...] flower-ridden images of shepherds seducing shepherdesses under intense blue skies. [...] Lord Akeldama's ceiling depicted cheeky-looking cherubs up to nefarious activities' (*Soulless*, p. 224).

Like Wilde, Akeldama cultivates a flamboyant, witty, and eccentric persona with a personal, anachronistic style and a penchant for extravagant interior design, but he is also an intelligent and strategic thinker, and the young dandies who act as his 'drones' constitute a fashionable spy network that spans across London: 'The *Morning Post* would pay half its weekly income for the kind of information he seemed to have access to at any time of night' (*Soulless*, p. 47). Through his networks of fashionable gay men acting as spies at social events across London, Akeldama indeed mobilizes what Cook has outlined as a hidden urban scene in Victorian London: '[The homosexual] was repeatedly linked to a social scene based around the theatres, parks, streets, and bars and restaurants of major European cities, and was shown to have a particular personal investment in urban life.'[138] Cook's study maps out London's hidden infrastructures of male homosexuality. Beyond the Cleveland Street scandal, which suggested the existence of such networks to the public in 1889, gay men re-purposed well-known public places such as Hyde Park or Oxford and Regent Street as cruising grounds, met in luxurious and cosmopolitan hotels such as the Ritz or the Savoy, at the Alhambra or St James theatre, private clubs in Cleveland Street, or public urinals, for example near Berkeley Square, Piccadilly Circus, in Woodstock Street close to Oxford Circus, or Danbury Place off of Wardour Street in Soho. Urban figures such as telegraph boys were implicated in homosexual networks, as were soldiers through 'Mrs Truman's tobacconist shop', from where liaisons could be initiated, and the Victoria Hotel and Anderton's appeared in blackmail scandals.[139] Lord Akeldama's network of dandy spies exists in a similar way, namely as an alternative and yet very public mapping of London. As such, he and his gay dandies do not exist on the margins of, but are fully integrated into London's social infrastructures, much like their historical counterparts. In fact, Lord Akeldama's address in 31 Russell Square is 'that very location [...] where Wilde spent his final night in London on 19 May 1897 before his exile to France'.[140]

Lord Akeldama encapsulates, catalyzes and re-presents a popular Victorian reception of male homosexuality as embroiled in the decadence movement and with allegations of effeminacy, evident in Max Nordau's polemic *Degeneration* whose publication in English in 1895 influenced the Wilde trials, and Havelock Ellis's 1897 theory on *Sexual Inversion*. This notion of the homosexual as an 'invert' prevailed well into the twentieth century, complemented somewhat by German sexologist Magnus Hirschfeld's theory of homosexuals as a 'third sex'. Lesbian women however remained sparsely theorized, as Sally Ledger observes: '[T]hose women who wanted to write about lesbian love only had the vocabulary made available to them by late-Victorian sexologists and a handful of naturalist and decadent writers.'[141] Radclyffe Hall's now-classic *The Well of Loneliness* (1928), intent on sparking a public debate about lesbian love, exemplifies this, as it only had recourse to Ellis's concept of 'sexual inversion': 'On the one hand', Ledger deliberates, the novel 'did at least make lesbian love visible; but, on the other hand it reinforced the sexologists' pathologisation and morbidification of lesbian sexuality.'[142] The novel's reception history somewhat illuminates queer history across the twentieth century because, as Heather Love notes, it has 'repeatedly come into conflict with contemporary understandings of the meaning and shape of gay identity' because its bleak depiction of lesbian love is 'out of step with the discourse of gay pride'.[143]

Genevieve Lefoux, a French inventor and Carriger's steampunk response to these historical currents, must consequently be read in this context. Genevieve is introduced as 'the most beautiful female', and wearing her 'hair cut unfashionably short, like a man's' (*Changeless*, p. 79):

> [T]he woman was also dressed head to shiny boots in perfect and impeccable style—for a man. Jacket, pants, and waistcoat were all to the height of fashion. A top hat perched upon that scandalously short hair, and her burgundy cravat was tied into a silken waterfall. Still, there was no pretence at hiding her femininity. Her voice, when she spoke, was low and melodic, but definitely that of a woman (p. 80).

Nally identifies this cross-dressing inventor as a figure who 'has assumed a masculine role in all areas of her life', 'very much a stereotypical lesbian', and an example of post-feminist attempts to represent queer identity that end up 'one-dimensional, homophobic or employed in order to naturalize heterosexuality', because her '*difference* to other women [...] essentially leaves heterosexuality untouched as the status quo'.[144] While this reading may tie in with 'invert' theories, Genevieve's femininity is not negated by her cross-dressing as we see in the excerpt above. Instead, her attire enacts steampunk's play with gender performativity through Victorian fashion, calling up music hall stars like Vesta Tilley, and the fact that she is always elegant, charming, attractive, and confident also undermines negative stereotypes about 'butch' lesbians.

Genevieve's relationship with urban spaces is not embedded in an alternative geography, but she does use and re-purpose urban spaces in typically steampunk ways: She owns a notoriously fashionable hat shop, 'Chapeau de Poupe', on Regent Street. Underneath this public front (connected to femininity and self-fashioning) is a hidden laboratory, in which she builds Alexia's weaponized parasol, or a weaponized mechanic octopus with which she destroys half of Mayfair in search for her kidnapped son. The 'octomaton', one of the more outrageous steampunk forms of transport, might illustrate Madame Lefoux's willingness to transgress boundaries in order to preserve her personal integrity and her family, translated into the physical urban sphere.

While Lord Akeldama and Madame Lefoux constitute playful, nuanced, and semi-ironic homages to the gender discourse of the *fin de siècle*, Nally not unreasonably warns that 'commonly vaunted tropes about male sexuality' and the 'masculinized woman' makes the 'characters bear the burden of visual markers of homosexuality, as markers of difference, with the result that heterosexual sexuality is ultimately invisible and rendered the norm'.[145] However, whereas many pop culture texts do deploy queer identities as easily legible against a conventional, heteronormative status quo, Carriger's series complements

Akeldama and Lefoux with a number of other, less visibly coded queer identities, beginning with Alexia's bisexuality. Not only is Carriger's Parasolverse one of few to include queer characters at all (and not just in order to undermine Thatcherite ideals through urban Gothic), but they are positively everywhere. There are Lefoux's lover Angelique, an angelic blonde lesbian, Lord Maccon's beta Professor Lyall, the unassuming, straight-passing professor-type later revealed to be bisexual, 'Biffy' a gay man evolving from Lord Akeldama's favourite drone to werewolf alpha, other drones (named characters include the Viscount Trizdale and Emmet Wilberforce Bootbottle-Fipps [Boots]), and the deceased, but notorious, bi- or pansexual Alessandro Tarrabotti, Alexia's father. In the 'Custard Protocol' series centred on Alexia's daughter Prudence, we find in Primrose and Madame Sekhmet two feminine lesbian women, in Rodrigo a libertine who 'under modern terminology [...] would likely identify as pan', and in Anitra a feminine-passing trans-woman understood by other characters as 'aravani', or 'hijra', an Indian concept for a 'third gender'.[146] Similar to how diverse female characters provide a spectrum of feminine representation, this variety of queer characters relieves Akeldama and Lefoux of the burden of representation and also undermines the stereotypes to which they pay homage by adding nuance and individuality. This spectrum of queer identities less legible within a Victorian gender discourse about 'invert' lesbians and effeminate dandies challenges rather than re-iterates them and quietly undercuts a heteronormative status quo in different ways. Carriger further challenges the heteronormative conventions of the romance genre itself through the publication of her two tie-in novellas that focus, respectively, on Lefoux's lesbian romance (*Romancing the Inventor*, 2016), and Lyall and Biffy's gay romance (*Romancing the Werewolf*, 2017).

Queer Representation and Steampunk

Carriger's Parasolverse is an example of how steampunk may utilize the neo-Victorian aesthetic in combination with social retrofuturism in order to craft alternative gender genealogies in which LGBTQA+ identities are represented in positive ways. Such a desire echoes powerfully with the endeavours of queer decadents at the *fin de siècle* itself, as Joseph Bristow outlines[147]: Oscar Wilde, Vernon Lee, and Michael Field (Katharine Bradley and Edith Cooper) mobilized the decadent mode and its ability to articulate and represent androgyny as ambiguous sexuality to create a 'defiant homoerotic aesthetic' that 'inspired late-Victorian writers to consider how they might modify, rework, and even imagine anew sexual modernity.'[148] This is perhaps most clearly illustrated in

Wilde's story, 'The Portrait of Mr. W. H.' (1889), in which three men become entangled in a quest to prove that the mysterious addressee of Shakespeare's Sonnets, Mr W. H., was an 'effeminate' young actor, so much so that one of them, Cyril Graham, forges a portrait and later commits suicide.[149] Like the Willie Hughes of the portrait, Graham is also coded as an 'effeminate', 'splendid creature' to whom Mr Erskine is 'absurdly devoted'.[150] As Bristow argues, Wilde's outline of a quest to 'realise one's own personality on some imaginative plane out of reach of the trammelling accidents and limitations of real life' and portrait of historical fiction-making as 'an artistic desire for perfect representation'[151] constitutes a historicist impulse to unearth genderqueer people in history, even if that 'entails faking and appropriating history in the face of contravening empirical facts'.[152] Graham's forgery and the fact that Wilde actually commissioned his own portrait of Mr W.H. (now lost) from illustrator Charles Ricketts show that such a desire to see queer identities mirrored in history and so legitimized was strong enough that queer histories had to be invented where they could not be recovered: 'This historicist impulse to recover the queer past, even though it may well involve acts of preposterous distortion, defines one of most potent aspects of literary decadence.'[153] This is an intriguing parallel to the steampunk mode.

However, Bristow also outlines that the ambiguous, genderqueer characters unearthed and re-imagined in Wilde's, Lee's, or Field's fiction were often figures associated with pain, doom, punishment, and death, and that their histories invoked a queer experience of loneliness and tragedy, because, as Wilde's own example so powerfully illustrates, such a narrative echoed the late-Victorian queer experience.[154] Whereas the queer historicism constitutes an interesting trajectory between *fin-de-siècle* subculture and the present-day, we have seen through the example of Hall's *Well of Loneliness* that these narratives of queerness as painful and isolating no longer correspond with contemporary LGBTQA+ identities' desire to be represented in positive ways. In fact, queer fan criticism has in recent years actively campaigned against a prevalent narrative trope called 'Bury Your Gays',[155] in which especially lesbian and bisexual women often die or go insane. Fans argue that LGBTQA+ characters being defined by plot arcs that invariably end in misery and death normalize a meta-narrative of queerness as inherently doomed, which runs counter to the ideals of pride culture.[156] Not least, this trope echoes the paradoxically Victorian poetic justice that kills off the 'Fallen Woman' in many post-feminist media. Both instances constitute a bizarre survival of Victorian narrative conventions in which transgressions on gender norms are punished.

Against this background, it is especially important to note that none of Carriger's characters, queer or not, are punished in such a way. Whereas queer couples in the Parasolverse experience the usual trials and tribulations of the romance plot, they all find love and happy endings eventually. Their survival does not depend on them 'passing' as heterosexual – like Alexia in her femininity, they are free to conform or rebel on their own terms, in ways that echo present-day queer communities. The series therefore shows how steampunk may provide a space in which gender genealogies may be re-traced backwards into a formative past, explored with regard to how that past reflects our identities and their histories back at us, but also how such genealogies may be re-projected and re-evaluated on the terms of the present. Queer histories of the closet, hiding, persecution, and suffering in secret can be re-cast into an anachronistic fantasy in which happy endings are feasible and the ideals of pride culture are synthesized into an alternative genealogy. So, like Wilde, steampunk may not only realize 'an artistic desire for perfect representation',[157] but moreover, I suggest that Eve Kosofsky Sedgwick's concept of reparative reading, a mode that prioritises texts' 'empowering, productive as well as renewing potential to promote semantic innovation, personal healing and social change'[158] and which 'looks to a work of art for solace and replenishment rather than viewing it as something to be interrogated and indicted'[159] here migrates from reading practice into the very fabric of the steampunk story-world: 'Because the reader has room to realize that the future may be different from the present, it is also possible for her to entertain such profoundly painful, pro-foundly relieving, ethically crucial possibilities as that the past, in turn, could have happened differently from the way it actually did.'[160]

This may most fruitfully be illustrated by Prudence's wedding to Madame Lefoux's son Quesnel, where

> Madame Lefoux caused a stir by dancing openly with Miss Imogene. Until Lord Falmouth ['Biffy'] ostentatiously led his beta [Lyall] out onto the floor. Then Lady Kingair joined them, a monumentally uncomfortable but militant-looking Aggie Phinkerlinkton on her arms. When Lord Akeldama, a twinkle in his eyes, offered his arm to Percy [Primrose's twin brother], Percy only sighed and joined them. [...] There was sure to be a scandal in the papers – ladies dancing with ladies was one thing, but *gentlemen* dancing with *gentlemen*? At a wedding? That was beyond even the supernatural set. But Rue (who was happily dancing with Tasherit [Madame Sekhmet]) seemed pleased with this probable outcome. Quesnel was amiable enough not to care about social standing. He swirled around with one of Lord Akeldama's more impressively dressed drones. (p. 67)

In this scene, queer characters openly dance with one another, but heterosexual characters also dance with partners of the same gender, so that heteronormative conventions are playfully dissolved into an open display of solidarity and acceptance.[161] What is more, when Lord Akeldama suggests that 'Progress never did come cheap to high society, sweetling', and Primrose wonders 'how dancing can change the course of civilisation', Prudence comments: 'Give it a chance' (p. 68). This exchange suggests that by making this non-normative dancing fashionable, heteronormative gender binaries may in the long run be destabilized and so afford a degree of visibility and normalization to queer identities. As playful and light as this scene is, it also exemplifies the imaginative power inherent in steampunk's fantastic alternative genealogies.

Conclusion: Reclaiming Gender through Steampunk

A chapter on genealogies and reception histories may well be concluded with its own. About thirty years after *Les Fleurs du Mal* and the conceptualization of modernity as intrinsically tied to the experience of the modern metropolis, coupled with what would later be realized as the flâneur figure, the New Woman emerges in London as a collective symbol of female emancipation. A cross-media phenomenon and composite ideal, she is both quintessentially female (although her femininity is debated), and quintessentially urban, and she provides a legible iconography emblematic of the ongoing debates that inform her. The bicycle comes to symbolize her independence and her mobility alongside the practical and much derided bicycling costume which accompanies it. The suffragist, likewise, is enshrined in the public imagination in her white dress and purple, white, and green sash, campaigning in public spaces such as Hyde Park or Oxford Street. Female journalists, writers, and artists encroach on urban space, carving their own trajectories through the city, reflect on and write about it, and so become visible participants in the phenomenon of modernity. As Steve Pile suggests, 'What makes the city a city is not only the skyscrapers or the shops or the communication networks, but also that people in such places are forced to *behave* in *urban* ways.'[162] As such, the New Woman also actively participates in the making of modern urban space in line with Massey's theory.[163] The urban sphere of late-Victorian London is not only the stage on which women's agency and independence are enacted physically and performatively, but indeed the very space that legitimizes this empowerment.

The New Woman has become a cornerstone in an imagined feminist teleological genealogy of steady emancipation, not least because as a collective ideal, she provides a legible iconography, but that iconography masks a variety of debates that were in no way monolithic, and also depends on evolving frameworks of what constitutes 'feminism'. Still, it is evident why neo-Victorian or steampunk fiction gravitates towards the New Woman as an ideal with which modern audiences are invited to identify. However, while neo-Victorian heroines may be presented as empowered because they self-fashion independently or access urban space in exciting ways – riding motorbikes, investigating shady magicians, or scaling the Natural History Museum – the complex legacy of post-feminism and the persistence of certain sexist tropes in media also trouble and challenge their alleged empowerment. Neo-Victorian heroines such as Irene Adler or Mina Harker and steampunk Action Girls like Veronica Hobbes or Eliza Braun are conceived as feminist ideals whose sexual liberation emancipates them and sets them apart from the conventional Victorian women who are imagined to be 'stuffy' and 'repressed', and who draw attention to and ideally also overcome the latent sexism imagined to pervade the Victorian age. However, such alleged empowerment not only pits the anachronistically modern heroine against the 'ordinary' Victorian women who are so dismissed and judged inferior, but it is also often undermined by the persistence of sexist tropes, which ultimately hamper if not foreclose the text's ability to imagine viable alternatives.

The corset perhaps encapsulates how present-day feminism can depend on a Victorian Other against which we may define ourselves as liberated, when in reality it is part of a material history that is much more complex, and female body images today are no less subject to those aesthetic pressures we perceive to be at work in the Victorian age. On the contrary, as Margaret Stetz observes, not only is the same scrutiny not applied to male dress and bodies, but to invite present-day audiences to identify against rather than with their Victorian counterparts means ignoring how Victorian fashion acted as a marker of respectability which allowed women – including the bicycling New Woman and the suffragist – to access socio-political arenas of activity and activism in important ways.[164] Feminist critique of Victorian legacies and neo-Victorian portrayals must be sensitive to the ideological undercurrents which inform its readings.

Moreover, post-feminist critique, informed by second-wave ideals, may sometimes lack the vocabulary to account for these perplexing legacies. Fourth-wave feminism, especially in connection with fan criticism and its re-evaluation of the politics underlying representation in mainstream media, may provide ways in which we can articulate what feminism must still strive to achieve, irrespective of whether or not women choose non-traditional pathways or make post-feminist lifestyle choices. This has become increasingly important since 2016, widely called the MeToo era, where we are faced with how patriarchal power structures in politics, the work place, the entertainment industry and popular media itself have re-appropriated feminist achievements into a system where women may imagine themselves to be empowered because they have achieved the second wave's goals (participation in public life, sexual liberty) while still being silenced, curtailed, exploited, and objectified on a large and systematic scale. These developments cannot be productively understood within the parameters of individual, post-feminist lifestyle choices. They are part of a much wider, patriarchal cultural logic that still governs Western societies, and for which fourth-wave feminism must find ways to account, because it has become clear that they impact women's lives in important ways regardless of how traditional or radical they chose to be in their femaleness. Examples of how activism has attempted to do so include social media campaigns, international Women's Marches, or the public cleansing of Hollywood's entertainment industry of sexual harassers, as well the so-called 'pussy hats' or the reclamation of phrases like 'nasty woman' or 'nevertheless, she persisted' from misogynistic discourse. These all suggest that femininity is becoming newly politicized in fourth-wave activism.

Alexia Tarabotti, heroine of Gail Carriger's Parasolverse, defies such a patriarchal cultural logic, instead reclaiming her femininity by enjoying it on her own terms. Carriger's supernatural romance might look frivolous, whimsical, and possibly conservative, but as this chapter shows, Alexia succeeds in enacting both female agency and femininity in ways that suit her purpose, counter to many female characters in other steampunk fictions. In addition to those examples already discussed, this includes James Blaylock's *St. Ives* series in which women are largely angelic wives or people to be rescued. *The Difference Engine*, although radical in many ways, still configures Ada Byron, revered Queen of Engines, or Sybil Gerard as 'sexual appendages of the hero or to threatened objects of technological stalkers and government conspiracies'.[165] Mark Hodder's alternative universe in his *Burton and Swinburne* series (2010–2015) is indeed born out of the erasure of its most iconic female presence, Queen Victoria, who is killed in an early assassination attempt, thus giving way to 'Albertian London'. Lavie Tidhar's Milady in the *Bookman* series (2010–2012), a brash and cynical Black woman, is still victimized and crippled by a male villain before emerging as a newly powerful, but fractured cyborg. On the other hand, interesting and empowered female characters may be found in Philip Reeve's *Mortal Engines* series (2001–2006), Cherie Priest's *Clockwork Century* series (2009–2014), Nisi Shawl's *Everfair* (2016), or P. Djéli Clark's *The Black God's Drums* (2018) and *Master of Djinn* (2021), for example.[166] Indeed, Priest stated that writing women back into history, even anachronistically, is important because it means saying 'We were here and we were doing things' and challenges 'our ideas about who we *were*.'[167]

This is equally true and important for LGBTQA+ identities wishing to see themselves reflected and so legitimized in history, a desire they share with their Victorian counterparts, but who reject tragic narratives of isolation and pain because they find it projects a problematic message incongruous with the ideals of pride culture. Here, too, steampunk may use its hyper-Victorian retro-speculation to collapse timelines and teleologies and deconstruct simplistic binaries between 'then' and 'now', 'Them' and 'Us', replacing outdated gender discourses, now considered harmful, with a positive genealogy of queerness that also challenges heteronormativity in creative and playful ways. This fantastic fiction-making, albeit non-mimetic and anachronistic, echoes the desire of queer aesthetes to 'realise one's own personality on some imaginative plane out of reach of the trammelling accidents and limitations of real life', and may provide an imagined reconciliation with queer histories of the closet.

Steampunk, I argue, is at its most productive and potentially radical when it mobilizes and critically interrogates genealogies constructed around such categories as gender, race, or class, and collapses rather than reinforces binaries between past and present, male and female, liberation and repression, and so on. The tensions that emerge from such an anachronistic double-exposure may, instead of neatly affirming audiences' self-perception as 'having come this far', prompt a re-evaluation of that perception sparked by curiosity. Unlike some neo-Victorian fiction, where sexuality may become 'the battlefield between the supposedly radical Victorian subcultures (e.g., nymphomaniacs, cross-dressers, pornographers, lesbians) and the normative anti-sexual discourses of the Victorian bourgeoisie', Carriger's steampunk offers vicarious fantasies and envisions a retrofuturist setting in which women and non-heterosexual characters alike interrogate and undermine such readings by simply living independently and on their own terms.[168] Steampunk may, consciously or not, re-vitalize discourses of the Victorian age itself that have become obscured by canon formations and reception history. In such a way, steampunk may include or make visible ideas, people, and perspectives familiar today but which we struggle to identify reliably in the (Victorian) past because the vocabulary we use has only evolved in recent decades. Anywhere else, we run the risk of a retroactive diagnosis when we evaluate the past with newer vocabularies of the present, but in steampunk, both contemporary contexts and present-day perspectives may be playfully juxtaposed and so generate creative tension, holding, in Haraway's terms, 'incompatible things together, because both or all are necessary and true' for us.[169] By layering, contrasting, and remixing past and present, steampunk can include both and so, in James Carrott's approximation of a Wildean paradox, become 'more true because it's not'.[170]

Notes

1. Mike Perschon, 'Useful Troublemakers: Social Retrofuturism in the Steampunk Novels of Gail Carriger and Cherie Priest', in *Steaming Into a Victorian Future*, ed. by Julie Anne Taddeo and Cynthia J. Miller (Lanham: Scarecrow Press, 2013), pp. 21–41, p.35, p. 36.
2. Claire Nally, *Steampunk. Gender, Subculture, & the Neo-Victorian* (London: Bloomsbury 2019), p. 217, p. 227.
3. Charles Baudelaire, *The Painter of Modern Life*, (New York: Da Capo Press, 1964 [1863]). *The Flâneur*, ed. by Keith Tester (London: Routledge 1994). Shields, Rob, 'Fancy footwork: Walter Benjamin's notes on *flânerie*', in *The Flâneur*, ed. by Keith Tester (London: Routledge 1994), pp. 43–60. Martina Lauster, 'Walter Benjamin's Myth of the Flâneur', *MLR*, 102:1 (2007), 139–156. Walter Benjamin, *Charles Baudelaire: a Lyric Poet in the Era of High Capitalism*, trans. by Harry Zohn (London: Verso Books, 1997).
4. Keith Tester, 'Introduction', in *The Flâneur*, ed. by Keith Tester (London: Routledge 1994), pp. 1–21, p. 6.
5. Tester, p. 2.
6. Walter Benjamin, *The Arcades Project*, trans. by Kevin McLaughlin and Howard Eiland (New York: Harvard University Press, 2002), p. 41.
7. Laura Mulvey, 'Visual Pleasure and Narrative Cinema', *Screen*, 16:3 (1975), 6–18.
8. Janet Wolff, 'The Invisible Flâneuse: Women and the Literature of Modernity', *Theory, Culture, & Society*, 2:3 (1985), 37–46, p. 41.
9. Wolff, p. 45, original emphasis.
10. Griselda Pollock, *Vision and Difference: Feminism, Femininity and Histories of Art* (London. Routledge, 1988), p. 71.
11. Teresa Gómez Reus and Aránzazu Usandizaga, 'Introduction', in *Inside Out: Women negotiating, subverting, appropriating public and private space*, ed. by Teresa Gómez Reus and Aránzazu Usandizaga (Amsterdam: Rodopi 2008), pp. 19–33, p. 19.
12. Deborah Epstein Nord, *Walking the Victorian Streets: Women, Representation, and the City* (Ithaca: Cornell University Press, 1996), p. 82.
13. Deborah L. Parsons, *Streetwalking the Metropolis: Women, the City and Modernity* (Oxford: Oxford University Press, 2000), p. 4.
14. Parsons, p. 42.

15 Nead, *Victorian Babylon*, p. 70.
16 Wendy Parkins, *Mobility and Modernity in Women's Novels, 1850s-1930s: Women Moving Dangerously* (London: Palgrave Macmillan, 2009), p. 11.
17 Lauren Elkin, *Flâneuse: Women Walk the City in Paris, New York, Tokyo, Venice and London* (London: Chatto Windus 2016), p. 11.
18 Janet Wolff, 'Foreword', in *Inside Out: Women negotiating, subverting, appropriating public and private space*, ed. by Teresa Gómez Reus and Aránzazu Usandizaga (Amsterdam: Rodopi 2008), pp. 15–18, p. 19.
19 My focus lies on Carrier's adult romance series, 'The Parasol Protectorate', but I will also discuss one of the two YA series, 'The Custard Protocol' series. This study prioritizes steampunk fiction set in London and re-thinking London in interesting ways. YA often veers towards fantastical second-world settings or prioritizes character over setting, but there exists a rich and varied corpus of steampunk YA, such as Carriger's 'Finishing School' series, or the fiction of Kenneth Oppel, Cassandra Clare, Philip Reeve, Scott Westerfield, Kady Cross, Andrea Kremer, or Adrienne Kress.
20 Marianne Berger Woods, *The New Woman in Print and Pictures: an Annotated Bibliography* (Jefferson: McFarland & Company, 2009). Lena Wånggren, *Gender, Technology and the New Woman* (Edinburgh: Edinburgh University Press, 2017), pp. 13–20.
21 Angelique Richardson and Chris Willis, 'Introduction', in *The New Woman in Fiction and Fact: Fin-de-Siècle Feminisms*, ed. by Angelique Richardson and Chris Willis (London: Palgrave Macmillan, 2001), pp. 1–38, p. 1.
22 Talia Schaffer, 'Nothing but Foolscap and Ink: Inventing the New Woman', in *The New Woman in Fiction and Fact: Fin-de-Siècle Feminisms*, ed. by Angelique Richardson and Chris Willis (London: Palgrave Macmillan, 2001), pp. 39–52, p. 39; Sally Ledger, *The New Woman: Fiction and Feminism at the Fin de Siècle* (Manchester: Manchester University Press, 1997). Ann Heilmann, *New Woman Fiction: Women Writing First-Wave Feminism* (London: Palgrave Macmillan, 2000). *A New Woman Reader*, ed. by Carolyn Christensen Nelson (Peterborough: Broadview Press, 2001). Ann Heilmann, *New Woman Strategies: Mona Caird, Olive Schreiner, Sarah Grand* (Manchester: Manchester University Press, 2004). Marion Shaw and Lyssa Randolph, *New Woman Writers* (Tavistock: Northcote House Publishers Ltd, 2007). *The History of British Women's Writing, 1880–1920*, ed. by Holly A. Laird (London: Palgrave Macmillan, 2016). Lyn Pykett, *The "improper" Feminine: The Women's Sensation Novel and the New Woman Writing* (London: Routledge, 1992). Gail Cunningham, *The New Woman and the Victorian Novel* (Lanham: Rowman & Littlefield Publishers, 1978). Linda Dowling, 'The Decadent and the New Woman in the 1890's', *Nineteenth-Century Fiction*, 33:4 (1979), 434–453. *Victorian Women Writers and the Woman Question*, ed. by Nicola Diane Thompson (Cambridge: Cambridge University Press, 1999).

23 Schaffer, 'Foolscap and Ink', p. 45.
24 Ledger, *The New Woman*, p. 3.
25 Wånggren, p. 3.
26 Sarah Wintle, 'Horses, Bikes, and Automobiles: The New Woman on the Move', in *The New Woman in Fiction and Fact: Fin-de-Siècle Feminisms*, ed. by Angelique Richardson and Chris Willis (London: Palgrave Macmillan, 2001), pp. 66–78, pp. 66–67.
27 Schaffer, 'Foolscap and Ink', p. 35.
28 Richardson and Willis, p. 22.
29 Wånggren, p. 62.
30 Anna Despotopoulou, *Women and the Railway, 1850-1915* (Edinburgh: Edinburgh University Press, 2016), p. 3.
31 Ana Parejo Vadillo, *Women Poets and Urban Aestheticism: Passengers of Modernity* (London: Palgrave Macmillan, 2005), p. 37.
32 Parejo Vadillo, *Women Poets*, p. 70.
33 Parejo Vadillo, *Women Poets*, p. 76, p. 196.
34 Parejo Vadillo, *Women Poets*, p. 196, p. 116.
35 Lisa Hager, 'British Women Writers, Technology, and the Sciences, 1880–1920' in *The History of British Women's Writing*, 1880-1920, ed. by Holly A. Laird (London: Palgrave Macmillan, 2016), pp. 59–71, p. 60.
36 Ledger, p. 155, also: Walkowitz, *City of Dreadful Delight*, p. 6.
37 Ella Hepworth Dixon, *The Story of a Modern Woman*, ed. by Steve Farmer (Peterborough: Broadview Press, 2004 [1894]), p. 106.
38 Dixon, p. 76.
39 Valerie Fehlbaum, 'Paving the Way for Mrs Dalloway: The Street-walking Women of Eliza Lynn Linton, Ella Hepworth Dixon and George Paston', in *Inside Out: Women negotiating, subverting, appropriating public and private space*, ed. by Teresa Gómez Reus and Aránzazu Usandizaga (Amsterdam: Rodopi 2008), pp. 149–166, p. 162.
40 George Paston (Emily Morse Symonds), *A Writer of Books*, ed. by Margaret D. Stetz and Anita Miller (Chicago: Chicago Review Press, 1998 [1898]), p. 37.
41 Anna Sparham, *Soldiers and Suffragettes: The Photography of Christina Broom* (London: Philip Wilson Publishers, 2015).
42 Lynne Walker, 'Locating the Global/Rethinking the Local: Suffrage Politics, Architecture, and Space', *Women's Studies Quarterly*, 34:1/2 (2006), 174–196, p. 182.
43 Seminal contributions made by Elaine Showalter, Sandra M. Gilbert and Susan Gubar, Adrienne Rich, Julia Kristeva, bell hooks, Audrey Lorde, or Margaret Atwood, and Ursula K. Le Guin.
44 See, for example: Andrew King, 'The Sympathetic Individualist: Ouida's Late Work and Politics', *Victorian Literature and Culture*, 39:2, 2011, pp. 563–579. Lisa Hager,

'Embodying Agency: Ouida's Sensational Shaping of the British New Woman', in *Rediscovering Victorian Women Sensation Writers*, ed. by Anne-Marie Beller and Tara MacDonald (London: Routledge, 2014), pp. 90–101. Lyn Pykett, 'Fin-de-Siècle Ouida: A New Woman writing against the New Woman?', in *The History of British Women's Writing, 1880–1920* ed. by Holly A. Laird (London: Palgrave Macmillan, 2016), pp. 35–46.

45 Stéphanie Genz, *Postfemininities in Popular Culture* (London: Palgrave Macmillan, 2009), p. 2.

46 Angela McRobbie, *The Aftermath of Feminism: Gender, Culture, and Social Change* (London: SAGE Publications, 2009).

47 'In the British and American media, "postfeminism" has been used from the late 1980s onwards to refer to a supposed obsolescence of feminism, pitting the stereotype of the older, serious, sour-faced second-wave feminist against the fun-loving, pole-dancing, carefree younger postfeminist who grew up listening to the "girl power" band Spice Girls.' Antonija Primorac, *Neo-Victorianism on Screen: Postfeminism and Contemporary Adaptations of Victorian Women* (London: Palgrave Macmillan, 2018), p. 98; Antonija Primorac, 'The Naked Truth: The Postfeminist Afterlives of Irene Adler', *Neo-Victorian Studies*, 6:2 (213), 89–113.

48 Imelda Whelehan, *Modern Feminist Thought: From the Second Wave to 'Post-Feminism'*, (New York: New York University Press, 1995).

49 Genz, p. 2, p. 20.

50 McRobbie, p. 1.

51 Primorac, *Postfeminism*, p. 5; Rosalind Gill, 'Postfeminist media culture: Elements of a sensibility', *European Journal of Cultural Studies*, 10:2 (2007), 147–166.

52 'Screen texts offer the pleasures of a nostalgic return to an era of perceived gender certainties for a generation of viewers who take feminism's achievements for granted and who do not have a memory of its struggle', Primorac, *Postfeminism*, p. 17.

53 Genz, p. 4.

54 Genz, p. 94.

55 Genz, p. 7.

56 Perschon, 'Useful Troublemakers'.

57 Primorac, *Postfeminism*, p. 14.

58 Primorac, p. 98.

59 Primorac, p. 99.

60 Primorac, p. 104.

61 Primorac, p. 90.

62 Primorac, pp. 42–43.

63 Nally, p. 200.

64 Nally, pp. 200–201.

65 Nally, p. 204.

66 Nally, p. 203.
67 Nally, p. 203.
68 Nally, p. 203.
69 The umbrella term for Carriger's fictional steampunk universe, in which several of her series are set: The 'Parasol Protectorate' (*Soulless*, 2009; *Changeless*, 2010; *Blameless*, 2010; *Heartless*, 2011; and *Timeless*, 2012.) Another cycle begins with Alexia's daughter Prudence: The 'Custard Protocol' series (*Prudence*, 2015; *Imprudence*, 2016; *Competence*, 2018; *Reticence*, 2019). Also a few tie-in novellas (*Romancing the Inventor*, 2016, and *Romancing the Werewolf*, 2017); Perschon, *Steampunk FAQ*, p. 158.
70 Nally, pp. 217, 135, 227.
71 Nally, p. 227.
72 Rosalind Gill, *Gender and the Media*, (Malden: Polity Press, 2007), p. 269.
73 For example, her reading of Kate MacAllister's *Steamed*.
74 Jennifer Cooke, 'Introduction', in Jennifer Cooke (ed.), *The New Feminist Literary Studies* (Cambridge: Cambridge University Press, 2020), pp. 1–10, p. 4. See also: Nicola Rivers, *Postfeminism(s) and the Arrival of the Fourth Wave. Turning Tides* (London: Palgrave, 2017). Jane Pilcher and Imelda Whehelan 'Mainstreaming or New Activism? Gender Studies and Gender Politics', in Jane Pilcher and Imelda Whehelan (eds.), *Key Concepts in Gender Studies*. 2nd Edition (London: SAGE Publications, 2017), pp. xiii–x. Rosemary Clark-Parsons, *Networked Feminism. How Digital Media Makers Transformed Gender Justice Movements* (Oakland: University of California Press, 2022).
75 Ealasaid Munro, 'Feminism: A Fourth Wave?', *Political Insight*, September 2013, 22–25, p. 23; Tegan Zimmerman, '#Intersectionality: The Fourth Wave Feminist Twitter Community', *Atlantis*, 38:1 (2017), 54–70. Also: Jennifer Baumgardner, 'Is There a Fourth Wave? Does It Matter?', *Feminist*, 2011, https://www.feminist.com/resources/artspeech/genwom/baumgardner2011.html (accessed 26 April 2020); Henry Jenkins, Sangita Shresthova, Liana Gamber-Thompson, Neta Kligler-Vilenchik, and Arely Zimmerman, *By Any Media Necessary: The New Youth Activism* (New York: NYU Press, 2016).
76 Munro, p. 23.
77 Henry Jenkins, 'Welcome to Convergence Culture', *Confessions of an Aca-Fan*, 19 June 2006, http://henryjenkins.org/blog/2006/06/welcome_to_convergence_culture.html (accessed 28 April 2020).
78 Cooke, 'Introduction', p. 4.
79 Kira Cochrane, *All the Rebel Women: The rise of the fourth wave of feminism*, ebook, (London: Guardian Shorts, 2013). Prudence Chamberlain, *The Feminist Fourth Wave: Affective Temporality*, (London: Palgrave Macmillan, 2017).
80 As Munro notes, fourth wave has generated its own language which lends itself to character limits and hashtagging: 'The realisation that women are not a homogenous

group has brought with it a set of new terminologies that attempt to ensure that those who hold a given identity are not spoken for, or carelessly pigeonholed. For newcomers, the vocabulary can be dizzying, from "cis" (a neologism referring to those individuals whose gender and sexual identities map cleanly on to one another) to "WoC" ('women of colour') and "TERF" ('trans-exclusionary radical feminists').' Munro, p. 25.

81 Rivers, *Turning Tides*, p.16.
82 Primorac, *Postfeminism,* p. 106.
83 Eckart Voigts, '"Victoriana's Secret": Emilie Autumn's Burlesque Performance of Subcultural Neo-Victorianism', *Neo-Victorian Studies* 6:2 (2013), 15–39, p. 15.
84 Voigts-Virchow, 'Hermeneutics', p. 20.
85 Marie-Luise Kohlke, 'Sexsation', p. 346. Heilmann and Llewelyn, too, underline the 'nostalgic fetishization of the taboo, the secret and forbidden in a world of sexual over-exposure, a disingenuous belief in the radical nature of a society no longer under the shadow of what Michel Foucault conceptualised as the "repressive hypothesis"'. Heilmann and Llewellyn, p. 107; Michel Foucault, *The History of Sexuality*, 1978.
86 Kohlke, 'Sexsation', p. 67.
87 Primorac, *Postfeminism,* p. 93.
88 New Zealand granted women the vote in 1893. The novel is set in 1896.
89 'The limit of the Willing Suspension of Disbelief for a given element is directly proportional to its awesomeness.' Anon., 'The Rule of Cool', *TvTropes*, n.d., https://tvtropes.org/pmwiki/pmwiki.php/Main/RuleOfCool (Accessed 20 July 2020).
90 An eclectic martial art and self-defence method comprised of elements of boxing, jujitsu, cane fighting, and French kickboxing, developed in 1898 by Edward William Barton-Wright and made famous through Conan Doyle's Sherlock Holmes stories.
91 Mann, *Affinity Bridge*, p. 26.
92 Founded in 2004, TvTropes is a popular wiki that catalogues storytelling tropes across a variety of media, from television and film to literature, comics, video games, music, and advertising.
93 Anon., 'Distress Ball', *TvTropes*, n.d., https://tvtropes.org/pmwiki/pmwiki.php/Main/DistressBall (Accessed 28 April 2020).
94 Genz, pp. 153–154.
95 Sophia MacDougall, 'I Hate Strong Female Characters', *New Statesman*, 15th August 2015, https://www.newstatesman.com/culture/2013/08/-hate-strong-female-characters (Accessed 26 April 2020).
96 Anon., 'Faux Action Girl', *TvTropes*, n.d., https://tvtropes.org/pmwiki/pmwiki.php/Main/FauxActionGirl (Accessed 28 April 2020).
97 Pip Ballantine and Tee Morris, *Phoenix Rising: A Ministry of Peculiar Occurrences Novel*, (New York: Harper Voyager, 2011), p. 2.

98   Anon., 'Action Girl', *TvTropes*, n.d., https://tvtropes.org/pmwiki/pmwiki.php/Main/ActionGirl (Accessed 28 April 2020).
99   Pip Ballantine and Tee Morris, *The Janus Affair: A Ministry of Peculiar Occurrences Novel*, (New York: Harper Voyager, 2012). While the motorcycle, in its earliest version, was invented as early as 1885, we can assume that this machine is a techno-fantastical anachronism.
100 *Phoenix Rising*, p. 57.
101 Primorac, *Postfeminism*, p. 99.
102 McDougall, n.p.
103 Gail Carriger, *Soulless* (London: Orbit Books, 2009).
104 Amy Montz, '"In Which Parasols Prove Useful": Neo-Victorian Rewriting of Victorian Materiality', *Neo-Victorian Studies*, 4:1 (2011), 100–118, p. 108.
105 Montz, p. 108.
106 'It won several awards, and within a year was being developed into a manga version for Yen Press that was released in 2011. The Parasol Protectorate series is easily one of the (if not the) most successful steampunk series ever published. Carriger dominates steampunk lists on Goodreads, which is ironic given that early criticism Carriger received had determined that her books weren't "steampunk enough" due to the lack of focus on technology. Looking at steampunk lists today; it seems that the whimsical paranormal steampunk adventure Carriger pioneered is where the genre thrives best.' Perschon, *FAQ*, p. 164.
107 Marie-Luise Kohlke and Christian Gutleben, 'What's So Funny about the Nineteenth Century?', in *Neo-Victorian Humour: Comic Subversions and Unlaughter in Contemporary Historical Re-Visions*, ed. by Marie-Luise Kohlke and Christian Gutleben (Amsterdam: Brill Rodopi, 2017), p. 1.
108 Gutleben, 'Fear is Fun' pp. 303, 310–311, Kohlke and Gutleben, 'What's So Funny?', p. 3.
109 'Moreover, by re-presenting period terminology, outmoded attitudes, and questionable ideological discourses in order to comically deconstruct them, neo-Victorian humour becomes implicated – even if only ironically – in their reproduction, inadvertently giving them new life and keeping them in cultural circulation.' Kohlke and Gutleben, p. 2.
110 Nally, pp. 84–85.
111 Gutleben, 'Fear is Fun', p. 12.
112 Nally, p. 130.
113 Nally, p. 130.
114 'She would have coloured gracefully with embarrassment had she not possessed the complexion of one of those "heathen Italians", as her mother said, who never coloured, gracefully or otherwise. (Convincing her mother that Christianity had, to all intents and purposes, originated with the Italians, thus making them the exact opposite of heathen, was a waste of time and breath.)' Carriger, *Soulless*, p. 11.

115 Christine Bayles Kortsch, *Dress Culture in Late Victorian Women's Fiction: Literacy, Textiles, and Activism*, (Farnham: Ashgate, 2009). Margaret Stetz, 'Looking at Victorian Fashion: Not a Laughing Matter', in *Neo-Victorian Humour: Comic Subversions and Unlaughter in Contemporary Historical Re-Visions*, ed. by Marie-Louise Kohlke and Christian Gutleben, (Amsterdam: Brill Rodopi, 2017), pp. 145–169. Dru Pagliosotti, '"People keep giving me rings, but I think a small death ray might be more practical": Women and Mad Science in Steampunk Comics', in *Neo-Victorian Humour: Comic Subversions and Unlaughter in Contemporary Historical Re-Visions*, ed. by Marie-Luise Kohlke and Christian Gutleben, (Amsterdam: Brill Rodopi, 2017), pp. 213–146.

116 Primorac, *Postfeminism*, p. 15.

117 Mary Anne Taylor, 'Liberation and a Corset: Examining False Feminism in Steampunk, in *Clockwork Rhetorik: The Language and Style of Steampunk*, ed. by Barry Brummett, (Jackson: University of Mississippi Press, 2014), pp. 38–60. Martin Danahay, 'Steampunk and the Performance of Gender and Sexuality', *Neo-Victorian Studies*, 9:1 (2016), 123–150, p. 127; Julie Anne Taddeo, 'Corsets of Steel: Steampunk's Reimagining of Victorian Femininity', in *Steaming Into a Victorian Future*, ed. by Julie Anne Taddeo and Cynthia J. Miller (Lanham: Scarecrow Press, 2013), pp. 43–65.

118 Montz, p. 116, original emphasis.

119 Montz, p. 111.

120 Gail Carriger, *Changeless* (London: Orbit Books, 2010), p. 144–145.

121 Montz, p. 109.

122 Nally, pp. 232–233.

123 Gail Carriger, *Changeless*.

124 Gail Carriger, *Heartless* (London: Orbit Books, 2011).

125 Nally, p. 218.

126 Gail Carriger, *Imprudence: Book Two of The Custard Protocol* (London: Orbit Books, 2016), p. 61.

127 McDougall, also echoed here: 'Screw writing "strong" women. Write interesting women. Write well-rounded women. Write complicated women. Write a woman who kicks a**, write a woman who cowers in a corner. Write a woman who's desperate for a husband. Write a woman who doesn't need a man. Write women who cry, women who rant, women who are shy, women who don't take no sh*t, women who need validation and women who don't care what anybody thinks.' Quoted in Lauren Cooke, 'How We're Written', *Huffington Post*, 25 April 2014, https://www.huffingtonpost.com/lauren-cooke/how-were-written_b_4834218.html (accessed 28 April 2020).

128 Molly Westerman, 'How Steampunk Screws with Victorian Gender Norms', *bitchmedia*, 15 January 2014, https://www.bitchmedia.org/post/how-steampunk-screws-with-victorian-gender-norms (accessed 28 April 2020).

129 Lisa Hager, 'Queer Cogs: Steampunk, Gender Identity, and Sexuality', *Tor.com*, 4 October 2012, https://www.tor.com/2012/10/04/steampunk-gender-sexuality/ (accessed 28 April 2020).
130 Nally, pp. 241, 235.
131 Gail Carriger, 'Researching Fluidity & Representing it in Fiction', *Gail Carriger*, 24 May 2019, https://gailcarriger.com/2019/05/24/researching-gender-fluidity-representing-it-in-fiction-the-5th-gender-by-gail-carriger-custard-protocol-san-andreas-shifters-tinkered-stars-behind-the-magic/ (accessed 28 April 2020).
132 Gail Carriger, 'Is Alexia Bisexual?', *Reader Q&A*, 2016, https://www.goodreads.com/questions/647353-is-alexia-bisexual-i-ve-wondered-about (accessed 28 April 2020).
133 More on dandyism and steampunk in: Stefania Forlini, 'The Aesthete, the Dandy, and the Steampunk; or, Things as They Are Now', in *Like Clockwork. Steampunk Pasts, Presents & Futures,* ed. by Rachel A. Bowser and Brian Croxall (Minneapolis: Minnesota UP, 2016), pp. 97–126.
134 Napoleon Sarony, 'Oscar Wilde 1882', *MetMuseum.org*, n.d., https://www.metmuseum.org/art/collection/search/283247 (accessed 23 April 2020).
135 Nally, p. 237.
136 Matt Cook, *London and the Culture of Homosexuality 1885-1914* (Cambridge: Cambridge University Press, 2003), p. 84. Richard Freiherr von Krafft-Ebing, author of *Psychopathia Sexualis* (1886), one of the first texts on sexual pathology, especially homosexuality, sadism, and masochism.
137 Talia Schaffer 'Fashioning Aestheticism by Aestheticizing Fashion: Wilde, Beerbohm, and Male Aesthete's Sartorial Codes', *Victorian Literature and Culture*, 28:1 (2000), 39–54.
138 Cook, p. 83.
139 Cook, p. 19, pp. 27–28.
140 Nally, p. 236.
141 Ledger, p. 142.
142 Ledger, p. 144.
143 Heather Love, *Feeling Backward: Loss and the Politics of Queer History* (Cambridge: Harvard University Press, 2007), p.100–101; 'During the 1970s, the novel was attacked primarily for its equation of lesbianism with masculine identification; in the years of the "woman-loving-woman," it was anathema with its mannish heroine, its derogation of femininity, and its glorification of normative heterosexuality.' p. 100.
144 Nally, p. 234.
145 Nally, p. 240.
146 Carriger, 'Researching Gender Fluidity', n. p.
147 Joseph Bristow, 'Decadent Historicism', *Volupté: Interdisciplinary Journal of Decadence Studies*, 3.1 (2020), 1–27.

148 Bristow, p. 8, 4.
149 Oscar Wilde, 'The Portrait of Mr W. H.', in *The Complete Works of Oscar Wilde: Stories, Plays, Poems, & Essays*, (New York: HarperCollins, 2008), pp. 1150–1202, p. 1151.
150 Wilde, p. 1153, 1152.
151 Wilde, p. 1150.
152 Bristow, p. 10
153 Bristow, p. 10.
154 Bristow, p. 5.
155 'The Bury Your Gays trope in media, including all its variants, is a homophobic cliché. It is the presentation of deaths of LGBT characters where these characters are nominally able to be viewed as more expendable than their heteronormative counterparts.' Anon., 'Bury Your Gays', *TvTropes*, n.d., https://tvtropes.org/pmwiki/pmwiki.php/Main/BuryYourGays (accessed 28 April 2020), n. p.
156 Eve Ng and Julie Levin Russo, 'Envisioning Queer Female Fandom', *Transformative Works and Cultures* 24 (2017), n.p. Elizabeth Bridges, 'A Genealogy of Queerbaiting: Legal Codes, Production Codes, "Bury Your Gays", and "The 100 Mess"', *Journal of Fandom Studies*, 6:2 (2018), 115–132.
157 Wilde, p. 1150.
158 Katrin Röder, 'Reparative Reading, Post-structuralist Hermeneutics and T. S. Eliot's Four Quartets', *Anglia* 132:1 (2014), 58–59.
159 Rita Felski, *The Limits of Critique* (Chicago: The University of Chicago Press, 2015), p. 151.
160 Eve Kosofsky Sedgwick, 2003. *Touching Feeling: Affect, Pedagogy, Performativity* (Durham, North Carolina: Duke University Press, 2003 [1985]), p. 146.
161 Gail Carriger, *Reticence: The Custard Protocol: Book Four* (London: Orbit Books, 2019).
162 Steve Pile, *Real Cities: Modernity, Space and the Phantasmagorias of City Life* (London: SAGE Publications, 2005), p. 1, original emphasis.
163 Massey, p. 107.
164 Stetz, 'Not A Laughing Matter'.
165 Clayton, *Charles Dickens in Cyberspace*, p. 111.
166 These are not set in Victorian London, however, but, respectively in a post-apocalyptic future, across the United States, the Belgian Congo, a steampunk-ed New Orleans, and an alternative Cairo.
167 Carrott and Johnson, *Vintage Tomorrows*, p. 82.
168 Eckart Voigts, '"Victoriana's Secret": Emilie Autumn's Burlesque Performance of Subcultural Neo-Victorianism', *Neo-Victorian Studies* 6:2 (2013), 15–39, p. 21.
169 Haraway, p. 291.
170 Tedx Talks, *Vintage Tomorrows: James H. Carrott at TEDxSonomaCounty*, Video, YouTube, posted by Tedx Talks, 19 June 2013, https://www.youtube.com/watch?v=MT9WWyAFHpE, 8:05–8:10 (accessed 28 April 2020).

Conclusion: An Exercise Bicycle for the Mind

Whereas post-Victorian fiction was a presence throughout the twentieth century,[1] steampunk itself notably emerges at the collapse of the industrial paradigm and so both marks and is produced by a pivotal shift in the West's relationship with the Victorian past, namely when that past becomes 'weird and archaic'. As its original, functional infrastructures become disentangled from their initial purpose, the (tactile, volatile, quaint) Victorian aesthetic instead becomes a vehicle for cultural soul-searching, as popular fiction ponders the oncoming and later, the evolving digital age. Indeed, steampunk curiously, if quietly, parallels and even chronicles cyberpunk's evolution, as its once-niche thought experiments – like hyper-cities, human-machine hybridity or symbioses, and AI – become tangibly and legibly mainstream. 1990s steampunk and neo-Victorian Gothic especially demonstrate how the Victorian past is increasingly re-signified, de-coupled from nostalgic notions of heritage and continuation, and instead re-positioned as a radically defiant Other whose quirks, fissures, and marginalized subcultures crucially undermine neo-liberal meta-narratives. That this (re-)signification of the Victorian era's legacy through its ever-fascinating, '(would-be) *transcended otherness*, alternately gothically horrid and cheerfully quaint',[2] is an ongoing cultural struggle is demonstrated by the fact that, just as in Thatcherite politics, selective, reactionary 'Victorian' meta-narratives have once again been mobilized in the Brexit era to service a British identity of political power and exceptionalism that conveniently ignores the era's prosperity as dependent on pervasive colonial violence. Then as now, in its rebellion against such meta-narratives, Victorian London provides both stage and substance for an essential, imagined 'Victorian-ness', even if steampunk consciously veers away from a domestic middle class and instead gravitates towards urban underdogs, deviants, and misfits who make visible the instability of the social contract, or speak back from the margins to the city as global nexus.

Indeed, steampunk London itself emerges as a globalized phenomenon mutable to, but not dependent on, various cultural contexts. Both the American-based seminal steampunk of Gibson, Sterling, and the Trifecta, for example, and the hyper-Gothic Ripperature of British authors Moore, Newman, and Ackroyd responds to respective neo-liberal meta-narratives of the 1980s. However, the American contingent focuses on the newly archaic weirdness of the industrial paradigm, while the British authors explore the Gothic as a cynical counterpoint to Thatcherite nostalgia. Nonetheless there is no markedly British (or, at that, US-American) steampunk to identify: Of these authors, only Newman's novel is really steampunk-adjacent, but Moore is of course creator not only of the hyper-Gothic *From Hell*, but also the eclectic, intertextual, and iconically steampunk *Leage of Extraordinary Gentlemen*. Mann, while British, demonstrates markedly less cultural acuity with regard to the Victorian East End than both Newman and the Canadian Peters, whose work not only creatively re-works Dickens and Morrison, but also mobilizes both Gothic and cyberpunk impulses. Indeed, steampunk Londons illustrate that access to or understanding of Victorian London is not culturally or locally contingent: Both Canada-based Ubisoft and California-based Ready at Dawn, after all, utilized extensive material and historical research to create steampunk Londons that felt 'authentic' to global audiences irrespective of whether or not they were familiar with or had access to the material city. Thus, the textual building blocks from which the steampunk Londons in this study are sourced – classic literature, painting, archival material, and indeed, neo-Victorian media such as film adaptations – have become increasingly and equally accessible to steampunk creators across the world. How these creators engage with this virtual archive – whether they unquestioningly re-iterate well-known stereotypes, re-work lesser-known historical texts, or confer with experts – depends therefore on their intentions and interests. Whereas, for example, the creators of 1990s British Ripperature demonstrate perhaps a more darkly ironic and cynical approach to the Victorian past, so do Californian Powers and Canadian Peters in the 1980s and 2000s, respectively, and second-wave steampunk is characterized more palpably by a somewhat whimsical curiosity regarding the Victorian past, whether written by UK-based Moore, US-based Carriger, or Morris and Ballantine from New Zealand. Iterations of steampunk London are therefore less dependent on real or material cultural experiences of 'the Victorians' than the transmedia imaginary fostered between knowledge communities across the anglophone world and how audiences relate to the latter. Nonetheless, steampunk Londons may respond to culturally specific or changing perceptions of what 'the Victorians' signify in shared memory – with all the stereotyping, blind spots, and misinterpretations that might entail.

Alongside its encapsulating of changing relationships with the Victorian past, steampunk also traces popular audiences' evolving media literacy. Where early steampunk relied on time travel frame narratives, in the era of memes, mainstream audiences have come to read through layered and complex transmedia pastiches quickly and effortlessly. Post-modern natives like the millennials and younger generations indeed more likely encounter adaptations, remixes, pastiches, and parodies of classic texts or genre tropes (like, for example, *Frankenstein*) before (if at all) engaging with primary texts themselves, and so develop the ability to decode steampunk's anachronistic, cross-genre worlds from context. This also means steampunk's anachronistic remix may become more mainstream. Recent neo-historical and neo-Victorian media illustrate this, among them Giorgos Lanthimos' *The Favourite* (2019), *The Great* (Hulu, 2020 to present), and *Poor Things* (2023), Apple TV's *Dickinson* (2019–2021), Autumn de Wilde's colourful *Emma* (2020), and Armando Iannucci's *The Personal History of David Copperfield* (2020): All approach the past with a blend of sincerity and highly stylized quirkiness that is not quite anachronism, thereby paradoxically drawing attention to historical distance while also rendering the past newly approachable to wider audiences. As such, they mark a departure from heritage-focused films of the Merchant Ivory variety, leveraging anachronistic remix strategies that steampunk has over the years rehearsed.

Steampunk mobilizes this popular transmedia literacy to leverage resonant tensions that arise from retro-speculative interventions into an era of large technological, political, and social change, thereby inviting audiences to re-evaluate the past from a critical, post-colonial perspective. Its bold and usually easily identifiable retro-speculations somewhat ironically make the steampunk past more accessible for wider audiences: Whereas Victorian and neo-Victorian fiction often prefigures an existing knowledge or at least interest in the nineteenth century, steampunk's speculative impulses, while perhaps enhanced through previous knowledge, nonetheless confront each reader with the same, unfamiliar setting and hence the same learning curve about the fictional setting. As such, steampunk is inherently participatory and collaborative, not just in the external sphere of its maker culture, but on a fundamental, hermeneutic reader level, prompting readers to actively and continuously re-evaluate their position in relation to the past. However, its actualization of historical processes into exciting thought experiments about the route not taken may also clash in paradoxical ways with steampunk's proclivity for action-driven adventure and romance, particularly when immersive scenarios of 'playing the past' situate the latter as a defamiliarized Other in which real dangers necessitate actionable, morally unambiguous choices: Find artefacts, liberate orphans, stop rebels, revenants, robot octopi, or nefarious mad scientists, escape the body-switching werewolf, and so on. In some cases, if not always, such choices depend on a simplified, stereotypical juxtapositions of 'good' and 'bad' Victorians or historical forces that invite an easy identification with the progressive Good Guys.

Indeed, steampunk lays bare persistent stereotypes and prejudices about 'Victorian-ness' and the Victorian past, especially when foregoing radically re-thinking identity and instead merely re-hashing familiar stereotypes that affirm readers' preconceptions about identity, belonging, gender, sexuality, or race. For example, like much neo-Victorian fiction, steampunk is frequently content to present a 'strong', liberated female character as reader proxy and relegate most other Victorian women to oblivious, tut-tutting complacency, if not caricatures of patriarchal repression. Whereas presentism is potentially an asset in steampunk, without equally engaging in the socio-historical texture and its discourses, the generative tension fails to manifest, and steampunk's critique falls flat. Interrogated and re-deployed, the Victorian East End's racial anxieties may be leveraged into counter-cultural satire (*Anno Dracula*), but ignorantly re-produced, they only replicate a foggy backdrop for the same biases (*The Affinity Bridge*). In the same vein, projecting a presentist heroine who rejects the demonized corset and the allegedly cumbersome skirts risks patronizingly obscuring the many and nuanced ways in which real Victorian women lived within, challenged, or defied patriarchal structures. Not only does this reveal a selective, superficial engagement with the nineteenth century and its memory on the part of authors and readers, but also a collective failure to transcend the current feminist moment. The fact that, in neo-Victorian and steampunk fiction alike, rebellious transgression is so often recuperated into patriarchal narrative logic through the male gaze or sexual violence suggests that we may be able to identify systemic inequality and trauma-inducing oppression, but are limited in our ability to actually envision radical alternatives. In positioning readers towards easily identifiable historical wrongs and congratulating them for recognizing their injustice, these ultimately conservative narratives effectively stake our modern enlightened identity on our capacity to identify moral gestures. Steampunk has the potential to complicate a convenient hindsight perspective in which the past may be more easily evaluated and judged by collapsing binaries of 'Them' vs 'Us' in tandem with 'Past' and 'Present' – but its potential to envision radical alternatives only corresponds to our own.

Steampunk may realize this potential in creative and inclusive ways. Its retro-speculation becomes an especially valuable tool in re-centering historically marginalized identities and crafting reparative meta-narratives of agency, liberation, and joy, particularly for audiences who usually see themselves mirrored in history only in stories of oppression, trauma, or self-denial. Steampunk's blatant retro-speculation may write aspirational fantasies back into history without trivializing or obscuring those networks of power and discourse whose traumatic legacy we must still confront, or erasing the struggles of those who brought about change. The 'accessible empowerment steampunk provides for the marginalised'[3] is evident in its potential to include queer steampunks, steampunks of colour, or disabled steampunks – not least because here, walking aids, prosthetics, and wheelchairs provide easy and exciting opportunities for cosplay or cyborg characters. Many people of colour, as Pho notes, are 'drawn to steampunk subculture as a site of resistance against hegemony' because it 'rejects nostalgia in favour of transformative critique': It 'provides the artistic license for people of color to transmute traumatic cultural histories onto an empowering subculture identity.'[4] Indeed, whether post-colonially critical or joyfully reparative, steampunk fiction may so reflect 'the accountability that steampunks hold each other to in discussions about race, culture, and historic oppression'.[5]

That cities play a central role in such discussions is not least evident in steampunk's purposeful re-organization of collective memory as shaped by *lieux de mémoire*, but is also reflected in real events of recent years, be it women's marches, Black Lives Matter protests, or the so-called statue wars. The latter, as ongoing public debates about which historical agents to memorialize as cornerstones of identity meta-narratives in the public sphere, have resulted in the defacing of memorials of Civil War leaders in the US, the sinking of slave trader Edward Colston's statue into Bristol harbour in 2020, and ongoing discussions about Cecil Rhodes being immortalized in Oxford university's façade, and so recall *The Difference Engine*'s rewriting of public memory through Wellington memorials. These events exemplify modern communities re-evaluating the past from a critical, post-colonial perspective, enacting their Right to the City, and demanding agency in shaping the places where they live, as well as challenging the collective meta-narratives about power and participation that urban spaces signify. Like steampunk London, they illustrate how cities shape our identities, and how our cognitive mapping as individuals or collectives may relate to physical space. Steampunk typically gravitates to London as historical nexus and a powerful, internationally familiar memory figure to physically enact these critiques as thought experiments in a virtual sphere that is much easier to revise than the real city.

Steampunk often mobilizes Victorian London as the physical (though actually virtual) building blocks through which collective memory and cognitive mapping are encoded and may be creatively re-mapped. In so inviting audiences to vicariously explore a historically formative but retro-speculatively re-worked era, it prompts a continuous hermeneutic re-evaluation of city and memory in tandem, and so undermines perceptions of the past as fixed and deterministic. Instead, steampunk empowers audiences to imagine the past – and by inference, the present – as mutable to individual actions, and consequently themselves as politically aware agents in both spheres. After all, as Terry Pratchett reminds us: 'Fantasy is an exercise bicycle for the mind. It might not take you anywhere, but it tones up the muscles that can.'[6]

Notes

1. Notable proto-steampunk aesthetics may be identified in Harper Goff's design for the Nautilus in Disney's *20,000 Leagues under the Sea* (1954), the Vincent Price films *Master of the World* (1961) and *City Under the Sea* (1965), as well as George Pa's movie versions of Wells' stories *War of the Worlds* (1953) and *The Time Machine* (1960). See: Perschon, 'Seminal Steampunk', p. 156. Also Onion, p. 140.
2. Kohlke and Gutleben, 'The (Mis)Shapes of Neo-Victorian Gothic', p. 12, original emphasis.
3. Pho, 'Punking the Other', p. 137.
4. Pho, 'Punking the Other', p. 135. Examples include the campy action comedy *Wild Wild West* (1999), which re-positions a black hero in the traditionally white-dominated Western genre and reckons with the outcomes of the Civil War, the afrofuturist steamfunk movement, launched in 2009, or the steampunk fiction of Maurice Broaddus, Nisi Shawl, Cherie Priest, and P. Djèlí Clark (which also widen the steampunk lens beyond London and Great Britain).
5. Pho, 'Punking the Other', p. 146.
6. Terry Pratchett, quoted in Paul Kidby, *Terry Pratchett's Discworld Imaginarium* (London: Gollancz, 2017), p. 9.

Bibliography

A New Woman Reader, ed. by Carolyn Christensen Nelson (Peterborough: Broadview Press, 2001).

Aarseth, Espen, 'Allegories of Space. The Question of Spatiality in Computer Games', in *Space Time Play. Computer Games, Architecture, and Urbanism: the Next Level*, ed. by Friedrich von Borries, Steffen P. Walz, and Matthias Böttger (Berlin: Birkhäuser Verlag, 2007), pp. 44–47.

Abbott, William T., 'White Knowledge and the Cauldron of Story: The Use of Allusion in Terry Pratchett's Discworld' (unpublished Master thesis, East Tennessee State University, 2002).

Ackroyd, Peter, 'Jack the Ripper and the East End', in *Jack the Ripper and the East End*, ed. by Alex Werner (London: Chatto & Windus, 2008), pp. 7–31.

Ackroyd, Peter, *Dan Leno and the Limehouse Golem* (London: Vintage Books, 2017 [1994]).

Alder, Emily, *Weird Fiction and Science at the Fin de Siècle* (London: Palgrave Macmillan, 2020).

Aldiss, Brian, and David Wingrove, *Trillion Year Spree: The History of Science Fiction* (London: Gollancz, 1986).

Ameel, Lieven (ed.), *The Routledge Companion to Literary Urban Studies* (London: Routledge, 2023).

Ameel, Lieven, and Sirpa Tani, 'Parkour: creating loose spaces? *Geografiska Annaler: Series B, Human Geography* 94:1 (2012), 17–30.

Ameel, Lieven, et al. (eds), *The Materiality of Literary Narratives in Urban History* (London: Routledge, 2019).

Anderson, Benedict, *Imagined Communities: Reflections on the Origin and Spread of Nationalism* (London: Verso, 1983).

Anon., '"Dear Boss" letter', http://www.casebook.org/ripper_letters/ (accessed 25 May 2018).

Anon., 'Action Girl', *TvTropes*, n.d., https://tvtropes.org/pmwiki/pmwiki.php/Main/ActionGirl (accessed 28 April 2020).

Anon., 'Bury Your Gays', *TvTropes*, n.d., https://tvtropes.org/pmwiki/pmwiki.php/Main/BuryYourGays (accessed 28 April 2020).

Anon., 'Distress Ball', *TvTropes*, n.d., https://tvtropes.org/pmwiki/pmwiki.php/Main/DistressBall (accessed 28 April 2020).

Anon., 'Faux Action Girl', *TvTropes*, n.d., https://tvtropes.org/pmwiki/pmwiki.php/Main/FauxActionGirl (accessed 28 April 2020).

Anon., 'The Rule of Cool', *TvTropes*, n.d., https://tvtropes.org/pmwiki/pmwiki.php/Main/RuleOfCool (accessed 20 July 2020).

Anon., 'Steampunk Week – Book Review: The Affinity Bridge by George Mann', https://www.thebooksmugglers.com/2010/04/steampunk-week-book-review-the-affinity-bridge-by-george-mann.html (accessed 19 June 2018).

Anon., 'The Affinity Bridge', https://www.kirkusreviews.com/book-reviews/george-mann/the-affinity-bridge/ (accessed 19 June 2018).

Arata, Stephen D., 'The Occidental Tourist: "Dracula" and the Anxiety of Reverse Colonialization', *Victorian Studies* 33:4 (1990), 621–645.

Ashley, Mike, *The Times Machines. The Story of the Science-Fiction Pulp Magazines from the beginning to 1950* (Liverpool: Liverpool UP, 2000).

Assmann, Jan, 'Cultural Memory', in *Cultural Memory Studies. An International and Interdisciplinary Handbook*, ed. by Astrid Erll and Ansgar Nünning (Berlin, New York, 2008), pp. 109–118.

Atkinson, Michael, 'Parkour, anarcho-environmentalism, and poesis', *Journal of Sport and Social Issues* 33:2 (2009), 169–194.

Baldick, Chris, 'Introduction', in *Oxford Book of Gothic Tales* (Oxford: Oxford University Press, 1992).

Ballantine, Pip, and Tee Morris, *Phoenix Rising: A Ministry of Peculiar Occurrences Novel* (New York: Harper Voyager, 2011).

Ballantine, Pip, and Tee Morris, *The Janus Affair: A Ministry of Peculiar Occurrences Novel* (New York: Harper Voyager, 2012).

Barber, Suzanne, and Matt Hale, 'Enacting the Never-Was: Upcycling the Past, Present, and Future in Steampunk', in *Steaming Into a Victorian Future*, ed. by Julie Anne Taddeo and Cynthia J. Miller (Lanham: Scarecrow Press, 2013), pp. 165–183.

Barlow, Aaron, 'Reel Toads and Imaginary Cities: Philip K. Dick, *Blade Runner*, and the Contemporary Science Fiction Movie', in *The Blade Runner Experience. The Legacy of a Science Fiction Classic*, ed. by Will Brooker (London & New York: Wallflower Press, 2005), pp. 63–82.

Barthes, Roland, 'Semiology and the Urban', in *The City and the Sign. An Introduction to Urban Semiotics*, ed. by M. Gottdiener and Alexandros Ph. Lagopoulos (New York: Columbia University Press, 1986), p. 87–98.

Baudelaire, Charles, *The Painter of Modern Life* (New York: Da Capo Press, 1964 [1863]).

Baudrillard, Jean, *Simulations*, trans. by Paul Foss, Paul Batton and Philip Beitchman (Los Angeles: Semiotext(e), 1983).

Bauer, N. et al., 'Vom Charakter der Details. Henry Mayhews Costermonger als Proto-Subkultur', in *Die Zivilisierung der urbanen Nomaden*, ed. by R. Lindner (Berlin: LIT, 2005), pp. 63–81.

Baumgardner, Jennifer, 'Is There a Fourth Wave? Does It Matter?', *Feminist*, 2011, https://www.feminist.com/resources/artspeech/genwom/baumgardner2011.html (accessed 26 April 2020).

Bayles Kortsch, Christine, *Dress Culture in Late Victorian Women's Fiction: Literacy, Textiles, and Activism* (Farnham: Ashgate, 2009).

Beaumont, Matthew. *Nightwalking. A Nocturnal History of London* (London: Verso, 2015).

Begg, Paul, *Jack the Ripper: The Definitive History* (London: Routledge, 2003).

Bell, Karl, 'Phantasmal Cities: The Construction and Function of Haunted Landscapes in Victorian English Cities', in *Haunted Landscapes. Super-Nature and the Environment*, ed. by Ruth Heholt and Niamh Downing (London: Rowman & Littlefield, 2016), pp. 95–110.

Bell, Karl, 'Through Purged Eyes. Folk Horror and the Affective Landscape of the Urban Weird', in *The Urban Wyrd 2: Spirits of Place* (Wyrd Harvest Press, 2019).

Belloc Lowndes, Marie, *The Lodger* (Oxford: Oxford University Press, 1996 [1913]).

Benjamin, Walter, *Charles Baudelaire: a Lyric Poet in the Era of High Capitalism*, trans. by Harry Zohn (London: Verso Books, 1997).

Benjamin, Walter, *One-Way Street* (London: Verso, 1997).

Benjamin, Walter, *The Arcades Project*, trans. by Kevin McLaughlin and Howard Eiland (New York: Harvard University Press, 2002).

Berger Woods, Marianne, *The New Woman in Print and Pictures: an Annotated Bibliography* (Jefferson: McFarland & Company, 2009).

Bird, Kathryn, '"Civilised society doesn't just happen": The Animal, the Law and "Victorian Values" in Kim Newman's *Anno Dracula*', *Neo-Victorian Journal* 7:1 (2014), 1–24.

Blade Runner, Final Cut, dir. by Ridley Scott, DVD (Los Angeles: Warner Brothers Entertainment, 2007 [1984]).

Blaylock, James P., *Homunculus* (London: Titan Books, 2013 [1986]).

Blaylock, James P., *Lord Kelvin's Machine* (London: Titan Books, 2013 [1992]).

Bloom, Clive, 'Jack the Ripper – a legacy in pictures', in *Jack the Ripper and the East End*, ed. by Alex Werner (London: Chatto & Windus, 2008), pp. 239–267.

Bloom, Clive, 'The Ripper writing: a cream of a nightmare dream', in *Jack the Ripper. Media. Culture. History*, ed. by Alexandra Warwick and Martin Willis (Manchester: Manchester University Press, 2007), pp. 91–109.

Booth, Charles, *Descriptive Map of London Poverty*, 1898.

Boulton, Harold, 'A Novel of the Lowest Life', British Review (9 Jan. 1897), 349, reprinted in Morrison, Arthur, *A Child of the Jago*, ed. by Peter Miles (Oxford: Oxford University Press), pp. 176–177.

Bowser, Rachel A. and Brian Croxall (eds), *Like Clockwork. Steampunk Pasts, Presents & Futures* (Minneapolis: Minnesota UP, 2016),

Bowser, Rachel A. and Brian Croxall, 'Introduction: Industrial Evolution', *Neo-Victorian Studies*, 3:1 (2010), 1–45.

Bridges, Elizabeth. 'A Genealogy of Queerbaiting: Legal Codes, Production Codes, "Bury Your Gays", and "The 100 Mess"', *Journal of Fandom Studies*, 6:2 (2018), 115–132.

Bristow, Joseph, 'Decadent Historicism', *Volupté: Interdisciplinary Journal of Decadence Studies*, 3.1 (2020), 1–27.

Brooker, Peter, 'Imagining the Real: *Blade Runner* and Discourses on the Postmetropolis', in *The Blade Runner Experience. The Legacy of a Science Fiction Classic*, ed. by Will Brooker (London & New York: Wallflower Press, 2005), pp. 263–277.

Brooker, Will, 'Introduction: 2019 Vision', in *The Blade Runner Experience. The Legacy of a Science Fiction Classic*, ed. by Will Brooker (London & New York: Wallflower Press, 2005), pp. 13–24.

Bruno, Giuliana, 'Ramble City: Postmodernism and "Blade Runner"', *October*, 41 (1987), pp. 61–74.

Butler, Judith, *Gender Trouble: Feminism and the Subversion of Identity* (New York: Routledge, 1999).

Professor Calamity, 'My Machine, My Comrade.' *Steampunk Magazine*, 3:1 (2007), pp. 24–25.

Calvino, Italo, *Invisible Cities*, trans. by William Weaver (London: Harcourt Brace & Company, 1972).

Cannadine, David, 'A case of [Mistaken?] Identity', in *Sherlock Holmes: The Man Who Never Lived and Will Never Die*, ed. by Alex Werner (London: Penguin Random House, 2014), pp.13–55.

Carriger, Gail, 'Is Alexia Bisexual?' *Reader Q&A*, 2016, https://www.goodreads.com/questions/647353-is-alexia-bisexual-i-ve-wondered-about (accessed 28 April 2020).

Carriger, Gail, 'Researching Fluidity & Representing it in Fiction', *Gail Carriger*, 24 May 2019, https://gailcarriger.com/2019/05/24/researching-gender-fluidity-representing-it-in-fiction-the-5th-gender-by-gail-carriger-custard-protocol-san-andreas-shifters-tinkered-stars-behind-the-magic/ (accessed 28 April 2020).

Carriger, Gail, 'Researching Gender Fluidity & Representing it in Fiction', *Gail Carriger*, 24 May 2019, https://gailcarriger.com/2019/05/24/researching-gender-fluidity-representing-it-in-fiction-the-5th-gender-by-gail-carriger-custard-protocol-san-andreas-shifters-tinkered-stars-behind-the-magic/ (accessed 28 April 2020).

Carriger, Gail, *Blameless* (London: Orbit Books, 2010).

Carriger, Gail, *Changeless* (London: Orbit Books, 2010).

Carriger, Gail, *Heartless* (London: Orbit Books, 2011).

Carriger, Gail, *Imprudence: Book Two of The Custard Protocol* (London: Orbit Books, 2016).

Carriger, Gail, *Reticence: The Custard Protocol: Book Four* (London: Orbit Books, 2019).

Carriger, Gail, *Soulless* (London: Orbit Books, 2009).

Carrott, James H., 'Punking the Past: The Politics of Possibility', in *Steampunk Magazine*, 9 (2012), 70–71.

Carrott, James H., and Brian David Johnson, *Vintage Tomorrows* (Sebastopol: O'Reilly, 2013).

Carstocea, George, 'Uchronias, Alternate Histories, and Counterfactuals', in *The Routledge Companion to Imaginary Worlds*, ed. by Mark J. P. Wolf (New York: Routledge, 2017), pp. 184–191.

Catastrophone Orchestra and Arts Collective, the. 'What then, is Steampunk? Colonizing the Past So We Can Dream The Future', *Steampunk Magazine*. 1. (2006), 4–5.

Chalupský, Petr, 'Crime Narratives in Peter Ackroyd's Historiographic Metafictions', *European Journal of English Studies*, 14:2 (2010), 121–131.

Chalupský, Petr, *A Horror and a Beauty: The World of Peter Ackroyd's London Novels* (Prague: Karolinum Press, 2017).

Chamberlain, Prudence, *The Feminist Fourth Wave: Affective Temporality* (London: Palgrave Macmillan, 2017).

Chisholm, Alex, 'The Pall Mall Gazette, 8th Sept 1888', http://www.casebook.org/press_reports/pall_mall_gazette/18880908.html (accessed 25 May 2018).

Chisholm, Alex, 'The Star, 1st Sept 1888', http://www.casebook.org/press_reports/star/s880901.html (accessed 25 May 2018).

Chisholm, Alex, 'The Star, 8th Sept 1888', http://www.casebook.org/press_reports/star/s880908.html (accessed 25 May 2018).

Clark-Parsons, Rosemary. *Networked Feminism. How Digital Media Makers Transformed Gender Justice Movements* (Oakland: University of California Press, 2022).

Clayton, Jay, *Charles Dickens in Cyberspace: The Afterlife of the Nineteenth Century in Postmodern Culture*, (Oxford: Oxford University Press, 2003).

Clifford, David et. al., *Repositioning Victorian Sciences: Shifting Centres in Nineteenth-century Scientific Thinking* (London: Anthem Press, 2006).

Clute, John. 'Vive?', in *Look at the Evidence* (London: Gollancz, 1996 [1991]).

Cochrane, Kira, *All the Rebel Women: The rise of the fourth wave of feminism*, ebook, (London: Guardian Shorts, 2013).

Cook, Matt, *London and the Culture of Homosexuality 1885–1914* (Cambridge: Cambridge University Press, 2003).

Cooke, Jennifer. 'Introduction', in Jennifer Cooke (ed.), *The New Feminist Literary Studies* (Cambridge: Cambridge University Press, 2020), pp. 1–10.

Cooke, Lauren, 'How We're Written', *Huffington Post*, 25 April 2014, https://www.huffingtonpost.com/lauren-cooke/how-were-written_b_4834218.html (accessed 28 April 2020).

Corelli, Marie, 'A Word about "Ouida"', *Belgravia* 71, March 1890, repr. in Ouida, *Moths*, ed. by Natalie Schroeder (Peterborough: Broadview Press), p. 567.

Coverley, Merlin, *Psychogeography* (Harpenden: Pocket Essentials, 2006).

Coville, Gary, and Patrick Luciano, 'Order out of chaos', in *Jack the Ripper. Media. Culture. History.*, ed. by Alexandra Warwick and Martin Willis (Manchester: Manchester University Press, 2007), pp. 56–70.

Crawford, Joseph, 'The Urban Turn: Gothic Cityscapes before *The Mysteries of London*', unpublished conference paper given at *The Urban Weird* organized by Open Graves, Open Minds & Supernatural Cities (University of Hertfortshire, 6–7 April, 2018).

Crawford, Joseph, *Gothic Fiction and the Invention of Terrorism. The Politics and Aesthetics of Fear in the Age of the Reign of Terror* (London: Bloomsbury, 2013).

Csicsery-Ronay, Istvan, *The Seven Beauties of Science Fiction* (Conneticut: Wesleyan University Press, 2011).

Cox, Jessica, 'Canonization, Colonization, and the Rise of Neo-Victorianism.' *English* 66:1 (2017), 101–123.

Cunningham, Gail, *The New Woman and the Victorian Novel* (Lanham: Rowman & Littlefield Publishers, 1978).

Curtis, L. Perry, Jr., *Jack the Ripper and the London Press* (New Haven: Yale University Press, 2001).

Curtis, L. Perry, Jr., 'The pursuit of angles', in *Jack the Ripper. Media. Culture. History.*, ed. by Alexandra Warwick and Martin Willis (Manchester: Manchester University Press, 2007), pp. 29–45.

Danahay, Martin, 'Steampunk and the Performance of Gender and Sexuality', *Neo-Victorian Studies*, 9:1 (2016), 123–150.

Danahay, Martin. 'Steampunk as a Postindustrial Aesthetic: "All that is solid melts in air"', *Neo-Victorian Studies*, 8:2 (2016): 28–56.

Daskalaki, Maria, Alexandra Starab and Miguel Imasa, 'The "Parkour Organisation": inhabitation of corporate spaces', *Culture and Organization*, 14:1 (2008), 49–64.

Davies, Paul, *The Art of Assassin's Creed: Syndicate* (London: Titan Books, 2015).

de Bruin-Molé, Megen, '"Now with the Ultraviolent Zombie Mayhem!": The Neo-Victorian Novel-as-Mashup and the Limits of Postmodern Irony', in *Neo-Victorian Humour. Comic Subversions and Unlaughter in Contemporary Historical Re-Visions*, ed. by Marie-Louise Kohlke and Christian Gutleben (Leiden: Brill Rodopi, 2017), pp. 249–276.

de Bruin-Molé, Megen, *Gothic Remixed: Monster Mashups and Frankenfictions in 21st-Century Culture* (London: Bloomsbury, 2020).

De Certeau, Michel, *The Practise of Everyday Life*, trans. by Stephen F. Rendall (Berkeley: University of California Press, 1984).

Deleuze, Gilles. 'Postscript on Control Societies,' in *Negotiations: 1972–1990* (New York: Columbia University Press, 1990), pp.177–182.

Despotopoulou, Anna, *Women and the Railway, 1850–1915* (Edinburgh: Edinburgh University Press, 2016).

devinsupertramp, *Assassin's Creed Syndicate Meets Parkour in Real Life!* Video, YouTube, posted by Devin Graham, 7 July 2015, https://www.youtube.com/watch?v=HFRscoOkkb8 (accessed 15 February 2020).

Dickens Charles, *The Old Curiosity Shop* (Ware: Wordsworth Editions Limited, 2001 [1840]).

Dickens, Charles, *Nicholas Nickleby* edited by Michael Slater (London: Penguin, 1986 [1838–39]).

Dickens, Charles, *Dombey and Son* (London: Penguin, 1970 [1848]).

Dickens, Charles, *The Mystery of Edwin Drood* (Cambridge: Penguin Classics, 2011 [1870]).

Disraeli, Benjamin, *Sybil; or, The Two Nations*, ed. by Thom Braun (London: Penguin, 1980 [1845]).

Dixon, Ella Hepworth, *The Story of a Modern Woman*, ed. by Steve Farmer (Peterborough: Broadview Press, 2004 [1894]).

Dobraszczyk, Paul, *Future Cities: Architecture and the Imagination* (London: Reaktion Books, 2019).

Doctorow, Cory, 'The Difference Engine: A Generation Later', in: *The Difference Engine*, by Gibson, William, and Bruce Sterling, 2nd Edition. (New York: Random House, 2011 [1990]), pp. vii–xi.

Dodge, Martin, and Rob Kitchin, *Mapping Cyberspace* (London: Routledge, 2017).

Domsch, Sebastian, 'Monsters against Empire: The Politics and Poetics of Neo-Victorian Metafiction in *The League of Extraordinary Gentlemen*', in *Neo-Victorian Gothic. Horror, Violence, and Degeneration in the Re-Imagined Nineteenth Century*, ed. by Marie-Louise Kohlke and Christian Gutleben (Leiden: Brill Rodopi, 2012), pp. 97–122.

Doré, Gustave, and Blanchard Jerrold, *London. A Pilgrimage* (New York: Dover Publications, 1970 [1872]).

Dowling, Linda, 'The Decadent and the New Woman in the 1890's', *Nineteenth-Century Fiction*, 33:4 (1979), 434–453.

Doyle, Arthur Conan, 'The Man with the Twisted Lip', in *The Complete Sherlock Holmes* (New York: Barnes & Noble, 2012 [1891]), pp. 158–198.

Doyle, Sir Arthur Conan, 'A Study in Scarlet', in *The Penguin Complete Sherlock Holmes* (London: Penguin, 2009 [1887]), pp. 15–87.

Doyle, Sir Arthur Conan, 'The Adventure of the Blue Carbuncle', in *The Penguin Complete Sherlock Holmes* (London: Penguin, 2009 [1892]), pp. 224–256.

Doyle, Sir Arthur Conan, 'The Red-Headed League', in *The Penguin Complete Sherlock Holmes* (London: Penguin, 2009 [1892]), pp. 176–189.

Doyle, Sir Arthur Conan, 'The Resident Patient', in *The Penguin Complete Sherlock Holmes* (London: Penguin, 2009 [1894]), pp. 422–434.

Doyle, Sir Arthur Conan, 'The Sign of Four', in *The Penguin Complete Sherlock Holmes* (London: Penguin, 2009 [1890]), pp. 89–159.

Duperray, Max, '"Jack the Ripper" as Neo-Victorian Gothic Fiction: Twentieth-Century and Contemporary Sallies into a Late Victorian Case and Myth', in *Neo-Victorian Gothic. Horror, Violence, and Degeneration in the Re-Imagined Nineteenth Century*, ed. by Marie-Louise Kohlke and Christian Gutleben (Leiden: Brill Rodopi, 2012), pp. 167–196.

Elkin, Lauren, *Flâneuse: Women Walk the City in Paris, New York, Tokyo, Venice and London* (London: Chatto & Windus, 2016).

Ella, 'Ouida', *The Victoria Magazine* 28, March 1877, repr. in Ouida, *Moths*, ed. by Natalie Schroeder (Peterborough: Broadview Press), p. 565.

Ellis, Kirk, and Ru Weerasuriya, *The Blackwater Archives. The Art of The Order: 1886* (San Francisco: Bluecanvas, Inc., 2015).

Elmore, Rick, '"The bindings are there as a safeguard": Sovereignty and Political Decisions in *BioShock Infinite*', in *BioShock and Philosophy: Irrational Game, Rational Book*, ed. by Luke Cuddy (Oxford: Wiley Blackwell, 2015), pp. 97–105.

Epstein Nord, Deborah, *Walking the Victorian Streets: Women, Representation, and the City* (Ithaca: Cornell University Press, 1996).

Esser, Helena, 'What Use Our Work: Crime and Justice in Ripper Street', *Neo-Victorian Studies,* 11:1 (2018), 141–173.

Fehlbaum, Valerie, 'Paving the Way for Mrs Dalloway: The Street-walking Women of Eliza Lynn Linton, Ella Hepworth Dixon and George Paston', in *Inside Out: Women negotiating, subverting, appropriating public and private space*, ed. by Teresa Gómez Reus and Aránzazu Usandizaga (Amsterdam: Rodopi 2008), pp. 149–166.

Felski, Rita, *The Limits of Critique* (Chicago: The University of Chicago Press, 2015).

Ferguson, Christine, 'Surface Tensions: Steampunk, Subculture, and the Ideology of Style', *Neo-Victorian Studies*, 4:2 (2011), 66–90.

Finch, Jason, *Literary Urban Studies and How to Practice It* (London: Routledge, 2021).

Fiorato, Sidia, 'Theatrical Role-Playing, Crime and Punishment in Peter Ackroyd's *Dan Leno and the Limehouse Golem*', *Pólemos: Journal of Law, Literature and Culture*, 6:1 (2012), 65–81.

Fischlin, Daniel, Veronica Hollinger, Andrew Taylor, William Gibson and Bruce Sterling. '"The Charisma Leak": A Conversation with William Gibson and Bruce Sterling', *Science Fiction Studies,* 19:1 (1992), 1–16.

Fisher, Mark, *The Weird and the Eerie* (London: Repeater Books, 2017), p. 40

Forlini, Stefania, 'Technology and Morality: The Stuff of Steampunk', *Neo-Victorian Studies*, 3:1 (2010), 72–98.

Forlini, Stefania, 'The Aesthete, the Dandy, and the Steampunk; or, Things as They Are Now', in *Like Clockwork. Steampunk Pasts, Presents & Futures,* ed. by Rachel A. Bowser and Brian Croxall (Minneapolis: Minnesota UP, 2016), pp. 97–126.

Foucault, Michel, 'Of Other Spaces', trans. by Jay Miskowiec, in *Architecture / Mouvement/ Continuité, October* 1984. pp. 1–9. Unpublished lecture, given 1967.

Foucault, Michel, *The History of Sexuality*, 1978.

Foucault, Michel, 'The Birth of Biopolitics', in *Ethics: Subjectivity and Truth,* ed. by Paul Rabinow (New York: New Press, 1997), pp. 73–80.

Frayling, Christopher, 'The house that Jack built', in *Jack the Ripper. Media. Culture. History.*, ed. by Alexandra Warwick and Martin Willis (Manchester: Manchester University Press, 2007), pp. 13–28.

Freud, Sigmund, 1919. 'The "Uncanny"', in *The Standard Edition of the Complete Psychological Works of Sigmund Freud, Volume XVII (1917–1919): An Infantile Neurosis and Other Works* (London: Hogarth Press, 1955), pp. 217–256.

Fuchs, Michael, '"Things Are Not as They Seem": Colonialism, Capitalism and Neo-Victorian London in The Order: 1886', in *The New Urban Gothic. Global Gothic in the Age of the Anthropocene,* ed. by Holly-Gale Millette and Ruth Heholt (London: Palgrave Macmillan, 2020), pp. 41–56.

Gadamer, Hans-Georg, *Truth and Method* (Wahrheit und Methode), (New York: Continuum, 1989 [1960]).

Galton, Francis. 'Eugenics: Its Definition, Scope and Aims' in *The Fin de Siècle. A Reader in Cultural History c.1880–1900*, ed. by Sally Ledger and Roger Luckhurst (Oxford: Oxford University Press, 2000 [1904]), pp. 329–333.

Ganteau, Jean-Michel, 'Vulnerable Visibilities: Peter Ackroyd's Monstrous Victorian Metropolis', in *Neo-Victorian Cities. Reassessing Urban Politics and Poetics*, ed. by Marie-Louise Kohlke and Christian Gutleben (Leiden: Brill Rodopi, 2015), pp. 151–174.

Gary, Drew, *London's Shadows. The Dark Side of the Victorian City* (London: Bloomsbury, 2010).

Gauld, Tom, *Tom Gauld on psychogeographers*, cartoon, *The Guardian*, 22 Sept. 2017, https://www.theguardian.com/books/picture/2017/sep/22/tom-gauld-on-psychogeographers-cartoon (accessed 17 June 2018).

GDC, *World of Dishonored: Raising Dunwall*, Video, YouTube, posted 22 February 2016, https://www.youtube.com/watch?v=LOQDbSvpFtY (accessed 15 February 2020).

Genz, Stéphanie, *Postfemininities in Popular Culture* (London: Palgrave Macmillan, 2009).

Geyh, Paula, 'Urban free flow: a poetics of parkour', *M/C Journal. A Journal of Media and Culture* 9:3 (2006), n.p.

Gibson, William, 'The Art of Fiction'. *The Paris Review*, 2011 https://www.theparisreview.org/interviews/6089/william-gibson-the-art-of-fiction-no-211-william-gibson (accessed 10 March 2018).

Gibson, William, 'Life in the Meta City', *Scientific American*, posted September 2011, https://www.scientificamerican.com/article/life-in-a-meta-city/?redirect=1 (accessed 7 March 2020).

Gibson, William, *Neuromancer* (London: Gollancz, 2016 [1984]).

Gibson, William, *Pattern Recognition* (London: Penguin Random House, 2003).

Gibson, William, *Virtual Light* (London, Spectra, 1994).

Gibson, William, and Bruce Sterling, *The Difference Engine*, 2nd Edition. (New York: Random House, 2011 [1990]).

Gilbert, Pamela, 'Ouida and the other New Woman', in *Victorian Women Writers and the Woman Question*, ed. by Nicola Diane Thompson (Cambridge: Cambridge University Press, 1999), pp. 170–188.

Gill, Rosalind, 'Postfeminist media culture: Elements of a sensibility', *European Journal of Cultural Studies*, 10:2 (2007), 147–166.

Gill, Rosalind, *Gender and the Media* (Malden: Polity Press, 2007).

Gilman, Sander L., "Who kills whores?' 'I do,' says Jack: race and gender in Victorian London', in *Jack the Ripper. Media. Culture. History.*, ed. by Alexandra Warwick and Martin Willis (Manchester: Manchester University Press, 2007), pp. 215–228.

Goldsworthy, Vera, *Inventing Ruritania: The Imperialism of the Imagination* (New Haven: Yale University Press, 1998).

Gómez Reus, Teresa and Aránzazu Usandizaga, 'Introduction', in *Inside Out: Women negotiating, subverting, appropriating public and private space*, ed. by Teresa Gómez Reus and Aránzazu Usandizaga (Amsterdam: Rodopi 2008), pp. 19–33.

Götz, Ulrich, 'Load and Support. Architectural Realism in Video Games', in *Space Time Play. Computer Games, Architecture, and Urbanism: the Next Level*, ed. by Friedrich von Borries, Steffen P. Walz, and Matthias Böttger (Berlin: Birkhäuser Verlag, 2007), pp. 134–137.

Graham, Stephen, 'Vertical Noir', *City*, 20:3 (2016), 389–406.

Grimes, Hilary, *The Late Victorian Gothic: Mental Science, the Uncanny, and Scenes of Writing* (Farnham: Ashgate, 2011).

Gross, Cory, 'A History of Misapplied Technology. The History and Development of the Steampunk Genre', *Steampunk Magazine*, 2. (2007), 54–61.

Gunning, Tom, 'Re-Newing Old Technologies: Astonishment, Second Nature, and the Uncanny in Technology from the Previous Turn-of-the-Century', in *Rethinking Media Change. The Aesthetics of Transition*, ed. by David Thorburn and Henry Jenkins (Cambridge: MIT Press), pp. 39–60.

Gurr, Jens Martin, *Charting Literary Urban Studies. Texts as Models of and for the City* (London: Palgrave Macmillan, 2021).

Gutleben, Christian, '"Fear is Fun and Fun is Fear": A Reflexion on Humour in Neo-Victorian Gothic', in *Neo-Victorian Gothic. Horror, Violence, and Degeneration in the Re-Imagined Nineteenth Century*, ed. by Marie-Louise Kohlke and Christian Gutleben (Leiden: Brill Rodopi, 2012), pp. 301–326.

Hadley, Louisa, *Neo-Victorian Fiction and Historical Narrative. The Victorians and Us* (London: Palgrave Macmillan, 2010).

Hager, Lisa, 'British Women Writers, Technology, and the Sciences, 1880–1920' in *The History of British Women's Writing, 1880–1920*, ed. by Holly A. Laird (London: Palgrave Macmillan, 2016), pp. 59–71.

Hager, Lisa, 'Embodying Agency: Ouida's Sensational Shaping of the British New Woman' in *Rediscovering Victorian Women Sensation Writers*, ed. by Anne-Marie Beller and Tara MacDonald (London: Routledge, 2014), pp. 90–101.

Hager, Lisa, 'Queer Cogs: Steampunk, Gender Identity, and Sexuality', *Tor.com*, 4 October 2012, https://www.tor.com/2012/10/04/steampunk-gender-sexuality/ (accessed 28 April 2020).

Haggard, Robert F., 'Jack the Ripper and the threat of outcast London', in *Jack the Ripper. Media. Culture. History.*, ed. by Alexandra Warwick and Martin Willis (Manchester: Manchester University Press, 2007), pp. 197–214.

Hall, Stuart, 'Notes on deconstructing "the popular"', [1981], republished in *Essential Essays*, Volume 1 (Durham: Duke University Press, 2019), p. 347–361.

Hantke, Steffen, 'Difference Engines and Other Infernal Devices: History According to Steampunk', *Extrapolation* 40:3 (1999), 244–254.

Haraway, Donna. 'A Cyborg Manifesto. Science, Technology and Socialist-feminism in the Late Twentieth Century', in *The Cybercultures Reader*, ed. by David Bell and Barbara M Kennedy (London: Routledge, 2000), pp. 291–324.

Hardy, Pat, 'The Art of Sherlock Holmes', in *Sherlock Holmes: The Man Who Never Lived and Will Never Die*, ed. by Alex Werner (London: Penguin Random House, 2014), pp. 135–157.

Harkness, Margaret, *In Darkest London* (London: Black Apollo Press, 2003 [1889]).

Harvey, David, 'The Right to the City', *New Left Review*, 53 (2008), 23–40.

Harvey, David, *Rebel Cities. From the Right to the City to the Urban Revolution* (London: Verso, 2012).

Haugtvedt, Erica, *Transfictional Character and Transmedia Storyworlds in the British Nineteenth Century* (London: Palgrave Macmillan, 2022).

Hebdige, Dick, *Subculture. The Meaning of Style* (London: Routledge, 1979).

Heidegger, Martin, *Being and Time*, trans. by Joan Stambaugh (New York: SUNY Press, 2010 [1927]).

Heilmann, Ann, *New Woman Fiction: Women Writing First-Wave Feminism* (London: Palgrave Macmillan, 2000).

Heilmann, Ann, *New Woman Strategies: Mona Caird, Olive Schreiner, Sarah Grand* (Manchester: Manchester University Press, 2004).

Heilmann, Ann, and Mark Llewellyn, *Neo-Victorianism. The Victorians in the Twenty-First Century, 1999–2009*, (London: Palgrave Macmillan, 2010).

Hills, Matt, 'Counterfictions in the Work of Kim Newman: Rewriting Gothic SF as "Alternate-Stories"', *Science Fiction Studies*, 30:3 (2003), 436–455.

Ho, Elizabeth, *Neo-Victorianism and the Memory of Empire* (London: Bloomsbury, 2012).

Ho, Elizabeth. (ed.), Special Issue: Neo-Victorian Asia, *Neo-Victorian Studies*, 11:2 (2019).

Hutcheon, Linda, *A Poetics of Postmodernism. History, Theory, Fiction* (Routledge: New York, 1988).

Huxley, Thomas Henry. 'Evolution and Ethics' in *The Fin de Siècle. A Reader in Cultural History c.1880–1900*, ed. by Sally Ledger and Roger Luckhurst (Oxford: Oxford University Press, 2000 [1893]), pp. 238–241.

Huxtable, Sally-Anne, '"Love the Machine, Hate the Factory": Steampunk Design and the Vision of a Victorian Future', in *Steaming Into A Victorian Future*. (Lanham: Scarecrow Press, 2013), pp. 213–234.

Iser, Wolfgang, *The Implied Reader: Patterns of Communication in Prose Fiction from Bunyan to Beckett* (Baltimore: Johns Hopkins University Press, 1972).

Iser, Wolfgang, 'The Rudiments of a Theory of Aesthetic Response', in *The Act of Reading: A Theory of Aesthetic Response* (Baltimore: Johns Hopkins University Press, 1978).

Jackson, Louise A., 'Law, order, and violence', in *Jack the Ripper and the East End*, ed. by Alex Werner (London: Chatto & Windus, 2008), pp. 99–139.

Jagoda, Patrick, 'Clacking Control Societies: Steampunk, History, and the Difference Engine of Escape', *Neo-Victorian Studies* 3.1 (2010), 46–71.

Jameson, Fredric, *Postmodernism. Or, The Cultural Logic of Late Capitalism* (London: Verso, 1991).

Janssen, Flore, 'Margaret Harkness: "In Darkest London" – 1889', https://www.londonfictions.com/margaret-harkness-in-darkest-london.html# (accessed 10 June 2018).

Jay, A. Osborne, 'The New Realism: To the Editor of the Fortnightly Review', *Fortnightly Review,* 67, 1897, pp. 314), reprinted in Morrison, Arthur, *A Child of the Jago*, ed. by Peter Miles (Oxford: Oxford University Press), pp. 178–179.

Jay, Mike, *Emperors of Dreams: Drugs in the Nineteenth Century* (Cambridgeshire: Dedalus, 2011).

Jenkins, Henry, 'Narrative Spaces', in *Space Time Play. Computer Games, Architecture, and Urbanism: the Next Level,* ed. by Friedrich von Borries, Steffen P. Walz, and Matthias Böttger (Berlin: Birkhäuser Verlag, 2007), pp. 56–60.

Jenkins, Henry, *Textual Poachers: Television Fans and Participatory Culture* (London: Routledge, 2013 [1992]).

Jenkins, Henry, '*Textual Poachers*, Twenty Years Later: A Conversation between Henry Jenkins and Suzanne Scott' in *Textual Poachers: Television Fans and Participatory Culture* (London: Routledge, 2013 [1992]), pp. vii–li.

Jenkins, Henry, 'Welcome to Convergence Culture', *Confessions of an Aca-Fan*, 19 June 2006, http://henryjenkins.org/blog/2006/06/welcome_to_convergence_culture.html (accessed 28 April 2020).

Jenkins, Henry, *Convergence Culture. Where Old and New Media Collide* (New York: New York University Press, 2008).

Jenkins, Henry, Sangita Shresthova, Liana Gamber-Thompson, Neta Kligler-Vilenchik, and Arely Zimmerman, *By Any Media Necessary: The New Youth Activism* (New York: NYU Press, 2016).

Jeter, K.W., *Infernal Devices* (Nottingham: Angry Robot, 2011 [1987]).

Jeter, K.W., *Morlock Night* (Oxford: Angry Robot, 2011 [1979]).

Jordan, Jane, 'Ouida: The Enigma of a Literary Identity', *The Princeton University Library Chronicle*, 57:1 (1995), 75–105.

Jordan, Jane, '"Romans Français Écrits En Anglais": Ouida, the Sensation Novel and Fin-De-Siècle Literary Censorship', in *Rediscovering Victorian Women Sensation Writers*, ed. by Anne-Marie Beller and Tara MacDonald (London: Routledge, 2014), pp. 102–118.

Kennan, George F., *The Decline of Bismarck's European Order. Franco-Russian Relations 1875–1890, 1981* (New Jersey: Princeton University Press, 1979).

Kerr, David, 'Doré, (Louis Auguste) Gustave', Oxford Dictionary of National Biography, http://www.oxforddnb.com/view/10.1093/ref:odnb/9780198614128.001.0001/odnb-9780198614128-e-67162 (accessed 8 June 2018).

Kershen, Anne J., 'The immigrant community of Whitechapel at the time of the Ripper murders', in *Jack the Ripper and the East End*, ed. by Alex Werner (London: Chatto & Windus, 2008), pp. 65–97.

Kidby, Paul, *Terry Pratchett's Discworld Imaginarium* (London: Gollancz, 2017).
Kirchknopf, Andrea, '(Re)workings of Nineteenth-Century Fiction: Definitions, Terminology, Contexts', *Neo-Victorian Studies*, 1.1 (2008), 53–80.
King, Andrew, 'The Sympathetic Individualist: Ouida's Late Work and Politics', *Victorian Literature and Culture*, 39:2 (2011), 563–579.
Kohlke, Marie-Luise, 'Introduction: Speculations in and on the Neo-Victorian Encounter', *Neo-Victorian Studies*, 1.1 (2008), 1–18.
Kohlke, Marie-Luise, 'Sexsation and the Neo-Victorian Novel: Orientalising the Nineteenth Century in Contemporary Fiction', in *Negotiating Sexual Idioms: Image, Text, Performance*, ed. by Marie-Luise Kohlke and Luisa Orza (Amsterdam: Brill Rodopi, 2008), pp. 53–79.
Kohlke, Marie-Luise, 'Tipoo's Tiger on the Loose: Neo-Victorian Witness-Bearing and the Trauma of the Indian Mutiny', in *Neo-Victorian Tropes of Trauma: The Politics of Bearing After-Witness to Nineteenth-Century Suffering*, ed. by Marie-Luise Kohlke and Christian Gutleben (Amsterdam: Brill Rodopi 2010), pp. 367–398.
Kohlke, Marie-Luise, 'Mining the neo-Victorian Vein: Prospecting for Gold, Buried Treasure, and Uncertain Metal', in *Neo-Victorian Literature and Culture: Immersions and Revisitations*, ed. by Nadine Böhm-Schnitker and Susanne Gruss (London: Routledge, 2014), p. 21–37.
Kohlke, Marie-Luise, and Christian Gutleben, 'The (Mis)Shapes of Neo-Victorian Gothic: Continuations, Adaptations, Transformations', in *Neo-Victorian Gothic. Horror, Violence, and Degeneration in the Re-Imagined Nineteenth Century*, ed. by Marie-Louise Kohlke and Christian Gutleben (Leiden: Brill Rodopi, 2012), pp. 1–50.
Kohlke, Marie-Luise, and Christian Gutleben, 'Troping the Neo-Victorian City', in *Neo-Victorian Cities. Reassessing Urban Politics and Poetics*, ed. by Marie-Louise Kohlke and Christian Gutleben (Leiden: Brill Rodopi, 2015), pp. 1–42.
Kohlke, Marie-Luise, and Christian Gutleben, 'What's So Funny about the Nineteenth Century?', in *Neo-Victorian Humour: Comic Subversions and Unlaughter in Contemporary Historical Re-Visions*, ed. by Marie-Luise Kohlke and Christian Gutleben (Amsterdam: Brill Rodopi, 2017).
Konrad Wojnowksi, 'Simulational Realism – Playing as Trying to Remember', *Art History & Criticism*, 14:1 (2018), 86–98.
Kontou, Tatiana, and Sarah Willburn, *The Ashgate Research Companion to Nineteenth-Century Spiritualism and the Occult* (Ashgate: Farnham, 2012).
Koven, Seth, *Slumming: Sexual and Social Politics in Victorian London* (Princeton: Princeton University Press, 2004).
Lynch, Kevin. *The Image of the City* (Cambridge, Massachusetts: MIT Press, 1960).
Lacan, Jacques, *Seminar, Book I: Freud's Papers on Technique, 1953–1954* (New York: Norton, 1998).
Lambot, Ian, 'Self-Build and Change: Kowloon Walled City, Hong Kong', *Architectural Design*, 87:5 (2017), 122–129.

Lambot, Ian, and Greg Girard, *City of Darkness: Life in Kowloon Walled City* (Pewsey: Watermark Publications, 1993).

Lapointe, Tanya, and Denis Villeneuve, *The Art and Soul of Blade Runner 2049* (London: Titan Books, 2017).

Latour, Bruno, *We Have Never Been Modern*, trans. by Catherine Porter (Hemel Hempstead: Harvester, 1993).

Lauster, Martina, 'Walter Benjamin's Myth of the Flâneur', *MLR*, 102:1 (2007), 139–156.

Lavery, Grace E., *Quaint, Exquisite. Victorian Aesthetics and the Idea of Japan* (Princeton: Princeton University Press, 2019).

League of S.T.E.A.M., The, '"Here Comes the Bride" – Adventures of the League of STEAM', Video, YouTube, posted by The League of S.T.E.A.M., 24 November 2011, https://www.youtube.com/watch?v=CHY1U9wxv2o (accessed 20 June 2018).

Ledger, Sally, *The New Woman: Fiction and Feminism at the Fin de Siècle* (Manchester: Manchester University Press, 1997).

Lessing, Lawrence, *Remix. Making Art and Commerce Thrive in the Hybrid Economy* (London: Bloomsbury, 2008).

Lefebvre, Henri, 'The Right to the City', in *Writings on Cities*, ed. by Eleonore Kofman and Elizabeth Lebas (London: Blackwell, 1996), pp. 147–159.

Lefebvre, Henri. *The Production of Space* (Oxford: Basil Blackwell, 1991).

Lévy, Pierre, *Collective Intelligence. Mankind's emerging world in cyberspace* (New York: Perseus Books, 1997).

Lewis, Barry, *My Words Echo Thus: Possessing the Past in Peter Ackroyd's Novels* (Columbia: University of South Carolina Press, 2007).

Lichtenstein, Rachel, and Iain Sinclair, *Rodinsky's Room* (London: Granta Publications, 1999).

Llewelyn, Mark, 'What Is Neo-Victorian Studies?', *Neo-Victorian Studies*, 1.1 (2008), 164–185.

Lombroso, Cesare. *Crime. Its Causes and Remedies*, trans. by Henry P. Horton (London: [unknown], 1911).

London, Jack, *People of the Abyss* (London: [Penguin], 1977 [1903]).

Love, Heather, *Feeling Backward: Loss and the Politics of Queer History* (Cambridge: Harvard University Press, 2007).

Lovecraft, H. P., *Supernatural Horror in Literature* (New York: Dover, 1973).

Luckhurst, Roger, 'The contemporary London Gothic and the limits of the "spectral turn"', *Textual Practice* 16:3 (2002), 527–546.

Luckhurst, Roger, *The Invention of Telepathy, 1870–1901* (Oxford: Oxford University Press, 2002).

Luckhurst, Roger, 'The weird: a dis/orientation.' *Textual Practice* 31:6 (2017), 1041–1061.

Luckhurst, Roger, *Science Fiction* (Cambridge: Polity Press, 2005).

Lyotard, Jean-François, 'About the human', in *The Inhuman: Reflections on Time*, trans. by Geoffrey Bennington and Rachel Bowlby (Cambridge: Polity Press, 1991).

MacArthur, Sian, *Gothic Science Fiction from 1818 to present* (London: Palgrave Macmillan, 2015).

MacDougall, Sophia, 'I Hate Strong Female Characters', *New Statesman*, 15 August 2015, https://www.newstatesman.com/culture/2013/08/-hate-strong-female-characters (accessed 26 April 2020).

Makai, Péter Kristóf, 'Video Games as Objects and Vehicles of Nostalgia', *Humanities*, 7, 123 (2018), 1–14.

Mann, George, *The Affinity Bridge*: A Newbury and Hobbes Investigation, (New York: Tor, 2009).

Marriot, John, 'The imaginative geography of the Whitechapel murders', in *Jack the Ripper and the East End*, ed. by Alex Werner (London: Chatto & Windus, 2008), pp. 31–63.

Marx, Karl, *Capital. An New Abridgement* (Oxford: Oxford World's Classics, 2008 [1867]).

Massey, Doreen, *For Space* (London: SAGE Publications, 2005).

Mayhew, Henry, *London Labour and the London Poor. Vol. II.* (London: Frank Cass and Company Limited, 1967 [1862]).

McRobbie, Angela, *The Aftermath of Feminism: Gender, Culture, and Social Change* (London: SAGE Publications, 2009).

Meikle, Denis, *A History of Horrors. The Rise and Fall of the House of Hammer* (Lanham: Scarecrow Press, 2009).

Meyer, Christina, and Monika Pietrzak-Franger (eds), *Transmedia Practices in the Long Nineteenth Century* (London: Routledge, 2022).

Mighall, Robert, *A Geography of Victorian Gothic Fiction. Mapping History's Nightmares* (Oxford: Oxford University Press, 1999).

Mitchell, Kate, *History and Cultural Memory in Neo-Victorian Fiction. Victorian Afterimages* (London: Palgrave Macmillan, 2010).

Montrose, Louis, 'Renaissance Literary Studies and the Subject of History', *Studies in Renaissance Historicism*. 16:1 (1986), pp. 5–12.

Montz, Amy, '"In Which Parasols Prove Useful": Neo-Victorian Rewriting of Victorian Materiality', *Neo-Victorian Studies*, 4:1 (2011), 100–118.

Morrison, Arthur, 'What is a Realist?', *New Review*, 16/94 (Mar. 1894), 326–336, reprinted in Morrison, Arthur, *A Child of the Jago*, ed. by Peter Miles (Oxford: Oxford University Press, 2012 [1896]), pp. 179–181.

Morrison, Arthur, 'Whitechapel. From "The Palace Journal", April 24, 1889', https://www.casebook.org/victorian_london/whitechapel3.html?printer=true (accessed 19 June 2018).

Morrison, Arthur, *A Child of the Jago*, ed. by Peter Miles (Oxford: Oxford University Press, 2012 [1896]).

Mulvey, Laura, 'Visual Pleasure and Narrative Cinema', *Screen*, 16:3 (1975), 6–18.

Münch, Ole, 'Henry Mayhew and the Street Traders of Victorian London — A Cultural Exchange with Material Consequences', *The London Journal*, 43:1 (2018), 53–71.

Munro, Ealasaid, 'Feminism: A Fourth Wave?', *Political Insight*, September 2013, 22–25.

Murail, Estelle, and Sara Thornton, 'Dickensian Counter-Mapping, Overlaying, and Troping: Producing the Virtual City', in *Dickens and the Virtual City: Urban Perception and the Production of Social Space*, ed. by Estelle Murail and Sara Thornton (London: Palgrave Macmillan, 2017), pp. 3–34.

Nally, Claire, *Steampunk. Gender, Subculture, & the Neo-Victorian* (London: Bloomsbury 2019).

Nead, Lynda, *Victorian Babylon. People, Streets and Images in Nineteenth-Century London* (New Haven & London: Yale University Press, 2000).

Nevins, Jess, 'Introduction: the 19th-Century Roots of Steampunk', in *Steampunk*, ed. by Ann and Jeff VanderMeer (San Fransisco: Tachyon, 2008).

Newman, James, *Videogames* (London: Routledge, 2004).

Newman, Kim, 'Afterword', in *Anno Dracula* (London: Titan Books, 2011 [1992]), pp. 449–456.

Newman, Kim, 'Annotations', in *Anno Dracula* (London: Titan Books, 2011 [1992]), pp. 42–442.

Newman, Kim, *Anno Dracula* (London: Titan Books, 2011 [1992]).

Ngai, Sianne, *Our Aesthetic Categories. Zany, Cute, Interesting* (Cambridge: Harvard University Press, 2012).

Ng, Eve, and Julie Levin Russo. 'Envisioning Queer Fandom', *Transformative Works and Cultures* 24 (2017), n.p.

Nielsen, Holly, 'Reductive, superficial, beautiful – a historian's view of Assassin's Creed: Syndicate', *The Guardian*, 9 December 2015, https://www.theguardian.com/technology/2015/dec/09/assassins-creed-syndicate-historian-ubisoft (accessed 15 February 2020).

Nora, Pierre, *The realms of memory: Rethinking the French Past* (New York: Columbia University Press, 1999).

Nordau, Max. 'Degeneration', in *The Fin de Siècle. A Reader in Cultural History c.1880–1900*, ed. by Sally Ledger and Roger Luckhurst (Oxford: Oxford University Press, 2000 [1895]), pp.13–17.

Oldridge, Darren, 'Casting the spell of terror: the press and the early Whitechapel murders', in *Jack the Ripper. Media. Culture. History.*, ed. by Alexandra Warwick and Martin Willis (Manchester: Manchester University Press, 2007), pp. 46–55.

Onega, Susana, 'Family Traumas and Serial Killings in Peter Ackroyd's *Dan Leno and the Limehouse Golem*', in *Neo-Victorian Families. Gender, Sexual and Cultural Politics*, ed. by Marie-Louise Kohlke and Christian Gutleben (Leiden: Rodopi, 2011), pp. 267–296.

Onega, Susana, *Metafiction and Myth in the Novels of Peter Ackroyd* (Columbia: Camden House, 1999).

Onion, Rebecca, 'Reclaiming the Machine: An Introductory Look at Steampunk in Everyday Practise', *Neo-Victorian Studies*, 1:1 (2008), 138–163.

Padua, Sydney, '2D Goggles, or The Thrilling Adventures of Lovelace and Babbage.' http://sydneypadua.com/2dgoggles/ (accessed 12 March 2018).

Pagliosotti, Dru, '"People keep giving me rings, but I think a small death ray might be more practical": Women and Mad Science in Steampunk Comics', in *Neo-Victorian Humour: Comic Subversions and Unlaughter in Contemporary Historical Re-Visions*, ed. by Marie-Luise Kohlke and Christian Gutleben (Amsterdam: Brill Rodopi, 2017), pp. 213–146.

Parejo Vadillo, Ana, *Women Poets and Urban Aestheticism: Passengers of Modernity* (London: Palgrave Macmillan, 2005).

Parkins, Wendy, *Mobility and Modernity in Women's Novels, 1850s–1930s: Women Moving Dangerously* (London: Palgrave Macmillan, 2009).

Parsons, Deborah L., *Streetwalking the Metropolis: Women, the City and Modernity* (Oxford: Oxford University Press, 2000).

Paston, George (Emily Morse Symonds), *A Writer of Books*, ed. by Margaret D. Stetz and Anita Miller (Chicago: Chicago Review Press, 1998 [1898]).

Perschon, Mike, 'Doctor Who: the Girl in the Fireplace', *Steampunk Scholar*, 29 Nov 2013. http://steampunkscholar.blogspot.de/2013/11/doctor-who-girl-infireplace.html (accessed 12 March 2018).

Perschon, Mike, 'Seminal Steampunk: Proper and True', in *Like Clockwork. Steampunk Pasts, Presents, & Futures*, ed. by Rachel A. Bowser and Brian Croxall (Minneapolis: Minnesota UP, 2016), pp. 153–178.

Perschon, Mike, 'The Steampunk Aesthetic: Technofantasies in a Neo-Victorian Retrofuture' (unpublished doctoral thesis, University of Alberta, 2012).

Perschon, Mike, 'Useful Troublemakers: Social Retrofuturism in the Steampunk Novels of Gail Carriger and Cherie Priest', in *Steaming Into a Victorian Future*, ed. by Julie Anne Taddeo and Cynthia J. Miller (Lanham: Scarecrow Press, 2013), pp. 21–41.

Perschon, Mike, *Steampunk FAQ. All That's Left to Know About the World of Goggles, Airships, and Time Travel* (Milwaukee: Applause Theatre & Cinema Books, 2018).

Peters, S.M., *Whitechapel Gods* (New York: Roc Books, 2008).

Pho, Diana M., 'Objectified and Politicized: The Dynamics of Ideology and Consumerism in Steampunk Subculture', in Taddeo and Miller (2013): 185–212.

Pho, Diana M., 'Punking the Other: On the Performance of Racial and National Identities in Steampunk', in Bowser and Croxall (2016): 127–152.

Pike, David. L., 'Afterimages of the Victorian City', *Journal of Victorian Culture*, 15:2 (2010), 254–267.

Pike, David, 'Steampunk and the Victorian City', in *Like Clockwork. Steampunk Pasts, Presents & Futures*, ed. by Rachel A. Bowser and Brian Croxall (Minneapolis: Minnesota UP, 2016), pp. 3–31.

Pilcher, Jane, and Imelda Whehelan. 'Mainstreaming or New Activism? Gender Studies and Gender Politics', in Jane Pilcher and Imelda Whehelan (eds), *Key Concepts in Gender Studies*. 2nd Edition (London: SAGE Publications, 2017), pp. xiii–x.

Pile, Steve, *Real Cities: Modernity, Space and the Phantasmagorias of City Life* (London: SAGE Publications, 2005).

Pollock, Griselda, *Vision and Difference: Feminism, Femininity and Histories of Art* (London: Routledge, 1988).

Powers, Tim, 'Introduction', in *Morlock Night*, by K.W. Jeter (Oxford: Angry Robot, 2011 [1979]).

Powers, Tim, *The Anubis Gates* (London: Orion Books, 1983).

Primorac, Antonija, *Neo-Victorianism on Screen: Postfeminism and Contemporary Adaptations of Victorian Women* (London: Palgrave Macmillan, 2018).

Primorac, Antonija, 'The Naked Truth: The Postfeminist Afterlives of Irene Adler', *Neo-Victorian Studies*, 6:2 (2013), 89–113.

Primorac, Antonija, and Monika Pietrzak-Franger (eds). Special Issue: Neo-Victorianism and Globalisation: Transnational Dissemination of Nineteenth-Century Cultural Texts, *Neo-Victorian Studies*, 8:1 (2015).

Pulham, Patricia, 'Mapping Histories: The Golem and the Serial Killer in *White Chapell: Scarlet Tracings*, and *Dan Leno and the Limehouse Golem*', in *Haunting and Spectrality in Neo-Victorian Fiction*, ed. by Rosario Aras and Patricia Pulham (London: Palgrave Macmillan, 2010), pp. 157–179.

Pykett, Lyn, 'Fin-de-Siècle Ouida: A New Woman writing against the New Woman?', in *The History of British Women's Writing, 1880–1920* ed. by Holly A. Laird (London: Palgrave Macmillan, 2016), pp. 35–46.

Pykett, Lyn, *The "improper" Feminine: The Women's Sensation Novel and the New Woman Writing* (London: Routledge, 1992).

Ramsell, Catherine, '"The Affinity Bridge" Is an Enormously Fun Steampunk Novel', https://www.popmatters.com/125702-the-affinity-bridge-by-george-mann-2496193023.html (accessed 19 June 2018).

Rance, Nicholas, '"Jonathan's great knife": *Dracula* meets Jack the Ripper', in *Jack the Ripper. Media. Culture. History.*, ed. by Alexandra Warwick and Martin Willis (Manchester: Manchester University Press, 2007), pp. 124–143.

Ready At Dawn, *The Order 1886* (2015), developed by Ru Weerasuriya, PlayStation 4, Sony Computer Entertainment.

Reeve, Philip, *Mortal Engines* (London: Scholastic, 2018 [2001]).

Reyes, Xavier Aldana. *Body Gothic. Corporeal in Contemporary Literature and Horror Film* (Cardiff: University of Wales Press, 2014).

Richardson, Angelique and Chris Willis, 'Introduction', in *The New Woman in Fiction and Fact: Fin-de-Siècle Feminisms*, ed. by Angelique Richardson and Chris Willis (London: Palgrave Macmillan, 2001), pp. 1–38.

Ricoeur, Paul, 'Narrative Time', *Critical Inquiry*. 7:1 (1980), 169–190.

Ricoeur, Paul, *Time and Narrative*, Vol. 1. (Chicago: Chicago UP, 1984).

Ricoeur, Paul, *Time and Narrative*, Vol. 3. (Chicago: Chicago UP, 1988).

Rivers, Nicola. *Postfeminism(s) and the Arrival of the Fourth Wave. Turning Tides* (London: Palgrave, 2017).

Roddy, Sarah, Julie-Marie Strange and Bertrand Taithe. 'Henry Mayhew at 200 – the "Other" Victorian Bicentenary', *Journal of Victorian Culture*, 19:4 (2014), 481–496.

Röder, Katrin, 'Reparative Reading, Post-structuralist Hermeneutics and T. S. Eliot's Four Quartets', *Anglia* 132:1 (2014), 58–59.
Romero Ruiz, Mara Isabel, 'Detective Fiction and Neo-Victorian Sexploitation:Violence, Morality and Rescue Work in Lee Jackson's *The Last Pleasure Garden* (2007) and *Ripper Street*'s 'I Need Light' (2012–16)', *Neo-Victorian Journal*, 9:2 (2017), 41–69.
Ross, Ellen, 'Deeds of heroism: Whitechapel's ladies', in *Jack the Ripper and the East End*, ed. by Alex Werner (London: Chatto & Windus, 2008), pp. 181–217.
Roukema, Aren, 'Mind Wars: H.G. Wells, Edward Bulwer-Lytton and the Boundaries of Science Fiction', unpublished paper delivered at the conference 'War and Peace: 10th Annual Conference of the Victorian Popular Fiction Association' (Institute for English Studies, University of London, 3–7 July 2018).
Rowley, Stephen 'False LA: Blade Runner and the Nightmare City' in *The Blade Runner Experience. The Legacy of a Science Fiction Classic,* ed. by Will Brooker (London & New York: Wallflower Press, 2005), pp. 203–212.
Rubenhold, Hallie, *The Five: The Untold Lives of the Women Killed by Jack the Ripper* (London: Transworld Publishers, 2019).
Said, Edward, *Orientalism* (London: Penguin Classics, 2003 [1978]).
Sammon, Paul M., *Future Noir: The Making of Blade Runner* (New York: HarperCollins, 2017 [1996]).
Samuel, Raphael, 'Mrs Thatcher's Return to Victorian Values', *Proceedings of the British Academy*, 78, 9–29.
Sarony, Napoleon, 'Oscar Wilde 1882', *MetMuseum.org*, n.d., https://www.metmuseum.org/art/collection/search/283247 (accessed 23 April 2020).
Schaffer, Talia, 'Fashioning Aestheticism by Aestheticizing Fashion: Wilde, Beerbohm, and Male Aesthete's Sartorial Codes', *Victorian Literature and Culture*, 28:1 (2000), 39–54.
Schaffer, Talia, 'Nothing but Foolscap and Ink: Inventing the New Woman', in *The New Woman in Fiction and Fact: Fin-de-Siècle Feminisms*, ed. by Angelique Richardson and Chris Willis (London: Palgrave Macmillan, 2001), pp. 39–52.
Schaffer, Talia, *The Forgotten Female Aesthetes: Literary Culture in Late-Victorian England* (Charlottesville: University Press of Virginia, 2000).
Schillace, Brandy, *Clockwork Futures. The Science of Steampunk and the Reinvention of the Modern World* (New York: Pegasus Books, 2017).
Sedgwick, Eve Kosofsky, 2003. *Touching Feeling: Affect, Pedagogy, Performativity* (Durham, North Carolina: Duke University Press, 2003 [1985]).
Sella, Marshal, 'The Remote Controllers', https://www.nytimes.com/2002/10/20/magazine/the-remote-controllers.html (accessed 19 June 2018).
Shaw, Marion, and Lyssa Randolph, *New Woman Writers* (Tavistock: Northcote House Publishers Ltd, 2007).
Shelley, Mary, *Frankenstein, or The Modern Prometheus* (Oxford: Oxford Classics, 2008 [1818]).
Shields, Rob, 'Fancy footwork: Walter Benjamin's notes on *flânerie*', in *The Flâneur*, ed. by Keith Tester (London: Routledge 1994), pp. 43–60.

Siemann, Catherine, 'Some Notes on the Social Problem Novel', in *Steaming Into A Victorian Future.* ed. by Julie Anne Taddeo and Cynthia J. Miller (Lanham: Scarecrow Press, 2013), pp. 3–21.

Siemann, Catherine, 'The Steampunk City in Crisis', in *Like Clockwork. Steampunk Pasts, Presents & Futures,* ed. by Rachel A. Bowser and Brian Croxall (Minneapolis: Minnesota UP, 2016), pp. 51–72.

Simmel, Georg, 'The Metropolis and Mental Life', in *The Sociology of Georg Simmel,* ed. by K.H. Wolff (Glencoe, IL: Free Press, 1950 [1903]), pp. 409–426.

Sinclair, Iain, *Downriver (Or, The Vessels of Wrath): A Narrative in Twelve Tales* (London: Paladin, 1991).

Sinclair, Iain, *Lights Out for the Territory: 9 Excursions in the Secret History of London* (London: Granta, 1997).

Smith, Andrew, *Gothic Literature* (Edinburgh: Edinburgh University Press, 2007).

Smith, Clare, *Jack the Ripper in Film and Culture. Top hat, Gladstone Bag, and Fog* (London: Palgrave Macmillan, 2016).

Soja, Edward, *Postmetropolis. Critical Studies of Cities and Regions* (Oxford: Blackwell Publishers, 2000).

Soja, Edward, *Thirdspace: Journeys to Los Angeles and Other Real-And-Imagined Places* (Oxford: Blackwell Publishing, 1996).

Sparham, Anna, *Soldiers and Suffragettes: The Photography of Christina Broom* (London: Philip Wilson Publishers, 2015).

Spencer, Herbert. 'The Principles of Sociology.' in *The Fin de Siècle. A Reader in Cultural History c.1880–1900*, ed. by Sally Ledger and Roger Luckhurst (Oxford: Oxford University Press, 2000 [1876]), pp. 321–326.

Sterling, Bruce (ed.), *Mirrorshades. The Cyberpunk Anthology* (New York: Ace Books, 1986).

Sterling, Bruce, 'The User's Guide to Steampunk', in *The Steampunk Bible,* ed. by Jeff VanderMeer and S.J. Chambers (New York: Abrams Image, 2011), pp. 11–12.

Stetz, Margaret D., 'Neo-Victorian Studies', *Victorian Literature and Culture*, 40, (2012), 339–346.

Stetz, Margaret, 'Looking at Victorian Fashion: Not a Laughing Matter', in *Neo-Victorian Humour: Comic Subversions and Unlaughter in Contemporary Historical Re-Visions*, ed. by Marie-Luise Kohlke and Christian Gutleben, (Amsterdam: Brill Rodopi, 2017), pp. 145–169.

Stevenson, Robert Louis, *The Strange Case of Dr Jekyll and Mr Hyde* (Oxford: Oxford Classics, 2006 [1886]).

Sussman, Herbert, 'Cyberpunk Meets Charles Babbage: The Difference Engine as Alternative Victorian History', *Victorian Studies,* 38:1 (Autumn 1994), 1–23.

Sussman, Herbert, *Victorians and the Machine: The Literary Response to Technology* (Cambridge: Harvard UP, 1968).

Suvin, Darko, *Metamorphoses of Science Fiction. On the Poetics and History of a Literary Genre* (Bern: Peter Lang, 2016 [1979]).

Sweet, Matthew, *Inventing the Victorians* (London: Faber and Faber, 2001).
Taddeo, Julie Anne, 'Corsets of Steel: Steampunk's Reimagining of Victorian Femininity', in *Steaming Into a Victorian Future*, ed. by Julie Anne Taddeo and Cynthia J. Miller (Lanham: Scarecrow Press, 2013), pp. 43–65.
Taddeo, Julie Anne and Cynthia J. Miller (eds), *Steaming Into a Victorian Future* (Lanham: Scarecrow Press, 2013).
Tatsumi, Takayuki, 'Transpacific Cyberpunk: Transgeneric Interactions between Prose, Cinema, and Manga', *Arts*, 7:9 (2018) n.p.
Taube, Alaksejs, 'London's East End in Peter Ackroyd's *Dan Leno and the Limehouse Golem*', in *Literature and the Peripheral City*, ed. by Lieven Ameel, Jason Finch, and Markku Salmela (London: Palgrave Macmillan, 2015), pp. 93–110.
Taylor, Mary Anne, 'Liberation and a Corset: Examining False Feminism in Steampunk, in *Clockwork Rhetorik: The Language and Style of Steampunk*, ed. by Barry Brummett (Jackson: University of Mississippi Press, 2014), pp. 38–60.
TEAMSUPERTRAMP, *Behind The Scenes – Assassin's Creed Syndicate Meets Parkour in Real Life*, Video, YouTube, posted by Devin Graham, 6 July 2015, https://www.youtube.com/watch?v=c2dlOR4CdR4 (accessed 15 February 2020).
Tedx Talks, *Vintage Tomorrows: James H. Carrott at TEDxSonomaCounty*, Video, YouTube, posted by Tedx Talks, 19 June 2013, https://www.youtube.com/watch?v—T9WWyAFHpE, 8:05–8:10 (accessed 28 April 2020).
Tenniel, John, 'The Nemesis of Neglect', cartoon, in *Punch*, 29 Sept. 1888, https://commons.wikimedia.org/wiki/File:Jack-the-Ripper-The-Nemesis-of-Neglect-Punch-London-Charivari-cartoon-poem-1888-09-29.jpg (accessed 10 June 2018).
Tester, Keith, 'Introduction', in *The Flâneur*, ed. by Keith Tester (London: Routledge 1994), pp. 1–21.
The Flâneur, ed. by Keith Tester (London: Routledge 1994).
The History of British Women's Writing, 1880–1920, ed. by Holly A. Laird (London: Palgrave Macmillan, 2016).
The Matrix, dir. by the Wachowskis, DVD (Los Angeles: Warner Brothers Entertainments, 1999).
The Routledge Companion to Urban Imaginaries, ed. by Christoph Lindner and Miriam Meissner (London: Routledge, 2018).
Traill, H.D., 'The New Realism', *Fortnightly Review*, 67, 1897, pp. 63–73, reprinted in Morrison, Arthur, *A Child of the Jago*, ed. by Peter Miles (Oxford: Oxford University Press, 2012 [1896]), pp. 175–176.
Tylor, Edward, 'Primitive Culture' in *The Fin de Siècle. A Reader in Cultural History c.1880–1900*, ed. by Sally Ledger and Roger Luckhurst (Oxford: Oxford University Press, 2000 [1871]), pp. 317–321.
Ubisoft, *Assassin's Creed: Syndicate* (2015), directed by Marc-Alexis Côté, Scott Phillips, and Wesley Pincombe, PlayStation 4, Ubisoft.
Urban Imaginaries. Locating the Modern City, ed. by Alev Çınar and Thomas Bender (Minneapolis: University of Minnesota Press, 2007).

VanderMeer, Jeff, and S.J. Chambers, *The Steampunk Bible* (New York: Abrams Image, 2011).

Vaughan, Laura, 'Mapping the East End labyrinth', in *Jack the Ripper and the East End*, ed. by Alex Werner (London: Chatto & Windus, 2008), pp. 219–237.

Victorian Women Writers and the Woman Question, ed. by Nicola Diane Thompson (Cambridge: Cambridge University Press, 1999).

Vidler, Anthony, *The Architectural Uncanny* (Cambridge, MA: MIT Press, 1992).

Voigts, Eckart, '"Victoriana's Secret": Emilie Autumn's Burlesque Performance of Subcultural Neo-Victorianism', *Neo-Victorian Studies* 6:2 (2013), 15–39.

Voigts-Virchow, Eckart, 'In-yer-Victorian-face: A Subcultural Hermeneutics of Neo-Victorianism', *Lit: Literature Interpretation Theory*, 20 (2009), 108–125.

Wagner, Thomas M., 'The Affinity Bridge', http://www.sfreviews.net/mann_affinity_bridge.html (accessed 19 June 2018).

Walker, Lynne, 'Locating the Global/Rethinking the Local: Suffrage Politics, Architecture, and Space', *Women's Studies Quarterly*, 34:1/2 (2006), 174–196.

Walkowitz, Judith R., *City of Dreadful Delight* (Chicago: University of Chicago Press, 1992).

Wånggren, Lena, *Gender, Technology and the New Woman* (Edinburgh: Edinburgh University Press, 2017).

Warner, Horace, *Spitalfields Nippers* (London: Spitalfields Life, 2014).

Warwick, Alexandra, 'Blood and ink: narrating the Whitechapel murders', in *Jack the Ripper. Media. Culture. History*, ed. by Alexandra Warwick and Martin Willis (Manchester: Manchester University Press, 2007), pp. 71–90.

Warwick, Alexandra and Martin Willis (eds), *Jack the Ripper. Media. Culture. History* (Manchester: Manchester University Press, 2007).

Weber, Max, *The City* (Glencoe, IL: Free Press, 1958).

Webster, Andrew, 'Building a better Paris in Assassin's Creed Unity. Historical accuracy meets game design', *The Verge*, 17 April 2019, originally published 31 October 2014, https://www.theverge.com/2014/10/31/7132587/assassins-creed-unity-paris (accessed 15 February 2020).

Wells, H.G., 'The Time Machine', in *H.G. Wells. The Great Science Fiction* (London: Penguin Classics, 2016 [1895]) pp. 1–90.

Werner, Alex (ed.), *Jack the Ripper and the East End* (London: Chatto & Windus, 2008).

Westerman, Molly, 'How Steampunk Screws with Victorian Gender Norms', *bitchmedia*, 15 January 2014, https://www.bitchmedia.org/post/how-steampunk-screws-with-victorian-gender-norms (accessed 28 April 2020).

Whalen, Zach, and Laurie N. Taylor, *Playing the Past: History and Nostalgia in Video Games* (Nashville: Vanderbilt University Press, 2008).

Whelehan, Imelda, *Modern Feminist Thought: From the Second Wave to 'Post-Feminism'*, (New York: New York University Press, 1995).

White, Hayden, *Metahistory: The Historical Imagination in Nineteenth-Century Europe* (Baltimore: Johns Hopkins Univ. Press, 1973).

Whitsun, Roger, *Steampunk and Nineteenth-Century Digital Humanities. Literary Retrofuturisms, Media Archaeologies, Alternate Histories* (London: Routledge, 2017).

Wilde, Oscar, 'The Portrait of Mr W. H.', in *The Complete Works of Oscar Wilde: Stories, Plays, Poems, & Essays*, (New York: HarperCollins, 2008), pp. 1150–1202.

Wilde, Oscar, *The Complete Works of Oscar Wilde. Stories, Plays, Poems, & Essays* (New York: Harper Perennials, 2008).

Willis, Martin, 'Jack the Ripper, Sherlock Holmes and the narrative of detection', in *Jack the Ripper. Media. Culture. History.*, ed. by Alexandra Warwick and Martin Willis (Manchester: Manchester University Press, 2007), pp. 144–158.

Wintle, Sarah, 'Horses, Bikes, and Automobiles: The New Woman on the Move', in *The New Woman in Fiction and Fact: Fin-de-Siècle Feminisms*, ed. by Anquelique Richardson and Chris Willis (London: Palgrave Macmillan, 2001), pp. 66–78.

Wise, Sarah, 'Arthur Morrison: "A Child of the Jago" – 1896', https://www.londonfictions.com/arthur-morrison-a-child-of-the-jago.html [accessed 15 June 2018].

Wise, Sarah, *The Blackest Streets. The Life and Death of a Victorian Slum* (London: Vintage Books, 2008).

Wittenberg, David, *Time Travel. The Popular Philosophy of Narrative* (New York: Fordham University Press, 2013).

Wojnowksi, Konrad, 'Simulational Realism – Playing as Trying to Remember', *Art History & Criticism*, 14: 1 (2018), 86–98.

Wolf, Mark J.P., *Building Imaginary Worlds: The Theory and History of Subcreation* (London: Routledge, 2014).

Wolfe, Gary K., *Evaporating Genres: Essays on Fantastic Literature* (Middleton: Wesleyan University Press, 2011).

Wolff, Janet, 'Foreword', in *Inside Out: Women negotiating, subverting, appropriating public and private space*, ed. by Teresa Gómez Reus and Aránzazu Usandizaga (Amsterdam: Rodopi 2008), pp. 15–18.

Wolff, Janet, 'The Invisible Flâneuse: Women and the Literature of Modernity', *Theory, Culture, & Society*, 2:3 (1985), 37–46.

Wolfreys, Julian, *Writing London. Materiality, Memory, Spectrality* (London: Palgrave Macmillan, 2002).

Wolfreys, Julian, *Writing London: The Trace of the Urban Text from Blake to Dickens* (London: Palgrave Macmillan, 1998).

Wolfreys, Julian, and Jeremy Gibson, *Peter Ackroyd. The Ludic and Labyrinthine Text* (London: Palgrave Macmillan, 2000).

Yeo, Eileen, 'Mayhew as a Social Investigator', in *The Unknown Mayhew. Selections from the Morning Chronicle 1849–50*, ed. by Eileen Yeo and E. P. Thompson (Harmondsworth: Penguin, 1973) pp. 56–109.

Yu, Timothy, 'Oriental Cities, Postmodern Futures: "Naked Lunch, Blade Runner", and "Neuromancer"', MELUS, 33:4 (2008) 45–71.

Zimmerman, Tegan, '#Intersectionality: The Fourth Wave Feminist Twitter Community', Atlantis, 38:1 (2017) 54–70.

Index

A Child of the Jago (Arthur Morrison) 9, 58
Aarseth, Espen 100, 109
Abberline, Inspector Frederic 64–5
Ackroyd, Peter 73–5, 77, 86, 200
   London 73, 76–8
   Psychogeography 86
Action Girl 151–2, 162, 164, 171
Adaptation 9, 62, 66, 72, 120
Adler, Irene 152–5, 157, 164–5, 185
adventure 3, 16, 23–5, 158, 162, 201
   genre conventions 108, 122, 131
   and gender 145, 148, 161
   in video games 38, 42, 44, 114, 124–7
   exploration 56
aestheticism 17, 146, 177, 196
aesthetics 54, 87, 122, 204, 214
Affinity Bridge, The (George Mann) 79–80, 87, 202
Airship 2, 11, 115, 124–5, 164, 171, 175, 221
Akeldama, Lord. *See* Carriger, Gail
Altered Carbon 119–20
Alternative history 10, 31–2, 36, 41–3, 86–8, 123
Ameel, Lieven 7
American New Right 19
American Rust Belt 28
Analytical Engine 30–1, 37, 76–7
Anno Dracula (Kim Newman) 10, 73–80, 85–6, 124, 126–7, 202
   As Counterfiction 51, 54–5, 64–72
Anubis Gates, The (Tim Powers) 19, 21, 25, 47, 222
Arata, Stephen 94, 69
Assassin's Creed 9–10, 100–1, 107–8, 111–13, 120, 130, 164
Assmann, Jan 5
Atkinson Grimshaw, John 56, 109, 122
Austen, Jane 66, 167

Babbage, Charles 30, 76
Baker Street 105–6

Ballantine, Pip. *See also* Morris, Tee, 146, 162, 200
   Ministry of Peculiar Occurrences Series, The 146, 162
Barthes, Roland 66
Baudelaire, Charles. *See also* Flâneur 142–5
   Painter of Modern Life, The 142
Baudrillard, Jean 101
Bazalgette, Joseph 34, 103
Belgravia 153
Bell, Karl 4, 25, 52
Belloc-Lowndes, Marie 107, 60
Benjamin, Walter 22, 143
bicycle 146–50, 163–4, 168, 175, 184–5, 204
   bicycling costume 146–50, 171, 184
   and the New Woman 145, 148
Bierce, Ambrose 24
BioShock 10, 121, 126, 133
BioShock: Infinite 121
Bismarck, Otto 71
Blade Runner 15, 29, 101
   Aesthetics 117–126
   Tyrell Corporation 119, 138
   'Tears in Rain' monologue 128
Blaylock, James P. 9, 15–6, 21–3, 30, 42
   Langdon St. Ives Series 20, 22, 186
Bloom, Clive 63, 69
Booth, Charles 104
   Poverty Map 58
Booth, William
   In Darkest London 55–6
Bowser, Rachel A.
   and Brian Cox 86
Braun, Eliza, *see also Ministry of Peculiar Occurrences Series, The* 158, 162–5, 173, 185
Bristow, Joseph 181
British Empire, the. *See also* Colonialism, Imperialism. 41, 61–9, 107, 125–9, 132, 150, 159

Index

Bury Your Gays 182
Butler, Judith 151
Byron, Ada. *See* Lovelace, Ada.
Byron, George Gordon 25, 30–1, 36

Caird, Mona 146
Calvino, Italo 99, 129, 130, 133
Cannadine, David 105–6
Captain Swing 40
Carriger, Gail 155–6, 168, 171–2, 177, 181, 186, 141, 146
   Parasol Protectorate, The 10, 146, 167–7, 180–1, 187, 186
   Soulless 177–8
   Changeless 170, 177, 180
   Blameless 174
   Tarabotti, Alexia 165–75, 177, 180–3, 186, 171–2, 192, 155
   Conall Maccon 172–4, 177
   Lord Akeldama 177–8, 181
   Geneviève Lefoux 71–2, 177, 179–80
   Custard Protocol Series, The 169, 174, 181, 192, 189
   Finishing School Series, The 169
Carrott, James 188
Catastrophone Orchestra, the 2
Clayton, Jay 31
Cleveland Street Scandal, the 68, 71, 178–9
Clute, John 1, 32
Coleridge, Samuel Taylor 19, 27
colonialism. *See also* British Empire, Imperialism. 108, 115, 120, 127, 141, 199
Conan Doyle, Sir Arthur 57, 106–7, 117, 130
Contagious Diseases Acts 171
convergence culture 7, 59, 66, 91–4, 156, 192
Cook, Matt 178
counter-culture 15, 21, 29, 51
counterfiction 10, 32, 54, 65–3, 78, 86, 124
Coverley, Merlin 77
Croxall, Brian
   and Rachel A. Bowser 86
Csicsery-Ronay, Istvan 32, 42
cultural memory 5, 32, 146
Custard Protocol Series, The. See Carriger, Gail
Cyberpunk 9–10, 15–16, 51, 81, 132, 199–200
   and *The Difference Engine* 28–30, 37–8, 43
   and *Blade Runner* 15, 29, 117–21
   and video games 101, 122–8
Cyberspace 29, 83, 101, 106, 119
Cyborg Manifesto, The (Donna Haraway) 125

Dandy 177–9
Darwin, Charles 124
De Bruin-Molé, Megen 54, 85
De Certeau, Michel 66
decadence 18, 64, 146, 179–8
Dickens, Charles 100–2, 108–9, 124, 130, 200
   Dickensian London 10, 21, 55, 81, 103, 107, 134
   Edwin Drood 57
   Bleak House 55
   Old Curiosity Shop, The 103
   Nicholas Nickleby 102
Difference Engine, The (Bruce Sterling and William Gibson) 9, 16, 28–32, 37–9, 41, 203
Dishonored 10, 121–2, 126, 133
Disraeli, Benjamin 31
Dobraszczyk, Paul 118
Doré, Gustave 9, 53, 56–7, 63, 81–2, 104, 122
   London, A Pilgrimage 56
Dorian Gray, The Picture of (Oscar Wilde) 52, 57
Dracula (Bram Stoker). *See also Anno Dracula* 52, 65–72, 126

East End, The 9–10, 18, 86–87, 200, 202
   in early steampunk 22–7, 35–9
   and Jack the Ripper 52–64, 68–78
   in second-wave steampunk 80–85, 157, 163
   in video games 123–8
East India Company 115, 126, 132
Eddowes, Catherine 60, 65, 67, 79
Ellis, Havelock 179
emplotment 19, 42
Epstein Nord, Deborah 144

Faber, Michael 51
Fallen Woman 144, 154, 164, 174–6, 182

Fan criticism 156, 160–1, 165, 175–6, 182
Faux Action Girl (*see also* Action Girl) 156, 165
feminism 141–2, 145–7, 151–3, 155–9, 161, 185
   activism 150, 159
   genealogies 10, 159, 171, 176
   First Wave 159
   Second Wave 156, 175
   Third Wave (*see also* post-feminism) 151
   Fourth Wave 176
   ideals 151–2, 161, 185
Ferguson, Christine 23
Field, Michael (Katharine Bradley and Edith Cooper) 148, 181
Fingersmith (Sarah Waters) 51
Flanders, Judith 109
Flâneur 10, 142–6, 163, 184, 188
   Flânerie 7, 72, 144
   Flâneuse 143–5, 149
Foucan, Sebastien 112
Foucault, Michel 15, 49, 99, 133, 193, 212
Frankenstein (Mary Shelley) 85, 201
Freud, Sigmund 18, 52
From Hell 51, 62–4, 200

Gadamer, Hans-Georg 116
Galton, Francis 52
Genz, Stéphanie 152, 161
Gibson, William 36, 117
   and Bruce Sterling (*see also The Difference Engine*) 1, 9, 16, 28–32, 36–43
   Neuromancer 15, 29, 37, 101
Gissing, Georg 73, 75–6, 78, 95
Graham, Stephen 120
Grand, Sarah 146, 167
Great Exhibition, The 32
Great Stink, The 34, 38–9, 43
Gutleben, Christian 68
   and Marie-Luise Kohlke 6, 8, 24, 53, 55, 64, 167

Hadley, Louisa 51
Hager, Lisa 176, 190
Haggard, Rider H. 154
Hall, Radclyffe 179
Hall, Stuart 6, 66

Hantke, Steffen 23, 42
Haraway, Donna 4, 151, 215
   The Cyborg Manifesto 12, 125
Hardy, Thomas 146
Harker, Mina. *See also Dracula, League of Extraordinary Gentlemen* 152–7, 161, 165, 185
Harvey, David 9, 16, 22, 38, 43, 118
Hebdige, Dick 23
Hepworth Dixon, Ella 149
hermeneutics 19, 116, 120, 129, 140, 193
Heterotopia 8, 53, 99, 127
   in video games 114, 118–20, 129, 133
Hills, Matt 21, 66, 92–3
Hirschfeld, Magnus 179
Ho, Elizabeth 52
Hobbes, Veronica (*see also* Newbury and Hobbes) 79, 96, 157–64, 173, 185
Hobsbawm, Eric 5
Holmes, Sherlock 10, 120, 163
   in adaptations 153
   and Jack the Ripper 57, 62, 65–77, 69
   Holmes' London 105–7, 112, 130
hooks, bell 190
Hope, Anthony 65, 71
Hyde Park
   and the New Woman 148, 150, 158, 168, 184
   in steampunk fiction 169, 171
   in video games 124
   in queer history 179

imperialism. *See also* British Empire, Colonialism 30, 64, 125, 132, 168
Indian Mutiny, the 125
Infernal Devices (K. W. Jeter) 25, 27
Iser, Wolfgang 11

Jagoda, Patrick 31, 33, 36
James, Henry 146
Jameson, Fredric 8, 28, 29, 118
Janus Affair, The. See also Ministry of Peculiar Occurrences Series, The 158, 173
Jenkins, Henry 7, 59, 66, 68, 79, 121
   convergence culture 7, 59, 66, 91–4, 156, 192
Jerrold, Blanchard 56, 90, 211

Kelly, Mary Jane 60, 67
Kensington Museum 18, 32–3, 35, 103
Kohlke, Marie Luise 6, 8, 158
    and Christian Gutleben 6, 8, 24, 53, 55, 64, 167
Kosofsky Sedgwick, Eve 183
Kowloon Walled City 119
Krafft-Ebing, Richard Freiherr von 178

Labouchère Amendment 177
Lacan, Jacques 8, 19
Lakshmibai 125–7
League of Extraordinary Gentlemen, The (Alan Moore) 66, 154, 200
Ledger, Sally 147, 179
Lee, Vernon 181
Lefebvre, Henri 16
    Production of Space 7, 22, 51, 99
    Right to the City 9, 38, 43
Lefoux, Geneviève. *See* Carriger, Gail
Lessing, Lawrence 67
Levy, Amy 148
Lévy, Pierre 59
Limehouse Golem, The (Peter Ackroyd) 52–7, 72–8, 86
London Labour and the London Poor (Henry Mayhew) 9, 16, 20
London, A Pilgrimage (Gustave Doré, Blanchard Jerrold) 56
London, Jack 58
Lord Kelvin's Machine. *See* Blaylock, James P.
Love, Heather 19
Lovecraft, H. P. 24–5
Lovelace, Ada 36–7, 186
Luckhurst, Roger 18, 25, 28, 55, 76–7
Ludgate Hill 56, 109

Maccon, Connall. *See* Carriger, Gail
Machen, Arthur 24
mad scientist 30, 85, 160, 164, 173, 202
maker culture 2, 201
Mann, George 79, 80, 146, 160, 200
    The Affinity Bridge 79–80, 87, 202
Married Women's Property Act 171
Marx, Karl 3, 41, 75–6, 83–4, 108
    Marxist theory 9, 17, 39, 43
    Marxist historiography 41
    Marxist revolution 31, 41

masculinity (toxic) 154–6, 168
Massey, Doreen 10, 100, 102–4, 113–8, 130, 184
Mayhew, Henry 46, 206
    London Labour and the London Poor 9, 16, 20
McDougall, Sophia 195
MeToo 157, 176, 185
Meynell, Alice 148
Mighall, Robert 53, 55
Ministry of Peculiar Occurrences Series, The (Pip Ballantine and Tee Morris) 146, 162
Mohhanty, Chandra 151
Montrose, Louis 18
Montz, Amy 166, 170–1
Moore, Alan 52, 62–3, 66, 154, 200
    From Hell 51, 62–4, 127, 200
    League of Extraordinary Gentlemen, The 66, 154, 200
Morlocks (*see also* Wells, H. G., *Time Machine, The*) 16–8, 21
Morris, Tee. *See also* Ballantine, Pip 146, 162, 200
    Ministry of Peculiar Occurrences Series, The 146, 162
Morris, William 3, 70
Morrison, Arthur 53, 65, 70, 81, 200
    A Child of the Jago 9, 58–9

Nally, Claire 142, 154–6, 167, 175, 178, 180
Natural History Museum 32, 164, 185
Nead, Lynda 103, 144
Neuromancer (William Gibson) 15, 29, 37, 101, 106, 117, 119
New Woman 10, 141–52, 154–60, 171, 174–5, 184–5
Newbury and Hobbes Series (George Mann) 79, 146, 160
Newman, Kim. *See Anno Dracula*
Ngai, Sianne 24
Nora, Pierre 32, 49
Nordau, Max 17, 179

Old Jago (*A Child of the Jago*) 58, 70, 124
Old Nichol 58
Oldridge, Darren 62
Order 1886, The 10, 100–1, 114–5, 123–9, 131–3

Orientalism 53, 56–7, 64, 70, 78
   in *Blade Runner* 118
   and Neo-Victorianism 158
Osborne, Jay 58

Painter of Modern Life, The (Charles Baudelaire) 142
Panoptic perspective 10, 102–19, 128–9
Parejo Vadillo, Ana 148
Parkins, Wendy 145
Parsons, Deborah 144
Perschon, Mike 1, 23, 141, 175
Pho, Diana M. 3, 6
Pike, David 8, 30
Pile, Steve 184
Poe, Edgar Allan 142
Pollock, Griselda 222, 144, 188
popular culture 6, 9, 153–4, 157–8, 164
popular fiction 1, 10, 15, 199
popular memory 1, 4, 51, 53–4, 100, 123
post-feminism 151–61, 171, 174–5, 180–3, 185–6
Powers, Tim 9, 15, 19, 21–3, 26–7, 200
   The Anubis Gates
Pratchett, Terry 66, 93, 204
Primorac, Antonija 6, 13, 151, 191, 222
psychogeography 7, 10, 54, 72–8, 86

Quatermain, Allan (*see also* League of Extraordinary Gentlemen) 154–5
queer 176–84, 187, 203
   activism 156
   histories 146
   theory 151

Radcliffe, Ann 52, 70
Reeve, Philip
   The Mortal Engines 186
remix 54, 67, 78–9, 85–7, 176, 201
reparative reading 4, 183, 203
Richardson, Angelique 147
Ricoeur, Paul 19, 45
Ripper, Jack the 53–4, 59–87, 108, 127
   Ripperature 52, 72–3, 76, 125–7, 200
   Ripper murders (*see also* Whitechapel murders) 9, 59, 65, 68, 74, 77, 81
   Ripper mythology 62– 68
   Ripperologists 69
Ritchie, Guy 153, 165

Rodinsky's Room (Rachel Lichtenstein) 75
Rohmer, Sax 58, 65
Ruskin, John 3

Sand, George 144
Sarony, Napoleon 178
Schaffer, Talia 147
Schreiner, Olive 146
Shawl, Nisi 186
Simmel, Georg 107, 16, 135, 224
Simpson, Nick 167
Sinclair, Iain 73, 77
Soja, Edward 37, 99–101, 118, 130
Spencer, Herbert 52
Spivak, Gayatri 151, 155
St. Paul's Cathedral 56, 108–9, 117
Steampunk Bible, The (Jeff VanderMeer) 3, 42
SteamPunk Magazine 2, 132
Stenbock, Count Eric S. 65, 71
Sterling, Bruce 9, 12–3, 16, 27–8, 48–9, 211
   and William Gibson
   Difference Engine, The
   Steampunk Bible
Stetz, Margaret D. 185
Stevenson, Robert Louis 52, 61
Stoker, Bram
   Dracula 52, 65, 67, 69, 126
strong female characters 193, 219
subculture 2, 15, 23, 155–7, 163, 203
   urban 29, 42–3
   Victorian 131, 182, 187, 199
Suffragists 150, 158–9, 184–5
Sussman, Herbert 30–1, 36
Swinburne, Algernon 65

Taddeo, Julie Anne 170
Tarrabotti, Alexia. *See* Carriger, Gail
Tennyson, Lord Alfred 65, 70
Terra incognita 53, 56, 69, 82
Tesla, Nikola 124, 127–8
Textual Poachers (Michel de Certeau) 66
textuality of history 77, 86
Thatcher, Margaret 28, 51
   Thatcherite politics 52, 181, 199
   nostalgia 51, 200,
   'Victorian Values' 71, 86
thirdspace 99–101, 130
Time Machine, The (Wells, H. G.) 9, 16–7

Time travel 16–20, 25, 42–4, 107, 201
Transmedia 2–9, 15, 59, 65, 100, 200
   literacy 111, 123, 201
   memory 54
   story-worlds 68, 72, 78, 80, 86
TvTropes 160–1
Tyrell Corporation. *See Blade Runner.*

uncanny 54–55, 85
   and the urban 62, 64, 73, 81
Urban Gothic 7, 52–5, 81, 87, 181
Urban habitus 22, 38–41, 107, 143
Usandizanga, Arànzazu 144

Vampires 25, 55, 61, 79
   in *Anno Dracula* 65–72
   in Carriger's fiction 165–77
   in *The Order 1886* 115, 126–7
video games 2, 9–10, 100–2, 107, 111–5, 121–133
Villeneuve, Denis 120
Voigts, Eckart 131, 157

Walpole, Horace 52
Wånggren, Lena 147
Warwick, Alexandra 61
Waters, Sarah
   Fingersmith 51

Weber, Max 22
Wedekind, Frank 60, 65
Weird 27–8, 35, 43, 200
   and archaic 3, 168, 199
   fiction 24–6, 43
Wellington, the Duke of 31–2, 203
Wells, H. G. 42, 76, 177, 147
   Time Machine, The 9, 16–18
Werewolves
   in Carriger's fiction 168–72, 181
   in *The Anubis Gates* 25, 202
Westenra, Lucy (*see also* Dracula, Anno Dracula) 67
Westermann, Molly 176
Westminster 33, 109, 128
   Westminster Bridge 124–5
   Westminster Palace 103, 108–15, 124, 127
White, Hayden 18, 41
Whitechapel Gods (S. M. Peters) 10, 80–5, 87, 124
Whitechapel murders (*see* Ripper, Jack the)
Wilde, Oscar 52, 57, 65, 167, 177–9
   and queer historicism 181–3, 188, 201
Woolf, Virginia 149

www.ingramcontent.com/pod-product-compliance
Lightning Source LLC
Chambersburg PA
CBHW071829300426
44116CB00009B/1491